A Westminster Wedding

by

Kathleen Buckley

A Westminster Wedding

Cover Art by *Tina Lynn Stout.*

The Wild Rose Press, Inc.
PO Box 708
Adams Basin, NY 14410-0708
Visit us at www.thewildrosepress.com

Publishing History
First Edition, 2022
Trade Paperback ISBN 978-1-5092-4171-2
Digital ISBN 978-1-5092-4172-9

Published in the United States of America

The door was thrust open, and a stranger strode in, a footman following in his wake, remonstrating, "Sir! Sir! You cannot—"

The newcomer halted in the middle of the room, booted feet apart, crop in hand, hat still on his head. He was dusty, a little less than average height, whipcord lean, and browned by outdoor life. Angry as a hornet, too.

Verity squeaked. The earl, viscount, and Halliwell rose while the vicar murmured that he and his mate must take their leave. They slipped out, keeping as much room as they could between themselves and the newcomer.

"I do not believe we are acquainted, sir." The earl's bland observation might have been uttered in a coffee house or assembly.

"I'm Ambleton."

The name conveyed nothing to Barding or Popejoy.

Miles said, "Mistress Rachel's father?"

"I am, damme, and where is she? By God, sir—begging your pardon, ladies—" He seemed to note the presence of females for the first time and whipped off his tricorne. He hesitated for a moment as if wondering what to do with it, before tucking it under the arm that held his crop.

Dedication

For W.D.B., M.D.

Westminster Wedding—a Whore and a Rogue married together.

~The Universal Etymological English Dictionary,
N. Bailey, London, 1737

Cast of Main Characters

Julia St. John—living apart from her family as Mrs. Julia Perry, she has no future

Cecilia St. John—Julia's young half sister

Miles Halliwell—the Earl of Barding's man of business, indispensable to the family

Adam Bryden—Halliwell's capable assistant

Lionel Stretton, Earl of Barding—head of the Stretton family

Caroline, Lady Barding—the earl's wife, matriarch in training

Lavinia, Dowager Countess of Barding—the earl's mother, the family matriarch

George Stretton, Viscount Popejoy—the Earl of Barding's oldest son and heir

Eustacia Stretton, Viscountess Popejoy—George's wife, concerned about her fertility

William Stretton—the earl's second son, deceased

Peter Stretton—the earl's youngest son, in Italy for the last seven years

Georgie Popejoy—Viscount Popejoy's son, about three years of age

Verity Winston—Caroline's orphaned niece who lives with the family

Dr. Broxon—a skillful, if rather eccentric, physician

Hilda Ernst—Lavinia, Lady Barding's companion

Hiram St. John, Baron St. John—father of Julia and of her half siblings, Cecilia and Martin

Augusta St. John—Julia's stepmama and Cecilia and Martin St. John's mother

Timothy Sykes—tutor to Viscount Popejoy's children

Marcia Brant—governess to Viscount Popejoy's

children
Rachel Ambleton—a young lady hiding in London
Samuel Ambleton—Rachel Ambleton's father

Chapter 1

Early April, 1740

Two letters arrived the same day. In the previous two years, she had received a total of six, the last having been but a month past. Easter was coming; could this be news of her life's resurrection? To return to society would be heaven. To have friends again, to have a hot bath whenever she wanted, to attend the theater and entertainments, to have time to read. She missed her family...or her father and Cecilia and Martin, anyway.

As far past her youth as she was, there might still be a man who would think her a desirable wife. A widower with children, like Theo Manning, who would take her away from her father's house and her stepmother. She might choose gowns in colors that became her.

Julia St. John, spinster, known to her neighbors in Handley, Dorset, as the widow Julia Perry, dared not hope.

At first reading, she could not take in the meaning of Papa's letter. Having learned the father's identity, he believed they could make an advantageous disposition of Jeremy, if the natural father's family wanted him, as now seemed likely. Julia was not to discuss this matter with anyone. An unnecessary warning, when she had no one in whom to confide—as if she would! He would advise her of further developments.

The letter acted upon her like sal volatile, jarring her back to life. Welcome, yet not an entirely pleasant sensation. The news itself was not the only shock. Her father had never spoken of the boy as anything but "the brat," when he could not avoid referring to him. Having decided from the first not to grow fond of the baby, Julia never spoke the name he had been given, either. At the time, it seemed sensible, like not naming a puppy or kitten one was not allowed to keep. Seeing the child's name in her father's bold, careless hand seemed to confirm that a change might come.

What did he mean by "advantageous"? Nurse would become the father's family's expense, but the saving would be minor. Of course, Papa could lease out or sell High Farm rather than supporting her tiny household there, but the saving or gain would have little effect on the St. John finances. In fact, supporting her in their home would be more expensive, as she could not wear in London the old, plain clothing suitable here. Unless he was thinking ahead to the cost of educating the boy at university or settling him in some occupation requiring a substantial outlay for an apprenticeship? Or the purchase of a commission? Possibly.

But Julia would be freed from raising the child, which would be a relief to her, and she would be home. Perhaps Papa had missed her, even if he was not given to voicing his affection.

The other letter was addressed in her half sister's handwriting. She broke the pink wafer seal. How surprising that their father had let her write under separate cover. Previously she had added her own addendum to his letter, meaning it was necessarily brief and he read it. Cecilia was seldom able to confine herself to a single sheet otherwise. She loved writing and receiving letters, which seemed unusual in one who had not enjoyed her lessons. Maybe it was because she was never silent if there were anyone to talk to. In the absence of a live body, she poured out her thoughts in letters.

Dearest Julia,

I fear I am responsible for the current agitation. I knew at once that I should have kept silent, but when I saw the obituary, I cried out, "Dead!" without thinking, and as both Papa and Mama were present, they questioned me until I revealed what I had sworn never to speak of. Then Papa read the notice and grew thoughtful. He and Mama closeted themselves in the bookroom, and the next thing I knew, Papa said he would write Jeremy's other family to see if they wanted him. So you see it was just as well I was taken by surprise; it is a piece of luck for you! You will be able to go on with your life somewhere at least, dear sister. Please do not mention when you write next that I have written to you. I'll contrive to have the boot boy send it without Papa's knowledge.

Did you hear that Theo Manning has married? The bride is that odd Laura Sloan, who digs up Viking remains or some such thing. She will hardly have time for her pastime now that she is taking care of his children. Are you not glad you were not called upon to bring them up?

Papa hopes to secure me a husband with a title, mayhap a viscount or higher. That is another good result of my unconsidered reaction.

Your loving sister,
Cecilia

Oh, Cecilia. The familiar blend of affection and exasperation washed over her. When Cecilia was still in the schoolroom, it had been obvious that (with the help of a very fine dowry) she could make an excellent marriage, having inherited her dazzling looks and liveliness from some earlier ancestress than Augusta, who was bracket-faced and possessed apricot-colored hair she claimed was blonde.

Julia, having inherited her father's height and sharply cut features together with a quiet nature, would not. Papa and Stepmama had been sure Cecilia would make a brilliant match. Now their wish might come true.

Theo Manning. Quite the nicest man she had ever met. He had been nine-and-thirty, only twelve years older than she, and having several children meant he was not overly concerned about her remaining breeding years. She would undoubtedly be raising his children now if not for the unhappy events two years past.

She buried the letters under the tea in her tea caddy with the miniature that had been her mother's wedding gift to Papa. He had given it to Julia, perhaps less to console her on Mama's death than because Sally Suttle St. John's laughing, informal pose did not suit his notions of propriety.

****

It was an emergency, of course. It always was, with the Earl of Barding's family, the Strettons. Lucky they were in town. Miles Halliwell had an appointment this afternoon, but that could wait until another day.

"Bryden!" Miles called.

"Sir?" His assistant popped into his office like a rabbit from a burrow. Adam Bryden had come from Lanark in Lowlands Scotland intent on making his fortune in London. He would likely succeed.

"I need a message sent to the baronet, begging off from this afternoon's meeting. You may say 'tis related to an unexpected death." Barding's letter did not say so, indeed did not say much about the reason for his summons, but the earl's second son having died a month ago, it might be true. At least the earl, his countess, and the dowager countess were in London. Parliament being in session, the Earl of Barding felt it his duty to attend in spite of mourning. His heir, Viscount Popejoy, and his lady had retired to the Strettons' seat near Banbury. Had it been necessary to attend the earl—and his formidable mother—there, Miles would have had to cancel at least a week's worth of appointments. There was very little he would not do for the Bardings.

He read the letter again before leaving for Barding House. The urgency was clear in spite of Lord Barding's obscure phrasing. As Lionel Stretton, Earl of Barding, was not ordinarily incoherent, Miles concluded the matter was one of such delicacy that details could not be trusted to paper and ink. What the devil was it this time? One thing was clear: Barding's elderly mother, still very much the head of the family, was concerned. How, the letter did not make clear. She might be furious or worried, but it would not be a minor matter. Miles preferred not to imagine what would cause Lavinia, Dowager Countess of Barding, anxiety.

She must be near eighty. Ordinarily she got what she wanted without help. Was it possible her mind was beginning to fail her? It would hardly be surprising with the weight of her responsibilities. Barding was a good property owner, but he did not possess his mother's business acumen.

Lavinia, Lady Barding, would purse her lips at that description; no member of the aristocracy cared to have "business" coupled with his or her name. But according to Whitacker, their previous man of business and Miles's mentor, Lavinia had begun investing family money before she was thirty, when her husband had been absent for months in the Netherlands. On his return, he found their finances much the better for Lavinia's management and ceded most financial decisions to her. At his death, her son never thought of trying to take on the responsibility. For her part, Lavinia always appeared to defer to him.

Grief for William, the earl's second son, might play a part. William had died last month without issue. Yet why would it only now cause concern? Unless it was the succession. George, the earl's heir, had only one son. Peter, the remaining son, was five-and-twenty, studying art and architecture in Italy. In theory he might marry and produce offspring. No one in the family expected it, least of all Miles, who had been sent to Italy three years ago to ask him to come home and been roundly refused. They could hardly expect Halliwell to do anything about their lack of potential heirs.

The phrases "astounding news," "the Dowager Countess wants immediate action," and "you will sift the matter thoroughly" suggested something a little out of the usual sphere of a man of business. Miles would do it, whatever it was. He owed all he was and had to the Strettons.

****

They met with him in the library. The earl tended to treat him as a nephew of whom he was moderately fond. Caroline Stretton smiled warmly and asked how he did, as if he were an acquaintance. George, Viscount Popejoy, the heir, treated Miles like an old friend. Halliwell did not trespass upon their kindness. He was merely their man of business. He had never quite understood Lavinia Barding's attitude. She was neither friendly nor unfriendly. Yet he must have been brought to live there with her consent, if not her blessing. Had she refused to allow his presence, he would certainly not have been taken into their home. Had it helped that he did not resemble the Strettons, who ran to blond or very light brown hair, blue eyes, and a stocky frame which made them look shorter than they were? He could never ask, and she would never volunteer the information. Over the years, however, she had sometimes shown him a degree of approval, which, God help him, he cherished.

She did value his usefulness. Her son and grandsons were neither stupid nor notably clever, except for Peter, who had removed himself from the family for most purposes, and whose intelligence was artistic rather than practical.

After a few preliminary remarks amounting to "I rely on you to clear up this deucedly awkward matter quickly," Barding fell silent and turned to his mother. Caroline, his countess, continued to sit silently, working at some piece of embroidery. Did she ever resent her mother-in-law's influence?

Lavinia Barding did not speak immediately. It was clear that the impression of her distress conveyed by the earl's letter had been misleading. She was intent on some course of action. Caroline Barding, however, was frowning slightly. She might merely be trying to decide between two shades of embroidery silk.

"Lady Barding, how may I serve you?" He directed his question halfway between the ladies.

Lavinia's face, still handsome despite age, strong features, and crape-like wrinkles, showed nothing. "It was no secret that William was something of a libertine. That was no great thing in itself. Most men use whores or keep mistresses."

Barding shifted uncomfortably. His mother glanced at him, and he drew himself up and pretended he had not been embarrassed while Miles did not permit his amusement to show. The earl was less bothered by the plain speaking than by the speaker being his mother.

"I don't know whether he sired other bastards—"

What?

"But William did not succeed in getting Laura with child, which does make me wonder…"

"Really, Mama, this is beside the point, is it not?"

"No, it is not, Barding. Let me complete my instructions to Halliwell."

The earl subsided.

"We received a letter recently from a Hiram St. John, who styles himself Baron St. John. I do not recognize the name, but his direction was given as Kensington Square, rather than a coffee house."

She was aware that a man bent on nefarious activity or wishing to conceal his actual name and address could receive his correspondence at a coffee house. He need only tell the proprietor whatever name he pleased and ask him to hold any messages to be picked up.

"I see." A compliment on her astuteness would be patronizing. Prompting her was unnecessary. She would proceed at her own rate.

"St. John asserts that William seduced his daughter and got her with child."

"We are concerned, as you can imagine, Halliwell. Hrmpf."

Lavinia Barding and Miles exchanged glances. Caroline Barding gave her eyebrows a rueful quirk.

"What did the writer want, my lady?"

The first sign of unease appeared: a slight crease between her perfectly arched eyebrows. "He did not ask for anything…specifically. He merely informed us of the boy's existence. Barding, the letter, please."

Her son passed her a folded letter. She held it out to Miles. "Read it for yourself, and tell me what you think."

The hand was educated, though not as careful as a clerk's would be. Precisely the style one expected of a gentleman who was neither scholarly nor meticulous.

…seduced my girl at a house party and got her with child…name's Jeremy…toddling now…happy to continue taking care of the boy discreetly of course…what's done is done, but I thought you should know…

"A very odd communication," he allowed. "It's vague, except for the child's name. Alleged child," he qualified. "Have you written for additional details?"

"Of course. We have not yet received a reply; we received this only yesterday." She granted him a minuscule smile. "I don't know whether you recall that one of William's names was Jeremy? It was Caroline's favorite brother's name."

"Thank you for reminding me, my lady. I'd forgotten. Its use suggests the author knows something about William beyond the fact of his death."

"I know you will understand the significance of the timing, also."

"Ay. One would expect the girl's father to write as soon as he knew she was ruined or at least as soon as he knew she was with child. Or when the baby was born. To wait this long, coincidentally until after William is no more, certainly raises questions. What is it you wish me to do?"

"I have little doubt we will receive a prompt reply. Then we shall know what we will do."

He rather wished she had postponed sending for him until she had received further information, while priding himself on the Bardings' reliance on him.

"The letter was too subtly worded for me to ascertain whether it constituted an attempt at extortion. If it is, do you intend to prosecute St. John?"

"You are being ridiculous, Halliwell. Why would we pay to conceal William's peccadillo? His reputation was known in our circle, and as he was already married, he could not be expected to wed the chit. Nor do I care if it is an attempt to squeeze us. We will not pay. It will be St. John's girl's reputation which will suffer."

"I'll begin by finding out who these people are. When we know who we are dealing with, it may shed some light on their motive."

Lavinia twisted the emerald ring on her finger. "If St. John's claim seems credible, determine whether the child is William's."

"That may be impossible, my lady." He seldom

encountered a problem he could not put right. On the other hand, this was not a legal or accounting issue.

"I have great faith in your abilities, Halliwell."

He permitted the dowager countess's statement to warm him for a moment. "Assuming I find this 'Jeremy' is likely to be Mr. William Stretton's, what do you want done?"

A pause. At the periphery of his vision, Caroline Barding's hungry gaze told him. William had always been her favorite in spite of his failings.

"I want the child," Caroline said.

Chapter 2

Miles did not tell Bryden the subject of the meeting, beyond saying it involved a few tedious details resulting from William Stretton's death. The earl had harrumphed at the end of the meeting and mumbled that he and the Ladies Barding preferred that the existence of a possible Stretton bastard be kept secret, even from Halliwell's assistant. An odd request, when the dowager countess admitted William's habits were public knowledge.

Lavinia added, "Why blacken the girl's name unnecessarily? The more who know of the allegation, the more likely gossip will spread."

He began to investigate the St. John family's finances and reputation immediately on leaving Barding House. The task required no different skills from those he employed to determine businesses were sound and well run. He could meet with other sources he used tomorrow. Then he would catch up on the work he had put off to meet with the Bardings.

****

"You are efficient." Lavinia Barding continued to read the report Miles had delivered an hour before. As he could not entrust the research to Bryden, he had gone to a man who dealt in information. He was known by those who used his services to be trustworthy, and Halliwell had never found him mistaken in any background he had provided. He ordinarily gave verbal reports only; his clients took notes if needed. Whitacker, whose clerk Miles had been, had introduced him; Markham was selective in accepting clients. If he did not wish to deal with someone who approached him, he was merely a gentleman who had retired from an importing business. Whoever had claimed he could supply information must have been confusing him with another, or else was playing a prank. Miles had written the report from his own obscurely phrased notes and from memory.

As you stressed the need for haste, I could not be as thorough as I would wish. I will continue to dig into the St. Johns' background and supplement this report as soon as possible.

Baron St. John's income derives as follows. Approximately one-tenth from the estate, St. John Underhill, Marchmoor, Staffordshire. St. John Underhill has been in the St. John family since it was inherited from a cousin in 1622. The title dates to 1689; apart from being created Baron St. John, the most remarkable achievement of any member of the family (in recorded history) was Hiram St. John's courtship and marriage to the late Sarah Joan Suttle, daughter of Jonah Suttle, owner of a pottery. She combined beauty, charm, an extremely large dowry, and no social graces whatsoever. I am told there is probably no kitchen in the southern half of England that does not possess at least one baking dish or pitcher or bowl from the Suttle kilns.

Nine-tenths from investments (Consolidated Funds, rents from London properties). The investments were purchased with Sarah Suttle's dowry. The St. Johns have no significant debt.

Sarah, Lady St. John, died of lung fever in 1719. Five months later, Lord St. John married Augusta Cynthia Barre, daughter of Sir Gerald Barre, baronet. The Barres are of ancient lineage with several illustrious members. The title was received in 1611, when James I instituted the baronetage to raise money for the support of troops in Ireland. The Barres are well thought of, with a reputation for probity and strict propriety. The current Lady St. John lacks beauty and charm but has done much to erase the stigma of St. John's first wife.

Children: Julia, nine-and-twenty, by Sarah St. John; Martin, twenty, and Cecilia, eighteen, by Augusta St. John.

Julia St. John, a spinster, went to companion an elderly lady connection of Augusta St. John's two or three years ago. The old lady had a property to leave, and it was hoped she would bequeath it to Lady St. John, or to her children. As the woman was a distant relative and I could not learn where the property is, I can tell you no more about it, or of Mistress Julia's whereabouts. Of her it is said she is much like her mother as to her sense and good heart, though not in beauty, and with no suggestion of the shop about her.

Cecilia is expected to marry well as she is a diamond of the first water and well dowered. She is described as "a sweet, lively miss." I am not certain what this means, but my informant mentioned he had known a girl who was fond of climbing trees and once rode a sheep. Her woolly mount at last deposited her in a mud puddle. He said he would have described her as lively and also rather sweet. That Cecilia has not already married is ascribed to her mother's ambition and also to her desire the girl should outgrow those lively tendencies, whatever they are.

Martin is a pleasant young man, no wilder than many, and more responsible than most. He is already conscious of his future as the next Baron St. John.

Nothing to the family's detriment has come to my ears and they are generally liked, except Lady St. John, who is said to be a finickal mistress and lacks the warm-hearted manner of the first Lady St. John. This is the opinion even of servants and others who disapproved of Sally St. John's mercantile origin.

"I suppose we can acquit them of deceiving us," she remarked, "unless something in their letter contradicts your intelligencer."

St. John's letter arrived the next day.

****

"You've another letter, Mistress Perry," Riggs commented. "The third in less than two months. You'll be getting as much mail as parson and his lady soon." The shop did double duty as the post office and hub of gossip. No doubt the proprietor had mentioned it to anyone who came in and would continue to do so until everyone in Handley knew. There were few secrets in a village.

Except one. Julia owed her neighbors' belief she was a widow rather than an immoral woman to several lucky circumstances: she was not a young girl, she wore a pretty wedding ring set with an aquamarine, and on her arrival in full mourning, she had leaked tears at any reference to her family or her late husband. Remarks meant to be consoling, such as "You have a token to remember him by, at least," brought forth more tears.

She had lived at High Farm almost a year before she emerged from the worst of her melancholy.

Today's letter clarified certain details only by implication. Her father wrote to advise her that a representative of the family would be coming to interview her. They had already been shown the letters relating to the seduction. The writer had never used names, only terms of endearment like "dearest" and "my love" and signed them as "your cavalier," "your supplicant," and twice, by a nickname, "Will o' the Wisp." The tricks of a practiced seducer! Nevertheless, the family had identified the hand as their son's. "I have no doubt you will be exceeding discreet with the fellow they are sending to you and not agree to give the boy up to them unless they agree we may see him regularly," the letter ended.

She had never been happy about her decision, but it was too late to regret it. The reproaches, the tears, the fits of vapors, all of them having to be concealed, the promises everything would work out, were past and dead as Caesar. Papa and Stepmama's fury not only at the fact but at their daughter's refusal to name the man and, even worse, to let the child go, had all faded. Papa was now quite pleased with this turn of events. How ironic. Soon she would be free. Or freer than she had been for the last two years.

Her lips tightened at the thought of all she had lost or given up. Foolish to give way to bitterness! If she were a better person, she would accept her situation and be thankful it was no worse. Yet she could not help longing for the things she had enjoyed when she was young: long walks or rides at St. John Underhill, dancing, parties, good conversation. Then after her youth was past, she had savored Theo Manning's admiration.

Admittedly, interesting talk was in short supply at London entertainments. There had been a good deal of silly chatter when she was a girl, though at least it often led to laughter. When was the last time she had laughed? Perhaps as one aged, merriment came more seldom. In the last two years, there had been no one to laugh with, in any case.

She enjoyed reading, but it was difficult to get books. She had read and reread the few she had brought with her, and her father occasionally sent her one or two, but he read little except the newspapers, and her stepmother considered reading unfeminine and an unnecessary expense besides.

She knew people to greet when she met them at church or in the shops. They were acquaintances rather than friends, and she did not exchange visits with them. If she grew friendly with them, they would be bound to ask about her family and her late husband. She had worn deepest mourning on her arrival in Handley and had kept to herself ever since. Janet Campbell, the boy's nurse, had let it be understood "the widow Perry" had leased the house from the owner.

The parson's wife, who might have made an effort to welcome her into parish activities, was in poor health and her duties shared out among several active parishioners. None of them had thought to approach Julia. Perhaps she might have made friends if she had not feared the necessity for more lies. There would be no way to avoid lying in reply to any personal question.

And she was tired in all ways: tired of being alone and lonely, and weary from performing tasks she had never been trained for. Janet Campbell cared for the child, except for washing his clothing and bedding, which was sent out to a laundress with the rest of their clothes. A woman came in for half a day to cook and do the worst of the cleaning. The maid helped Janet in the nursery. The child and meal preparation took precedence, as they must. The neglected work, dusting, sweeping, washing her few delicate items which could not be sent to the washerwoman, like her prettier caps, brushing and mending her clothing, and shopping for food and other necessities often fell to Julia.

Until today, her future had stretched out as a series of identical days, world without end. She would not look ahead to a happier future yet, however. Her father had promised her before she came to live in Handley that it would be only for a few months, until the baby could be sent to a foster family. She could not bear to be disappointed again.

She did wish he had thought to give her an idea of when to expect the family's agent. It was bound to be awkward. Still, there were the letters, and there was the boy. Too much to drink on William's part, which anyone who knew him would believe, and desperation on hers. Yes, that would explain it.

Chapter 3

When Barding provided him the St. John female's direction, High Farm, Handley, Dorset, he had expected a tenant cottage on the outskirts of the village. In Handley, however, he was directed to a lane—such as it was!—at the end of the village and told to look for the green door and shutters.

The lane meandered up a gentle slope for a mile before he found a two-story stone house with shutters and door of a deep, rich green. High Farm indeed; it was situated on what he would have called a rise. A flower garden bloomed with harebell, yarrow, and meadowsweet behind a low stone wall. White curtains fluttered in the open windows. While one would not let an erring daughter live in a hovel, this dwelling was better than his imagination had painted. He glimpsed the corner of a cow shed or stable at the back and possibly a vegetable garden. Perhaps she had been provided with a gardener and housekeeper as well as the nurse.

The door opened to his knock. A slim woman of thirty or so stood before him. Her blue gown, snow-white kerchief concealing her from neck to whatever bosom she possessed, and equally white cap covering her hair betokened a housekeeper.

"My name is Miles Halliwell. I am here to speak with Mistress Perry."

"Please come into the parlor, Mr. Halliwell. I'll have your horse taken around to the back and given water, if you permit?" Her voice was well bred and soft; a gentlewoman left in straitened circumstances by an improvident father or husband, probably.

"Thank you. I'm sure Coffee would appreciate a drink."

She smiled a little doubtfully. "Follow me, please." The passage led past a door to the kitchen toward a handsome enclosed stair. She turned to the left and stopped at the door of a plainly furnished room.

"It will only take me a moment."

No doubt he would have to wait longer than that while the St. John chit was informed of his presence and prinked for it. The parlor was square and furnished with simple furniture, some of which Queen Elizabeth might have used if Her Majesty had happened to call at High Farm. The starkness was relieved by an old Turkey carpet and a number of bright cushions on the chairs and settle. The room had the feeling of a home. Different from Charfield, of course, but cozy in a way his own lodgings were not. Perhaps a dwelling needed a woman's touch to be welcoming.

Somewhere at the back of the house he heard a voice, then brisk footsteps.

"The gardener's boy will remove, er, Coffee's saddle and bridle and give him water. He said he—your horse—seemed not to require walking to cool down. The boy hopes to be a groom and is very knowledgeable about horses. Please do be seated." She sat down on one of the chairs near the fireplace, making an inviting gesture at its mate.

"I trust Mistress Perry will join us shortly."

Did the housekeeper know the truth about the "Perry" girl and the child? If not, her mistress would no doubt dismiss her. He would have to make sure the woman did not linger outside the door to eavesdrop.

"Sir, I am Julia Perry."

Julia Perry was certainly the name of the mother of William's by-blow. At that moment, Miles knew what he had overlooked in his notes and the report he had written and had failed to remember when St. John's letter arrived with the direction of High Farm.

His face must have betrayed him, for she turned pink.

"I beg your pardon! I was expecting…" He could not end, "a younger female." He recovered himself. "I was expecting you would have a housekeeper or companion." Not his best effort. Good God, how had he not remembered that Julia was the older sister?

"You thought I would be a heedless, silly girl. Perfectly understandable." Her voice revealed nothing.

Meeting her amber eyes, he read pain. He could say nothing soothing to alleviate it.

"I did assume you would be quite young and naïve. I was acquainted with William Stretton. He never showed much interest in ladies of sense and character, having neither himself. I trust I do not give offense." He would have left off the last sentence had he believed Julia Perry, or Julia St. John, loved William. Having seen her, he could not believe it. His half brother's taste had run to petite, well-rounded females of no great intellectual power.

"No, sir." Color tinged her cheeks again.

Shame at having let herself be seduced, and at her age, no less. He had given some thought to how to proceed in this unfamiliar situation. The only instruction Lavinia Barding had given him was "Make sure the brat is William's."

That casually issued order worried him the most. Miles had had little exposure to babies and young children. He had come to live at Charfield Hall when he was three, only slightly younger than George, but he had no memory of what George had looked like at that age. William must have been born soon after his own arrival, but he retained no memory of it. Neither he nor George had spent much time in the baby's presence, or in Peter's before he was three or four. The countess and the dowager countess might remember what the Stretton babes had looked like—women often did, he understood, or thought they did—but no Stretton would dignify the St. Johns' claim by going to view Will's bastard. Besides, the arrival of a member of a noble family would stir talk. However, the Stretton ladies had provided some help: they had shown him miniatures of the three boys as infants and a painting of the family done about the time Peter was a year old, when his older brothers were six and four, and his sister eight.

Would he be able to see any similarity in the baby's features? He would have to rely on clues and instinct, not the degree of proof he preferred. The situation was delicate. He must avoid implying disbelief in Lord St. John's claim the child had been sired by William Stretton, at least until he was certain it was a lie.

Caroline Barding wanted the boy to be William's son and inclined to believe St. John's assertion that his daughter had borne William Stretton's by-blow. Like her mother-in-law and the earl, she also wanted

22

evidence. Halliwell doubted they had recalled that Julia St. John was several years older than William. What of it? William probably had impregnated the girl. Woman. Julia St. John was not the kind to attract William as a rule. While it might seem out of character, odder things happened when a man was bowsy. The letters sounded like the sort of drivel he'd expect from William. Failing to shoulder his responsibility was not out of the question for Will, either.

Now he had met Julia St. John, the story was less convincing, not because she was unattractive and older, but because Miles could not believe she would yield to his drunken blandishments.

A second consideration was St. John's behavior. Why wait so long to write to Barding? If St. John had been purse-pinched, transferring responsibility for the child's rearing would make sense, assuming they cared about the child more than they cared about their daughter's reputation. They had not simply placed the baby with some poor family in exchange for a small fee.

If William had not been married, they would surely have expected him to marry the girl. If she did not discover he was married until she realized her condition, they could not have sought to remedy matters by a quick marriage, not to William, at least. A duel or a demand for a substantial settlement would be the likely result. A family able to give a good dowry would have little trouble finding a gentleman willing to marry a ruined daughter, even if he knew about the pregnancy.

The revelation following hard on William's death had first appeared to be an attempt to pass off the baby as William's now he was unable to deny it. But if her family did not need William to contribute to the baby's maintenance, there was no point in mentioning the matter. Why reveal the boy's existence and their daughter's shame?

Unless William had been informed and simply ignored it. Knowing William, this would not be inconceivable. Ah, possibly not the best choice of words. But if he had not responded, why had there been no subsequent letter? If Miles were the father of a chit in Julia St. John's predicament and his first letter had gone unheeded, he would have written the earl, or approached him at his next stay in London. Or hunted down the seducer and thrashed him.

The only explanation which would account for waiting until the boy was in leading-strings was that the family hoped to preserve the girl's reputation. They had kept her indiscretion a secret, because here she was, living under an assumed name. When he had inquired at the public house for directions to High Farm, she had been described as "the Widow Perry, poor lady. Not got over the loss of her husband, she hasn't." Evidently no scandal attached to her in Handley. Remarkable, though not impossible, if she had been sent to some midwife who offered a discreet house for lyings-in. If the resulting baby had been placed in someone's care immediately, Julia could have returned home from a long sojourn with the mythical, now deceased, relative in a distant county, and resumed her unblemished life. It might not have served with a young, flighty miss but could pass unquestioned with an old maid of serious demeanor. Yet here she was with the child some eighteen months old. The whole affair raised questions in his mind. Miles did not like mysteries, most especially when they involved the Bardings.

"Mistress Perry, I apologize for the seeming impertinence, but under the circumstances, I feel I must ask you a few questions for my employer's satisfaction." To make sure they were not buying a pig in a poke. "Buying" was not the right word, when no request for money had been made. "Accepting" a pig in a poke. If the child had been fathered by some other man who could not be approached, or was impecunious, passing off the by-blow as William's might seem a golden opportunity. His habits were no secret, and he was unable to deny having had a liaison with the St. John woman. The problem was, why bother when they were not asking for money? The woman and her bastard were settled here, out of sight and out of mind, and Markham had heard no whisper of scandal when he delved into the St. Johns' reputation. While the St. Johns were not well known in the upper levels of London society, Markham's informants cast wide nets. If there had been something to learn, he would know of it. A spinster daughter sent off to be a companion to an old lady was common enough to cause no talk.

Her cheeks reddened, a perfectly understandable reaction in a well-bred female. "Of course."

"How did you first meet Lord William?"

"At a fair in London, sir. A group of my friends went."

"Did he rape you?"

"Uh…no?" It was not quite a question, but it was less than a denial. "I mean, no. Of course not."

A strange reaction. He could not dismiss the possibility outright if William had been drunk. It might explain how he had come to prey upon a plain old maid. Why would Mistress Julia deny it? Better to admit to being raped than to being wanton or foolish enough to allow herself to be seduced.

"Will you tell me where the seduction took place?" The wonder was how any girl of good family ever lost her virtue before marriage, as carefully chaperoned as they were. Or were supposed to be. If he ever married and had a daughter, he would do better.

"It was at a house party over the Christmas holidays."

"By whom was it given?"

She swallowed. "I fear I no longer recall."

She was lying to protect the hosts.

Ten years ago, on Friday, June 19th, at the Moon & Stars Assembly Rooms, a pretty young lady, the daughter of an attorney, had caught Miles's eye. As luck would have it, Whitacker, the Bardings' then man of business, was acquainted with the family and introduced him. Letitia Bellingham was a delightful girl, sweet without being insipid, with a lively interest in everything. They danced the minuet together and conversed at supper, discovering how much they had in common. He remembered the night as if it were yesterday: the room, the music, her blue mantua, one shade darker than her eyes. He subsequently called upon her. It would only have been a matter of time before he spoke with Letitia Bellingham's father. He had never been romantickal, and still she had made an impression upon him that might linger until his last breath.

Surely a serious-minded lady should be able to remember a meeting less than three years ago, when she had been sufficiently struck by the man to give up her virginity. Unless it had already been long gone; that was a possibility. His lips tightened.

"Were you there with your family?"

"Yes. But a number of young people were present, not only those who had come with their families but also some university friends of the son of the house. All of the younger guests were full of high spirits and not as carefully chaperoned as they should have been. It was a rambling old house with many nooks and crannies, perfect for a game of hide-and-seek."

She spoke of the young people, not seeing herself as one of them. She was not, of course, no more than William had been. He mentioned that fact.

"No. Several of us were old enough to act as chaperons. Some of the girls and boys were rather too high-spirited. I and one or two others thought it best to be at hand. William had had a good deal of punch and came along, saying it sounded like excellent sport, near as good as blindman's buff."

Now, that rang true.

"In such a game, at night after the men at least had been drinking, I would have thought only a chaperon for each young lady could have prevented a couple from stealing off to clicket like a pair of foxes in the shrubbery. Or the linen closet or some unused bedchamber."

Her flushed face and rapid breathing were either anger or the prelude to humiliated tears. Before he could frame the next brutal question, she took several deep breaths to compose herself. "I cannot blame you for not understanding how it was, when I don't understand it myself. I was patrolling, as you might say,

27

listening for sounds of misbehavior rather than looking for the one who was hiding. William and I met in a passage in the older wing, which seemed a likely place as none of the rooms were occupied—they were drafty and still furnished in the style of a century ago. He suggested we hunt for miscreants together, as he would be able to deal with any drunken boy we found. Some of the striplings had taken unaccustomed amounts of punch or had flasks of brandy with them. It seemed no more than sensible."

"Yet you ended the evening with your petticoats around your waist."

She continued after a wince at his coarseness. "We came to one little chamber in which the curtains were open. Moonlight was flooding in. I was going to pull them across the window, to spare the bed hangings and carpet from fading in sunlight. 'Stay a moment, 'tis a pretty sight,' William said. 'Let us admire it.' The gardens below were as mysterious as a fairy land, all pearly light and ebony shadows. Then he kissed me."

"As you appear to be a sensible woman, I find it difficult to understand how your fall from grace came about from a mere kiss in the moonlight."

She did not reply immediately. Finally she sighed. "Mr. Halliwell, I was unmarried at an advanced age, having never really been courted. I met Lord William at a fair, as I have said, and he talked to me rather than hurrying off in search of younger, prettier females immediately after we were introduced. As a man, you cannot understand how flattering his attention was. He spent a little time with me at each of our meetings."

The last phrase was revealing. Clearly there had been more than the first meeting and then the house party. She would say more if he waited. Most could not abide silence. Almost she surprised him when an even longer pause ensued before she went on.

"It was very disarming not to be ignored, and to converse with a handsome man about subjects other than parish activities or the weather. When he kissed me, it stirred feelings I hardly recognized. I do not suppose I need spell out the rest."

No. "What did you talk about?"

"What?"

"You have said that you and Lord William conversed. What did you discuss?"

"Oh…everything and nothing. The theater, gossip, amusing incidents one or the other of us had seen."

"Did you know he was married?"

"The subject never came up. Neither of us had any thought of marriage. We were simply acquaintances."

Those who knew William Stretton found him amiable. He was also selfish and could be boorish when he was cup-shot, though Miles doubted his female relatives knew about that. On second thought, Lavinia might. Unfortunately for his character and those around him, he possessed wheedling ways and a boyish artlessness which often won him forgiveness. His manner might ingratiate him with any lady; he had always been able to win Caroline, Lady Barding's, forgiveness despite her acknowledgement of his faults. That Julia St. John had been enchanted did not surprise him. That William would have bothered with her did.

Acquaintances, and yet they had carried on a clandestine correspondence.

"How did it happen that you exchanged a series of letters?"

"The day after the fair, he sent me a note with a posy. I wrote to thank him."

He had found that staring fixedly—at a steward or bailiff he suspected of working a jig with the accounts, or a dishonest merchant—discomposed his prey. It served its purpose. She commenced fiddling with her handkerchief.

"Did it not cause comment when this token was delivered?"

"I-I was out of the house. Shopping. His messenger met me as I returned."

She was lying. He need not ask how the coincidence occurred. It would have been arranged at their first meeting. Her replies would have been sent by her maid or some other trusty servant. Almost certainly her maid. 'Twas a common mistake to hire a young maid for a girl. The chit would be as foolish and romantickal-minded as her mistress. "And the other letters?"

"Must we discuss this, sir? I confess I was immoral, and it gives me great pain to remember how I made the wrong decision at every turn."

"I need not inquire further. Please forgive my habit of thoroughness. I would like to see Jeremy."

She rose, saying only, "Come with me."

He followed her up the narrow, oak-paneled stair to one of four small bedrooms. She pushed open the door and spoke without entering the room. "Nurse Campbell, this gentleman would like to see the child."

Julia St. John stood aside. He waited for her to enter, but she shook her head. "I will wait for you in the parlor." She turned away and disappeared down the staircase without a backward glance.

Chapter 4

Miles smiled at the woman, a sharp-featured, sharp-eyed woman in her middle years, and asked her name.

"Janet Campbell, sir."

He could see a request for his name hovering on her lips before she folded them, remembering her place. Scotland was in her voice; presumably she did not hold with truckling overmuch to Englishmen.

A small child stood within a baby walker, staring at him doubtfully.

"Come, Master Jeremy." Nurse Campbell held out her hand, and the boy trundled toward her.

"How old is he?"

"A year and a half."

"Nurse, I am a bachelor and know little of infantry. What can you tell me?"

"The lad scarce needs the walker, but the fire being lit today I've put him in it so I can take my eyes off him while I tidy the chamber. He's quick in all his ways and knows enough words to ask for most things he wants. Sometimes he'll go into a pet because he doesn't know what to call a thing. He's not finickal. He's no worse than any child of his age, and better than some."

More than he cared about, when he had inquired only to get the woman talking. The important thing was, Jeremy Perry or St. John did resemble the pictures of George, William, and Peter he had seen. Flaxen hair might darken; blue eyes were simply blue eyes, unless they were uncommon vivid; and a small child's nose and chin would change a good deal by the time he was grown. It was possible any young child with fair hair or brown hair and pale blue eyes might look like any other with the same characteristics. But the child could be William's: Master Jeremy's ears were the same shape as Halliwell's half brothers'—wider at the bottom than at the top. This did not prove he was William's son. He might equally have been George's or the earl's. Peter had been in Italy for years.

"A fine-looking boy. I suppose you have been with Mistress Perry's family for many years?"

She could not keep the pride out of her voice. "Ay, he's a good wee mannie. I was Mistress Julia's nurse."

Jeremy was fortunate to have one person who was fond of him. Almost angry for no reason he could think of, Halliwell made his way down the stair.

In the parlor, he found the woman seated at a little gateleg table supporting a tea tray. She poured a bowl and offered it. "Will you take milk? Sugar? 'Tis only bohea, not green tea."

"Milk, please." He accepted the little bowl on its saucer. "You have a fine, healthy son."

"Yes." As she poured her own tea, he was able to study her. She was neat and suitably clad yet bore an indefinable air of being uncared for, like a child's toy left too long on a shelf. Appropriate! The woman had been an old maid when she encountered William.

"I am surprised that the Earl of Barding heard from Lord St. John rather than from you." When he had supposed the mother was a young, silly chit, it had not seemed odd. After meeting her, he could not imagine Julia St. John requiring an intermediary unless she thought a letter from a baron would carry more weight. "What was it you hoped for from this?"

"Hoped for?" she repeated as if she did not understand the question.

"Why did St. John write to the Earl of Barding about the child's existence? What did he expect? What did you expect?"

"I don't know. It was not my idea." Her bewilderment sounded genuine even to his cynical ears.

"Let me restate the question. Why not when you found yourself pregnant?"

The woman bit her lip at the blunt term. "It seemed best not to say anything. My family hoped to conceal my disgrace."

"And it appears they succeeded. But now something has changed to make informing the earl desirable, or the loss of your reputation less undesirable." At her stricken expression, he found himself strangely reluctant to interrogate her, though he knew she was lying at least in part.

"My father saw the notice of Lord William's death and wrote to me that he meant to inform Lord Barding. He seemed to think the family might wish to assume responsibility for the boy. I don't know why."

"You did not ask? As it involved your reputation, I would think you would have some curiosity about the reason for his decision."

Her smile lifted the corners of her mouth fractionally. "When a female is dependent upon her father for support, she would be unwise to question his actions."

That tart answer rang true. Even a man might hesitate to oppose someone who was his means of support. The Bardings did not refuse to take his advice even when it ran counter to what they wished. At the same time, however, he served them to the best of his ability, however inconvenient. "I concede the point. Thank you for your assistance. I will make my report to the earl. When I have received further instructions, I will inform you."

"Very well."

Something in her face suggested curiosity.

"Do you have any questions before I go?"

"It is really no business of mine. However, I cannot help wondering why the earl would want him."

A loving mother had every right to be concerned for her son's future and how he might be treated by his father's family. But why would Julia St. John care, when she obviously had no interest in the boy? " 'Tis not the earl but his lady who wishes him to live at Charfield Hall. Lord William was his mother's favorite, and he had no legitimate children."

Should he reassure her about Jeremy's future, if the Bardings took him? It would not be a bad life for William's natural son, as Miles could testify. He would be brought up decently, educated, and placed in a suitable profession.

"Do you know how long it will take to hear from Lord Barding?"

"I intend to stay at Shaftesbury, and he will write to me there." He should go back to London but might have to turn around again almost at once. His account would set forth the evidence and leave it to the Bardings to decide. The earl had provided him a groom to carry his report, as the Bardings would return to their country home as soon as Parliament rose. Far quicker to send it by messenger than by the post from Shaftesbury, the nearest town of any size, to London, whatever the General Post Office claimed.

****

The earl's, or rather the dowager countess's, answer came more quickly than he had expected. Barding had written it, but from certain clues, Miles suspected it had been at his mother's dictation. She did not trust a man to see a baby's resemblance to other family members. It would be necessary for them to view the child. Parliament would adjourn three days hence; the following day, the family would depart for the country. The earl had already sent to Charfield to dispatch his old traveling coach to Shaftesbury, by which Miles was to bring the child, its nurse, and the mother to Oxfordshire. There Jeremy Perry could be inspected by the family and compared to pictures of the other boys.

Miles spent longer thinking about the postscript than about the body of the letter. *I summoned Lord St. John to meet with me.* Miles felt sure Lavinia had been present. *He earnestly desires that if we take Jeremy, the St. John family be permitted to maintain a relationship with the child. Lady St. John, who accompanied the baron, fairly begged that our families be on visiting terms as Julia St. John cannot bear the thought of letting her son go entirely. They would not have written to me, the baron claimed, but that they had grown concerned for the child's upbringing as a gentleman, situated as he was, with no adult male influence and no boys but the sons of farmers to play with as he grows up. He says there are few gentlemen's families living nearby, and Mistress Perry, as she is called, would not be accepted without an introduction from someone known to them.*

The letter's last line was untrue. An introduction from the vicar would be enough to give Mistress Perry a place among the local gentry. Or would it? They would naturally ask about her family connections: what part of the country she came from, how she found herself a widow living on her own. She would have to spin a tale that could not be discovered to be a lie. Possible but difficult.

His next thought was, how fortunate for the boy that the family did not wish to hide him away and forget him. A purely emotional response, of course, and like all reactions rooted in the heart rather than the head, unwise. He had been cared for by one side of his family; what more did anyone need? *How would my life have turned out if my mother's family had not cast her out, if they had, or if she had not been an orphan?* He wished he knew more about the woman who had given him birth.

His intellect picked out one line to dissect. He had seen no sign that Julia St. John was such a doting mother she could not bear to give up her bastard son. She had not entered the nursery with him. That proved nothing: she might have found it painful to contemplate surrendering the boy, or else wished to let him see the child and speak with the nurse without her constraining presence. She had shown no emotion except when he had humiliated her with his questions. He could not fault her either for maintaining her control or being shamed by having to recount her loose behavior.

But she had never spoken Jeremy's name, which struck him as peculiar, like an almost complete lack of connection to her son. She had given him birth and lived in a modest home, not a mansion like Charfield, where it would be possible to ignore his presence. Not that the earl's children had gone unnoticed. The Bardings took an interest in their offspring, which was not true of all noble families.

Julia St. John's lack of emotion was troubling. He was not in the habit of revealing strong feelings himself. Julia St. John was neither stupid nor impulsive: her speech and bearing were too controlled. Then how could he explain her liaison with William? Unconsidered behavior was common enough in young, innocent girls led astray by a man's attentions. But Julia had somehow got a son without the excuse of inexperience or having to whore to survive, and he doubted it was the result of drink.

With a stab of remorse, he wondered if his own mother had been just the same. He could not recall her face or guess at her age, but she had sung to him and played with him. She must have been a good mother. Julia St. John or Perry, whatever she cared to call herself, was not.

The family's concern that the boy be brought up a gentleman did make sense. Still, St. John could afford to send the boy to school in a few years and then have him trained for some profession or genteel trade. Why involve the Bardings?

He would write Markham, requesting certain further information.

****

She could not quite put the matter out of mind,

though for several days her chief thought was of how much she disliked Miles Halliwell. His questioning had felt like a rape. Yet what else could she expect when any decent person would condemn a female who had not only yielded to a seducer but had schemed to evade chaperonage with equally heedless, headstrong friends. She could sympathize with a girl cozened into losing her virginity in innocent circumstances. Lying about one's destination and companions to attend a fair, then carrying on a clandestine correspondence with a gentleman showed a wild disregard of both propriety and common sense. But it had been William Stretton's idea to meet at the house party.

After a week, she began to wonder what was happening in the world beyond High Farm. Of course, one could not expect to hear in a matter of days; it would likely be weeks or a month before she heard anything more. Until she did, Julia would not permit herself to either speculate or hope.

Then she was busy with household matters. Janet Campbell gave her a list of the quantity of linen needed to make several shirts, caps, and bed gowns, as the boy was outgrowing the old ones. She would send Billy to Shaftesbury for those and a few other things they needed. She was going to the back door to tell him to leave the weeding to his son and ready the horse and cart when a rap at the front of the house interrupted her.

"Good morning, Mistress Perry." Billy's son had already taken the reins of Miles Halliwell's horse. Why did the man standing at the door bring the Devil to mind? He was not ill-favored or sinister in any obvious way. His hair was chestnut, and his features were good if austere. It might be his eyes, the gray of dirty ice.

"Good morning, sir. Have you more questions for me or Mistress Campbell? Come into the parlor."

The maid peeked out of the kitchen.

"Betty, bring the tea tray and some of the saffron cake to the parlor."

He interrupted her inquiry as to how he found the accommodations at his inn with a brusque "I have received instructions from Lord Barding, who also sent a letter from your father." He offered her a letter sealed with the St. John signet. "You will wish to read it first."

Knees weak, Julia sank onto the bench by the window. Breaking the seal, her heart sank. The Bardings wanted to see the child before reaching a decision though her papa thought they would accept him. She was to accompany Jeremy to their estate.

Betty brought in the tray with the tea service and murmured, "Ma'am?"

Julia unlocked the tea canister and measured out the tea by habit. When it had been only a question of living in a village where she knew no one, she had been able to ignore her dishonor. To impose upon the earl's family who would despise her for immorality and with the sin of lying on her soul, was unthinkable. How could she possibly face them?

The proposed visit was another delay. Yet once that ordeal was past, she could finally return to her own life. She should have been able to go home a year ago without fuss. First that promise was broken, and now she was expected to lie to an earl! Lying to his man of business had been almost more than she could bear.

"The traveling coach should arrive in two days' time to take you, your son, and his nurse to the manor. I will accompany you to assure your comfort at the inns.

I think we must plan on the journey requiring three days. Do you know if the boy is a good traveler?"

"He has never gone on any journey since we came here when he was a baby."

"Well, we will stop when we must to let him recover if he should prove queasy."

"Is it really necessary that I go? Janet Campbell has cared for him from the beginning, and Betty often acts as nursery maid. I can spare her to assist Nurse. If the earl and his family wish to keep the boy, it would not be necessary for Betty or for Nurse to return here if the Bardings are willing to keep them on. Nurse Campbell and Betty are familiar to him and know his routine."

"The earl and his lady and the dowager countess wish to meet you."

Her cheeks heated; she wanted to lower her eyes to avoid meeting Halliwell's gaze. Their eyes had met once at their first meeting. She had thought his were the eyes of an executioner: cold and implacable.

More humiliation before it would be done. She would have to do it, both for her family and herself. Once she was free, she would put it all behind her.

"Then certainly I will come." Under the circumstances, she really had no choice.

"You may bring the maid, too, of course. A fourth child at Charfield even temporarily will require an additional nursery maid, but I must ask: will the nurse and maid gossip about this?"

"Janet Campbell knows the truth and is utterly loyal to me. She was my own nurse until my stepmother replaced her and was with my mother's family before I was born. The others have been given to understand that my late husband's family did not approve of our marriage, hence their slighting of us. It will be necessary to explain our visit somehow."

"There will be no difficulty about that. The Bardings are known for taking in distant relatives in distress."

Distress was a very apt description of her state one cold March afternoon a little more than two years ago when she made the choice that led to this day.

****

She had found Augusta St. John present when she went to her father's study at his summons, a sure sign she was to be berated. This time she knew she deserved it. Her stepmother did reproach her though with less heat than expected. Nor did Augusta persist when Papa muttered, "What's done is done. Now we must preserve our family's reputation."

Julia's first reaction on hearing her father's plan was disbelief, followed by hurt. She managed to respond, "I hardly think that will answer, Papa. When a young female goes on an extended visit to some distant relative, there is bound to be talk."

Augusta frowned. "But you are not a young female. You have been on the shelf for years. We need only say my godmother is in failing health and needs a companion. We will hint she may decide to leave her property to me or to Cecilia, if she should take a fancy to her. Everyone will understand."

Julia wanted to retort that if she were to be the old lady's companion, perhaps Augusta's godmother would leave her the property. The remark would invite a sharp rebuke as being frivolous: Augusta's godmother had been dead for some years.

"I have never asked anything of you before, Julia.

41

Surely you can do this for me, or if not for me, for our family." Her father's conciliating tone shamed her, despite a sudden, mutinous thought. She felt more like a poor relation than a member of their family. She and Mama had been a family. When present, her father had hardly noticed her.

Julia had tried to win his regard without success while Cecilia had learned to capture his attention by the time she was three or four. Even if Julia still had any hope of earning his affection, she could not have exercised her little half sister's coquettish ways. If Papa had been immune to her mother's beauty, warmth, and charm, what chance had Julia ever had to deserve his love?

If she did as he requested, he might be grateful to her. Or not. For the first time in her life, Julia argued. She pointed out that a scheme depending upon a web of lies was wrong. Living apart for a time would not be a great sacrifice, if it were no more than that. But she did not like to lie. Although the Ten Commandments only forbade bearing false witness against a neighbor, she chose to take it as a prohibition against lying except perhaps in the rarest circumstances. Surely there could be no justification for it here.

When she persisted, her father said, "Your mama"—*My stepmother!*—"thinks you refuse to help because you are jealous of Cecilia. I cannot believe you are so selfish, Julia. Remember that it is not only her chances for a good marriage you would hurt, 'tis also Martin's. As my heir, he can make an excellent marriage if no scandal attaches to us."

Her half brother, Martin, was the one to whom she felt closest. He teased her sometimes, and always had a sympathetic word or a surreptitious glance of rueful sympathy when his mother belittled her.

"I cannot decide so quickly, Papa. I must have time to think."

"What is there to think of?" he shouted, losing patience. "By God, Julia, I despair of you. I support you, and you will repay me by doing as I say."

"Hush, St. John. The servants will hear."

He did not threaten to turn her out, perhaps because he knew that to cast off a spinster daughter would be a scandal of another sort—and would not solve their problem.

Augusta, for once the more temperate of the two, hurried into speech. "Julia, please consider the matter carefully before you refuse. I own 'tis monstrous awkward, yet it need not be a disaster if we all do our part. Think of how this little mistake will reflect on all of us. You know how sensitive Cecilia is. She is overset at the thought of the humiliation and talk."

This was a restrained description. Cecilia was keeping to her chamber, alternately weeping, sulking, and lamenting, as she sometimes did if denied some treat. No one would take notice of it unless it lasted more than a day or two. Stepmama added after a pregnant pause, "At least do not utterly refuse so quickly. You know how distressing it is for all when Cecilia is in a taking."

Her father and stepmother were determined to see Martin respected and Cecilia a titled married lady. That was the crux of the matter: to achieve those ends, no breath of scandal must touch the family.

****

Halliwell asked how long she would need to

43

prepare for the journey, rousing her from her contemplation of the tea bowl clutched in her hands as if its heat could warm her. Shifting it to hold between thumb and forefinger as her governess had taught her, she replied, "A day. We do not have much to pack." She had seven gowns, two of them full mourning, the others gray or brown or lavender, a color that somehow turned her face sallow. She need only take four, with their necessary under-petticoats, shifts, and accessories, and a night-rail. Her stay with the Bardings would be brief. Apart from essential garments, she would take her Bible, prayer book, the miniature of her mother, and the recent letters from her father and sister. She could not bear to be parted from the little ivory oval depicting Mama as a girl of eighteen, and she did not care to leave the letters where they might be found.

According to Miles Halliwell, Banbury and Charfield Hall were about one hundred miles from Handley. Julia had been prepared for some awkwardness on the journey. Miles Halliwell did not approve of her, and his cold manner did not bode well for three days in each other's company. However, the morning of their departure began better than she expected. Julia had forgotten he would not be in the coach, which was as full as it could be with herself, Janet Campbell, Betty, the boy, and the hamper of things Janet would need to care for him on the road.

Halliwell rode. As he passed the coach to speak to the coachman about their first change of horses, she gave him credit for horsemanship. Whatever else the man might lack, he sat his horse well, hand light on the reins, muscular thighs gripping his mount's sides. The first two hours after they left Handley were the best, unfortunately.

They had been on the road for less than half a day when the journey began to feel like an eternity. Fortunately, the weather was cool, for they had to keep the carriage windows closed because of the dust. This might have made the interior cozy. With three adults and a small child, the atmosphere soon grew stuffy.

"No!"

Earlier, the boy and Nurse Campbell had been counting cows and sheep in the fields they passed and sometimes a horse or dog. She thought they'd got up to four-and-thirty, or at least Nurse had. By her own count, this was the fifteenth "No!"

"No bikket!" he shrieked in response to Janet Campbell's offer of a piece of shortbread.

She returned it to the basket of food, toys, and other necessities. "Mistress Perry, might you ask Mr. Halliwell if we could stop for a few minutes?"

Julia, sitting beside Betty with her back to the horses because facing backward did not agree with the boy and he needed to have Campbell beside him, lowered the window and put out her hand to wave to Halliwell. It was the agreed signal for a needed stop— the fourth—and eliminated the need for her to poke her head out into the dust cloud raised by the wheels and the horses' hooves.

Coming level with the window, he inquired, "An immediate halt? Or at the next inn?"

She glanced at Janet.

"Master Jeremy needs only to run after a ball for a time to stretch his legs. Then he will be ready to rest in the coach." She did not use the word "nap" which the boy knew.

He did sleep after playing for a time on the grassy verge and staring at sheep and lambs in the field. When he woke, he played with a string of big, brightly colored beads, sliding them back and forth and making them rattle. Then he was hungry. He stared out the window again and babbled incomprehensibly. Janet answered. She seemed to understand him.

"Ay, 'tis a cow. The milk you drink comes from a cow."

"Unggg!"

Julia leaned her aching head back and closed her eyes.

Chapter 5

Five days later, each all but identical to the one before, Halliwell rode up beside the coach window and tapped on it. Perhaps the lines at the corners of his hard gray eyes came from squinting in the sun or perhaps he was as tired as she. He was dusty, too. She felt a lock brush her ear, come free from her closely dressed hair. When she tucked it up under her cap, it was stiff and dry with the same dust. When the boy's nose ran, the snot was dark with it. Even keeping the windows closed, every time they opened one to speak to Halliwell or to catch a little breeze to cool them or because Betty sometimes felt queasy, dust penetrated.

She rolled the window down.

"Another hour, I think, or not much more."

"Thank God." Julia wanted to bathe away dust and sweat and wash her hair, dress in clean clothing, sit quietly, and sleep with no loud voices from a taproom to disturb her rest. The inns they had expected to stay in would have been comfortable and quiet. Instead, they had put up at any accommodations they could find for the additional nights on the road.

She wanted to be away from the boy's stare and his pouting. Betty's usual cheer had faded into endurance. Janet alone was unperturbed. As Julia uttered this heartfelt comment, a stench filled the coach. Halliwell recoiled; Janet lowered the other window and observed,

"We will be needing to stop so I can tidy the laddie. Mistress, it would be well to keep both the windows down and never mind the dust."

"I see a steeple and cottages ahead. Likely there's a pothouse if not an inn. Will it do?"

"Oh, ay, sir," Janet said.

****

Charfield Hall stretched out asymmetrical wings to embrace the visitor. The oldest part was said to date to the reign of Edward I. Piecemeal additions over four centuries had turned a simple medieval hall and buttery into an irregular sprawl. The once-separate chapel stuck out from one wing at an odd angle; the floor plan was confusing and inconvenient. All the same, Miles always enjoyed the sight of Charfield Hall when he returned. As a small boy he had been fascinated by the stone used for the walls: light in color but thickly studded as a good plum cake with pebbles of different colors.

He was not a family member, though he had lived there from three until seventeen. Yet Charfield felt like home in a way his comfortable London lodgings did not. Perhaps if he owned a property someday, it would feel as welcoming as Charfield Hall.

The family summoned him to Charfield once or twice a year to discuss investments or major expenditures. This visit might be different, as all depended on what the family decided about the child. Perhaps he would be escorting Julia Perry back to Handley as soon as the coach horses were rested, with or without her son, or he might be here a week or more. 'Twas hard to plan when nothing was sure. Miles liked certainty.

Unlike his usual sojourns, he would probably not

be occupied most of the day. Having not been able to bring his work with him—Bryden would need it—he would have to find some way to fill the hours. He had not often had an entire day free since he left school, except Sunday. He enjoyed his work and he needed to make money, but still, he could have taken a brief holiday once in a while. Other men of the middling or professional class did. Mayhap the lack of family made a difference.

Well, he would idle when the Strettons did not require his attention. He could fish, as he and George had often done as children. They had been friends of a sort as they were almost of an age. That ended after George left for Harrow and Miles was sent to the local parson's grammar school. At Harrow, George formed friendships with other sprigs of the nobility and gentlemen's sons. When one or two came to Charfield with him between the school terms, they addressed him as Popejoy. No one in the family had ever called him anything but George. His position as the earl's heir suddenly mattered.

His own education took a different turn. The other boys, sons of local gentlemen, kept their distance. If they did not know he was a bastard, they understood at least he was not of their class. All the same, the little grammar school had been a good choice. The Reverend Mr. Seaton's interest had lain with natural philosophy and mathematics, so that in addition to subjects suitable to a gentleman, Miles had learned some useful skills and discovered he liked figures. Numbers did not have moods or worry about propriety or what others would think. They had no expectations and were never unreasonable.

The library was also open to Miles; neither the earl nor George was bookish, and the earl had a separate room in which to manage estate matters and his correspondence. Miles could spend some time reading for pleasure. His duties should not be pressing; the onus to decide about the Perry boy's future was on Lavinia, Caroline, and the earl.

He met George in the passage outside the library.

"Miles? Would you come with me to look at the boy?"

Halliwell agreed. However tentatively phrased the request, it could not be refused. They had played together as boys, but George would be earl one day. If Lord Popejoy hesitated to venture into the mostly female world of the nursery, Miles would accompany him.

They found Georgie and Jeremy supervised by both nurses in the room that had been exclusively Georgie's to play in. Nurse Willett was mending some small white garment while Janet Campbell sat knitting.

"Thought I'd look in and see how the lads were doing this morning. Getting along? Any scuffling or shoving?"

Viscount Popejoy had always jerked out phrases when nervous, as when he had been called to account for some boyhood mischief.

"Not a bit of it, my lord." Willett's flat statement drew Halliwell's attention. The nurse's lips were a thin line, echoing her furrowed brow. Resentment of the new child or Campbell?

Jeremy was playing with a set of wooden blocks. On his last school holiday before leaving for Italy, Peter had asked the estate carpenter to provide him with a number of small oaken blocks. Much of that visit had been devoted to painting the sides with pictures, letters, and numbers. William, predictably, had made fun of him.

Julia's son worked with fierce attention and stacked four, lining up the sides with animals.

"Got a kitty, a horse, a chicken, and a puppy. Like animals, do you?"

Startled, the boy's hand twitched as he tried to add a fifth block and dropped it. His face puckered, but he did not cry. He frowned over the blocks for a moment, selected one with a cow instead of a pig, and set it atop the others.

George Popejoy sighed almost inaudibly. His heir, nearly three, sat several feet away surrounded by a drum, a collection of toy soldiers, and half the blocks, staring at one in his hand.

"G'morning, Georgie. How's my boy today?"

A listless mumble in reply.

"I've had days like that m'self. Mostly mornings." He laughed uneasily. "When we were little, m'brothers and I fought wonderful battles with those soldiers. Can't really do it by yourself but mayhap when Jeremy's a bit older…"

"He's out o' sorts today, my lord. Having another child around's a change, and little ones don't like change. Once he's used to the notion, a playmate could do him good."

"Bound to. We'll be going." He nodded pleasantly at both women before striding out.

In the passage, he asked, "Do you remember being that age? Georgie's age?"

"I was brought here around then." Nurse Willett

was correct: children liked everything to stay the same, and it hadn't. How long had he been a lump of misery? Impossible to tell now, when his early memories were only fragmentary. Someone, perhaps Barding, had taken him and George to the stable and showed them the horses. Another time he and George were playing in the garden, and Miles had been stung by a bee.

"I'd forgot you were about Georgie's age when you came to stay. I think I was a wild brat and you were quiet, but maybe that was when we were older."

"It's a long time ago." Miles did not care to think of it. The Bardings' nurse had been kind, but she wasn't his mother.

"The thing is, Eustacia's not best pleased. Doesn't want William's by-blow here or not sharing the nursery and schoolroom with Georgie, Alethea, and Amelia anyway. Says he shouldn't be brought up thinking he's one of the family."

"No chance of that." If he had not been taken in to be reared at Charfield Hall while still in leading strings, he would have been thrown on the parish or sent to an orphan house. If he had survived childhood, he might have spent his life as a laborer until overwork, accident, or gin killed him. Instead he had had enough to eat, a place to sleep, and the privilege of sharing George's lessons. He had not been one of the family.

Popejoy glanced at him piercingly, opened his mouth to speak, and closed it again. "Quite so…I don't know how to set her mind at rest."

Miles summoned a faint smile. "Don't you think Lavinia, Lady Barding, will take care of it?"

"A point. What I'd like to know is, what was Will doing to seduce a female like Julia St. John. Julia

52

Perry."

"Curst if I can guess. We'd better call her Perry, however."

"Oh, of course. Don't want to embarrass her family."

"Do you mean to look in on your daughters as we're here?"

"They'll be at their lessons with Brant. I won't interrupt 'em. That governess terrifies me. I'm always afraid she'll ask me a question I can't answer." He clapped Miles on the back as they reached the intersecting passage. "I'm off to visit the kennels. I want to take a look at Bluebell's litter."

Miles thought he would see how Julia was settling in. To his surprise, she had not left her bedchamber.

"I couldn't wander around the house as if I were a guest, sir," she explained.

"You are a guest, Mistress Perry. Wouldn't you like to take the air in the garden? There aren't many flowers yet, but 'tis still a pretty place."

"But what if I'm summoned by one of the family?"

"The footman at the end of this passage or the one in the hall downstairs will inform whoever is sent that you are in the garden."

She agreed hesitantly, seeming overwhelmed by shyness. Not surprising, perhaps, given Charfield Hall's size and history and her own lack of acquaintance with the upper reaches of the peerage. Recalling how insignificant he had felt at Charfield as a boy, he exerted himself to tell her amusing stories about the neighborhood and the servants and tenants until she was at ease and even laughed.

****

Her first full day at Charfield, an invitation to dine with the family arrived with her morning chocolate. The maid who brought it asked her preferences for breakfast, which followed after a suitable interval for chocolate-drinking. The previous day, supper had been served to her in her bedchamber. As they had arrived in the midafternoon, dusty, disheveled, and tired, this was no insult. She had been introduced to the dowager countess and Caroline, Lady Barding had summoned the housekeeper to show her to a chamber.

"You will want to bathe and rest after so long a journey," Lavinia Barding said. Julia was grateful for the reprieve from the questioning she dreaded.

In a pleasant bedchamber, she was provided with a deep, steaming tub, scented soap, enough towels for two or three, and a maid to assist with her bath and clothing. Bliss, after two years of occasional inconvenient baths. Heating enough water, hauling it upstairs, and then emptying the tub again was not something to be done often in a house with few servants. She had usually carried the heavy can up the narrow stair herself. By the time she had enough water for a minimal bath, it was no more than lukewarm.

She had not expected such a gracious welcome. While she had been commanded to bring the boy to his paternal relatives, she had anticipated seeing little of the family herself. It boded well for William Stretton's by-blow, if they accepted him. He would have the best of everything.

The invitation to dine with the family surprised her. She had never met or perhaps even seen any of the Strettons other than William. The Earl of Barding, possessed of an old title, politically influential as well as rich, moved in the highest circles. A title alone did not guarantee acceptance in the beau monde. Julia's father was merely the third Baron St. John. Worse, his fortune had come from marriage to her mother, only child of the owner of Suttle Pottery. Jonah Suttle had prospered, as his inexpensive, boldly decorated earthenware proved popular among the poor and middling sort. Sally's accent and lack of early training in the graces and deportment expected of a lady closed her out of polite society, and so the marriage that raised the St. Johns' fortune did not raise their standing. Augusta's people had never moved much in London society, despite a long, respected history. This could not outweigh the St. John family's reputation for being not quite genteel. Even so, Julia might have been welcome at the Bardings' table. Because she was ruined, the mother of a bastard, her inclusion was unforeseen.

That Halliwell had sought her out to assure himself of her comfort had also been unexpected. He had a wealth of anecdotes about the local people and their customs, going back many years. She could almost imagine he had witnessed those events himself. The Bardings' man of business clearly took an interest in all aspects of the family and its seat, not merely its finances. She had known he was painstaking; now she realized he was kind as well. He had been thoughtful during their journey, too, though at the time she had been so exhausted and apprehensive she had scarcely noted it.

At the midday dinner, as the dowager countess explained in her note, she would meet the family's various relations and dependents. She was not to think it would be an elaborate or formal meal, as they were in mourning, and " 'tis ridiculous to be strictly formal in the country when 'tis a family dinner." They would talk privately later.

The maid assigned to Julia opened the door to the soft double tap.

"I will escort Mistress Perry to dinner, if she is ready?"

She started up from the chair where she had been sitting, surprised Halliwell would fetch her. What a relief it was to be decently gowned in one of her few suitable garments. She had worn it no more than once or twice in the last two years. It was a pity the robe à la française did not fit as it ought. She had lost weight; there had been no time to alter it when she found how low in flesh she had grown. But Molly had arranged Julia's filmy kerchief so cleverly that it did not gape at the bosom, though the bodice was loose. She was clean, her hair dry, pinned up in little curls, and covered with her best lace-edged linen cap.

She went downstairs, fingers resting on Halliwell's arm tentatively. The touch of Theo Manning's arm had never felt so intimate. Perhaps it was only that Theo was familiar to her, or mayhap that he was a less impressive figure. Clad in a suit of excellent cut in a rich green, Miles Halliwell belonged here, as once she might have, before her life went awry. How strange the family's man of business fitted these surroundings so well. He might be a relation of some exalted family, to judge from his manners and speech when he was not acting the inquisitor. He was more attractive than she had realized. The reflection was driven from her mind by the thought of facing the Stretton family in the next few minutes.

He cleared his throat. "Have you been made comfortable, Mistress Perry? Is there anything you would like that has not been provided?"

"Everyone has been kinder than I deserve." *Including Miles Halliwell.*

Halliwell's head turned sharply toward her. "You are a gentlewoman, ma'am."

Her eyes widened, and her lips moved to form a word. But after a moment all she replied was, "Thank you, sir. That is good of you."

In the drawing room, after she had made her curtsies to the dowager countess and Caroline, Lady Barding, Miles Halliwell presented her to the Earl of Barding and the earl's heir, George, Viscount Popejoy, and his lady. Then she met a whole crowd of lesser folk. She could only be glad Molly had told her who would be present, with verbal sketches of each: Caroline's orphaned niece, Verity Winston; Lavinia's companion, Hilda Ernst; the Popejoys' daughters' governess, Marcia Brant; and their son's tutor, Timothy Sykes. Julia's surprise must have shown: a tutor for a lad of three? Molly had explained it was a tradition with the family. The previous earl had not believed in leaving small boys completely to the governance of nurses and nursery maids.

In spite of her misgivings, after two years of living almost as a recluse, Julia enjoyed the mild pleasure of dining with the family and its various dependents. She was seated between Timothy Sykes, the tutor, and Hilda Ernst, Lavinia's stolid companion. It might have seemed like a snub to most. She suspected it was intended not to draw attention to her, as being placed at the earl's or countess's hand would have done, and she was grateful for the thought.

Hilda, whose papa had come to England with George I's entourage, was a spinster in her fifth decade and had little conversation. She might have been chosen by the dowager countess for those very qualities: Lavinia, Lady Barding, did not seem a woman to suffer chattering fools gladly. While Hilda was intent upon dissecting her portion of trout and Sykes was conversing with Eustacia, Lady Popejoy, Julia followed the ebb and flow of talk farther along the table. Part of a remark from the earl to his heir carried: "...will get him back."

Lord Popejoy replied, "I hope so, and the sooner the better. I don't know what to do..." The rest of that sentence was lost as from the corner of her eye, she saw Timothy Sykes lean toward Eustacia Popejoy and speak earnestly. His voice was soft, audible only because Mistress Ernst was silent and the tutor was speaking urgently.

"Ma'am, I am concerned about Master George. He shows no interest in things which ought to fascinate him, like the puppies in the stable."

"He is no more than a baby, too young to have much expected of him."

"My lady, my own little brothers were as active as kittens at the same age. So also is my sister's son."

"Children do not all grow at the same rate. I am sure 'tis no more than a stage. But if you wish, I mean to work in the physic garden tomorrow after breakfast. You may speak to me then."

The exchange had had a peculiarly informal tone, which surprised Julia. The viscountess had hardly addressed more than the most commonplace civilities to

Miles Halliwell, who seemed almost a member of the family, and otherwise paid as little attention to him as she would to a footman. Perhaps she assigned Sykes a higher place in the social ladder because he was the nephew of a marquess, as Molly had informed her. The marquess and his brother were not on speaking terms, but still, the connection gave even a tutor a certain luster.

Having left nothing but the fish bones on her plate, Mistress Ernst addressed a comment to Julia.

"It was convenient that Halliwell was able to act as your escort, Mistress Perry. He is ordinarily here only infrequently, though of course he often comes to the London house when we are there. He was not due to make his mid-year visit for another month, but Lord Barding saw no harm in his coming early."

Hilda Ernst meant to depress her pretensions, if she had any. Some response seeming necessary, Julia remarked, "The family's affairs must keep him busy."

"He will be staying longer than usual, I understand, I suppose because the family has been all on end, with Mr. William Stretton's death and other matters. He has a gentlemanly air, though I believe his antecedents are not elevated and he is hardly more than a tradesman, after all."

"Such a sad loss for the family," Julia murmured and pretended to be absorbed in her own food.

She was pondering on the grave demeanor of the earl, the countess, Lavinia, and Lord Popejoy when Sykes asked her if she had seen the sights in Banbury. They had passed through the town, but by then she had been too tired to pay much attention. Someone always needed something from Banbury, he said. Mistress

Perry should accompany whatever lady went next to the pretty little town. The viscountess, perhaps, who shopped there regularly for treats for the children. Julia expressed appropriate interest while her mind was elsewhere. The maid had had little to say about Eustacia Popejoy. After meeting her, Julia understood, for the viscountess was all but invisible among the chief members of the family. Lady Popejoy seemed to hold no place in the hierarchy.

Talk became general, a surprising degree of informality in an earl's household. But then, she had never visited an earl before. Perhaps they were not all dignified and rigid. Her stepmother would never countenance such a free exchange at her table.

Lavinia Barding asked whether Julia had recovered from her journey. She replied that in spite of the number of days on the road, she had been restored by a good night's sleep.

"Come, Mistress Perry, tell me more about Jeremy." Caroline picked up the thread. "He is nearly to the age of being into everything, is he not? My sons were terrors when they were two and three." Had it not been difficult to travel with a very young child, and in the same coach, too? Julia admitted the boy had been a little fretful and bored, but he had also regained his spirits, according to Nurse Campbell.

The viscount asked whether she rode. They could find a mount in the stable for her if she did.

"I used to ride. I had a roan mare but left her behind when I moved to the cottage in Dorset. I was sorry to leave my pretty Anaret, but I could not keep her there."

"Anaret!" Caroline exclaimed. "From Eliza

Haywood's novel?"

Julia smiled ruefully. "Silly, I know, but I was taken with the name, my lady, and one couldn't use it for a child. My kitchen cat is called Amena."

Caroline laughed. "I named my old gelding Mr. Standfast, from *The Pilgrim's Progress*, you know. Disrespectful, perhaps, but very apt."

Julia began to relax. Perhaps her stay at Charfield Hall would not be an ordeal.

To her relief, Lavinia, Lady Barding asked few probing questions. The matriarch's harsh features and sharp eyes had intimidated Julia at first sight. She knew a personage when she saw one. But she made only the ordinary inquiries one might ask of a new acquaintance: how many siblings did Julia have? Were they married?

Somehow, this was not what Julia had expected of her first meeting with the Bardings. She rather liked them, with the exception of Eustacia, who had scarcely looked at her and had contributed little to the conversation. The dowager countess was the power in the house. Interesting that she and Caroline appeared to be as thick as inkle-weavers, rather than competing for dominance.

The Barding household ran smoothly under their control. Did they ever have weeks of loud voices, tears, recrimination, and entreaties? Julia doubted it.

Chapter 6

"You have seen and spoken with Julia, however briefly," Lavinia noted dryly. "We have now all seen Jeremy." Her well-schooled face showed some trace of emotion, though Miles could not read it.

Finally Lionel Barding broke the silence. "Try as I will, I can't see any resemblance. All babies look much alike, in my experience."

Two female heads turned with the precision of a military drill.

"He's beyond babyhood." That was Caroline.

Lavinia added, "Men seldom notice these things. A child of that age begins to show the family features, if indeed it is family."

"I must agree with Lord Barding," Eustacia stated. "The brat shows no likeness to my little Georgie."

Popejoy, who had been sitting silently, made a little sound in his throat. It might have been a suppressed cough or a snort of laughter. Miles schooled his face to impassivity. No one pointed out that Georgie bore no resemblance to his papa or to his grandpapa or his uncles Peter and William. He was round-faced and small-eyed, with little, plump hands. Miles did not suppose he would grow out of it. His mother was a prettier version of the same pattern.

The miniatures were laid out on the table. The portrait of the boys had been propped up against the back of a chair. Lavinia's forefinger hovered over the miniature of the earl as a young boy. "See his ear. The heavy lobe tapering to a rather narrow top is not common. Here it is again, in George. It is not as evident in Peter." She smiled. " 'Faun ears,' he called them once. It is not an inapt description, though 'tis more true of his than of others."

A kind way of saying his were more delicate than those of Peter's brothers and father, which seemed more suitable to rustics than gentlemen. Miles's thoughts drifted. He must resemble his mother's family. He could not recall her features now, except that she had dark rather than fair or red hair. His clearest memory apart from fragments of his mother reading to him was of their last walk together, when she had slipped on a patch of ice and fallen down. The woman next door, who had sometimes taken care of him, picked him up and hurried him into her own cottage despite his crying for his mama.

"He has curls, too, just as William and Peter did. George missed them, somehow," Caroline said.

"Halliwell, what does that expression mean? Do you not think the child is William's?"

"My lady, I am only a man and therefore not clever at seeing family features in young children, but even I noticed the, er, faun ears."

"Yet you are troubled by something? Come, we pay you for your good sense and advice."

The first thing that came to his mind was the one that troubled him most. "I find it difficult to imagine Mr. William Stretton seducing Mistress Perry."

"It does seem odd of William," Caroline remarked pensively.

Lionel Barding snorted. "William would tup anything in petticoats. I beg your pardon for the vulgarity, Caroline, Eustacia." He did not include his mother in the apology. She had grown up in the days of Charles II's notably licentious court and lacked patience for mealy-mouthed circumlocutions.

"When he had drunk deeply, I believe he was not particular," Popejoy agreed.

Miles had been thinking of Julia Perry, rather than William's habits. He could not imagine her losing her wits to moonlight and a libertine's practiced flattery. Unless she had also drunk too much that night? People did act inconsistently at times. What weighed against it was her description of how it had come about, which had sounded strangely flat.

"My lords, my ladies, I am waiting to receive further information which might cast more light upon St. John's claim. I hoped to confirm one or two points."

"What need?" Caroline asked. "We have examined the letters, and they appear to be in William's handwriting. The style is what I would expect from William. We have seen the boy."

Miles cast a glance at Lavinia. "The hand is not much different from Mr. Peter Stretton's." He did not add "or Lord Popejoy's," which would embarrass the latter and provoke an outburst from Lady Popejoy. "I believe all Mr. Carstaires's students formed their letters in much the same way." He did, himself. The dowager countess raised one elegant eyebrow. She understood what he had left out.

"The simplest explanation is the most likely." Lionel Barding sometimes seemed like a nonentity compared to his mother, no more than a figurehead.

The image was deceiving: he lacked his father's vivid character and his mother's masterful nature and financial acumen. One tended to forget he possessed commonsense and decency to an uncommon degree, unless one had heard him speak in Parliament, as Miles had on several occasions.

"I had not thought about the ears, but you are correct, Mama," the viscount conceded. "Jeremy Perry appears to be related to someone in our family." He cleared his throat and added awkwardly, "I know he's not mine. He can't be Peter's. William's the likely father, given his ways."

"Does it really matter whose get he is? We take care of our own," the earl said.

Huzzah! Anyone should be proud to have Lionel Barding for a father. The earl was correct. The actual father did not matter. He knew how much his lady wanted the boy to be Will's son. If others saw a resemblance, Caroline could convince herself Jeremy was William's, and the earl was willing to support the notion.

Eustacia sniffed.

"It's settled, then." Lavinia directed a benevolent smile around the table. "After all, Halliwell, you know we never have absolute certainty when we invest. Do we?"

"No, my lady."

Caroline fixed him with a gimlet eye. Really, she was growing very like her mother-in-law. "Will the old Scots nurse be willing to stay, Halliwell? And that girl, Betty, who acts as nursery maid? She should be glad to remain. I'm sure her wages here will exceed what she could earn in Dorset, and she is familiar to the boy."

"They both will, my ladies."

Lavinia nodded. "Very good. Caroline, I'm sure you will see to assigning Jeremy permanent lodging on the nursery floor and provide for anything he or Nurse Campbell need."

"You can't mean to house the by-blow here!" Eustacia's eyebrows rose toward her hairline.

"Of course he will remain here. How else could we see to his upbringing? Whyever did you think we'd brought them here? We—" Caroline stopped, evidently remembering almost too late that Eustacia had not married George until long after Miles Halliwell had left Charfield for London and could not know he had ever been anything more than the Bardings' man of business.

In her indignation, Eustacia did not notice.

"But to have him associate with Georgie and my little girls as if he were not illegitimate would be scandalous, Mama-in-law. Whatever would people think?"

Lavinia's own eyebrows rose. "I do not give a fig for public opinion. As we are lamentably short of legitimate issue, we will welcome Jeremy into our family. It will be good for Georgie to have a playmate." This was aimed at Eustacia, who had failed to provide the earl's heir with any other male children.

"Georgie is too gentle for rough play," the viscountess protested.

Caroline spoke with less patience than usual. "Eustacia, he is more than a year older than this child. Besides, it was an excellent thing for my boys to have several playmates. Even Peter, who was shy and bookish, benefitted. I have often seen an only son made a chicken-heart by maternal pampering and indulgence."

"It must be as you say, of course, my ladies." Eustacia pouted.

Lavinia inclined her head. "I am glad you all agree."

The viscount had said neither yea nor nay on the question of housing the boy, a wise decision as the one would lead to a curtain-lecture by Eustacia and the other to annoying his mother and grandmother.

"By the time we leave for town, the boy will be at home here. Now we must try to become more acquainted with little Jeremy's mother. I think tomorrow will do for an informal chat with Julia."

Eustacia twitched like a horse plagued by flies.

"We will discuss renovation of the nursery wing, now there is to be another child in residence. Except for the schoolroom, Georgie's room, and his nurse's room, nothing has been changed in near thirty years. That will serve as a convenient excuse."

It would not be all they talked about, of course.

"Barding, you and Popejoy will be excused from attendance, as she will be more frank without your presence. Oh, and you also, Halliwell."

****

Julia viewed the nursery floor with the ladies, with an eye to necessary changes. The Bardings' intention to make the boy's accommodations comfortable spoke well for his likely treatment at Charfield. However, it would have been more to the point for Janet Campbell to be present. Fortunately, Caroline, Lady Barding, had given enough notice of the tour that Julia had been able to consult the nurse.

"Fresh paint, and a lighter color this time, new curtains and carpets, and the chimneys must be swept," Lady Barding enumerated, counting on her fingers. "What else?"

"New mattresses for both the nurse's bed and Jeremy's," Lavinia, Lady Barding, said. "Eustacia, can you think of anything more?"

"No."

"Julia, thank you for mentioning the mattresses. Caroline and I might not have noticed how worn they were."

Janet Campbell had informed her of the mildewy odor.

"Caroline, we must all retire to my parlor to refresh ourselves with a dish of tea and become better acquainted." She smiled at Julia in the kindest way. It was almost convincing. The interrogation Julia had dreaded was at hand.

"Green tea or black? I find the green quite bracing, but sometimes one wants something soothing. The green is singlo and the black, souchong. Caroline, will you pour?"

At Julia's request, Caroline supplied her with a bowl of souchong with milk and set about pouring green tea for Lavinia and Eustacia. She chose the souchong herself.

The dowager countess and Caroline both supported their tea bowls with thumb under the bottom, forefinger and middle finger on the rim. Thank goodness, she had been taught the same elegant grasp, though her governess said it was also permissible to use only the forefinger on the rim. Eustacia clutched the delicate Chinese cup as if fearing to drop it.

"We have no doubt Jeremy is William's son," Caroline stated. "Naturally, we will keep him. And as you are his mother, we would like to get to know you, as you are now a member of the family, if unacknowledged. It will be easier without the men."

"We were surprised to hear from Lord St. John that our William had a son of whom we were unaware. Or to be more exact, that we had not learned of it earlier." Lavinia smiled, a sweet elderly lady commenting upon the weather.

"We find it very puzzling," Caroline added.

Two pairs of eyes turned to her. Eustacia sat glumly contemplating her tea bowl. Julia held her shoulders back to prevent any appearance of hunching over in shame. But they could not fail to see her heated face.

"You will understand that I told no one of my foolish, immoral error until I knew there was to be a child. When I realized my predicament and had no choice but to tell my parents, I did not reveal the name of the man who was my partner in sin."

"Why not, dear?"

She chewed her lip, trying to think. "I don't know how to explain it, except that I was not thinking very clearly. I had ruined myself. I did not want to ruin his life as well." She could not tell them the real reason.

"Did you inform him of the result of your, mmmm, mutual indiscretion?" While Caroline Barding bore no physical resemblance to her mother-in-law, there was a likeness between the two, an impression of keen intelligence.

"Yes."

"Did he not offer to save your reputation by

marrying you?"

Julia's heart thumped. "No. He said he could not because he was married." Had that not been true? Dear God, how much trouble and misery could have been avoided.

"You did not know until then?"

The dowager countess might well wonder at her ignorance. One would ordinarily be aware of such basic facts about the gentlemen one met.

"I met him at an informal gathering, and we were introduced by an acquaintance of a friend of my family." That was vague but surely enough. Mr. Halliwell would no doubt have reported everything she had told him.

"How very inattentive of your chaperon."

"I did not have one. I was an old maid beyond the age of needing one, and there were a number of us in the group."

As they were waiting for further enlightenment, she continued. Humiliating but necessary. "Friends of mine, married friends and relations of theirs, got up a party to visit Tottenham Court Fair. I went with them. 'Tis not a genteel event, but it did sound amusing."

"And was it?" Lavinia asked, interested. "I've never been to a fair and have always wondered."

"I suppose it was. It was crowded and noisy, and there were booths with food and trinkets to buy, but my chief memories are of William. You will think me a ninnyhammer, and I was, to be enthralled by nothing more than a fine day and amusing conversation."

"I do find it passing strange, Julia, for you appear to be a prudent young woman."

"I was six-and-twenty and unaccustomed to

70

gentlemen's admiration, my lady. Or feigned admiration. I am not beautiful or vivacious. After my first year or two in society, my father and stepmother gave up expecting me to make a good marriage and then to make any marriage at all. I abandoned any hopes I had in favor of being useful to my family as is the usual fate of unmarriageable girls. Going to Tottenham Court Fair was an adventure. Now I know William was only toying with me for lack of anything else to do, but I was smitten. It never occurred to me to ask if he were married."

"But in fact, the seduction took place elsewhere, I believe?"

"We chanced to be at the same house party at Christmas."

Her listeners knew what might happen at house parties. Ordinarily it would be between married ladies and their lovers or sometimes a young couple who were betrothed or almost betrothed.

"Well, Julia, we will draw a veil over those events. These things will happen."

"Not usually at my age. I was as naïve as any chit out of the schoolroom, having received so little male attention before. I assumed his interest was in marrying me, but looking back, he never spoke any word which could be construed as an avowal of interest."

"How many times after that did you see him?"

"Only once after we returned to town. When I knew I was enceinte, I wrote to him at his lodgings. He contrived a meeting and told me he could not marry me." Her mouth twisted. "He knew a fellow who might be willing to marry me, if I had a decent dowry as he supposed I must."

"I apologize for my late grandson's lack of conduct. He was charming but not always well conducted."

"Naturally you did not agree, as your heart had been engaged," Caroline murmured.

Julia would have liked to deny it but under the circumstances, could not. "Was it a lie?" The words erupted without her volition. "About his being married?"

"No. His widow, Laura, is living at a small manor we own. On hearing from St. John, I suggested she might like to live quietly while in mourning and asked her to make sure it is being adequately maintained, as it is rather out of the way and we seldom visit it. It would have been unkind to have her present when you and your son were here."

"But how will she feel on her return to find a strange child in the nursery?"

"She means to return to her own family at the end of her mourning. They live much of the year in London. She prefers town life, though William encouraged her to live at Charfield. I suppose we can guess why. I doubt she would realize there was another child in the house anyway. If she did, the statement that it was an orphaned distant relation would suffice. Laura does not possess an inquiring mind. And I am sure she will be marrying again soon after her mourning ends."

"It is very good of you to be willing to take the boy." The ordeal was almost over. "He will have so many more opportunities in your care than would be possible in mine."

"And we will be pleased to add you to our family." Caroline turned to Lavinia. "Aunt Maria's chambers would make a very satisfactory suite for Julia. They were newly painted and papered not long before Maria's death and the hangings and upholstery changed as well. The Chinese motif wallpaper in the parlor is pretty and not too—how shall I put it?—assertive. The curtains and upholstery can be replaced if you should find you do not care for the color."

"My lady…I do not need a suite of rooms. I will be leaving as soon as it is convenient for you to return me to Handley."

"Go back to Handley?" Caroline set her tea bowl and saucer down on the little table, her surprise manifest in her question.

"I'm sure 'tis a pleasant cottage and Dorset is well enough, but surely you will wish to remain here with Jeremy? We can arrange to have everything you want packed and brought here by carrier," Lavinia said.

Eustacia did not speak. She had been conspicuously quiet during the tour of the nursery and was probably thanking God for Julia's declared intention to leave.

"You cannot wish me to live here. It would be outrageous. The county would never stop talking of it, and the word would spread to London and everywhere else. 'Twould not be a year before it was known in the American colonies and the antipodes as well."

Lavinia's thin smile made clear what she thought of gossip. "I grant you, it would be inappropriate if William were alive. However, he is dead, and his widow wishes to return to her own family. I think she may have had an admirer who was less acceptable to her father than William. He will now seem like a very eligible beau for a widow. She is still young, after all, and childless. I do not approve of girls of seventeen being married off as she was, but William was prominent among her admirers, and her papa asked his intentions. He may not have been serious about Laura, and if we had not approved, he would not have cared. But she was a very suitable match, and it was time he married. I suppose we hoped it would steady him. It was not a wise decision on our part."

Caroline patted Julia's hand. "You cannot wish to leave your darling boy. I could never have parted with one of my children without breaking my heart. Many children are orphaned, which is unavoidable, but I cannot feel a child should be deprived of his mother if she be living."

At last Eustacia spoke up. "We should not overpersuade Mistress Perry if she wishes to go."

Her comment was ignored.

"St. John expressed your family's desire to maintain a relationship with your son as a condition of permitting us to take charge of him," Lavinia continued. "I quite understand that it might be uncomfortable for you to accompany us to London, but Jeremy will not visit London until he is much older. Your people will be welcome to come here to visit you and the boy." A significant pause. "Should you marry, we would of course want to keep Jeremy. It would make your marriage easier, and you could still have a relationship with him. When your family visited us here, what would be more natural than that you should join them?"

"I do not know what to say." Julia glanced around the table. Eustacia was frowning at her tea bowl again. "I do not want anyone to be made uncomfortable by my presence. It's possible to overlook a child who is confined to the nursery, but I could only be a reminder of an unfortunate incident."

"We will be happy to have William's son here, and we cannot deprive him of his mama."

"I have regretted all my life that my mother died when I was very young." The countess's smile was tremulous.

It seemed there was no more to be said, though Eustacia might air her opinion pretty freely to the viscount.

Chapter 7

Miles applied for an appointment with Lavinia the following morning. If she thought his concern justified, she could either inform Barding and Caroline, or summon Miles to meet with the three of them. To his surprise, she received him in her own parlor, a room he had never seen before. An old one, not much changed, perhaps, as three of the walls were covered in linenfold oak panels which probably dated back to the Tudors. The fourth wall was of plaster, painted a pale yellow. A closed door suggested an original much larger chamber had been divided into a bedroom and the parlor. The furniture might have been new when Lavinia had come here as the previous earl's bride. The silk upholstery was much newer, several shades darker than the wall, dating perhaps to when she moved from the countess's chambers. Lavinia Barding sat in a high-backed chair where light could fall upon her embroidery frame from a window. She gestured him to the matching armchair.

"I assume you wished to speak with me because you are troubled about William's son. It was clear to me earlier that you were withholding judgment. Yet you did not offer a differing opinion. Why?"

"I have little doubt you are correct that Jeremy is Mr. William Stretton's son. Even I can see the resemblance."

She smiled fractionally.

"What bothers me is that I am not sure Julia St. John is the mother."

"Pooh. What does it matter?"

"Would you welcome him if his mother was a maid, my lady?"

"Don't be ridiculous, Halliwell. Why would a young lady claim a maid's illegitimate baby as her own? He's a Stretton, and probably William's. That is what matters to Caroline. I—and Barding, too—do not care for the way some men get children on the wrong side of the blanket and leave them to be raised by the parish or starve. I will make sure Caroline does not spoil Jeremy as she did William. To be fair, she is wiser now. He will grow up to be a responsible gentleman. Like you."

This compliment nearly made him forget what he meant to say. "If his mother was a common tavern maid, it might be a case of trying to make a silk purse out of a sow's ear."

"Oh, pshaw. I've known men and women who overcame humble origins to be almost indistinguishable from gentry. Jeremy will have the benefit of good examples and a fine education. If we are to trade proverbs, remember 'clothes make the man.' Do you believe those foolish tales of nobly born men and girls whose gentility shines through though raised by peasants? I trust not! If we are all descended from Adam and Eve, what separates us from servants and plowmen and dairy maids apart from clothing and upbringing? Pray, don't tell anyone I said so, however. I recall hearing a gentleman was banned from Charles II's court for treating his servants with as much consideration as if they had been gentlefolk."

Miles had never before seen her rakehelly grin which invited him to laugh. Easy to see why she had been famed for her charm. He was not a social equal or intimate of the family. He resisted the invitation.

"As it makes no difference, I will excuse myself."

Before he could rise, she said, "No, stay. I am curious to know why you think Julia St. John is not Jeremy's mother."

"She has no notion of his habits, routine, or how to soothe him. I have not heard her speak his name or refer to him by any, er, fond nickname."

"Such as 'dear Georgie' or 'my little lamb'? Does she not babble baby talk to him?"

"I have never heard her address him in any way."

"You were not in the coach with them, were you? Your observations must have been limited to evenings at the inns where you stopped. She may have been tired or out of spirits by then."

However inappropriate to laugh spontaneously in his employer's presence, the idea was so far from the truth, Miles Halliwell could not restrain a bark of laughter. "We made a great many stops, my lady. The boy grew restless, or soiled himself, or we paused to get him milk or a bun or to let him play for a few minutes. Janet Campbell, the nurse, cared for him. She called him 'wee laddie,' 'sweet Jerry,' and 'lambkin.' "

"Oh! I had thought perhaps the roads were bad, or that it took them some time to pack and make arrangements. It never occurred to me the child might be a bad traveler."

The question was irresistible. "Lady Barding, if I may ask, did you ever take a journey with a child of that age?"

"Many times." A thoughtful pause followed. "Of course, the children were in a separate coach with their nurses. After I had three, we needed two coaches for them and their attendants. Yet I wish I could have had more. The death of my two youngest children grieved me more than I can say."

Seeing her pensive over deaths forty years past, Miles hesitated before proceeding. "At all events, I had a good many chances to see them together. Jeremy might not have been there, for all the attention Mistress St. John paid him, except when she winced at his tantrums."

"I grant you such a lack of interest is odd. I left my children's care to their nurses and nursery maids for the most part, though I tried to spend as much time with them as I could. I had a good deal to do overseeing the house, though my mother-in-law still lived. I do not like a muddled household. Then while my earl was away, there were other demands upon my time." Overseeing the estates and investing, she meant.

"High Farm is not Charfield Hall. The only servants were the nurse, a cook, and the maid of all work who also served as the nursery maid. There was a gardener and his boy for the outdoor work. The house has four bedchambers, not forty." He added, "I have a dim memory of my mother singing to me and teasing me to finish my porridge. I don't think I had a nurse."

"You did not." The absentminded statement was the most he had ever heard of his parentage from any member of the Stretton family. He had deduced his illegitimacy from veiled looks and oblique comments. "Her father was gentry of a minor sort. She went to live with her mother's relations when he died. Unpleasant people, I gather, who ignored her until she got with child, then hoped to extort money from Barding—my earl, you know, not Lionel—to support her." Lavinia sniffed. "Whitacker took their measure quick enough. We scotched their scheme by settling an annuity and a cottage on Lydia. When she died, you came to live here."

"Thank you for telling me." He could go through the Barding/Stretton files from the year of his birth until he was three and see if there was more information about his mother and her people. Whitacker had kept files going back to when he had set up his business near fifty years ago, and Miles had kept them all when he inherited from his former employer.

She gave a dismissive wave of one blue-veined hand. It was still graceful, the knuckles not much marked by arthritis. "It occurred to me only now you might not know." She went on without a pause. "I do see what you mean. In such close proximity, it is passing strange Jeremy's mother was not more involved in his care. It will make no difference here."

"She was reluctant to come to Charfield and thought it would be enough to send the boy and the nurse."

"Was she? Perhaps she felt meeting us would be awkward. She was startled at the idea she should make her home here, however, or even appalled. Why would she dislike the idea of living in comfort, even if she did not care to stay with Jeremy? She could easily ignore him."

"In Handley, she was accepted as a respectable widow. Here she faces being known as the mother of a by-blow. A whore, in the minds of most decent people."

The dowager countess studied the embroidery before her. "If it is seen we accept her as a distant connection, who in Oxfordshire will slight her?"

"No one overtly, perhaps, but she may still feel the shame. She might also wish to marry and have a home of her own, which would be difficult if her relationship with William is known."

The dowager countess ignored this. "The St. Johns have not cast her off. If Jeremy lives here and she returns to her family, her reputation will be preserved. They can see the boy here as if they were no more than acquaintances who had come to stay."

"I find it strange, then, that her family did not visit her once while she lived in Dorset."

"Never? Are you sure she did not visit them at their country home if not in London?"

"She did not." Seeing her expression, he asked, "Are you sure you and Lord Barding want to know the St. John family?"

"You reported they were unexceptionable."

"They are, in the sense that they are solvent, not known for any particular vices, and are members of the lower end of the beau monde. Rich, but the title is not old, and the money comes from Julia's mother who was a tradesman's daughter. I suspect them of wishing to improve their position. Who does not? There is nothing against it, unless they hope to do so by insinuating themselves into your family."

"That would explain a good deal, Halliwell. I wonder we did not think of it."

He allowed himself a slight smile. "My lady, your family has never needed to seek higher status."

"Fiddle-faddle. We have simply never cared to do

so. Scrabbling for position is vulgar, though I can understand it. She is a pleasant young lady, however, so I will speak with her tomorrow and see if I can tease out the truth. I dislike a puzzle."

Chapter 8

Julia followed the footman with all the enthusiasm of a convicted criminal on his way to the gallows. The dowager countess, despite her age, was every bit as clever as Miles Halliwell and the real power in the Stretton family. What more could she want to know? Or did she mean to offer money for Julia to go away, leaving Jeremy behind? Could she accept such an offer? The family wanted Jeremy, and her own family had made it plain they did not wish to ignore his existence. Granted, her presence might give them an additional excuse to forge ties with the Strettons, but she was not essential. To accept a bribe to go away would be demeaning and dishonest. She might have allowed herself to be bought off if she had had no other resources. As her father had agreed to settle money on her and provide her a house, she could afford to keep her remaining integrity, cold comfort as it might be.

"My dear, thank you for coming so promptly. I know our family meeting must have been an ordeal for you"—*Then why subject me to it?*—"but I'm sure you understand that we are interested in Jeremy. I have a few more questions that I feel are better asked privately."

"I will answer them if I can, Lady Barding."

The terrifying old lady smiled at her. As a girl Julia had sometimes amused herself by drawing ridiculous

83

pictures. Now she imagined a surgeon's lancet smiling.

"I sensed you are reluctant to make your home here, Julia. Will you tell me why?"

Whatever she had expected from the dowager countess, this was not it.

"When your family expressed an interest in taking the boy, I hoped for an opportunity to reclaim my own life."

Lavinia, Lady Barding studied her, expression unrevealing. "How do your family explain your absence? I do hope they did not put around that you died. That would make things difficult. Fatal to your chances of resuming your life as Julia St. John. Unless you emigrated to the Colonies, which would hardly be better than death, I would think." She shuddered gracefully.

"I am said to have gone to live with my stepmother's godmother, who had no one else who could care for her." The humor of the situation struck Julia for the first time. "The poor old lady has been dead for many years, really did have no close connections, and lived in the farthest wilds of Yorkshire, I think, or maybe Northumberland. I am not in favor of lying, but if one must, it is desirable the lie be watertight."

"Very sensible of your family. If Jeremy had been stillborn or died later as many infants do, you would be able to reappear. Or if, as now, someone took him to foster."

"Yes."

"I do not quite understand why your people did not put Jeremy to foster with some family. That is common enough when there is an embarrassment of this sort.

You could have gone home as soon as you recovered from the birth, your elderly relative having 'died.' Why did you not?"

The question posed a difficulty, as she could not tell the truth.

Two years ago her father and stepmother had urged the baby be given up as soon as it was born. Unless, of course, it was stillborn, as Augusta St. John had pointed out hopefully. Floods of tears had dissuaded Papa from finding a foster family. Augusta, making the best of it, admitted that some poor family raising the by-blow might be tempted to try blackmail.

Julia repressed an urge to lick her dry lips. How could she explain the irrational decision not to deal with the problem as any other respectable family would? Or why they would want to maintain a connection? "What if they died, leaving the child on the parish or to starve in the street? Or if they apprenticed him to a chimney sweep?"

"Quite unlikely in the country, where children are a valuable source of farm labor."

"Still, one would always worry," Julia replied. Holding the boy in reserve, as a sort of sentimental token or in case circumstances changed, had been madness. But Julia understood why her father and stepmother had agreed.

"One might if one were fond of the baby. But I do not believe you feel any affection for Jeremy. I am therefore bewildered by your keeping him when it would have been easy to have him fostered. Your family could have had his upbringing overseen by a trustee to make sure he was well cared for and received some education, if they were concerned about his welfare."

"I did what I did out of duty."

"Yet most women cannot help being fond of their babies. I suppose 'tis instinct, for otherwise I think a good many would not survive infancy. More than already die from the usual causes, I mean. I have known a mother who was indifferent to her child. I always thought it was because the birth was exceptionally hard and left her almost an invalid for months. Did you—"

Julia, blushing and feeling utterly unable to discuss childbirth, interrupted with a hasty, "My lady, I cannot bear to remember it." The screaming, the blood, her helplessness.

When the dowager countess did not continue, the pressure of silence finally forced her to say the one thing she could think of, which had the advantage of being partially true. "William Stretton charmed and seduced a respectable female, and only revealed he was already married when he was informed of his impending fatherhood. His exact words were, 'Well, damme. I'd marry you if I could, but my wife would object,' and he laughed. I hated him for that. Is it any wonder I have no feelings for his son?"

Lavinia sighed heavily. "No, perhaps not. And Caroline and I both owe you an apology. She was much younger then and because she and Lionel were temporarily out of charity with each other, she spoiled William. I was too taken up with the estate's affairs to notice she was overlooking or concealing some of his misdeeds. They were only the usual mischief for which George and later Peter were punished. Even when I became aware of the problem, I was slow to put a stop to it. He possessed such a sweet smile and winning ways, and I did not believe him to be malicious. As a result, he grew to manhood believing there would never be consequences. When he encountered one, he thought he could charm his way out of it. He too often succeeded."

They sat without speaking for a time.

"Well, you may put aside your duty now. We did not wish to deprive you of your child because Caroline in particular has strong views on the subject. However, if you are willing to turn him over to us, we are glad to have him. You must not hurry away, however, as if you came only to deliver the boy. When does your family go to your country home?"

"It always used to be at the end of June. I have not heard their intentions for this year."

"Then I think it would be best if you remained here for the present. Caroline will see to having suitable clothing made for you. What is appropriate for life in a country cottage is not what one would expect of a gentlewoman, not even one who has been caring for an elderly relative. Your new garments will be what a lady of your station should wear in the country or a provincial town if she were acting as companion to an ailing relation."

"I cannot let your family pay to outfit me."

"Nonsense, Julia. The cost is insignificant to my family, and we must put things as right as we can. Then after your people have gone to St. John Underhill, we will send you home to them. By the time your family returns to town for the opening of Parliament—your father does attend, I suppose?"

"He considers it his duty, my lady."

"Good. Then you will accompany them, and no

one will think it strange that you have returned from nursing the old lady. How better to be able to pick up your life than at your family home?"

"I don't think, that is, you need not go to so much trouble. I can go back to Handley."

"Nonsense, my dear, it's no trouble."

She remembered too late that her papa's last letter had suggested she should refuse to be parted from the boy. Her family could then visit her as would have been indiscreet at Handley. She had been so overset by the news she was to take him to Charfield that she had hardly taken notice of the rest. She now comprehended his statement as meaning they would have an excuse to visit the Bardings. She could not pretend reluctance to leave the boy, and the thought of her family descending on the Bardings made her feel sick.

"It will all work out, Julia. You must trust us."

There seemed nothing to say to that pronouncement.

****

Caroline scrutinized Julia from her neat little tricorne to her booted toes. "How well you look in that habit, Julia. How fortunate yellow is a good color for you, as it's mighty fashionable." She turned to Verity, attired in a blue that brought out the color in her eyes. "You should not ride too far today or gallop, I think, as Julia has not ridden for some time. The groom will be the best judge of how she goes on and what will be safe. Enjoy yourselves."

Julia had marveled at her image in the mirror over the console table. The petticoat and jacket were not as richly trimmed as some she remembered from before she had left London, having only some embroidery edging the buttonholes and the wide cuffs. Made up by the countess's sewing woman, rather than a fashionable tailor, it was what a lady who had been living retired in the country might possess. The other garments Lavinia and Caroline had insisted on bestowing upon her were just as becoming. They made her almost elegant. By comparison, the gowns she had taken with her into her banishment were not half as attractive—and they had been her best everyday clothing. Her stepmother had insisted she wear subdued shades of blue, claiming "blue looks well on anyone." Perhaps it might, but she never felt attractive in blue. Nor did the dove gray, dull browns, and grayish lavender flatter her, all of which Augusta St. John assured Julia would subdue the red tone in her hair. She stepped out jauntily to meet the groom and her mount, followed more sedately by Caroline's niece.

The weather had continued cool, more like a dry autumn than spring. Nevertheless, she looked forward to the opportunity to ride again. Nor did Verity distract her with chatter; she was a quiet girl. Perhaps too she was not a confident horsewoman. An experienced rider herself, even after two years without a horse, Julia was able to admire the scenery. She let her mind wander, smiling to remember Caroline's warning to Verity not to ride far or gallop for Julia's sake. If Verity ever rode at a gallop, it would be because her horse had bolted.

Verity was ready to turn back far too soon. Julia hoped eventually to see more of the property if she stayed at Charfield for a while and to gallop when possible. She could almost see the days and weeks stretching ahead as carefree and full of promise as Martin had viewed his school holidays. The Strettons were not as intimidating now that she knew them. Lavinia and Caroline were lively conversationalists; the earl and the viscount were kind. Marcia Brant held a variety of interesting opinions, and the tutor, Sykes, was well-informed. They must have been selected by the dowager countess, for Julia could not imagine Eustacia choosing to have her daughters taught natural philosophy and logic as well as the more ladylike accomplishments.

She found it hard to warm to Eustacia, possibly because Lady Popejoy reminded her of her stepmother: aware of her own consequence, far more so than either of the countesses. Her tendency to take a pet over inconveniences and fall into the vapors at difficulties was irksome, and, as Lavinia once observed, not helpful. Julia was able to shrug off Lady Popejoy's disapproval once she discovered Eustacia was judgmental of almost everyone. She even felt a bit sorry for her, as she clearly did not fit into the family, a fact of which she must be aware. Weighed against the friendship of the rest of the Strettons, the comfort of Charfield Hall, and freedom from worry, Eustacia was bearable. If not for her guilt, Julia could have been perfectly contented.

"I hope the sun and wind have not harmed our complexions," Verity murmured as they entered the house. "I seldom ride unless the countess chooses to go out. Lady Popejoy does not enjoy the exercise."

"Is it not safe to ride alone?"

"Oh, I couldn't! My poor mama would have considered it hoydenish."

"I did not mean quite alone. Of course one would have a groom in attendance. Otherwise, it would be impossible to remount if one should part company with the saddle."

"I would not be comfortable riding with a male servant unless a gentleman or another female were present."

Oh dear. Strait-laced as Augusta was, she saw no impropriety in a lady riding with only a groom, as long as he was a steady, older man.

"I wonder if Eustacia has any face wash against sunburn," Verity mused.

They entered the house windblown, even Verity, who seldom looked less than point-device, and yes, a bit pink.

****

The dowager countess looked around, faintly displeased. "It is not like Eustacia to be tardy. However, she visits Georgie in the nursery to say goodnight. She must have forgotten the time or perhaps he is fretful."

Caroline said, "I think we may as well go in, don't you? I am sure she will be with us shortly, and it does annoy Cook when we delay."

"I agree. We do not stand on ceremony Sunday evenings," she added in an aside to Julia, "having been at our most formal and on our best behavior at dinner, when the parson and his wife dine with us. You will have noticed that a worthy guest does not necessarily make for lively dinner conversation. Halliwell, take Mistress Perry in."

They would be eleven at table if Lady Popejoy appeared. At a formal meal, an uneven number would be awkward. Before they were seated, Eustacia swept in without a word of greeting or apology. "I want Georgie's nursery maid turned off at once and dragged before the magistrate for injuring my son."

"You are late, Eustacia." Lavinia Barding's voice noticeably lowered the temperature in the dining room.

"I must ask you to pardon me. I have made an alarming discovery in the nursery—"

Popejoy took her elbow. "Come, my dear, be seated. Perhaps you can explain your grievance to Mama and Grandmama after supper."

"I will not suffer her to stay in this house. She has beaten my poor little boy."

"What did he do?" George asked. "Have some of the pickled asparagus, Eustacia."

"He didn't do anything! She admits as much, but he is bruised, and what could it be but a beating or an accident, and she denies both."

"I wonder you cared to leave her with him if you think she has harmed the boy," Lavinia observed.

"I did no such thing. She is locked in the nursery floor linen closet." She turned to the earl. "Sir, will you not send for the magistrate?"

"If she is secure, let us wait until we have eaten. Sir Randall will be sitting down to his own supper now, and while I am sure he would sacrifice it for a murder or robbery, he might resent doing so for a few bruises on a toddling child. I have been told that when I was that age, I raised a lump on my head the size of a hen's egg, and I recall all f—three of my boys very often received scrapes, lumps, and bruises. Wait until young George is ten or twelve. That's when they begin to break their bones."

"Why not send a groom to Sir Randall now, asking him to come when he has finished his supper?"

"A very good notion, Mama. Thomas, see it done."

At a gesture from the earl, the footman departed.

Lady Popejoy was inclined to keep a fuss, as the phrase went, which was ill done. Even Julia's late mother, who was lacking in polish, would have suppressed her annoyance or distress before guests or servants. Julia reserved her opinion in light of the contretemps in the nursery, which might well be enough to overset a fond mother—or one prone to hysterics. Then Eustacia encountered Lavinia Barding's basilisk gaze and pressed her lips together instead.

Eustacia Popejoy's anxiety quelled for the moment, Lavinia and Caroline gently led the conversation into unexceptionable channels: the terrible winter and how cold 'twas for May. They would have no garden stuff if 'twere not for the glass house and the head gardener's good management.

By then Eustacia had recovered enough poise to contribute her own comment. "My cousin wrote me about the shocking riots in Norwich. She was terrified. The militia was able to put them down, though only half a dozen of the rioters were killed."

"They must have been suffering from the shortages of food and I suppose everything else, between the cold and the difficulty of transport. They were blanketed in thick snow from December until March although I believe no part of the country escaped untouched. Upon my soul, I heard that water sold for more than coals in London," the earl said.

"It did," Caroline added wryly. "I saw the household accounts."

Chapter 9

Julia and the other ladies were rising from the table at the countess's signal when Sir Randall Wilkinson was announced. He waved aside any suggestion he had hurried or cut short his meal. "We sup early on Sundays that the children may eat with us. It gives us a chance to polish their table manners more than can be accomplished in the nursery. Supper is better for the purpose than dinner, being shorter, and we are less likely to have guests to be shocked by their lapses. Now pray tell me what the matter is—"

"My son's nursery maid has beaten him," Eustacia interrupted.

The magistrate pondered. "Better to have left it to the nurse."

"He is bruised all over his body and he is only three!"

The earl and Sir Randall traded odiously male glances. Julia could sympathize to some degree; Eustacia must be extremely annoying on longer acquaintance than her own.

"Sir Randall will wish to examine young George's injuries." Lavinia Barding gave the last word a faint emphasis.

"Yes, he must do so at once. Come, Sir Randall, I will take you up to my son's chamber," Eustacia said.

"No, Eustacia. We must not all crowd into the

nursery. You will wait in the drawing room and compose yourself. Caroline, if you will take the ladies out? And perhaps Barding, Popejoy, and Sykes will not linger long over their port and will lend you their support." Lavinia Barding's suggestion carried the weight of a command.

The viscountess opened her mouth. Before she could utter any protest, the viscount said, "Excellent advice. Sir Randall will do better without anxious parents hovering, and there will be less disturbance in the nursery with fewer people. We will join the ladies in the drawing room shortly."

****

As soon as the other ladies had gone, Lavinia spoke. "Halliwell, you will come with us."

"Halliwell?"

The magistrate might well be as perplexed by his inclusion as Miles was. Wilkinson would be aware he worked for the Bardings; he might have heard rumors about his parentage.

"Halliwell is observant and sometimes makes connections others miss."

"I see." Sir Randall still sounded doubtful.

In the nursery, Mistress Willett pulled back the curtains, flooding Georgie's small bedroom with light. This late in the spring, the sun would not set for hours, making candles unnecessary. They gathered around the cot. "We will need to see George's bruises, Nurse."

At Lavinia's bidding, the stout little woman drew back the bed covers and raised the child's gown, all without waking him.

"Those marks do appear to be contusions, Lady Barding. Not where I would expect them, however. I think I must ask that you remove his shirt, although I dislike to wake the little fellow."

The boy mumbled a complaint but did not rouse.

"This on his arm appears to be a rash. Turn him, please, so I can see his back."

More bruises. "How would you explain these, Nurse? You must have many years of experience with small children and their mishaps. At Master George's age, mine were forever falling down and running into things."

She darted a glance at the dowager countess. "I know Lady Popejoy will have it Gertrude struck or beat Master Georgie, but I don't believe it. She's the gentlest girl, too gentle to manage a boy as active as most of them are. And Master Georgie don't run harum-scarum like most boys his age. He's a lamb that sits and plays quietly and never a tanterum from him."

"Peter was a quiet child. Though he did acquire the expected cuts and bruises and have outbursts, as all small children do."

"We must question the maid, then." Sir Randall straightened up and turned toward the door.

Was Miles the only one who suspected the nurse of holding something back? Should he speak? Lavinia was gazing at him contemplatively. "Sir Randall, if I may request a little more information?"

"By all means, Halliwell, as Lady Barding thought you would be helpful."

"Nurse, is he always this pale? How would you describe Master George's health in general?"

Her hands, clasped before her waist, twisted. "He's too young to play much out of doors, and besides, Lady Popejoy fears he might take a chill or some ailment.

He's not as brisk as I like to see a boy his age."

"Is he often ill?"

"He does catch every cold that's going around. Thank the Lord we've had no smallpox or scarlet fever or any of them nasty diseases in the neighborhood, for he'd catch them as sure as eggs. Sometimes I've thought he had a fever, but we keep a good fire in his room and dress him warm, so mayhap he is only overheated. It don't seem to lead to anything. He tires easy." Her eyes slid toward the dowager countess. "I don't tell her ladyship, the viscountess, my lady, on account of it throwing her into the dumps."

"I quite understand, Nurse."

"Would you say he was sickly?" Sir Randall frowned, studying the child.

"Not sickly, exactly, sir. Just not, well, not stout. If you know what I mean? Takes after his mother, I'd say, her suffering all kinds of ailments."

"I have always thought her quite robust," the dowager countess said.

"Ay, but she has megrims, my lady, and complains of her stomach and not sleeping sound."

Lavinia accepted the nurse's statement with no comment beyond a "Hmmm!" Halliwell suspected she believed Lady Popejoy's indispositions were more of the mind than the body.

"We will have the doctor look at him," Lavinia said. "I wish you had mentioned you thought him delicate, Nurse."

"Might be I should have told you, my lady. But there's nothing to catch hold of about him; 'tis all minor things. Not liking his dinner and tiring easy, that could be no more than he's growing. And Lady Popejoy don't like to hear that anything might ail the boy, so I don't tell her about the little things."

"In your place, I might do the same. But inform me in the future."

The nursery maid was hysterical and needed a nipperkin of brandy before she could answer sensibly, and then nothing to the point. The boy was not in such rude good health as her own little brothers. He was always having nosebleeds, and not because someone had hit him in the nose, poor little dear.

In the end, Sir Randall declined to arrest the girl and told Eustacia she might dismiss her if she wished, but that he for one did not believe she had mistreated the child. As the dowager countess made clear she agreed and thought it rather a case to be referred to the doctor, as it was probably only the green-sickness, nothing more was done.

Later, the elder Lady Barding spoke with Miles privately. "I knew I was correct to require your presence. I only wish we had known sooner that little George was not thriving as he should. I was wrong to assume Eustacia was fretting needlessly." She paused. "Eustacia fears she will not conceive again, which is a troubling thought." It was enough to worry them all: after Georgie, Peter was the only remaining heir. They must all hope Eustacia bore another son, or preferably two or three.

Halliwell had no difficulty following her train of thought when she went on. "Both Barding and I, and for all I know George as well, wrote to Peter when William died. He may not have received those letters yet, if he chanced to move from his last lodging. Did you not tell us when you returned three years ago that he wanted to spend time in Rome and Venice as well as Florence?

"Ay, my lady."

"He made his feelings about returning quite clear at that time. I pray he will reconsider now."

What could he say? George and William had ignored their younger brother or treated him with scorn: he was too young, too bookish, too gentle. Lionel Stretton encouraged him to do as his brothers and Miles did: spend every spare moment riding, swimming, and, later, learning to fence and shoot, though Peter's inclination was to study and to draw. The boy had followed Miles, who had allowed it, like a puppy. He was not quite one of the family either, and like Peter, sometimes preferred to sit quietly with a book. Before he could think of an appropriate remark, Lavinia spoke again.

"Peter looked up to you, Miles. I wish you would write and ask him to come home. My late husband was not a stupid or unfeeling man, but he regarded Peter's interests as fit only for tradesmen and females, and then only if they did not interfere with what he called their natural role. A gentleman must not make himself an object of derision by devoting himself to art. I did not handle him well. Neither Lionel nor I did enough to counteract his influence."

Miles found this unsurprising. The old earl had been a terrifying figure, who had once kicked his valet in the backside and sent him sprawling, roared when he was displeased, and whose orders were as inarguable as the king's. He was not unfair, however, and took a tolerant view of the boys' activities, though his understanding of why they had thought some action good did not save them from punishment.

"I will do so, my lady." She had inadvertently called him by his first name as she had when he was a child. He found it uncomfortable. Since he had completed grammar school and the earl foisted Miles upon his aging man of business as an additional clerk, Halliwell had maintained a formal distance from the family. Nor had he trespassed upon their good nature previously. He had always known he lived at Charfield on sufferance.

Before she could dismiss him, he added, "I am still waiting for a further report which may clear up some of our questions."

"I look forward to seeing it, but it's unlikely to make any difference. I believe Julia honest…in most ways. You will of course provide me a copy of whatever your man turns up, but our decision is made. Jeremy is a Stretton. You may go back to London."

He had learned as a child to guard his expressions. This time he failed, for she laughed and said, "Not today! You may leave in the morning."

"And Mistress Perry?"

"She remains with us until her family goes to the country. Then we will send her to them. She can return to town when they go for the Parliamentary session. I confess, her people have made it easy for her to return with her reputation intact."

"But, my lady…" He did not know what he objected to. Julia did not wish to stay with her child and if her family were willing to take her back, surely that was the best outcome for everyone. "Keeping her presence here a secret is impossible."

"And we have not tried. Julia St. John was never here. Our guest is Julia Perry, a respectable widow. You cannot have considered, Halliwell. The servants who go with us to London have been with us for many years and will not gossip. Her family and ours do not move in the same circles, so we will not meet unless they come to see Jeremy. You've said Julia cares nothing for her child, and I know 'tis true, so she will not be wanting to accompany them."

"Lady Barding, what of the viscountess?" If anyone revealed that Julia St. John was the Julia Perry who had come to Charfield with her illegitimate child, it would be she.

"Do you think Caroline and I cannot control her one way or another?" Lavinia's steely gaze dared him to return a negative.

Miles felt less confident than the dowager countess. While Eustacia's own best interest would be to avoid offending the other ladies, in a fit of pique she might speak before stopping to consider. "No, my lady, I am sure you will be able to deal with Lady Popejoy." Possibly after the fact, when it would be no help to Julia. He must trust that the earl and countesses would manage any problem that arose.

"Once back in society, Julia will marry, and her husband and new family will absorb her."

"She may not feel able to accept an offer of marriage, knowing what the man will discover on their wedding night."

"If Julia wishes to marry and feels she cannot form a connection for that reason, we will assist her."

Which meant Lavinia or the earl would find some suitable man who either owed them a favor or wanted to put them in his debt and smooth the way. Julia St. John might be unwilling to accept such help; she had a great deal of pride. Though she might not ever be aware the earl's family had steered a potential husband into her path. She needed to marry: a woman's only security was in marriage, and even then she might find herself destitute if her husband was improvident. In that event, the Strettons would take care of her because she was Jeremy's mother.

He departed in the morning with real regret, most of it concern for Julia. Misplaced, he knew. The Strettons took care of their own.

Chapter 10

When he arrived at his office two days later, Bryden greeted him with some surprise. "Mr. Halliwell, I was not expecting you."

"The matter was resolved. Is there anything I should deal with immediately?"

"No. You received the confidential letter you expected, and as you instructed, I sent a message to Charfield to inform you. That was yesterday. You must have passed the messenger on the road. I'll fetch it."

He read Markham's report, sipping claret. The man had agreed to give a written response to Miles's questions on the understanding that no names or identifying circumstances would be used.

"I apologize for the delay in this reply. I commenced inquiries on receipt of your letter but encountered difficulties. The valet is currently in Ireland at an estate where his new master has gone a-courting. After determining its whereabouts, I concluded that given the length of the journey, it would be best to wait to hear from you. I can employ someone discreet to make the inquiries, although the valet might be on his way back to London before anyone arrived.

It was not difficult to find the lady's maid. She is still in service at the family home where she serves the younger girl as she once served both young ladies. Because of this circumstance, I do not feel free to have someone question her. Her loyalty to the family, or her fear of being discharged, might seal her lips. There is also the risk she would inform the family.

Regarding your lady's direction, no one could recall the relation's name, apart from one thinking she had heard her referred to as Aunt Hattie or Aunt Hettie. I endeavored to discover if the family had an Aunt Harriet or Henrietta or anything similar, but apparently not, and the two persons with whom I spoke were not sure if the old body was an aunt or a great aunt or perhaps an aunt by courtesy or even a much older cousin. Neither recalled where she resided. The family has given out that she lives at some distance from anyplace mail is received and that her friends may write to J. at their London house, as they regularly send letters and packets by messenger or country carrier. The sister went with her to visit the old lady and remained for a few months while her mother was not in good health and did not feel capable of chaperoning the girl. Understandably, I surmise, as I have now heard her described as a "right handful." She is also very beautiful (I have seen her with my own eyes) and something of a minx.

I was able to learn something of the family's activities in the relevant period by striking up an acquaintance with the coachman. He's a garrulous fellow and remembered driving them to a certain baronet's Derbyshire manor. His memory was very clear, not because the drive was difficult but because of the company. Sir H. had two boys home from university and one from Harrow, and several of their friends, and the guests having been invited to bring their children, a number of them of similar age, the house was as full as *it could be, and very merry. The gentry amused themselves in their accustomed manner with hunting, games, music, dancing, and the like. There was no need to provide entertainment for the younger members of the party on up through the young men, for they managed to make their own diversions. I will not recount the stories he told me, but it was plain they were ripe for any mischief. W. was indeed present; he was a friend of the oldest H. son and was much looked up to by the others as an older, worldly-wise example.*

While the report stopped up a number of rabbit holes, it raised other questions in Halliwell's mind. Markham had done an excellent job of passing on the requested information in such a way that no one could connect it to the Bardings or anyone else. Miles wrote and sealed a letter to Lavinia summarizing his progress—or lack of the same—and tucked it into his pocket. He would deliver it to the General Post Office himself.

He possessed his soul in patience while reviewing the other correspondence that had come in during his absence. Only then did he go to the shelves of files and take down the one labeled "W. Perry." He would not have employed Bryden if he had distrusted him, but as the earl's family had specifically requested the matter be kept secret, setting up a file under a false name was a sensible precaution.

Taking it into his office, he filed Markham's letter and idly shuffled through the meager collection of notes and reports, remarking this or that random phrase. And there it was: the unnoticed thing that had been a tickle in his mind: the way Julia St. John had framed certain answers to his questions, her expressions, descriptions of her family.

He wished he could talk to her. No, first he wanted to question the valet. Once he had confirmed his suspicion, then he would...what? Inform Lavinia? It would make no difference to her or to Caroline or to the earl, for that matter.

It was now nearly six. Eager to get back to town, he had not stopped to eat on the way and had only drunk an ale while the horses were changed at about noon. He returned his notes to the file and made sure the cabinet holding the client files was locked. In the outer office, Adam Bryden was tidying his desk.

Tomorrow he would ask Markham to try to find out when William Stretton's former valet was expected to return. Rather, when his current master was expected back from Ireland. Someone at his house or lodging would know. That someone could be wheedled or bribed into giving the information.

****

When Julia went down to breakfast, she found Lavinia could only have come moments before, as she heard Lady Barding saying, "I will drink a cup of chocolate and look at my letters before I eat, James." When the dowager countess saw her, she added, "Julia, you have a letter, too." Another footman presented it on a silver tray. From her father; she recognized his hand. She tucked it into her pocket to read later.

The earl and viscount must already have finished their meal. Caroline was peering at a sheet which had been crossed and re-crossed in an effort to save paper and postage. Eustacia breakfasted in her bed as a rule, which made the meal Julia's favorite.

Julia was asking for tea and flummery caudle when

Lavinia gasped.

"Peter is coming home."

"He is?" Caroline's letter dropped from her fingers onto her caudle cup and slid off into her lap. "I feared he never would. What does he say?"

"Very little more. He received our letters informing him of William's death, regrets very much that he was unable to attend the funeral…" She frowned slightly.

Was the thought creasing Lavinia's forehead the one which had occurred to Julia? Did Peter's phrasing imply he would have been happy to see William buried? It certainly sounded like it.

"He thinks he should come home at least for a visit. He misses our joints of meat and good tea and gray weather." Lavinia smiled wryly. "If you will excuse me, I must inform Barding and Popejoy."

Before she could rise, Caroline stretched out a hand. "Stay until you have drunk your chocolate and eaten one of Cook's buns, at least. You know you weaken if you do not eat in the morning. The news will keep for another few minutes."

The dowager countess laughed a little. "You are correct, of course, Caroline. James, a bun, please. Have you tried them, Julia? Our cook makes them like the ones served at the Bun House in Chelsea."

"I will try one, my lady." The dough coiled around butter, sugar, spice, and currants was tempting.

"Does he say when he expects to arrive, Lavinia?"

"No. The letter is dated a few days after Easter. He says he will start back as soon as he can get passage on a ship. At least he will not have to travel to get to a port. He has recently been living in Livorno, he says, which is a busy trading center."

The news spread rapidly. The earl and Caroline were jubilant. Lavinia tried to conceal her relief. George said little but made jocular references to the fatted calf and the Prodigal Son, only growing serious long enough to add, "Not that Peter was prodigal. I was somewhat wild and an unthrift, and William was a profligate. I don't recall Peter ever overspent his quarter's allowance. Mayhap because paper and chalks and pencils and the like are less expensive than gaming and, er, carousing."

Caroline explained Peter had gone on the Grand Tour and then declined to return. It had been expected he would be away for two years or as much as three. The family had humored him for another year before sending Miles Halliwell to retrieve him, without success, three years ago.

The house was in a furor over Peter's long-awaited return: his room must be freshly cleaned and ready for him whenever he arrived and ingredients for his favorite dishes available. Verity decided to stay in to assist Caroline by inspecting Peter's bedchamber for necessary repairs and cleaning. "I am sure the chimney must be swept, the carpet beaten, the hangings and curtains taken down and aired," she said. "I hope there are no signs of mice in the drawers. That is always disgusting."

Rather than go alone (except for a groom, of course), Julia canceled her planned ride.

"We cannot assume he will be able to give us notice of his arrival," Caroline pointed out. "He seemed to understand our desire to have him home. I don't think he will linger once his ship docks, so he will reach us sooner than a letter would in all probability. We must have all in readiness."

The earl and the viscount rode out, supposedly to deal with some estate business, but perhaps to escape the feverish mood. "Stop in to see old Nurse Parr," Caroline called to Barding as he left. "She will remember what foods he particularly liked."

He glanced back, grinning, and replied, "Ay, she will. She was always partial to him."

Julia, undressing for bed, guiltily reflected on her own uselessness. She had already sent her maid to her own rest as Molly, like all the other servants, had been set to prodigies of cleaning. The maid, an expert needlewoman, was mending the frayed or moth-eaten bed hangings in Peter Stretton's chamber as there was no time to replace them. Something crackled as Julia removed her pockets. She withdrew the letter she had put away some fifteen hours before. She had not even glanced at it since.

My dear Julia,

I have received letters both from Barding and from the dowager countess. They are pleased with Jeremy Perry and praised you. You may well be astonished to be held in high regard by them under the circumstances! You need not concern yourself further about the boy.

Lavinia, Lady Barding, suggested that as your reputation has been preserved by our prudent arrangements, they should send you to St. John Underhill when we leave town. Lady Barding asserts this would permit us to bring you to London when we go back for the resumption of Parliament in November. We could then reintroduce you as having come home after your old lady was no more. While it might have answered had William Stretton's by-blow died or been fostered out in the normal way, it will not do under the new circumstances.

No good purpose will be served by your returning either to St. John Underhill or to London. Barding, and his mother, too, say they would be happy to keep you. However, your living at Charfield would also pose difficulties and you must decline any invitation to go to London. It will be most appropriate for you to say you are ashamed to show yourself in society and are happy to leave Jeremy in their care. You may return to Handley, saying the brat died during your stay with a distant relative or if you wish to live elsewhere, write me with some choices of towns you prefer. Common sense will persuade you that a fashionable town, or anyplace you might encounter someone we know, is out of the question.

I remain
Your loving father,
Hiram St. John

Heart pounding, she folded the sheet and tried to moderate her breathing. Perhaps if she went to bed immediately and thought only of pleasant things—*like Miles Halliwell's rare smile?*—she would escape the anticipated headache. Before taking off her stays, smock, and stockings, she slipped the letter into her Bible for safekeeping. The most inquisitive servant would not pry into that.

She settled into bed, concentrating on the pleasure of riding in Charfield's park. Even better, she had discovered a story of the ancient world in Charfield's well-stocked library. While her papa might have read the *Life of Sethos,* Augusta would never have approved

Julia or Cecilia reading any book written by a French *abbé*.

In spite of her efforts, her mind reverted to the letter. She would never be able to go back to her own life. Perhaps she been the only one who had believed she could resume her place in society. That would explain why her father had never found a family to take the child or mentioned any attempt to do so. She had not wept in two years. Now a few tears gathered in her eyes to drop onto the fine linen pillowcase.

****

The family naturally looked forward to seeing Peter after an absence of seven years, but when the first excitement had passed, Julia wondered why the gladness was alloyed by a certain tension in the earl, Caroline, Lavinia, and the viscount. The viscountess expressed temperate pleasure in the prospect of meeting Peter Stretton at last: he had already been on the Continent when she and George married.

Lavinia's eyes in particular showed stress not accounted for by the preparations for his return. The house was always well-kept, and the necessary work in Peter's bedchamber completed. Had the youngest son been so estranged from the family that they almost feared his return? A few words between Caroline and Lavinia overheard when they failed to notice Julia was near made plain the impression of dread: "He may not want to stop here long. We should not wish to keep him either, in light of the danger."

"Then we must make sure he does his duty while he is here."

Something about the terse exchange lodged in her mind, mayhap because her father's letter was festering

111

in her heart and the news on the same day about Peter's return had become inextricably linked to her own letter.

The agreement was that I could come home eventually. Her father and stepmother had pointed out that many parents lost small children to fevers or inflammations of the lungs or a dozen other causes. If Jeremy proved hardy, when he was aged six months or a year, they would turn him over to some family to foster. "You need only say he has died of whatever ailment you wish. It will not matter by then," her father had said. She had believed him, and indeed, he should have been correct. Cecilia would likely be married. But Cecilia had refused to consider several potential suitors. Julia imagined her parents' tolerance of her mulishness resulted from fear of a prolonged fit of the vapors.

Now there was nothing to look forward to except a quiet life in Handley or in some other country town. She would rather continue to live with the Strettons. They treated her almost as part of their family (always excepting Eustacia). The problem was that she would have to tell Lavinia she did not wish to be returned to her family or that they did not want her. She would have to give it more thought before deciding how to answer her father and what to tell Lavinia. She did not want to lie to the dowager countess. She had been misrepresenting herself for years and hated doing it. And apart from deceit being wrong, Lavinia was entirely too perceptive.

Chapter 11

Halliwell's meeting with the former valet took place about two weeks after his return from Charfield and two days after the man's return from Ireland. A letter requesting he meet to answer a few questions relating to the settling of William Stretton's estate, and assuring him he would be paid for his time, brought a reply that the fellow was happy to comply. As he lived at some distance from the offices of Whitacker & Halliwell, Miles had suggested a more convenient coffee house. The valet thanked him for his condescension in making it easy for him. He was welcome to think so; Halliwell's intention was to keep their conversation private.

After asking a few easy questions like *how long did you serve William Stretton?* Halliwell edged into the subject that interested him.

"Were you aware of any of Mr. Stretton's liaisons with ladies in the two or three years before his death?"

Eugene Walsh pursed his lips and tutted. "Not as such, sir."

What the devil does that mean? "Not as such, Mr. Walsh?"

"See you, it's not a 'yes' or 'no' question, really. Mr. Stretton was fond of the company of females of all sorts."

"I am interested in those with whom he had an

113

intimate relationship."

The boy came around to fill their cups. Walsh waited until he was out of hearing. "I'm no help, sir. I know there were women he bedded, couldn't help knowing when he came home with scent on his clothing. I could tell if he'd been with a lady by whether it was good perfume or not."

"We can narrow the field to ladies. Did he never mention a name? Send a letter to make an assignation? If you passed it to a groom or footman to take to the Penny Post, perhaps you noticed the name or direction." Unlikely William would have mailed a letter to Julia, when unmarried ladies did not receive letters from gentlemen outside their family, but worth asking.

"He sent replies to invitations he received, of course," the valet said slowly. "Arranging to meet a lady was something he'd do at an entertainment, most like. Easy enough to exchange a few quiet words with her. No need to put anything in black and white."

"Was there never a need to have a billet-doux delivered by hand?"

"Risk it falling into the husband's hands? No. Same as he wouldn't write by the Penny Post. Careful, Mr. Stretton was, when he was sober. And if he was in his cups, he wouldn't write." Walsh looked off over Halliwell's left shoulder. The fellow had had no difficulty meeting his eyes before.

"Did he only deal with married ladies or whores?"

A long hesitation.

"There was one young lady," Walsh admitted. "Like I said, he was careful, but this one time he broke his own rule. It wasn't what I could approve of, being likely to lead to trouble, but half a dozen times he had me carry notes. This was, oh, two years ago or more."

Bit by bit he drew the sordid story out of the valet.

"He knew where she'd be so I could deliver the note to her maid. I reckon they were so taken with each other the first time they met they arranged it then. After that, either she wrote to a coffee house where Mr. Stretton got letters under another name from some of his flirts or else he had a list of days and where she could be encountered, casual-like. Walking in the park between ten and eleven any nice day was one, shopping on a certain street was another. I don't rightly recall which day that was, nor the time."

"Was she unchaperoned? Did you walk up to the lady and give her the billet?"

"She always had at least a maid and sometimes there was another lady as well. But whether it was only the one or both, I never approached her. I'd pass it to the maid. She'd be walking behind them, so the dragon never saw me slip it into her hand."

"How many times did Stretton see her?"

"The first was Tottenham Court, the fair, you know. Not the place a decent girl should have gone. Her mama and papa can't have known where she was off to. From something the master let drop, I believe they thought she was going shopping with older cousins, one of them being betrothed, but it was all a ruse to go to the fair with the suitor and his friends. Mr. Stretton was introduced by one of them. Seems he was struck with the little baggage and joined their party. After that it was just the letters, until a house party."

"How did they both happen to be at the same party? I'd not think they moved in the same level of society."

"Ha! They didn't. He heard from the girl that her family was invited to stay over Christmas. The people giving the party were gentry and Mr. Stretton wouldn't know 'em as a rule, but he'd met the oldest son at university and they shared an interest in women, drink, and cards." The valet shrugged. "I don't suppose anyone knew he was married. Probably thought he was no more than a well-connected, handsome fellow who'd be a good catch for one of the young ladies." Walsh made a sour mouth. "I can't think what they were thinking of, to have ten or twelve young people present and not make sure they were chaperoned day and night. Boys down from university set loose with schoolroom chits—'tis a wonder they weren't all ruined."

"Your master was past boyhood."

"Ay, and should have known better. But I never saw a more beautiful girl. If he'd had no chance of sampling her, he'd have got over it soon enough, but between the letters back and forth and the occasional sightings, when he did get the chance, he took it."

"How many letters?"

"From him to her, half a dozen, I think. Maybe one more or less. From her to him, Lord! She wrote every week, nearly, by the Penny Post. Embarrassing, it was."

"What happened to them? They were not in his lodgings after his death." Going through the suite of rooms William had rented had been delegated to Miles.

"Couldn't let them be found, could I? Several of his women wrote him. He didn't always act like the gentleman he was born, but he wouldn't have wanted his flirts' scribblings used as evidence to divorce them. March was terrible cold. They made a nice fire."

"What happened after the house party?"

"Nothing much. Once he'd had her, that was that. At the end of his stay, he told her they had best stop writing and seeing each other until she was introduced into society. We both breathed a sigh of relief, because when that happened, she was sure to have a suitor or two with a title, and more than that with properties and fortunes. Her papa would choose the most eligible and hand her over. Even if Mr. Stretton was free to marry, no one would favor the girl marrying him over a titled or propertied cove."

Miles waited.

"It didn't turn out quite that way. A month or two later, the girl sent him a letter begging for a meeting. Mr. Stretton thought he'd better agree. He came home cursing his luck; she thought she was with child. We had a bad few weeks, my master thinking her father or brother would call him out on the one hand and on t'other, hoping they wouldn't for fear of hurting her reputation. After a while longer, when nothing came of it, we gave up worrying."

Miles asked a few more questions and let him go, his suspicion confirmed.

More pressing business prevented his writing that day, or for the next two days. He felt no guilt about the delay: what he knew made no material difference. It would not change the Strettons' decision about the little boy. He doubted very much it would affect their opinion of Julia. Nevertheless, he must report what he had learned, not only because it was his duty, but in fairness to Julia St. John.

Before he could clear his desk to write, however, he received a letter from Barding, delivered by a groom. "Were you instructed to take my reply back?"

Miles asked. He had not yet opened the sheet.

"Lor' love me, no, sir. Lady Barding, the old Lady Barding, said as you'd know what to do. Still, if you want to send a reply, I'll be spending the night at the house and starting back in the morning."

Halliwell dismissed the man with a tip. He had traveled fast and hard, judging by his dust-covered clothing and stiff movements, and would be the better for several pints of ale, a meal, and a bed.

The message was dismayingly brief, less than half a sheet. *Come at once. Peter is returning, and there are problems. We must discuss certain actions to be taken as quickly as possible. Barding.*

While Miles had written to Peter at Lavinia's request, it was unlikely the youngest Stretton brother should have received it yet. He might only be responding to the family's letters regarding William's death. Halliwell wished the earl had included a copy of whatever part of Peter's letter had provoked a reaction. Whatever the reason, it must be too sensitive to trust to a letter, even one carried by a trusted groom.

"Bryden, get me a place on the stage to Banbury tomorrow. It leaves from the Bell, Holborn. If there's no seat to be had, I'll go post. My errand won't wait until Thursday."

****

The post chaise was far more comfortable than the stage would have been. But even the unseasonable cool weather did not spare one the dust, the airlessness of the enclosed box, and hours of having one's bones rattled almost out of one's body. In its favor, the post chaise bowled along more speedily than the stage coach could have done, and he was not sharing it with as many as five other travelers, some of whom might have only a passing acquaintance with soap. Miles could not even read to take his mind off the discomfort, as the carriage's motion while he focused upon a book or document tended to bring on a severe headache.

He passed the time speculating fruitlessly on what problem awaited him at Charfield, when his mind did not wander to Julia Perry. Julia St. John.

Adams, the Charfield butler, arrived in the hall only moments behind Miles.

"I have informed Lord Barding and Lady Barding, the Dowager Lady Barding, and Lord Popejoy, of your arrival, Mr. Halliwell. They will await you in the library…though they understand you will wish to go to your room to tidy yourself."

"Thank you, Adams. I won't keep them waiting long."

When he entered the library after washing his face and hands and brushing his clothing as well as he could, four grim faces met him.

"Thank you for coming quickly, Halliwell."

"I am always happy to oblige you, Lord Barding."

"You may feel differently when we have outlined our problem," Lavinia said. "Barding, does the footman in the hall understand we are not to be interrupted?"

"He does."

The dowager countess's statement signified a true catastrophe. Surprising when he expected they would be looking forward to Peter's return.

The earl spoke. "We find ourselves in an extraordinary position. All our dependence is upon you." He let out a long breath. "We need your opinion and whatever advice you may think fit to give."

"Certainly, sir."

"Popejoy's heir is ill. We fear he will not recover."

In the silence that followed, Miles said, "Is it related to the bruising that worried Lady Popejoy when I was last here?"

"We all suppose it must be. He was dosed for the green-sickness, but it did no good. We have relied upon Dr. Broxon's skill for many years."

"I remember, my lady. He treated Lord Popejoy's broken leg before I went to London to work for Whitacker."

"And did not scruple to set the bone himself instead of leaving it to a bonesetter. Unfortunately, he does not know what is wrong with Georgie or how to treat it, though 'tis clear to all of us—"

"Most of us," Caroline interrupted.

"—except Eustacia—that he is extremely ill. The bruises that have no cause we can discover, the appearance of rashes, the bleeding at the nose, must all be related somehow. There are other things, too, but taken separately one might overlook them. Dr. Broxon has recommended good red beef and stout or porter's ale, but it has not helped. Sometimes the poor little fellow has no appetite, and he is losing weight."

"If something should befall young George," Lord Barding began, and stopped.

"Eustacia may not be able to give me another child," Popejoy said heavily. "She suffers from female complaints of various sorts since Georgie's birth."

"I see." Lord Barding had two living sons, but Miles did not care to venture into that extremely delicate subject. His statement confirmed what Lavinia had told him at his last visit. The little boy was nearly three, and the twins Amelia and Alethea, conceived two or three months before the viscount's marriage, six. While such a gap between pregnancies was no guarantee Lady Popejoy was unable to breed again, it did raise questions. Still, Georgie might recover from his ailment. Eustacia might die, leaving George a widower and able to remarry. Or George might die, leaving only Peter to sire the next generation of Strettons. He could not voice any of those things. He did say, "You mentioned that Mr. Peter Stretton is on his way back from Italy."

"He is, and we were relieved to hear it." Lavinia fixed her faded blue eyes on him. "Halliwell, you understand the difficulty. What would you recommend we do?"

There was only one possibility if in fact Eustacia could not produce another child. "Peter Stretton must be induced to marry and, er, procreate."

She gave a mirthless little choke of laughter. "We had got so far as that conclusion and rely upon you to persuade him."

"I will try. I cannot guarantee success." He would have said more, but the door opened suddenly and Eustacia stepped in, caroling, "Oh, there you all are. Mama-in-law, Verity and I are going into Banbury to choose lengths of cotton for dresses for the girls. They are growing too tall for their gowns. I thought Indian printed cotton would be pretty if any is available. Would you like to come with us? And you, too, of course, my lady, if you feel able," she added kindly to Lavinia.

"I think I must decline the treat, Eustacia. We have some business to discuss with Halliwell, and it cannot be put off."

"I must stay as well," Caroline said. "Do they also need new shoes? Their feet will be growing with the rest of them."

"La, I had not thought...but of course you are correct. Perhaps they had best come with us. Missing a few lessons will do them no harm." She fluttered out.

After a moment, George rose, went to the door, and listened for a moment before opening it. "Rafe, how did it happen that you let Lady Popejoy enter?"

"Begging your pardon, my lord, I left my place to answer the door, Mr. Adams having been called away for a few moments. 'Twas Parson, come to pay a call. I informed him the family was not at home. As I come back, I saw Lady Popejoy just going in."

George grunted, closed the door, and locked it.

Lionel Barding sat at the end of the long table, staring at his folded hands. With the long south-facing window behind him, it was difficult to make out his expression. "We must persuade Peter to marry. I agree with my mother; you are the fittest to attempt it. However, given the circumstances, we cannot count on his, ah, full cooperation. Even if he is willing..."

At the other end of the table, the strong bones of Lavinia's face and her hooded eyes were plainly visible, reminding Miles of the judge at a criminal trial he had attended. He had looked thus as he sentenced the man to death: implacable.

"That he is returning argues he has some family feeling, Barding. He may be willing to marry, even if not precisely the usual sort of marriage."

"If Peter is unwilling or, er, unable to provide a son, there is an alternative we hope he will accept, if you agree, Halliwell." The earl paused. "If you feel you cannot support it, the title may die out and the estates escheat to the Crown, as there are no surviving branches of our family. We have not been as prolific as many other noble houses."

George said, "No one has yet admitted that my son is dying. Dr. Broxon says there is hope where there is still life, and I am sure all of us pray daily that Georgie will be spared. But even if he is, can he regain full health? He might survive his current ailment only to be carried off by some other disease. But for a few slight indispositions, Eustacia seems healthy enough, though she has not recovered yet from Georgie's birth, which is troubling. I do not know if her parents lacked health or vigor. It's not something I feel I can ask. We must be prepared."

What had Miles's agreement to do with anything? The family told him what they wished to accomplish, and he did it. He said as much.

"Ay, Halliwell, you've never failed us yet. We could not ask for more loyal, efficient service than you have always rendered."

"And always with integrity and honor, which is not invariably the case with men who are in business." Lavinia rewarded him with a smile. "Which brings us to the reason you may balk at the solution we have struck upon. I admit it goes a bit beyond what one would normally ask."

"Your notion," Caroline said, "and a brilliant one."

"What, precisely, is it you want me to do?" His mouth had gone dry. Something was very much amiss.

The earl, viscount, and countess turned toward Lavinia.

"There is a hint of dishonesty in what I propose."

It was the first time he had heard Lavinia sound hesitant. He waited.

"Peter may well be reluctant to enter into marriage, and I confess I could not like to encourage a young lady to marry a man whose interest in her would be at best tepid. While there are women who do not care for the marriage bed and would be happy to marry only for a comfortable home, one cannot be sure of their feelings before the wedding. One certainly cannot inquire. The bride must be a gentlewoman, and it would be best if she could fit into our family comfortably."

Caroline's lips thinned. She would be thinking of Eustacia. Halliwell sympathized. He had still been only Whitacker's partner, but he remembered the furor when the Bardings had been presented with the accomplished deed: a Fleet Prison marriage, no banns, and no license. George had married Eustacia, who was pregnant, undoubtedly with the intention of forcing him into marriage. The aging, shabby-genteel aunt who had brought her up must have connived at helping Eustacia ruin herself. George had believed himself up to every rig of the knowing ones out to relieve a fellow of his money or possessions. Perhaps he was, in the case of card sharpers and doxies. His caution had not extended to a pretty, apparently genteel girl.

The Bardings had had to accept her and insisted on a quiet ceremony by special license, using "family opposition" as the reason, rather than trusting to the legality of the Fleet marriage. But for the pregnancy, they might have tried to pay her off and have the original marriage overturned in spite of the notoriety. But in the seven years since that scrambling wedding under the Rules of the Fleet, Eustacia had given birth only twice: to the twins Alethea and Amelia and then to Georgie.

The dowager countess was visibly steeling herself to explain. "When we first heard from Peter, it occurred to us that he and Caroline's niece Verity might marry. Like him, she is quiet, and she is biddable, as well. She would not be ideal, but what would you? She is available and would be grateful and discreet. Then after the doctor's last visit to Georgie, when we had to consider he might die, a better notion came to me. Julia St. John may be willing to marry Peter. She is an old maid, sensible and intelligent, and I do not think her family is as kind to her as they might be. Having her here has been no penance at all. I hope she is willing to agree."

"I can't think why she would refuse," Caroline said. "It would solve her difficulties as well as ours."

"My lords, my ladies, while I was in town I made some further inquiries. I was uneasy about certain details of the story Mistress Perry or St. John related. What I learned makes it certain that she is not Jeremy Perry's mother. When I interviewed Julia St. John, I was surprised to find her a woman of mature years when I expected a girl. Recently, I read my original notes again, which referred to the younger sister as 'lively,' and a more recent report called her 'a right handful.' Which would be more likely to attract William and be seduced? Finally, I spoke with William's former valet, who confirmed that Cecilia St. John was the one he seduced." He gave a brief account of his interview with Walsh. He should regret dashing their hopes, but he must share his conclusions now that

125

he knew they were relying on faulty information. The idea of Julia marrying Peter seemed wrong in some indefinable way in any case.

"Which St. John daughter birthed Jeremy makes no difference."

"But Mistress Julia's fertility is unproven."

"One may hope that she is fertile. After all, we could not be sure Verity would able to have a child. But we need not worry overmuch if only Julia will marry Peter."

"Why would Mistress Perry, as we've been calling her, be preferable to Verity?" What could they be thinking?

"We have a strong, healthy little boy in Jeremy, who is said to be her son and is unquestionably a Stretton." Seeing his blank expression, she continued, "Once they are married, we can see about making Jeremy legitimate."

"Marriage will not legitimate Jeremy, nor would adoption."

"No, we understand that. But I believe we have thought of a way around the problem." She pressed her lips together. She was nervous. Lavinia, Lady Barding, was worried. Miles felt himself break into a sweat. Rightly so, as it turned out.

Chapter 12

"If Peter and Julia had married at any time up to Jeremy's birth, even if they concealed the marriage, Jeremy would be legitimate." Lavinia's hooded eyes fixed upon his.

"But they didn't. They've never met. Peter hasn't even been in England in seven years."

"He might have been. We know he has been traveling extensively in Italy, and he is not a good correspondent. He might have returned, if only briefly."

Miles could have pointed out how unlikely it would be for someone who had been out of the country for years not to have visited his family. In Peter's case, he could not make that argument: if his half brother were not actually estranged from his family, neither would he necessarily seek them out.

The earl and countess and George had been listening with no indication of surprise or disapproval. He had sometimes suspected a strain of peculiarity ran in the Stretton bloodline. Miles said carefully, "Those things might all be true, but unless you are privy to some information I do not possess, they did not occur."

"But they might have."

"Merely alleging them will not serve. Someone is bound to question a two- or three-year-old secret marriage between a lady who has not been out of the country and a man who has not been in it."

"Not if there were a marriage license and both parties swore to it. With at least one reputable witness who could testify to its validity, and a peer of the realm who supports it."

He knew who the reputable person would be, too.

"What you are suggesting would be illegal. My knowledge of the law is limited to business matters for the most part. I can't tell you what the penalties might be, but at the very least, there would be terrible scandal attached to your name."

"Only if our little stratagem were found out, my boy," the earl commented.

"It would also be wrong. You would be asking Peter Stretton to acknowledge William's bastard in place of his own legitimate heir, if any."

"Doing so would relieve Peter of the trouble of getting an heir, though of course we'd like him to give the family one, if possible. And, ah, it would give him some protection in case..." George fidgeted.

Caroline said, "William's son would come before Peter and any son of his in the succession anyway."

"Only if the son were legitimate, my lady."

"We all know titles and estates have passed to men with no claim by blood at all. And Jeremy is a Stretton."

"Except that those heirs were born within the marriage even if they were begot by a lover. Too many people would know the marriage was a lie. Mistress Julia's family, for one." He cast a glance at Lavinia, who gazed back blandly before responding.

"Do you not think they will be happy to support the tale in the hope that under our auspices their younger girl will make a good marriage and they will all gain a foothold in the beau monde? Julia has not told us a great deal about the St. Johns, but I trust I know a hawk from a handsaw when I see one. Why would the St. Johns or the sister speak out? It would only damage her chance of marriage and lose her the benefit of a friendly connection with us, while Julia's secret marriage to a Stretton would only benefit her and the rest of the St. Johns. By this little ruse, we help everyone. Think how much better it would be for Jeremy to grow up an unquestioned Stretton." Lavinia's stare pierced him, as she knew it would.

"The valet I interviewed knows William Stretton seduced the younger girl."

"Faugh. He was decent enough to destroy William's collection of letters from his mistresses. I dare say he will never hear of Jeremy at all. He is only a valet, besides."

"Whatever the advantages of such a scheme, I think you have not considered all the difficulties. You may be correct about the desirable results, my ladies, my lords. But anyone in Italy who knows Peter did not leave during the relevant period is a risk. We could not prove he had returned except by testimony which might be called into question if someone else swore to his presence there. And there would be no way of proving the marriage. Alleged marriage."

"That is why we are consulting you, Halliwell, though it is a little outside the usual scope of your business. We will need a marriage certificate dated during whatever period Peter might have made a brief visit to England. And, I suppose, a special license, unless it should be easy to allege the banns were read."

"I think we would all be the better for a glass of

sherry," Caroline remarked brightly. "George?"

"Quite so, Mama." He stalked over to a cabinet.

Miles ignored the distraction. "You would need a forged—forged!—certificate. Most parishes record the reading of banns in the parish register. If I'm not mistaken, when the parties live in different parishes, the banns are read in both. If the banns for the alleged marriage did not appear in the register, that would cast doubt upon the validity of the marriage. The parson would certainly disavow so recent a certificate if he did not recognize the names of the parishioners."

George returned with a tray of glasses and a decanter of the pale dry sherry the earl preferred, and commenced to serve them.

Miles went on, "What you want would require finding a clergyman willing to write a certificate dated several years ago, somehow squeeze entries for the banns and the marriage into the register, and lie if questioned about it."

"You would have to bribe him. The parish register might be a problem," Lavinia conceded. "With a license, no banns would be required, which would remove part of the problem. With a special license, they could be married anywhere, which would make it easier to find a clergyman who would be willing to take a bribe. Surely the entry for the marriage could be written in between two other entries."

Halliwell took a deep breath followed by a swallow of wine. "Forging the license would require suborning a bishop or his chancellor or one of his surrogates. I do know that issuance of a license is sometimes recorded, and other documents are required as well: allegations about the couple and a bond. Those may also be recorded or filed. Obtaining a license to marry would not be easier."

"There's Gretna Green. I believe there's very little recordkeeping done, as almost anyone can perform the ceremony." Caroline added primly, "The daughter of a friend ran away to marry there."

This idea was comparatively simple to scotch. So to speak. "It might take as much as five or six days to travel to the Border, and as much to return. Mistress Julia could hardly have been absent from her family for a fortnight without someone noticing."

" 'A hit, a very palpable hit.' " The earl was amused.

Popejoy cleared his throat. "London may be the best place for a, er, clandestine marriage. Er, the Fleet, you know. A good many parsons conduct marriages there. Some may not be particularly good about keeping records."

"And more likely to be open to accepting a bribe." Barding was definitely smiling.

The gentlemen were not going to be the voice of reason as Halliwell had hoped.

He had been leaning forward. He sat back, steepling his fingers as he studied the four intent faces staring back at him. "To sum up, you are asking me to forge a marriage certificate and related documents and bribe an unknown number of persons. These are crimes. As I'm not an attorney, I don't know what the charges would be. Have you consulted your lawyer about this idea?" Why ask? He knew the answer.

The earl's eyebrows rose. "Jessen would not approve. You know what attorneys are."

He did indeed. "But what of Peter's own son, if he

marries and begets one? You cannot think it fair to deprive him of his place in the succession."

"We all know Peter is unlikely to marry if left to his own devices. If he did wed and father a son, admittedly there would be a degree of unfairness. In that contingency, we can make it right for any son or daughter of Peter's body." Lavinia's tone was gently chiding, as if he had entered the drawing room with mud on his boots.

"But..." His eyes touched on George before returning to the dowager countess.

Viscount Popejoy responded. "We must be practical, however unpleasant the reality. My countess's health has been delicate since Georgie's birth. Before, she seldom ailed. Her health and vigor was one of the things that drew me to her. She, ah... We have been concerned about Georgie's health. I fear he has not inherited his mother's strong constitution. But we have not been able to, ummm, provide Georgie a baby brother. I am not optimistic. Halliwell, you may not be aware she has miscarried twice. In spite of all she can do to conceive, she may not succeed, or she may miscarry again. In the unlikely event I found myself a widower, no one would wonder if I remarried within a year, but I do not expect it. Best Jeremy should be in the line of succession, given life's uncertainties."

"You have always been most resourceful in guarding our interests," Caroline observed, and gave him a kindly smile. "We feel sure you can find a way to make everything right."

"Setting aside whether I would be able to do it, would Mistress Julia St. John be willing to marry Peter?"

"I did not feel I could suggest it until we knew it was possible and whether you had any suggestions of how to do it. However, why would she not? She would be marrying into a family that values her, she would live in comfort, her reputation would be repaired, and really, what other chance is she likely to have?"

She deserved better than a marriage of convenience. Under the Bardings' patronage, she would have opportunities to make a marriage based on affection if not love. "As your man of business, it's my duty to warn you against attempting a fraud."

"We all understand that it's not strictly in accord with the law," Barding said. "Consider this: which is worse? A little tampering with forms and perhaps the register or letting our family name die out and the estate and title revert to the Crown? In the latter case, what will become of our tenants? My mother's very sound investments have made it unnecessary to get an Act of Enclosure to take away the tenants' rights to open fields and common land. Will the new owner hesitate to do so?"

"Of course, we cannot complete our plans until Peter is here," Caroline added. "We assume he would be willing, but we cannot know until we talk to him."

"We are asking you to look into the possibilities at this point." Lavinia bit her lip. "We cannot wait long. Julia's coming here with Jeremy and Peter's return make this the ideal opportunity to reveal a secret wedding. Concealing a clandestine marriage for two or three years is one thing, but once he has returned, it would be only natural to reveal it."

Heaven help him, they were serious, and none appeared to find anything wrong with the plan. The family had run mad. Yet he could understand their concern if the viscountess was unable to have another male child. If Peter had married…but he had not and might be relieved to be supplied with an heir.

Miles was not a member of the family, but still, they were important to him, not merely clients. He would give a great deal to have such close ties, though he never would. He had hoped he might, once.

The thought of Charfield passing to hands that might not esteem the rambling, inconvenient house and the servants and tenants was unexpectedly painful, too. He had known Charfield and those who lived within its bounds for nearly as long as he could remember.

Miles took a breath. "I will try to find out if it's feasible. I will not promise to carry it out if in my judgment the difficulty and risks are too great, precisely as I would not invest your money in some venture I believed would yield loss rather than profit." He could not refuse outright: he owed the Bardings too much. There would be time for them to think better of it.

"We knew we could count on you, Miles. You will set this in motion at once? We must be ready when Peter is home."

Which meant returning to London, though not until tomorrow. In the meantime, he might speak with Julia and sound her out.

Chapter 13

Miles Halliwell had arrived and, according to Molly, had immediately met with the family in the library. "…them as matter," as she put it. To Julia's surprise and disquiet, he sought her out after dinner and invited her to walk in the garden. She was flustered by the request. She was accepted by the earl's family; Halliwell could have no more questions. The sensation was strangely like being a girl again at her first ball.

Julia had thought him hard-faced and lacking in warmth at their first meeting. Since arriving at Charfield, she had discovered he possessed a softer side. There was no mistaking that the earl's family and servants thought well of him. Perhaps his icy demeanor was put on for professional reasons. Or had he suffered such hurts or losses that he chose to mask whatever he felt? She could scarcely fault him for it when she seldom felt free to reveal her own sentiments, though in her case, it was to avoid causing pain to another or brangling, or because ladies must hide discomfort or annoyance or be called hysterical or shrewish.

Hilda Ernst had referred to his origins; had she called them humble? He might have raised himself by his own efforts against great odds. If his breeding had been less than genteel, his harshness to her at Handley might be understandable, though she had hated him for it. Yet as his duty was to protect the Bardings' interests, he had to ensure she was not a scheming trollop seizing an opportunity to pass off her bastard to a wealthy family who might pay her to go away. The fact that her father and not she had approached the earl should have allayed such concerns, if one believed unconditionally in the honor of gentlemen. Mayhap he did not.

Her opinion of him had undergone a change on that interminable exodus from Handley. Halliwell had treated her, Janet Campbell, and Betty with every consideration. He had been solicitous of their comfort and displayed no irritation at the inns when the boy was difficult. He had even dandled him upon one knee so the boy could pretend to ride a horse, to his delight.

If not for the child's presence, the journey would have been as enjoyable as a coach trip could be, in spite of the tedium of jolting over bad roads. Even Halliwell's skill as an escort could not prevent their receiving teams of indifferent horses at some stages. He had apologized for one set of plodders.

"The earl keeps teams on the London road to facilitate his travel to town. On this route, even if he had cattle stabled, we would not be using them."

He did not explain, but she understood he meant to prevent talk of a female and a small child traveling with the earl's horses. It had been Halliwell who suggested full mourning to conceal her identity. Even in the inns' private parlors, she had managed not to show her face when any servant was present. He had mentioned in passing to the innkeepers or the servants that he was escorting his recently bereaved cousin to her family's home. She could only be grateful that he had so diligently guarded her privacy and reputation. It might have been at the earl's instruction, but still, he had been more attentive than his employer could have expected, exerting himself to converse with her at meals. She had learned he liked the country but also enjoyed the availability of newspapers, books, and the theater in London.

He made an effort to find treats for the child, certainly not part of his duty. The gingerbread had been a kind thought, though unfortunately it had unsettled the boy's stomach. Really, she must remember to call Jeremy by his name. It was not his fault he had been born.

They chatted idly for a few minutes: The primroses, sweet violets, and dog's mercury had finally come out in the chilly late spring. One often still needed a mantle or cape during the warmest part of the day. She was tolerably sure viewing the few flowers had not been his intention, though what he did mean was a mystery to her. As they paused by a bed of violets, Halliwell remarked that he preferred them to roses. She did also, which led to a discussion of other delightful or comforting odors: the yeasty aroma of baking bread, sheets smelling of lavender, the scent of rain in the night. Who would have supposed the stern man of business ever thought of such things?

They had come some distance from the house and no gardeners were in sight, nor was there any foliage to conceal a listener.

"Mistress Perry, I recently spoke with William Stretton's valet. I know Jeremy is not your child."

The plain statement struck her like a bolt of lightning. She opened her mouth to speak and closed it again. What could she say, after all?

"I honor you for your loyalty to your sister. Half

sister, I should say. Not many ladies would sacrifice themselves as you have."

She was still speechless when he said, "I apologize for taking you unaware. I should have begun by expressing my admiration for your unselfish devotion."

Her eyes prickled with tears. How odd to hear such a sentiment from someone who was almost a stranger. She swallowed hard, fighting down the urge to cry. "Thank you, Mr. Halliwell. I do not deserve such praise." It had taken her father and stepmother weeks of orders, pleading, promises, and threats to wear her down until she agreed to take the shame upon herself. They had not thanked her.

"I am familiar with the pressure to do one's duty. The sense of obligation to others, the feeling of guilt if one refuses."

He understood. How did he know?

"May I ask a rather impertinent question?"

The request steadied her: mere impertinence would not wound her, after some of his remarks in their initial meeting. "You may, sir, if you will answer one of mine."

"What is your question, Mistress Perry?"

"I know you met with the family earlier. Have you told them?"

"Yes, in passing. It made not the slightest difference to them. We conferred mainly about Peter Stretton's return."

The Bardings had treated her as if she were not lost to respectability. Amazingly, they had folded her into their family. "What do you wish to know, Mr. Halliwell?"

"Why did you agree to the pretense of being your

nephew's mother? It was a great sacrifice on your part."

"One does make sacrifices for one's loved ones, sir. By doing so, Cecilia was able to go home sooner after the birth than she would otherwise have agreed to do."

"I'd think she would be anxious to leave as soon as she could travel."

"She did not want him turned over to strangers until he was past the first, dangerous months. She was willing to leave if I stayed to oversee his care." Not precisely the truth but as close as she could come.

"Your family took considerable pains to preserve your reputation. Yet after a reasonable period, say six or eight months, Jeremy was not fostered out. It is not expensive to foster a child in the home of someone who wants a child or would welcome the money for its support. Presumably your sister went somewhere for her lying-in. The proprietor of such a place would know how to go about finding people to take the boy. Sometimes a middling family or even a more highly placed couple will secretly take a nobleman's bastard if they need an heir. Yet you have given up many more months than necessary to a child you do not love. Why?"

Much as she would have liked not to explain, Miles Halliwell knew so much about their family there was no point in concealing the truth. "Cecilia fancied herself in love with William Stretton. Even when she learned he was married, she was sure he loved her. To her, it was some great, tragic affair like Romeo and Juliet, though I am sure she never saw or read Shakespeare's play. Girls are born spinning such fancies." Even she herself had once believed in the possibility of love. "Although he made a jest of it on learning she was with child, she thought he was merely trying to raise her spirits. Therefore she did not want to give up his child despite knowing she could not keep it. Certainly my stepmother would not allow it. Cecilia did understand she could not trudge off nobly to give birth and raise her baby in a hovel somewhere."

"How did the plan to free you from responsibility for the child fail?"

"My father and stepmother meant to find a foster family for him. When the time came, Cecilia railed against the idea." And threw tantrums and had more vapors and wept and begged until they gave in.

"But why?"

"If you'd ever seen my half sister in a taking, you wouldn't ask."

"I mean, why did she care? Every year a few girls of good family make the same mistake, and they do the only thing they can. They give the child up to be raised by someone else. It's not necessarily a bad life."

At an odd, reluctant note in his voice, she raised her eyes from the graveled path to his face. Impassive as usual, it told her nothing.

"She was convinced that William's wife would die and William would marry her and legitimate his by-blow. As if he could! Foolish, but she was hardly more than a child herself, and had never made a decision more important than what color ribbons to buy."

"We convince ourselves of what we want to believe as readily as others deceive us. 'Tis a human failing."

"Not one of yours, I imagine, sir."

"Not for many years, at least." After a moment, he

went on. "You were pressed to raise the child. Was this meant to be permanent?"

"My father privately promised me that in a few more months, or perhaps a year, a family would be found for him. Cecilia would be told he had died, and I would be welcomed home. Our friends would be informed that Augusta's godmother, whom I was supposed to be companioning, had died. My father failed to find a suitable foster family."

"Possibly he and Lady St. John feared a recurrence of the vapors if they told Cecilia that Jeremy had died."

"No—" Her denial of Halliwell's dry remark caught in her throat. After Cecilia's storms of emotion over her pregnancy and Stretton's refusal to marry her, then over the prospect of giving Jeremy up to be fostered, she could not dismiss his suggestion. After a moment, she laughed in spite of herself. Cecilia would have become hysterical, and her papa and mama would have wished ardently to avoid yet another distressing round of wailing, sobbing, and refusing food.

"Then once she heard of William's death, she surrendered her expectations, and your father had no reason not to tell the earl?"

"Cecilia had never divulged her seducer's identity. She can be amazing stubborn. When she saw the obituary, she exclaimed and was induced to give up her secret. She never told us more than that he was a nobleman, and she was incorrect in that, as he was only the second son of a nobleman's heir."

"Do you regret accommodating your family's wishes?"

They had wandered out of the formal garden and into the long rectangle nearest the kitchen that provided vegetables and herbs. Another section was for medicinal plants. She paused to nip a sprig of rosemary and hold it to her nose, gazing at the physic garden beyond. It was unusually extensive and full of plants she did not recognize.

"It's not a question I can answer with a simple yes or no. It does not show me in a flattering light. Originally it was only a matter of preserving her reputation. I was already an ape leader with little chance of marriage and would always be a drain upon my family. Those were excellent arguments for my doing what was best for them."

"Knowing what is best or right to do does not make it easier, does it?"

"No. But what else could I do?" Why not be frank? The Bardings trusted Halliwell implicitly. "Augusta, my stepmother, ascribed my reluctance to my being jealous of Cecilia. I don't think I was, but my father never paid much attention to me and certainly Augusta didn't. They dote on Cecilia. I suppose Augusta might conclude I resented her. My stepmother and my father were set on Cecilia making a good marriage and rumors of the birth would have damaged her chances."

His faint smile blended sympathy and cynicism to a remarkable degree. "Most marriages are arranged with either monetary benefit or social advancement in mind. Not unreasonably; what is marriage but a business transaction of a sort? I'm told she is very beautiful. She might well catch the eye of some titled gentleman, or at least a man with excellent connections."

"She is charming, too, like a dazzling butterfly."

He muttered something inaudible.

"I beg your pardon?"

"If you must know, Mistress Perry, I said, 'Preserve me from the butterfly sort.' I suppose she is a lovely widgeon."

A bubble of laughter escaped her. When was the last time she had laughed even once in a day? "How did you know?"

"It goes with the vapors and allowing herself to be seduced."

"She was only turned sixteen at the time. I should have done a better job of chaperoning her."

"Was that not her mother's responsibility? You are a heroine, Mistress Julia, and deserve the Bardings' praise. Having William Stretton's son here has made Caroline, Lady Barding, happy."

She blinked away incipient tears. Weeping in Miles Halliwell's presence would be horrid: weak, foolish, humiliating. Worse, even, than returning to the house with reddened eyes, blotchy skin, and a clogged nose. With an effort, she admitted, "The thing I regret is not letting myself grow fond of him because I believed he would soon be taken from my charge." She forced a slight smile or perhaps more of a grimace. "Mayhap I never would have cared for him, given my loathing of how his father had ruined a girl still in the schoolroom. However, I would have tried, and perhaps he would have been some consolation."

"I understand your feelings. Yet are you really worse off now? No one knows Julia St. John was here with Jeremy Perry. The Bardings are willing to send you to your family's home later this summer so they can take you to town with them in the autumn. You've been gone too long for it to appear you went away merely to have a baby. It's a sound plan, and not much different from what you originally expected, though Jeremy will be fostered by his father's family rather than a farmer or tradesman. You would be able to take up the threads of your life. There is another possibility, too, which you might—"

They had come abreast of a stone bench at the garden's edge. She dropped onto it, head bowed. "I can't," she gasped, pressing her handkerchief to her eyes as she gave way to tears.

He sank down beside her. "Here, take mine. It's bigger."

Soft linen brushed the back of her hand. She groped for it, and her fingers met his. The brief touch shocked her out of her misery. Mortification followed. She mopped her face while trying to conceal her chagrin.

"Can you talk about it? What is it you can't do?" His voice was as gentle as if he were speaking to a skittish horse.

What a disgraceful display. The kindness in his commonplace words rather than the touch of his fingers dried up her tears. She could not recall the last time anyone had shown her sympathy. The comfort of it was utterly disarming, and she had not cried long enough for her nose to get stuffy. She took his handkerchief away from her eyes and folded it without looking at him, hoping the cool air on her heated face would serve to wipe out the evidences of weeping before they returned to the house.

When she could govern her voice, she said, "I can't go to St. John Underhill. They don't want me."

"Did they actually say as much?"

"Yes."

"He prefers you to remain here, as the Barding ladies do also?"

"No."

"What does St. John propose, then?"

"I can return to Handley, claiming Jeremy died on our visit to relations, or he will support me in some town out of the way where I can use my own name or the Perry name without meeting anyone who knows us. I am to plead shame as a reason not to stay with the Bardings."

"I am surprised you wanted to go home, when they appear to have treated you shabbily."

"It was my duty to protect Cecilia's reputation." Giving up a year or two of her life was worth it to deserve her father's affection. "I thought I would be able to go about in society again."

"Nothing prevents you from doing so. Your reputation is intact."

In a provincial town, she might be able to marry under her own name, but how would she explain her alienation from her family unless she simply lied and claimed they were all dead? Her husband would be sure to ask about the source of the money she received each quarter and he would find it came from Hiram St. John, leading to more questions. Her father might stop making those payments once she married; they had not discussed the possibility of marriage. He had told her what arrangements he would make for her and had not invited her to comment upon them. Ceasing to give her the small income on which she had lived in Handley would seem not unreasonable to most, if she married.

She would agree but for two facts. The gentleman

she might marry in such circumstances would hardly have more than a competence on which to support her and their children, if any. Perhaps it would not matter. However, if she had married while living under her father's roof, she would have been entitled to a substantial dowry provided in her mother's marriage settlements. How could Papa provide that money if she were living as Julia Perry? And if she used her own name, how could she explain to a prospective husband why she was living apart from her family?

"Even so, a spinster with no acquaintances in the neighborhood, with no family in evidence, and no wealth is unlikely to receive offers of marriage. Not acceptable ones, anyway. It would be like applying for a position as governess with no letters of reference."

"Difficult to take part in society in a place you are unknown, unless you are clearly in good circumstances," he admitted.

He was clever and observant, traits she ordinarily admired. From her household in Handley, he had probably been able to figure her income to the nearest half-crown.

He went on, "The people you'd meet would not be the sort of people you associated with in London. I can't see that serving. What has Lavinia suggested?"

"She doesn't know. How can I admit my family doesn't want me?"

"I doubt she would be shocked."

She was not able to look up at him. Nonetheless, she heard his amusement. From what she knew of the dowager countess, he might be correct.

"Mistress Julia, you may have another alternative. You would like to return to your rightful place in society, and I imagine you would like to marry?"

"Of course I would." She sighed, wishing it might be so easy.

"The first goal could be accomplished by the second. Would you object to a marriage of convenience, if the man were suitable and pleasant?"

She was blushing furiously, she knew it. This couldn't be a proposal…could it? Why would she think such a thing when she and Halliwell were scarcely acquainted? "Many marriages are made for practical reasons. I am not foolish enough to hold out for love."

"Then I suggest you ccasc worrying. Nothing is certain yet except that you need not go into exile again. Let the dowager countess make suitable arrangements. No one is better able to reintroduce you to London society."

"But my father—" She risked a glance at him and found he was studying her face.

"Leave it to the earl and Lavinia to make things right. It may be you are able to assist them."

Trusting Miles Halliwell's advice was easy. She wondered why, when she had begun by heartily disliking him. But however stern he might seem, he was also often kind, and she had no doubt of his intelligence.

"If you are ready to go in, we can enter through the door by the stillroom. We are unlikely to meet anyone in that passage. And if we did, they would think nothing but that you have been outside on a cool day."

The path leading through the kitchen garden was paved with slabs of stone, chamomile growing between them. One of the flags was not quite level. Julia stumbled and might have fallen if Halliwell had not caught her around the waist to hold her up. She found herself pressed against his side, his arm still around her. Breathing a little unevenly, she stammered, "Thank you," and made the mistake of looking up into his eyes. They no longer reminded her of ice. They were the soft gray of snow clouds, summoning up the image of a cozy fire, a feather bed, and a hot drink on a cold night.

"Are you all right?"

"Yes, thank you."

"Here, take my arm."

She twined her own arm around his. *How easy and comfortable.*

He cleared his throat. "I'll speak to the gardener about that paver. A fall on the walk could cause an injury."

Neither spoke again as they approached the house. Words would have spoiled that moment of connection, though all Halliwell had done was steady her when she tripped. Then he opened the door leading to the warren of storerooms and pantries near the kitchen, and a wave of scents washed over them: a faint odor of cooking and a stronger fragrance of dried herbs. Julia's nose wrinkled at something pungently aromatic.

They saw no one but Eustacia, her back to them at a long table in a room lined with shelves holding pots and flasks. Some of the apparatus on the table called to mind an apothecary's workroom. Some were unidentifiable. Julia's family had always bought their tonics, remedies, lotions, soap, and preserves. Even at St. John Underhill, where there was a stillroom, it was used only for making and storing jellies and jams and sometimes liqueurs.

Halliwell put his finger to his lips and led Julia past

without pausing. When they were through the door that closed off the stillroom passage from the servants' stair to the upper floors, he said, "It did not occur to me she might be there. No harm done, as she did not see us. Lady Popejoy is rather inquisitive."

" 'Tis most impressive. I had no idea she…" She had meant to say, "did something useful." She could hardly criticize a member of the earl's family to his man of business, however.

"Was less lazy than you supposed? More clever?"

Julia saved herself. "I had no idea she took an interest in the stillroom. Most ladies regard such activities as old-fashioned and unnecessary."

Her escort grinned, changing his usually guarded expression remarkably for the better.

"She had to find something not already in the hands of the two Ladies Barding," he replied, amused.

To her regret, in the morning, Miles Halliwell was gone. How very busy the earl kept him. Julia had seen the St. Johns' man of business once or twice in London, but he had never been summoned to St. John Underhill. Of course, her father had only one estate, while the earl had several, and she understood he had wide-ranging investments as well.

Chapter 14

In London, Miles took half a day to recover from too much travel in too short a period, and another half day to clear his desk and review the matters Bryden had dealt with. Everything was satisfactory; nothing was pressing. There was, alas, no way to postpone the task the Bardings had set him.

He did not know where to begin. How could Lavinia expect him to fulfill her orders? He had always been proud of his ability to solve problems, find answers, generally to do whatever the earl or dowager countess required of him. This was different. Placing an advertisement in the newssheets was not a possibility. Books on the law seemed unlikely to help. Consulting an attorney would at most yield the possible penalties for forgery of church documents and trying to pass off a bastard as a legitimate potential heir. He could not inquire of Barding's greenbag, Jessen, who was elderly and extremely correct. As the earl had said, he was sure to disapprove. How could he not, when Miles thought the idea wrong-headed at best. He was reluctant to discuss the earl's request with anyone else. And how was any honest man to find a forger or bribe whoever needed bribing?

The name popped into his mind: Simon Hayes. Like him, Hayes oversaw the business affairs of men who had money and either lacked the skill or the interest to manage their money themselves. Miles had met him several times, though he did not know him well. Hayes was a few years older, was considered discreet and trustworthy, and included a number of noblemen among his clients. Miles had also heard hints, not amounting even to a rumor, that the man had once assisted a client to recover some extremely embarrassing letters from a blackmailer. If true, this suggested Hayes had a certain skill in dealing with unusual situations. He wrote to request an appointment, explaining he needed advice rather than financial services. Two days later he was shown into Hayes's inner office.

After they had exchanged greetings and some remarks about the weather and current affairs, Hayes asked, "Now, you came for advice, I think? How can I help you?"

Miles had pondered the phrasing of his request. He could only hope Hayes would not be offended and throw him out. Yet, if he could not supply the needed information, Lavinia's design would have to be abandoned and the family could turn its attention to finding Peter a suitable younger bride with many years to breed. Julia would be able to marry someone else. It struck him that the second was equally important to him.

"I will pose this as a hypothetical," he said. "If one were to need a reliable person to perform a misdemeanor or series of misdemeanors, how would he go about finding one?"

The question did not appear to disconcert his listener. "How sure are you the acts in question are only misdemeanors?"

"I'm reasonably certain they do not rise to the level of felonies." In other words, not capital crimes.

"Is the person who would contract for the actions honest?"

"As honest as any man who solicits commission of an illegal or immoral or unethical act." He expected Hayes to laugh.

Instead, his response was, "I should have said, 'Is he of good character?' Will he use good faith in his dealings or will he attempt to cheat the man to whom he is referred? Testify against him in court?"

"Good Lord, no."

"Then I will suggest someone who can find a person to perform your hypothetical misdemeanors. He operates a sort of hiring hall for the criminal class. He won't cheat either party. You can find him Tuesdays and Thursdays at Job's Coffee House, St. Clement's Lane, Leadenhall Street. He will be at the round table at the back, left corner."

"How will I—that is, how will my client—recognize him?"

That did earn a brief smile. "The table is reserved for him. You or your client will also know him by his clothing. There won't be anyone dressed like him. If there is any uncertainty about it, ask one of the servers for Barlicorn."

Miles would far rather have heard that Hayes could not recommend anyone to commit even the mildest transgression.

****

"Mr. Peter Stretton to see you, sir. Isn't he supposed to be in Italy?"

Peter! "The Bardings recently informed me he was

on his way back. Send him in, Bryden."

Miles rose to greet him. When he had last seen Peter, he had been surprised to find the handsomest Stretton son's face had lost its boyishness. Foolish; at the time, he had not seen the lad for several years. Of course he would have changed. He had become a man. His finely cut features resembled the late earl's, though their grandfather had lacked the faun ears. Now he had fully matured, almost certainly in mind as well as body, or he would not have come back.

"Peter, welcome home. You're looking well." He would have greeted George or the late William formally, but Peter, five years younger, was his little brother. Half brother.

"Miles. You look successful." It did not sound like a compliment. Peter sighed and turned his tricorne in his hands.

"Sit down. Will you take a glass of claret? Or I've Madeira if you prefer."

"I don't suppose I can hope for ale?"

"Nothing could be easier. Bryden! Ale!"

Peter subsided into one of the armchairs before the desk. "Thank you."

"You must be tired. I well recall the rigors of foreign travel."

"It's not the travel. A ship's a great place for catching up on sleep. It's dreading what's at home. How bad is it going to be, Miles?"

"Wait until we have our ale. There are complications. How was Italy?"

"I might praise the beauties of Italy, the monuments, the history, the climate, and the food for hours." But when Bryden came in with a jug of ale and two silver tankards, Peter was confessing that he looked forward to roasts and Cheshire cheese, gingerbread and stout. The Scot departed, closing the door behind him.

After Peter had taken a long draught of ale, he asked, "What kind of complications?"

Miles told him about Jeremy.

"William." Peter made a disgusted noise. "Well, Mother and Grandmother will take care of the boy. He'll be all right. Won't he? I mean, you turned out well, even though I've realized in the last several years that the family may have failed you in some ways."

The statement took Miles by surprise. Had they? As they had failed Peter? On reflection, if the thought occurred to any Stretton, it would be Peter. He shrugged one shoulder. "Not really. I was treated fairly, I received an education and a profession. What more could I want?"

"Love? Or affection, anyway."

"Mine was a rhetorical question, Peter."

His half brother raised his tankard in salute. "Well! It doesn't sound too bad at the Hall, with William gone. Purgatory, maybe, but not Hell. Do the stages still run to Banbury on the same days?"

"They do. You may want to delay long enough to buy English clothing. Best to fit in if you insist on going by stage. Or I can arrange for a post chaise. Faster and more comfortable." Peter received an allowance from the estate. He had obviously been able to get by on it in Italy—his very Italian suit was of good quality—but it might have been stretched thin by his journey. "I haven't told you the worst yet."

A remark hovered on Peter's lips, banished by Halliwell's concluding sentence. Instead he exclaimed,

"*Corpo della santissima Vergine lavandaia! Maledetto da Dio e dal Papa!*"

"You are becoming more Italian by the minute," Miles replied to this heartfelt utterance, which was accompanied by an indescribable gesture toward heaven.

"It's not bad enough I return to the scenes of my youth, it must be to some disaster. Or brangling, anyway. Tell me the worst."

"I don't know how informed you have been about the family. I assume your grandmother or your mother or the earl have written occasionally, but whether the letters followed your wanderings around Italy and reached you is another matter."

"Or whether I threw them on the fire unopened."

"Fortunately, you at least received the one about William's death."

"I read them all, Miles. I couldn't help myself."

"Then you know George has only one son and a brace of daughters."

"I think Mother mentioned several years ago they had a boy."

"Georgie is about three now. I'd not accept a wager he will live to see four years."

"Sickly, is he? Poor little fellow. Poor George and Eustacia. Still, he may grow out of it."

"Do you remember Dr. Broxon? He views Georgie's health with the greatest concern."

"Broxon? I should think I remember him. You can't imagine how I wished for him, when I was lying ill at Florence. One visit from the local medico determined me to rely upon my landlady. What does he say is wrong with Georgie?"

155

"It reminds him of a form of the green-sickness, which he says is not limited to girls as most think. But as a young doctor, he attended a man with symptoms like Georgie's, and nothing did the slightest good. He has written several colleagues to inquire whether they have seen a similar affliction, and if so, what the result was."

"What a damnable thing. But Eustacia's a year or two younger than I, isn't she, so she has breeding years left. After all, our sister Ann is seven years older, and she's had eight or nine, two of 'em since I've been abroad. Imps, all of them, she informs me."

Ann Stretton, now Lady Vincent Harring, settled in Leicestershire, was the wife of a duke's second son. It should not be surprising she corresponded with Peter, but somehow, it was.

"Eustacia may not be able to have another child. Granted, miracles happen."

Understanding darkened Peter Stretton's eyes. "What of Laura? Is it possible William will have a posthumous heir?" He was grasping at straws.

Miles shook his head.

"Then there's no heir after Georgie except me."

"That's it."

"Disaster. Damnation. Small wonder they're worried."

"I realize it may be uncomfortable for you. But you decided to come home before you heard of this."

"They'll expect me to marry and secure the succession."

"I'm sure they hope you will agree to do so." As Miles did. He wished it need not be Julia.

"Isn't there some distant, misplaced heir we can

fall back on?"

"After George and little Georgie, it's your turn. If there is no heir, it all reverts to the Crown."

From Peter's expression, he was mulling over another Italian oath. "How much pressure will they bring to bear? Threaten to cut off my funds? It won't work. I was rather successful as a painter in Italy. Touring Englishmen bought my paintings by the dozen. I can support myself here if I have to."

"They're all aware of what they're asking of you. Most men of your age want to postpone putting their necks in a noose. Ermm, you may not have thought of it. Living in Italy and all."

His half brother's bitter laughter shook Miles. "I certainly had not thought of it yet."

"There may be a solution that would be minimally inconvenient."

" 'Minimally inconvenient'? Blood and blazes! To whom?"

"To you. They were delighted to hear you were coming back because they've missed you. I've missed you. Then this other curst thing came up. They understand that you prefer the Continent and that you might find England...difficult."

Peter groaned and rested his head against the back of his chair, contemplating the ceiling.

"All they ask is an heir to follow you if George does not get another son. Two would be better, of course, as life is uncertain."

"Nothing is more certain than that. When was the ceiling last washed? Or painted?"

"Uh, five years ago? Ten? Why?"

" 'Tis gray from smoke from the fireplace and

candles. London soot, too, if you ever open the windows. Don't you think it would be vastly improved by a mural representing the sky with a few high, puffy clouds and a circle of amorini pouring riches out of cornucopias and in the very center, a sun in the form of a guinea? Or there could be nymphs and satyrs instead. How patient you are, my dear. William would have knocked me into a mud puddle before I'd finished saying 'amorini.' "

"There's not a puddle in sight, and William is no longer with us." Persuading Peter might be more difficult than anticipated, and the family had not yet had a chance to rub him the wrong way. Really, it was amazing he had agreed to leave Italy.

Miles considered his next words carefully. "Even though I'm not a Stretton, the thought of Charfield passing to strangers sickens me. I remember you often sketched places around the property. All that beauty might be lost under a new owner." Trees cut down, the house altered to add a fashionable façade, small rooms thrown together, taking away the nooks and crannies where they had played, ancient oak paneling ripped out and replaced with wallpaper. "All the old servants might be turned off. The tenants—" The common lands enclosed, reducing the estate's people to hirelings or throwing them out of work entirely.

Peter waved a languid hand to cut him off. "I know. There's no choice." He sighed. "Have they any suggestions about how I am to find a bride? The girls I met before I set out on my Grand Tour must all be wed now unless they are old maids. I can't say I fancied any of them anyway."

"I will leave it for your grandmother to explain. I

urge you to consider her recommendation." Strike him blind, he was urging on Peter the same kind of bargain Julia St. John's family had forced upon her. But what other choice was there? "You might not have to remain long. You and your wife could live apart after a time."

Peter's lips twisted. "Will you share that post chaise with me, Miles? I'll want you to stand my groomsman."

"We won't rush you into marriage as fast as all that. Your family wants you to be as comfortable with the idea as possible."

Peter Stretton's mobile eyebrows expressed skepticism.

Chapter 15

They arrived in gusting wind, as if they'd been blown in. The homecoming appeared to be a success. Lavinia and Caroline embraced Peter; to Halliwell's surprise, Caroline wept. George clapped him on the back and muttered gruffly, "Glad you're home, little brother." The earl smiled, thanked him for coming, and after a moment observed with a trace of amazement, "You've grown up."

Eustacia said, "How glad you must be to be in England again. I can't imagine living in a foreign country for years."

Julia curtsied and murmured her pleasure at meeting him. Peter eyed her curiously. Miles had told him only that she was related to Jeremy and had accompanied him to Charfield to get him settled with his father's people.

"I wish they were glad to see me for my own sake, rather than because they expect me to produce an heir." Peter had joined Miles on the terrace late in the evening, after the others had gone to bed.

"They are. They missed you. If they were only relieved that you might agree to provide another Stretton child, they would have addressed the issue already. You can't charge Lavinia, Lady Barding, with being reticent."

"You might as well call her Lavinia; I know you

think of her that way. Admittedly, it would be awkward to call her Grandmama, despite her being your grandmother as much as mine."

"Impossible. She does not think of me as a grandson even in private. She thinks in terms of problems and results rather than emotion. It does make her easy to deal with."

"Sometimes I wish we had the warm, sweet kind of grandmother one hears of. My mother, now, may turn into a dear little old lady and be a delight to her grandchildren."

"I don't think I'd count on it, Peter. The elder Lady Barding is grooming her to be the next matriarch. She'll be a good one, too, if not as good as her teacher. I worry for the future of the Strettons when Eustacia inherits her mantle."

"She isn't up to their weight, is she? I never met her before I left."

"You wouldn't have. George met her somehow in London. He didn't consult the family."

"Oh, that explains a certain restraint in my mother's letters when she mentioned the marriage. I gather Eustacia doesn't understand what's going on, although I don't think she was especially glad to see me."

"She probably thinks you're a libertine who's been sowing your wild oats in Italy."

"I suppose she's heard the family's opinion of me."

"Quite unlikely." *And if they had ever hinted at it, Eustacia would either fail to understand or fail to hear.*

"Lavinia was the best of the lot. She didn't avoid asking me questions about my travels."

"She was interested." He could guess why she had

paid close attention to his rambles through the Italian states.

"Thank you for coming with me, Miles. It helps to have someone to talk to."

Miles ardently wished he had someone to whom he could unburden himself.

****

Miles Halliwell and Mr. Peter Stretton had arrived in the afternoon, too late for dinner but in time for supper. It might almost have been any collection of relatives welcoming an absent member with exclamations, hugs, and even tears. Miles Halliwell watched with no expression at all, though plainly he was counted as a friend as well as their man of business. As an onlooker with no connection to the family, Julia wondered at the strange constraint running under the greetings and questions about Peter's health, his journey, and his observations of Italy. He responded appropriately, but something was missing. *His heart is not in it.* And the family knew it and was worried. Except perhaps Eustacia, who had noticed nothing.

Julia toyed with the idea throughout supper, listening to Peter Stretton responding amiably to the remarks addressed to him. He was a handsome young man with exquisite manners and flashes of dry wit. His description of the Venetian carnival that preceded Lent made them all laugh; Eustacia regretted that they had nothing as amusing in England, though it sounded Papish.

"I preferred winter in the south, and spring and fall were often pleasant in most parts, but summer was hot and either very dry or else humid. And if you think 'tis cold and damp here, you have never wintered in a

Venetian palazzo," he observed in response to a question about the climate.

Remarkably, no one asked what he had been doing in Italy for so long, although Lavinia questioned him about his travels. By the end of the meal, Julia realized that while he answered any question, Peter Stretton initiated no topic and made no spontaneous comments. He brought to mind a clockwork device that performed its task without thought or feeling.

In the drawing room after supper, he did bestir himself to inquire about his nieces and nephew and ask when he might meet them.

George shifted uncomfortably. Eustacia hurried into speech. "It is too late today. They will be in bed. Tomorrow morning would be better."

Wind had been rattling the windows and whistling around the chimneys. Now it slammed against the panes. Julia inquired softly, "Did he like Italy so much?"

"Peter was always interested in the arts." Halliwell's reply was as oblique as much of the evening's conversation.

"I can understand going to see the monuments in Italy, but the arts flourish in England, too."

"Quite so." Halliwell lowered his voice. "However, he is interested in architecture, and where better to study its progress since ancient times than Italy? He paints, too, and naturally he was drawn by the opportunity to see the works of the masters there. I am sorry to admit none of us encouraged him. I am heartily glad to see him, but I will not be surprised if he leaves again. Italy suits him. "

"I see." It took no great perception to know the earl

and George, while both admirable in many ways, would be satisfied with a painting of a favorite horse or dog as long as its proportions and color were correct. Her own father and half brother would consider any deeper interest in art unmanly. Then Lavinia beckoned him, and Halliwell excused himself to attend the dowager countess, to Julia's regret.

Peter Stretton poured himself another cup of tea and ambled in Julia's direction. "May I join you?"

"Certainly, sir."

He took the chair Halliwell had vacated. His question, "I believe you are visiting from Dorset? How do you find Oxfordshire in comparison?" smacked of desperation.

"There appear to be more rivers here and more gentlemen's estates, and more chalk and stone quarries in Dorsetshire. My acquaintance with both Dorset and Oxfordshire is of the slightest, however." Wracking her brain for a topic, she asked, "Do you plan to remain here? Or live mostly in London or perhaps return to Italy?"

"I don't know. I have indulged myself by living abroad. Now I must decide what is best for my family."

He seemed rather unsure of himself, unlike Miles Halliwell, except in the second part of his reply. His people loved him and deserved his best efforts. She could not imagine Halliwell ever being in doubt about anything. He was watching them now while conversing with Lavinia. His expression was peculiar; what could he be thinking?

"At what time do you visit the nursery, Mistress Perry? May I accompany you?"

"Visit the nursery?" she repeated. She had not felt

so clumsy since she had first entered society.

"To see Jeremy?"

There was no wrapping it up in clean linen. "I can do nothing for the child that his nurse, Janet Campbell, cannot do better. I fear I have no motherly instincts." She gave him credit for a quick recovery after a moment's bewilderment.

"Nor do a good many other ladies. 'Tis unfashionable to dote on one's children, and some feel it spoils them. That is why Scots nurses are preferred by many families."

Julia agreed to this statement, Janet Campbell being a case in point, for although she was devoted to Jeremy in her brusque way, she did not hesitate to discipline him. She had been Julia's own nurse. "Are you fond of children, Mr. Stretton?"

"I am. Most of the time, anyway! I look forward to meeting my nieces and nephews."

Was it only embarrassment that caused the sensation of eyes other than Peter Stretton's upon her? No. Across the room, Lavinia Barding was watching her. She turned her attention back to Peter.

"I hope to sketch them, once they're comfortable with me. Children are both challenging and rewarding to draw as they do not sit still as an adult will, but by the same token, they are more open and spontaneous. I made sketches of some of the children at the *Ospedale degli Innocenti* in Florence."

"The...?"

"The Hospital of the Innocents. It was established in the fifteenth century to care for foundlings. I contributed several paintings of children to raise money for them. I have heard such a home is being organized in London. I hope it will be as well managed and funded."

"It sounds like an excellent notion, but how surprising to find such an innovation in a foreign country."

He said wryly, "Much as I love England, we are not first in every field of endeavor."

Most English people would disagree. It might not be only Peter Stretton's interest in art that set him apart. While she was trying to think of a rejoinder, Caroline called, "Julia, may I borrow Peter for a moment?"

"Of course, my lady." Peter was not hers to lend.

He did not seem to think the request odd, however, and wished her a good night with a smile, saying, "I will probably retire once I have spoken with my mother. The rigors of travel, you know."

Lavinia caught her attention and patted the seat of the settee. Julia smiled and obeyed.

"I hope you do not find our lack of social activities and company tedious," Lavinia said. "Our being in recent mourning discourages visits from the neighboring families. Then there is the problem of Georgie's ill health, as well."

"I have not been accustomed to much society in Handley, my lady. It is a pleasure to have the gardens to walk in and to be able to ride. I envy you the gardens. I have not seen a physic garden before, or any so prettily laid out."

"When I came to Charfield as a bride, it was a poor little patch, scarcely of any use, and we had to rely upon the apothecary for most things, which was not very helpful. Banbury being at some distance and little attention paid to the stocking of the stillroom, we were like to find ourselves without some ingredient necessary for a remedy. Over the years I improved it and, as I had time, learned to make oils of scented flowers and also of the herbs most used in cooking and remedies. One of my favorite pastimes was to make scented washing balls."

"Did you make the one in my room that has such a delightful scent of sweet peas, my lady?"

Eustacia, silently knitting some small garment in an armchair near the settee, glanced up. Lavinia drew her into the conversation. "No, that is Eustacia's doing. Her scented soap is much admired. I have given up all but touring the garden occasionally to give advice if Eustacia asks it. I passed the care of it to her, as she is interested in gardening and the making of all manner of decoctions, distillations, and oils. Those little cakes at supper owed their flavor to her oil of damask roses."

"I fear you flatter my attempts," Eustacia murmured, both embarrassed and pleased by the dowager countess's words. "I will be eternally grateful you taught me when I was utterly ignorant of gardens and distillation."

Peter having bade his mother goodnight, Caroline drifted over to sit in the other chair opposite Eustacia.

"I am glad you took to the art," Caroline said. "I must have been a bitter disappointment to my mama-in-law, as I cannot step into a garden in bloom without sneezing."

"For which I forgive you, as you are more than satisfactory in other respects, although I have enjoyed teaching Eustacia what I know."

"Isn't it very difficult?" Julia asked. Perhaps she could establish some common ground with Lady

Popejoy.

More warmly than she had addressed any previous remark to Julia, the viscountess replied, "It seemed so at first, but Grandmama-in-law is a good teacher. I watched carefully what she did when I assisted her, studied her book of medicines, salves, and curative waters, and took notes."

"Eustacia has built on what I taught her and makes extracts and oils of things I never thought of attempting, and which I always bought from the apothecary. She has excelled me, as I made remedies because it was a skill expected of a gentlewoman when I was a girl. I believe Eustacia loves it as Caroline loves embroidery and I loved riding and dancing before I grew unsteady."

Eustacia demurred and colored up.

The evening had passed pleasantly but ended earlier than usual. Lavinia rose first, announcing she would take her old bones off to bed.

"I will go up with you," Caroline said.

The earl added, "I won't be long in joining you."

George patted Eustacia's arm. "My love, you must be tired, with the excitement of Peter's arrival. Will you come upstairs now?"

"Oh...I suppose I should, Popejoy. I must be hagged. I did not sleep well last night." The viscount led his wife from the room.

Julia followed the others out, with a last surreptitious glance at Miles Halliwell. She had hoped they would be able to continue their talk, whether about Mr. Peter Stretton or crop prices or anything at all. He had a pleasant voice, asked her opinions, and listened to them. Her heart gave a skip when she saw he was looking back at her. She could not interpret his expression. Worried? Regretful? Wistful? Then the earl spoke close to his ear, and he directed his attention to Lord Barding.

Chapter 16

The day after their arrival, Miles suggested a ride around some of the Stretton boys' favorite places to play and down to the tiny village. They might take note of storm damage as they went. What he needed to tease from Peter was best done out of the hearing of others. They rode in companionable silence until they were well past the gardeners raking up debris from the storm.

Before he could speak, Peter said, "Father asked me to see him this morning. When I went to his study, I found my mother and Grandmama there as well. I was fairly trembling in my shoes. But they only wanted to repeat what you'd said, that the succession might rest upon me. They said it at greater length, however. They seemed to think I would be reluctant and talked about accommodating my wishes as much as they could. I promised to begin the hunt for a bride. They wanted to approve her before I committed myself. I agreed, of course."

"They are giving you time to get used to the idea. Lavinia will not wish to set your back up by rushing her fences."

"There's a mixed metaphor if ever I heard one. I will let the matter rest until it comes up. Look, there's where we used to swim. It wasn't as much fun after you and George went away to school, though. I didn't miss William when he left. But two or three of the village boys swam there, so we used to adventure together."

"I don't think the family thought about your being lonely once we were gone. So you had some friends. Good."

Reminiscently: "The miller's boy taught me to set snares. Lucky the gamekeeper never caught us."

"What could he have done? He wouldn't have delivered you to the magistrate. He couldn't thrash one of you and not the other. At most he could warn you not to do it again, or tell Lord Barding he'd caught you out."

"If he did, Grandfather never mentioned it."

Miles laughed. "Well, they were his rabbits. If he liked to let the pair of you harvest one or two, it was his choice. I take it the miller's son wasn't making a business of it."

"Zounds, no. We didn't do it often. He didn't even take them home for the pot. His father would have strapped him for it. We gave them to that old woman, Pansy, who had the simple son. Gypsy Pansy, that was it, in the tumble-down hut beyond the churchyard. She told the best stories. Sometimes a bag of apples found its way to her. Or some carrots or an onion or two from the garden."

"I suppose the gardener noticed and it was an open secret."

"I wonder I wasn't scolded and told to stop."

"Oh, well, nothing wrong with charity, is there? You have a kind family, Peter."

"Your family, too."

"Not really."

Peter smiled and shook his head.

"You haven't said much about your travels in Italy,

beyond a few observations on the sights everyone who visits Italy sees." How to phrase his question? "Did you take part in society in the cities you visited?"

"Not much. I had letters of introduction to various consuls and envoys and some of the titled Italians Father knew from his own Grand Tour, but I managed not to let myself be drawn into an endless round of entertainments. I went to Italy for the art."

Eliciting the information he wanted might require less subtlety and more directness. Peter should understand the family's intentions sooner rather than being ambushed by them later.

"Was there any period long enough that you might have traveled to England and back with no one able to swear you were in Italy at the time? No one who would matter, that is."

Peter turned his head to stare at him. His horse whuffed something that sounded like "Hmmmf."

"Why?"

Obviously Lavinia had not explained her plan. Miles had suspected as much. "Your grandmother has an idea which would dispose of several problems at one blow."

"Beyond my marrying and breeding for the sake of our illustrious line?"

"Ay."

"What idea? What problems?"

I knew I should have been present at the Bardings' conference with Peter.

"She has a grand design which would benefit everyone, or almost everyone. You may not feel it does much for you, beyond protecting you from rumors."

"R—" Peter closed his mouth on whatever he had

meant to say. "What does Grandmama have in mind?"

He avoided his half brother's eyes, preferring to stare at his horse's mane. "If you were to marry Julia, it would keep her in the family and provide her with a husband, which Lavinia hopes to do. Julia would be a far more suitable daughter-in-law for your mama than Eustacia is, or William's wife was. If you and Julia had a male child together, it would be another potential heir. You could return to Italy. No one, or very few, would wonder if your wife chose to stay here to raise the children in merry, civilized England."

"So the point of my marrying Mistress Perry would be to keep her in the family? Miles, I think I'm being insulted."

"No, no. Providing another potential heir is the chief priority. Your marrying Julia Perry would be the tidiest way of accomplishing all the desired ends."

"If I understood you, the 'desired ends' would be an heir after Georgie, which is perfectly reasonable. I don't feel obligated to dragoon Julia Perry into the family, however much Mama and Grandmama may wish it. I'm sorry they consider me such a disgrace that they want to pack me off to the Continent again. I suppose they greeted me warmly as a possible source of an heir presumptive. No doubt they think Mistress Perry will be glad to marry me, given her circumstances." Peter's eyes and mouth had gone hard and angry.

"It isn't like that, Peter."

Peter muttered something Italian under his breath. "Then why? Explain it to me."

Now they came to it. "Ah...Your mama is vastly taken with Jeremy, who is a healthy male child, as

Georgie is not. If you had happened to return to England briefly about two and one-half to three years ago, you might have impregnated a lady and married her secretly, or vice versa. Jeremy would be legitimate. This would provide at least one heir after you, even if you had no other son."

"This was Grandmama's plan? That I pretend to have come back, wed, and begot a son?"

"Yes."

To Halliwell's relief, his half brother's eyes crinkled with amusement. "It's a thousand pities she was not in the line of succession for the crown when Queen Anne died. She would have been a second Queen Elizabeth."

"I have often thought the same."

"Are they mad?"

"Ahhhh…" He could hardly admit he wondered the same.

"Are you mad?"

"I never used to think so."

"Miles, I'm just an idle fellow who likes architecture and paints pictures, but even I know that her scheme wouldn't make the child legitimate."

"No. But it might be possible to make it appear Jeremy was born within a marriage. Is there anyone who can swear to your being in Italy in the autumn of 1738? As long as you were married before Jeremy's birth and acknowledge him, it doesn't matter who fathered him. It would be best if you'd been in England in early winter of 1737 when he was conceived, of course."

"That's why you asked if I could have returned to England. But even if I had—"

"Forget your objections for a moment. I'll explain later."

Halliwell had seen that unfocused gaze before when Peter was concentrating on some problem. "December 1737? Where was I? I moved around a great deal. I need my drawing books to aid my memory." Peter's gaze turned inward, and he sank into a brown study, emerging from it only when they reached the village.

Peter clearly had friends. The blacksmith hailed him and chaffed him for having been away so long. An old lady with a market basket asked whether he'd been keeping out of mischief. The publican and his wife both spent a few minutes with them, the public house not being busy. They left much later, after a good deal of laughter and many sly references to Peter's boyhood exploits. Peter? Exploits? Halliwell had seldom seen him after Peter had been sent to school and Miles had gone to London to work for Whitacker.

Peter grew thoughtful. They were trotting along the road leading to Charfield's gate when he broke the silence. "Come to my room, and I'll look at my sketches and my notes to refresh my memory."

Halliwell gauged the sun's position. "Once we've shed our riding clothes and dirt, we will have to go down to dinner."

"I did not think it was so late. This insistence on set meal times is tedious."

"While you can get a meal at an inn at almost any hour, of some sort at least, one cannot expect the cook in a private house to be so obliging. You'll adapt."

"I hope so. I had forgotten what it was like to live at home. After dinner, we'll look at my sketches, assuming no one has something else planned for me."

"Is it like being a child again, with rules to follow and tasks set you?"

"Exactly like."

"Lavinia's scheme may not be workable if there was no period during which you could have got to England, wedded a lady, and returned to Italy. The sooner we determine it's impossible, the sooner the Ladies Barding can begin to resign themselves to Jeremy remaining a by-blow and you can get on with finding a bride and leaving the Barding hearth."

"They won't insist on my living here? William and his wife did, I hear."

"William chose to live here as he would otherwise have had to spend money on maintaining a separate home. It made it possible for him to live in lodgings in London and yet have money for his amusements, while his wife remained at Charfield."

****

After dinner, Barding and Popejoy went off to inspect the roof of a tenant's cottage damaged in the windstorm. Lavinia had instructions she wanted Miles to review and act upon at his convenience, which he understood to mean, after he had dealt with their current family matter. Caroline was speaking with the housekeeper about which curtains should be taken down to be shaken and aired and which should be replaced. Eustacia had eaten little and did not feel well. She intended to lie down. Marcia Brant, who was teaching the girls French, asked Julia to assist her by taking part in a simple conversation in that language as a demonstration. Miles concluded that lack of both household chores and company had reduced her to desperation for something to occupy her.

By unspoken agreement, Miles and Peter wandered upstairs.

Peter's bedchamber, given him when he left the nursery floor, was unchanged since then. He had occupied it only during vacations when he was at school, and then he had gone on his tour. He waved Miles to one of the two armchairs and went to a trunk at the foot of the bed. When he opened the lid, the reason for its presence was obvious. It was as full as could be of oversized bound volumes.

"Should I leave you to this task?" Miles asked. Peter would need hours to sort through them.

He laughed at Miles's expression. "They're like a diary. I date and title them. Wait, I'll get the ones beginning with Rome." Lifting out half a dozen, he set them aside, muttering, "That's this year." He counted out twelve more and they followed the first. Another twelve. "Here's 1738. And the last half of '37." He set this stack on the table between their chairs and commenced flipping through the first three, tutting, "Terribly hot summer.

"Rome at the beginning of October. I didn't mind the cooler weather, but I was told it was likely to be wet, with frequent cloudy days. I'd finished what I wanted to do, anyway. Ah, here's the road to Naples. Addison's *Remarks on Several Parts of Italy* praises Naples highly, and it is a pretty, pleasure-loving town. More to the point, there are various antiquities and curiosities to be seen nearby. Roman remains." He flipped past pages of drawings of catacombs, bridges of great height, little ruins by the side of the road, and some drawings entitled "From the ceiling of the

Chamber of Venus, behind her Temple" which depicted lust and strength in a manner more suited to a brothel than a drawing room.

"The date?"

"I left Naples in mid-November. I did not want to go north for the winter. Addison did not venture farther south, so I thought I would see what that end of the country was like and mayhap cross to Sicily. I never did get that far.

"Here: I met a fellow at an inn who told me about a town called Bari, so I went there instead. It's only about halfway down the Italian peninsula. I'd meant to start north in February to visit Padua and Venice, go west to Brescia and Milan, then to Genoa and back to Florence, and I did, eventually, but not until May. Bari was enchanting. Here's my view of the castle of Monte Sant'Angelo. A pretty little town."

"Who did you meet in those four or five months?"

"No one. No Englishman, I mean. No gentlefolk of any sort, in fact. It was refreshing. Towns of any size and interest are few in the south of Italy, which I suppose is why English travelers don't venture there. I was rather avoiding places I might encounter them. Young fools drinking and whoring their way through their Grand Tour, nursing sore heads while their guide or tutor tried to interest them in the sights grew tiresome. I lodged on a farm outside town. They thought I was mad but treated me like one of their family. Crazy Cousin Pietro, as it might be."

It was possible. "In five months you never met an English person? Or other foreign travelers?"

"I heard rumors of a German in one place, an old scholar of some sort, but never saw him. I wanted to enjoy the unspoiled Italian countryside, without hearing complaints about the accommodations, food, the inability of Italian servants to speak English or French or German or whatever."

"If you had wanted to return to England from where you were, how would you have gone?"

Peter's eyes half closed, thinking. "Bari is a port on the east coast. It would be convenient for sailing to Greece or Turkey or the Middle East generally, I suppose. Or I could have sailed from Salerno, south of Naples. An overland route would have taken too long."

"Thank God."

"I could have got to England and back in that time, certainly. I didn't, however."

"It doesn't matter if you didn't, if the family agrees you married secretly and there is a certificate and so forth to prove it."

"A forged certificate of marriage!" His eccentric half brother was appalled.

"Well, yes."

"You'd invent a fraudulent marriage, Miles?"

"I would rather not, though it would make your mother happy to have Jeremy pass as legitimate. However, the family's concerns over the succession are justified, and I have come to agree with them...more or less. I can't escape my duty. The difficulty is that, while I hope it will be impossible to obtain the supporting documents necessary to, er, prove Jeremy is not a bastard, we cannot rely on Lady Popejoy producing another child."

Peter chewed his lower lip. "That must be what Grandmama was tiptoeing around so delicately that I didn't understand."

"Turning Jeremy into a legitimate heir would be a neat solution to the problem and would secure a future for Mistress Perry. However, I don't want either you or Mistress Julia pressed to agree if either of you dislike the idea." Miles loathed it, himself. "You would be within your rights to refuse an arrangement that would make William's son your heir, which may not be possible anyway, if I cannot find someone to do the forgery. In that event, the family would have to accept that Jeremy will be raised as what he is." Peter would very likely refuse such an illegal, immoral scheme.

"As you were. I would be sorry if my mother were disappointed in this. I don't know how I would feel about rearing William's boy as if he were my own, perhaps giving him precedence over my own son, if I had one, in spite of liking what I've seen of Jeremy."

"I told them it would be an injustice. However, they would see to providing your son a suitable inheritance. On the issue of precedence, your mama pointed out that William's son would come before yours anyway, if only he were legitimate."

"I can hear her saying it." Peter's hearty laughter came to an abrupt end. "I understand my duty, Miles, but I want a lady I can be fond of. In fact, I insist on it. I hope my father will at least acknowledge Jeremy as William's if I do not agree."

"Then you need only marry some young lady you can tolerate long enough to get a couple of boys, then you can live apart. Lavinia and the rest might have to settle for that, which would mean you could return to Italy if you chose."

"To marry while planning to live apart from her as you've suggested is not the action of a gentleman. If I could not bear to live with her, how could I abandon my children to her? The more I think of it, the less I like the idea of wedding Mistress Julia, whatever admirable qualities she possesses. I won't do it, not even to satisfy everyone except myself."

Miles did not know whether to be saddened that Peter could not appreciate Julia's character and charms or glad. If he refused to marry her, Julia would be free to marry someone else who could value her at her true worth.

"I agree your wife must be someone you can like and respect, if you are willing to marry. Ordinarily, I would not approve of a man living separately from his wife and children." Unless he were cruel to his children or their mother. He knew Peter would cherish a family of his own as he himself would. He chose his next words with the greatest care. "None of us thought you would marry in the normal course of things. We realize you would be making a sacrifice in securing the succession. That's why the Ladies Barding thought you might be willing to offer for Julia, if we could find a way to make it appear Jeremy was legitimate. They hoped you would remain long enough to get another potential heir, too, but none of us want you to risk your life as well as your happiness."

Chapter 17

His little brother was a picture of blank incomprehension.

The spurt of exasperation Miles felt at Peter's apparent ingenuousness came out in his words. "Peter, whatever may go on in Italy and France, it's possible here to be hanged for sodomy. You might escape execution, as it's useful to be the son of an earl, but still receive some lesser punishment. But even the charge would be damaging. You and your family would survive the notoriety, but still…"

Peter opened his mouth and closed it again. His brows drew together. "The devil take it! You mean that nonsense William started my first year at school? You know what he was like."

William had been as irritating as a horsefly. He'd referred to Miles's illegitimacy at every opportunity.

"What he said about me was true, Peter. I am a bastard."

"He talked about it because he knew it bothered you. Do you remember when Father and Mother took Ann to London to be introduced into society? Before they went, William told her she had a figure like a boy and wouldn't be able to attract a man. He said it more than once in George's and my hearing."

Thinking back, Miles remembered those taunts.

"Miles, William already knew how to make his

tongue cut like a razor. Ann's weepiness and nervous affliction were believed to be nothing more than fright about her chances of making a good marriage. He never tried it with someone who might have thumped him or said anything in our parents' or Grandmama's presence that would call down retribution. Sometimes it was so subtly done, no adult who overheard noticed. In my case, it was only disparaging remarks about my drawing 'pretty pictures' as if it were an activity fit only for girls or not wanting to get muddy or jump walls on my pony. As if poor little Pudding was able to jump even a low wall! I suppose it gave my father and grandfather a wrong notion."

Remembering Peter's first vacation from school, Miles failed to suppress an "Errrmmm!"

A grin lighted up Peter's face. "Are you wondering how I survived my first term? William kept calling me 'miss' and mocking me and dropping hints to his friends about what a milksop I was. I ignored him because at first I didn't understand what he was hinting. I'd seen the way you ignored his stings made him furious, which made him keep trying, but there was no use letting him see it bothered me. He'd kept pecking away at Ann. Whatever I did, he'd keep on taunting me."

"I wonder none of his victims either broke his nose or tattled."

"He was clever about people, our late brother. He was in no danger of my giving him a clout on the snout. I was too much younger, and somehow he knew you wouldn't lose your temper and pummel him."

"I was living in your family's home on sufferance. Think how Lavinia and your mother would have reacted if I had given him a bloody nose."

Peter snorted. "Anyhow, I got tired of him pecking at me, and I finally figured out what he meant by it. I didn't start mincing and flourishing my scent-drenched handkerchief until we came home for Christmas. I did it once, giving him his own back, you know. It flustered him, and he let me alone. Then I thought, he won't want me doing this to humiliate him before his friends. And I certainly wouldn't have wanted to make a display of myself at school. I did try not to let anyone else here see my act, but I slipped a few times. That and his remarks must be how the rest of the family got the wrong idea. I never did it after that one holiday. I never needed to, either. William didn't want his friends to think his little brother really was a molly. Before you say anything, ay, it was foolish. I was also twelve. If I'd had sense, I'd have kept on ignoring him and seething inside."

"And I was never here during your school vacations after that Christmas, until you'd gone to Italy. I can't believe I never noticed he was bothering others as well as me."

"We were children or little more. Children are wrapped up in their own concerns. He was shrewd and took care who could hear him. God forbid Mama or Grandmama should realize he wasn't dear, charming William to everyone. I suppose they might have done that Christmas, except they were taken up with negotiating Ann's marriage."

"I'd forgotten that part." Miles and George, being almost the same age, had spent as much of every day as possible out of the house, the discussions and negotiations surrounding Ann Stretton's potential marriage to Lord Vincent Harring having reached fever pitch.

"When I visited you in Italy several years ago, I noticed you had several friends…"

"Artistic circles, Miles. You never saw me coquetting in the presence of a man. You also saw me with various young ladies."

"You never boasted of your conquests."

Peter snapped out a pungent Italian oath. "That's the behavior of a boor who's afraid he won't be thought manly if he doesn't brag about the women he's had. Do you?"

"Well, no."

"William did."

Neither said anything for a few minutes.

If Peter were willing to marry and settle down to produce successors to the title, the problem was solved. Miles would not have to try to arrange a fictitious marriage. Julia would not be pressed to marry Peter. Caroline would be sorry Jeremy could not be legitimated, but she would get over it. Before he spoke to the family, he had better clear up one point. Peter was frowning slightly, lost in his own reflections.

"Do you mean to marry for love?"

"Devil fetch me if I do. George married for love and only see how that has turned out. Can you imagine what Eustacia will be like as countess?"

"The thought has occurred to me."

"When one's family is reasonable, it's only rational to consider their wishes in choosing a spouse. The marriage affects them, after all. Grandmama's marriage was arranged. My mother was chosen by our grandparents, and that's been successful." A pause. "I

185

haven't met William's widow. Knowing William, I can't suppose it was a happy marriage, but was it appropriate?"

"Laura Stretton is shy, dutiful, and practical. I do not think she expected much from him. If they had had their own household, she would have managed it well and been satisfied. As it was, she was helpful to Caroline and Lavinia. I wish her a better husband for her second marriage. She is nothing like Caroline or Lavinia, but a woman of strong mind would have been a poor choice for William."

"Well, I reserve the right to refuse a lady they choose, but I'm not going to be difficult. I have no romantickal notions."

"Their first choice would have been Julia St. John."

"She is pleasant enough, but I prefer to select my own bride."

"You've had only a few minutes' conversation with her as far as I am aware. Apart from the family liking her, she is sensible and intelligent. She's the older daughter of Baron St. John. She is a suitable choice in all ways, and you claim not to care about marrying for love. Will you tell me what you object to?"

Peter made one of those Italianate gestures. He should probably be warned against using them while in England.

"She seems like a much older woman. Not in face and figure; it's her mind. She is not happy. I understand that a female with an illegitimate child is burdened with cares, but here she is among people who do not give a fig about Jeremy's parentage, which should relieve her of most of them."

"She's not Jeremy's mother; that honor belongs to her younger sister."

"Really? Mayhap that explains why she doesn't visit the nursery. Unless she simply does not like children."

"She never let herself become fond of the boy because she expected him to be fostered out. I have seen her helping the governess with the little girls, and they seemed to like her and she, them. Her father and stepmother persuaded her to pretend to be the boy's mother in order to spare the younger girl's reputation."

"That explains it. I'm not sure it makes it any better, because she must have an over-developed sense of responsibility. I suppose they encouraged her to feel guilty for not preventing her sister from ruining herself. She's too serious for me."

"She's delightful," Miles said without thinking.

"Your own sense of responsibility is tiresomely active. It's admirable and to our family's benefit, but I wouldn't care to share a house with it. I owe my family something, but do I owe them that much?"

"If you were female, some parents would say yes. Yours won't insist. Well, if you won't have Julia, we need only find you a young lady you like and your father and mother accept."

"I could go to London and find a bride. I'd have Father and Mama and Grandmama approve her first."

Ay, especially the dowager countess. "It might be best to let your family help you meet young ladies. You were only in town long enough to be presented at court before you embarked for Italy. Do you know how you would go about meeting marriageable ladies?"

He had nonplussed Peter, as he had expected.

"Uh...I could see if my friends from school have sisters?"

"Let us aim more narrowly. Your grandmother and mother between them must know every suitable family south of Hadrian's Wall. Before I discuss this with them, can you tell me what you would like in a bride and what you cannot tolerate? They may know of someone who would suit. At worst, they could suggest ladies with the right background and qualities." He knew the question was foolish; men seldom seemed to think about the matter. Apart from the girl being pretty or having a sizable dowry or both. Occasionally a gentleman demanded excellent breeding and connections. Most gave more thought to purchasing a horse than to choosing a wife.

To his surprise, Peter replied promptly. "She must be intelligent. Kind, too. I don't care for brittle, gossiping ladies. I would like her to have some appreciation of art. Good art, that is, not the vapid watercolors so many are taught to produce."

"Beautiful, I suppose?"

Peter tutted. "That's the least important thing. When I draw, I look for people with interesting faces. Faces you can read. Many society ladies permit themselves only a limited palette: artificial smiles, simpers, hauteur, pouts. Any truly spontaneous expression might cause wrinkles."

"Intelligent and kind should be possible. I'll speak with them tomorrow, unless you wish to take it up with them yourself?"

"Faith, no. It will seem less cold-blooded if they simply introduce me to an appropriate young lady or two."

Miles started down to supper with an unexpectedly light heart. Peter would marry and beget more Strettons, God willing. Miles would persuade Caroline and Lavinia there was no way to legitimate Jeremy. The task should be less difficult now that he could assure them of Peter's cooperation. The earl could acknowledge Jeremy as William's son; that would be a sop to Caroline, though Eustacia's reaction did not bear thinking of.

With the problem of the succession in hand, there was only Julia's difficulty to be dealt with. She needed to marry or must spend the rest of her life as someone's dependent, with no home of her own. If the Barding ladies could re-establish her in the beau monde, she might find a husband. Halliwell paused on the stair. *She will be another year older. Her only offers are likely to be from much older men or widowers with young children.* Julia deserved more. She should wed a man who appreciated her strength of character and her intelligence, who could give her the life appropriate to a baron's daughter. Mayhap Lavinia would have a solution. She usually did! But it was some time before his mind stopped churning with regret at what he could not have.

****

When he came down to breakfast later than usual, he was haunted by his night's dreams of amber eyes and hair that glinted red in the sun. Would he see her?

The earl and Popejoy were already in the estate office dealing with some tenant dispute. The governess took her breakfast in the nursery. The countess and the dowager countess were rising from the table. Julia Perry began to follow but sank back into her chair when

Lavinia said, "No, no, you have not finished your breakfast, Julia. Halliwell, when you have finished, please attend me in my sitting room. There is no need to hurry."

The footman poured him a cup of coffee. It was like the coffee served in France, rather than the usual English coffee house beverage. The earl had acquired a taste for it on his Grand Tour. Miles needed a cup before he could contemplate eating.

"Not quite enough sleep?" Julia asked. She resumed nibbling a buttered slice of raisin and currant breakfast cake, one of the cook's specialties. At her question, he discovered he had been staring at her without being aware of it. Her hair was as he remembered except that in his dream, by some happy circumstance, it had been loose around her bare shoulders and she had been laughing. The rest of her had been bare, too. Caught wrong-footed, he replied at random.

"No. Perhaps the moon was shining in through a chink in the curtains." Had he said something stupid? Had there been a moon?

"It was quite bright, for a half moon. I wish I had taken a walk in the garden before I retired."

The green gown became her very well, and today she had not swathed her shoulders and bosom in a tucker. She no longer looked uncared for, as he had thought at their first meeting. He must keep his gaze either on the view of the garden beyond the window or on her face. He wanted to say, "You should laugh more often." To do so would be quite impossible.

Instead he said, "So do I. We might have admired it together."

She blushed. His own face felt warm. He had not meant to say it; but why not? Ladies enjoyed a man's courteous attention without taking it seriously, and if Peter were not willing to marry her…Miles shied away from that thought. Besides, it would be good preparation for her return to society.

"I think you ride almost every day? Might I accompany you tomorrow or the next day, ma'am?" By all accounts, she was an accomplished horsewoman. He regretted not being able to play the truant and accompany her today.

"That would be pleasant, sir. Sometimes I go out with Verity, but she does not enjoy long rides and prefers not to gallop or jump."

"I have no objection to any of those activities. Tomorrow, then?" When she left to change into her habit for her ride, a faint floral scent drifted in her wake. He poured himself a second cup of coffee and chose a slice of mutton ham and a roll to fortify himself before presenting himself to the dowager countess. He would have to make sure the family did not require his presence in the morning, but they were usually reasonable and would not begrudge him a ride.

"Have you had a chance to speak with Peter?" Lavinia set aside her embroidery. Miles was tolerably sure the book cover was the same one she had been working on months ago. Caroline continued to work at her netting. "Is it possible, do you think?"

"Do Lord Barding and Lord Popejoy not wish to be present, my lady?"

"Like most gentlemen, discussion of marriage makes them fidgety. They prefer to leave the planning to us. You need not worry we will be interrupted by

Lady Popejoy. She requested the carriage to take her to Banbury to consult an apothecary."

"Very well. I spoke with Mr. Peter Stretton yesterday."

Before he could continue, Caroline said without looking up, "Miles, it is ridiculous to refer to your half brother in that manner when you are speaking with us. Be formal in the presence of strangers by all means, though I don't think your parentage is a secret from anyone who knows Barding well, but with us, simply 'Peter' will do."

"I'm not at all sure he would care to be called Simply Peter, Caroline." Lavinia's lips twitched. Miles had never seen her display whimsical humor. The morning was full of surprises.

"Perhaps not, but Miles smiled, Lavinia. It much improves your face." The latter was directed to Miles.

"Thank you, my lady. I think."

Then the dowager countess said, "Pray proceed," and he dragged his attention back to business.

"First of all, Peter has no objection to marriage and, ah, procreation. I find we were all misled by certain comments of M—William's, and by Peter's response to them."

"Good. That makes our plan feasible."

"I did sometimes wonder." The smooth, repetitive motions of Caroline's netting shuttle entranced him. He forced himself to look away and disregarded this remark in favor of addressing Lavinia's entirely too optimistic statement.

"Not quite, my ladies. He does not wish to marry Mistress Julia."

"Ah. It did not appear to me that the acquaintance

was thriving." Lavinia betrayed no disappointment. She was accustomed to dealing with things as they were rather than as she wished they might be, an attitude Miles appreciated.

Caroline sighed. "It would have been a tidy solution."

"We will not give up at once. Peter may change his mind when he knows her better. It would be the best arrangement all around, and Julia will not object, I am sure."

He did not say that Peter was unlikely to alter his opinion of Julia nor mention his own disapproval of Julia marrying only to oblige the Bardings. She had a great deal to offer a man of sense and deserved more than a marriage of convenience. Peter might be willing to enter into such a union with someone other than Julia, given his views on arranged marriages, but he also should insist on more.

"My ladies, my own opinion is that their marriage would be in the best interests of neither. He has no objection to an arranged marriage if he approves the lady, however."

"What a pity to have to give up a plan which had so much to recommend it." Caroline sighed.

"Except that the reason for it was illegal," Miles interposed.

Lavinia picked up her embroidery and studied it with disfavor. "Then we will begin reviewing young ladies who might suit. It is unfortunate that we are in mourning, but those we consider will understand the necessity."

"Please bear in mind that Peter prefers an intelligent, kind wife and will not be hard to please in the matter of appearance. It will be less difficult for you to determine which are foolish, selfish, or arrogant than it would be for a man, my ladies. He would prefer a lady with good artistic judgment, too."

"We will give some thought to possible matches for Peter and also for Julia. I am quite fond of her, and we cannot count on her father being of use." Lavinia gave a brisk nod and set down her embroidery again.

He made his bows and turned to go.

"There is something else. Julia is riding this morning. Molly, her maid, is busy assisting Caroline's maid and mine in the sewing room, and Julia's room was cleaned early, out of order. This is what you will do…"

"Is it necessary now, when you have all agreed to accept her?"

"It is."

It was the most unpleasant task the Bardings had ever required of him.

****

Mr. Halliwell's intent gaze had disconcerted her. At first she thought she must have a smudge on her face. Then she decided he was still half asleep, though he did not look drowsy. She had addressed him lest his coffee grow cold, and for a moment, she thought she sensed admiration in his eyes, which was ridiculous. After that, their conversation had taken a strange turn, more suitable for a ballroom than a breakfast table. The memory and the prospect of riding with him lifted her spirits. They needed it.

She must reply to her father's letter. Where would she go? Handley or some new neighborhood where she might take part in whatever limited society it afforded?

He had promised she could eventually return to London and a normal life. Now he had withdrawn that choice and cast her adrift. He would support her somewhere out of sight. He hoped his family—except for her!—could make use of their connection to the earl and countess in London. Her presence would cause talk, if the Bardings' servants mentioned her stay at Charfield with Jeremy.

During her isolation in Dorset, she had often thought of Mama. Since coming to Charfield Hall, she thought her mother's warmth and charm were oddly like that of Caroline and Lavinia Barding. In all other respects they were as different as could be. At the same time, she began to remember other things, like the slighting way Papa spoke to and of her mother. He had married her for the enormous dowry she brought with her. He had never paid much attention to Julia. Perhaps he ignored her because he had despised his wife.

Miles Halliwell's disapproval of her family's treatment and the Bardings' welcome stood out in stark contrast. Perhaps Julia's sole value to Hiram St. John was her availability to salvage Cecilia's reputation. She had not questioned whether her family were unfair to demand her sacrifice. None of them had thanked her or even acknowledged it.

A wave of fury washed over her, so unexpected and intense that her hands tightened on the reins: she had been treated badly and had never noticed or else supposed she deserved it. Her mount came to an abrupt halt.

"Be you all right, ma'am?" the groom called as he came up beside her.

"Yes, yes, I'm sorry to have been ham-handed,

Willis. I remembered something I left undone and should have attended to some time ago." Too much explanation to make to the man, but she did feel guilty for such a beginner's error in handling her horse. She patted its neck and silently promised a treat on reaching the stable.

If she did as her father wished, she would miss the Bardings. They were not related to her but treated her as one of themselves, or at least a friend. She would miss Miles Halliwell, too. He was a hard man who had infuriated her initially. If his background was humble, as Hilda Ernst claimed, his occasional harshness might be understandable. Only tough plants grow in thin, poor soil. But Halliwell was frequently kind, too. He was also utterly dependable. For proof, she had the Barding family's reliance upon him.

She had no desire whatsoever to be banished to some provincial town to live and die cut off from family and friends. Granted, in her present mood, she could dispense with her own family handily. Now that her half sister's future was secure, there was no reason not to look to her own.

It was time to confess the truth to Lavinia. Miles seemed to have unbounded faith in the dowager countess's benevolence and good sense, and nothing Julia had observed cast doubt upon his judgment in this regard.

"Willis, I think I must curtail my ride and return to the house now to take care of my forgotten task."

As soon as they reached the stable—and she had given Hestia a carrot by way of apology—she went straight to Lavinia Barding's parlor. The sooner she confessed, the sooner she would feel purged of her dreadful anxiety over her father's letter. She could scarcely concentrate on the necessary exchanges: she trusted Lady Barding was well? She had indeed enjoyed her ride. The civilities out of the way, she hurried ahead with her confession.

"My lady, you suggested I could join my family at St. John Underhill this summer and return to London with them in the autumn." After a painful pause, she continued. "My father's last letter made it clear I am not to go home. My stepmother never liked having me underfoot, and an aging spinster who cannot be treated quite like a poor relation would be even less welcome." She had intended to phrase her revelation more tactfully. Instead, the brutal truth emerged.

"Making it difficult to resume your previous life," Lavinia mused.

"I am welcome to return to Handley or slink away to some unfashionable town…" if she did not remain with the Bardings. She regretted revealing her bitterness; so lacking in a proper dignity and loyalty to family, however justifiable.

"Leaving the child with us. How strange. I'm sure your papa's letter to Barding claimed the St. Johns wanted to be part of Jeremy's life, in spite of never having visited you and Jeremy in Handley." Julia did not miss the satirical lilt in her voice. How had she known? Miles Halliwell, of course, who had ferreted out so much else about her.

"I am sorry to admit it, but I fear my father's notion or possibly my stepmother's, was to use Jeremy to establish a connection with your family." Humiliating to have to say it, but she could not bear to see her family impose upon the Bardings.

"Thank you, Julia, I appreciate your honesty. We suspected something of the sort. It's quite distressing, how embarrassing one's family can be sometimes. Tell me, how did you answer your father's letter?"

"I haven't. I was to decide where I would wish to live"—wish to live in obscurity and loneliness!—"and inform you I was too ashamed to return to my family and society. My own father does not want me even with an unsullied reputation."

"You are quite right not to wish to fade away in some provincial town. No need for it, either. Ordinarily one should try to fulfill one's responsibilities to one's relations unless their demands are ridiculous, which your father's have been."

She patted Julia's hand, almost bringing tears to her eyes again. What was it about another person's kindness to her that made her tear up?

"I hope we made it clear we are happy to have you. Would you not be willing to stay with us?"

She forced back the incipient tears by force of will. "I would be honored, but how can I stay when my family means to use William's bastard to insinuate themselves into your circle?"

"If the St. Johns become too encroaching, we will depress their pretensions. There's no reason Caroline and I cannot reintroduce you to society, once we return to town."

"But how will you explain me?"

"Whyever would we need to? You are a family friend who lent your support this summer after William's death and during Georgie's illness."

"They will wonder that I was staying with your family rather than my own."

Lavinia was gently amused. "My dear, I misdoubt most of our friends are aware of Baron St. John's existence. If they are, they will certainly understand why you have come to London with us, and so will anyone else."

Social advantage: the reason her father and stepmother had attempted to turn Jeremy into a ticket of admission to the earl's set. If they could manage it, Cecilia's beauty and charm might attract a nobleman.

"In town I would have to use my own name," she said slowly. "The servants here have known me as Julia Perry."

"Are you concerned that they will talk? They know they will be turned off without a character if they gossip about our family, and the ones who accompany us to London have been with us for years and are utterly trustworthy. In any case, if the question should arise, we will explain that you used another name because you were delivering Jeremy for his real mother, a friend of yours who was unable to travel."

The Bardings were well able to defend themselves, and Lavinia had no doubt they could protect her. She need not scruple to accept their invitation.

"Then I accept, my lady. Thank you."

"Excellent. I have no doubt we will find you a husband so you may be comfortable."

What could she say to this hopeful view of her chances? It was true she would like to be married. She even had a dowry, though it would not be large by her hosts' standards. She had thought, studying her face in the mirror since coming to Charfield, that she was not as plain and old as she had supposed. It must be the new gowns. Lavinia and Caroline had also insisted she leave off wearing the caps suitable to a matron, saying they were far too old for her. They pointed out that their own caps were smaller and more frivolous, and both of them were far older than she.

"A large, plain cap such as yours may be appropriate if you happen to be wearing a straw hat," Caroline admitted, "for the straw would otherwise catch in your hair. In the house, a little one with some lace and ribbons that complement one's gown is better."

And far more becoming, Julia conceded. Before she knew what they were about, she found herself in possession of several tiny, filmy caps trimmed with lace remnants. Their only function was decorative. They were far more attractive with her new wardrobe.

Mayhap a husband was not completely out of the question. A man like Miles Halliwell would be perfect: someone with the manners of a gentleman and not so wealthy that her dowry of five thousand pounds would not be welcome. A professional man or even a cit would be acceptable, if he were like Miles. Surely her father would not withhold her dowry?

Those were thoughts for the future. At the moment she must face the daunting task of writing to inform her father she would make her home at Charfield. Her courage might have failed her if her papa had been present. As he was not, 'twas only a matter of setting words down on paper. How could she phrase it to avoid his wrath? How pitiful to have to acknowledge that Lavinia and Caroline—and Miles—had been kinder to her than her own father. Well, she would not apologize for her decision or try to justify it. A polite inquiry after his health and that of her stepmother and Cecilia and Martin, and another two or three lines announcing her intentions, and it would be done.

Chapter 18

Did spies feel as soiled as he did? Perhaps not, or else they grew accustomed. Possibly he would feel it less had it been productive. No, he would have hated searching her possessions no matter what he found. The letters proved nothing, unless one chose to suspect the mention of some swain named Manning meant he had ruined her. It would make no difference to the earl's family, as they had intended to re-establish her in society when they believed she was Jeremy's mother. Nor did he care...except if it were true, she might be willing to overlook his lack of rank and family.

Leaving the passage on which most of the guest bedchambers were located, he risked going to Lavinia's parlor without requesting a meeting or being summoned. Turning the corner into the family wing, he came face to face with Julia, as if he had conjured her. She gave the little start he managed to suppress.

"Mr. Halliwell, good morning again."

"And to you, Mistress Perry." In a yellow habit, flushed and happy, with a few escaped tendrils of hair around her face, she was lovely to behold. Had he ever seen her in such good spirits before?

She appeared to be at a loss for anything else to say. He wanted to ask her if she would care to walk in the garden later; shame sealed his lips. "Well..."

"Well...I am on my way to help Verity in the

sewing room."

"Perhaps later we might see if any daffodils have come up?" He sounded like an idiot, the words forced out by a sudden, humiliating desire for her company.

"I would enjoy that. After dinner, perhaps?"

"I will anticipate it with pleasure."

Her glowing face assured him the suggestion had been welcome.

Lavinia, Lady Barding, took no offense at what her companion or Eustacia would have termed his presumption. When she called to him to enter, her first words were "How fortunate you are finished; I suppose you met Julia? Pray, tell the footman to ask Caroline to attend me."

He dispatched the man on duty on this errand and returned to sit waiting with Lavinia. She commented upon an item in the most recent London newssheet, only three days old, and asked his opinion.

The topic was meant merely to fill the time. He responded, at the same time admiring the cheerful room in which the dowager countess spent most mornings. The east-facing windows gave good light for needlework, not that she favored that pastime even now she no longer rode or tended the physic garden. Her embroidery frame served the same purpose as a hunter's blind.

Caroline tapped and hurried in without waiting for Lavinia's "Come!"

"Pray, sit. Miles, tell us if you found anything incriminating in Julia's rooms."

He summarized the letters he had found, concluding, "They prove St. John's intention to establish a connection with your family, as we already suspected."

"As Julia admitted to me this morning."

Caroline asked, "This suitor of hers, Manning? Could you deduce anything more from the letter?"

"He was a widower with children, the best and only aspirant to her hand, if indeed he was that. He cannot have been in love with her or he would have contrived to seek her out in her exile. And he married someone else." *The undiscriminating fool.* All the better for Julia, however. She deserved a husband who wanted more than a stepmother for his children.

"Could he not have been exercising gentlemanly restraint?"

"For two years, my lady? Would a man who loved her let her go so easily? If Manning had applied to St. John, I have no doubt he would have been discouraged, as otherwise St. John's ploy to present young Cecilia as chaste would fail. If he were refused, an ardent man would seek her out by his own efforts."

"Would you?" Caroline inquired with interest.

He had spoken too emphatically for a serious man who should speak of love or marriage in practical terms. "I would if I were determined to win that lady and no other." He hurried on to cover his embarrassment. "The most recent letter makes it plain her father and stepmother do not want her to return to the bosom of her family. No doubt they intend to use your family to find a husband for Mistress Julia's tiresome chit of a half sister."

He distrusted Lavinia's faint smile. "I take it you would not advocate Peter marrying her?"

"Deuce, no, my lady! Meeting the little baggage might send him back to Italy on the first available ship."

"Your conclusions about Julia St. John's past and honesty? We both know she has been guilty of some degree of deception."

"I would take my oath in court her only mistake has been to be dutiful to a family which does not value her." Miles cleared his throat to try for a more dispassionate tone. "I felt she was not truthful about something apart from not being Jeremy's mother. Now I believe it was no more than shame at her father's scheming." She had wept over her father's betrayal. While he should have told Lavinia, he did not regret having kept Julia's painful secret.

"Your findings and conclusions only confirm what Julia told me moments ago. She is just the sort we would have chosen for George, and we will be pleased to help her."

This comment seeming to indicate the end of their interview, Miles waited to be dismissed.

"Now, there is something else, Miles. For all Eustacia may deny it, 'tis clear Georgie is most extremely ill. I believe our good doctor is correct that his ailment is something far worse than green-sickness. We must see to it Peter marries as soon as possible. I trust he does not intend to waste time sowing any wild oats."

"From certain things he told me, I think he, hmmm, enjoyed himself in Italy. He does understand the urgency, my lady."

She nodded. "Excellent. We will want you to evaluate the backgrounds of the young ladies on our list of possible brides for Peter. I doubt there will be any surprises, but we will leave nothing to chance."

"If you will provide me a copy of your list, I will start back to town tomorrow." Another eighty-mile journey. He would travel back and forth like the ball in the French game of *jeu de paume* for no other client. He owed his profession to Barding having placed him with his man of business. Fortunately, Miles had liked the work and Whitacker had been pleased with him. But he would miss his ride with Julia.

"Miles, Barding prefers you to remain here until we have settled things with Peter. Your assistant is perfectly capable of doing the necessary research, is he not?"

"He is."

"I know it is somewhat inconvenient for you, but we would be very glad if you would agree. As usual, a groom will carry messages to and from your office. Will you need anything else? A separate room to use as an office, or an assistant to copy whatever letters you write?"

"I don't think so, my lady. The use of a groom would be helpful, however. Thank you."

Why did they want him at Charfield? To keep Peter company or to persuade him to change his mind about Julia or encourage him to court some other lady? The latter hardly seemed necessary as Peter was willing to marry to oblige his family. As long as it wasn't Julia, a cheering thought.

"Caroline, you have the list, don't you?"

"Of course." She passed a folded sheet to Miles.

"Then Miles can write to Bryden today, stressing the need for haste." She nodded at him.

He rose and bowed. "Good day, my ladies."

"Miles, one more thing," Caroline began. "I do not

think we tell you often enough how much we value your service to us. Also I owe you an apology. I regret I was not more caring when you first came to live here."

Caroline's admission rendered him speechless. He did not recall she had treated him much differently from George.

"Because I did not find out about you until your mama died when I was enceinte with William, my anger at Barding—he was still Popejoy then, of course—made me less gracious than I might have been, and far too lenient with William. But my wish that Jeremy could be legitimated was more because of the succession than because he is William's son. I hope Jeremy has the potential to be as fine a man as you are."

Despite the lump in his throat, he contrived to respond. "My lady, I never noticed any unkindness on your part. I was fortunate to have been brought here."

She smiled at him mistily. Whether her words were sincere or only meant to bind his loyalty yet more closely, his heart melted.

Lavinia appeared to be abstracted; he wondered if she had been following their conversation. Evidently she had.

"You turned out well, Miles. It is too bad Jeremy cannot be legitimated, but at least we have been partially successful. Peter will marry, and we must hope he sires enough boys to ensure the earldom survives. Barding means to acknowledge Jeremy as William's son. He will acknowledge you also."

"As he would have done when you came to live at Charfield, if I had not treated him to bouts of hysterics when I found out about you," Caroline said softly. "Had I not been breeding, I would have been more capable of reason. You may not be aware that females in that condition are subject to moodiness. I hope you will remember that fact when you marry."

An unexpected wave of affection for the Barding ladies overwhelmed him. He spoke without thought. "My ladies, a possibility occurs to me. It might not be necessary for Peter to wed Julia in order to make the boy legitimate. Apparently legitimate." Good God, what was he saying? The dowager countess's scheme had always been wrong-headed as well as illegal, and he had hoped there would be no chance of carrying it out. Now he was proposing a plan with even more difficulties. He must have taken leave of his senses. Mayhap insanity ran in the Barding blood.

Two sets of beady eyes focused on him. "How?" Steel rang in Lavinia's question.

"Peter spent five or six months in the Italian countryside without seeing anyone but the locals. It would have been possible for him to return to England briefly and marry, which is the plan you envisioned for Peter and Julia. But his bride wouldn't have to be Julia. Mistress Perry, as we've been calling her, has no attachment to the child, nor in spite of all their claims do the St. Johns. It's merely a question of finding a young woman of decent birth who was on her own during the time Peter might have been in England. She would have to be willing to lend herself to the deception, but many would do so for marriage to the son of an earl and a comfortable life."

Lavinia held up a white, elegant forefinger. "Will the St. Johns not be tempted to blackmail?"

"We know the younger girl, for whom they hope to make a brilliant match, was the mother, which they certainly do not wish to be revealed. Blackmail would be unlikely to tempt them unless Jeremy became the heir apparent. Would the St. Johns dare to try it when you could expose their daughter's fault and their attempt at blackmail? If she were married, her husband and his family would suffer as well.

"Your family tend to be long-lived. Lord Barding is likely to live for many years yet and will be followed by Lord Popejoy, who enjoys excellent health. It might be half a century before the title passed to Peter or to a son of his. A good deal might happen in those years. Julia's father and stepmother would likely be gone, her younger sister might be a grandmother who would not care to tell the world and its wife she had given birth to a bastard. It would bring scorn upon her husband, children, and grandchildren."

"A good point," Lavinia conceded. "Answer me this: how will you find a decent young woman willing to lie who was available in those months?"

"Young ladies are ruined every day. I may not find a nobleman's daughter, but I think a gentleman's daughter is not out of the question. Do you insist her father be of a certain rank? That would greatly increase the difficulty. Or would you settle for a well-brought-up cit's girl at a pinch?"

"I will settle for any decent young woman you can find who is acceptable to Peter. Caroline?"

"I agree."

He was not surprised that neither regarded a young lady's ruin as disqualifying her from the class of "decent young women."

"Miles, how do you plan to find her? And get a forged certificate, too?"

"I have the name and direction of a man who may be able to arrange such matters. I may not succeed. Perhaps Peter will not agree as he was not sure how he would feel about making Jeremy his heir in place of a son of his own. He may change his mind. It's not as though Jeremy would be certain to inherit the title: George and Eustacia might have another son." He added, "I told Peter his own son would receive a good inheritance so as not to be cut out entirely. The Barding estates can support the purchase of a property and money to pass to that son."

"Particularly as William is no more. I'm sorry, Caroline, but he was excessively expensive."

"I know. In fact, with Lavinia's and your wise investments, Miles, the family could make sure any of Peter's children had good inheritances."

"That might weigh with Peter. At the least, Jeremy will have the same upbringing for which I am grateful."

"If you succeed, you will have worked a miracle."

Belatedly, it occurred to him that he should have spoken to Peter and Julia first. Julia would not care about someone else posing as Jeremy's mother. Probably! One never knew with females, but she was a rational lady.

"I have not informed Bryden of the cause of my absences on your behalf and would not wish to involve him in this matter. I will have to return to London to see about finding the right young woman and the man who may be able to, er, take care of the details."

Lavinia and Caroline exchanged a glance; the countess spoke. "As you will not need to promote Julia's marriage to Peter, I believe we can dispense with your presence."

Chapter 19

Miles found Julia and Peter in the Long Gallery, studying the portraits of Strettons long dead.

"…skull cannot have been shaped like that, which leads me to suspect he cannot have been wall-eyed, either."

"If it is not a good likeness, so much the better," Julia agreed.

Hearing his footfalls, they both turned.

Peter read his expression. "What's wrong?"

"Nothing's amiss. Not precisely. I am glad to find you together." He paused to think how to put it.

"My mother…suggested…I should show Mistress Perry the portrait gallery." From his tone, Caroline's suggestion had been more of an order. The Barding ladies had meant to throw them together in the hope Peter would agree to marry Julia. Of course.

His own suggestion to the ladies, made in a moment's weakness, began to seem like a better idea. Otherwise, Julia and Peter might be forced willy-nilly into marriage. Peter, having consented to marry for the earldom's preservation, might resign himself to offering for Julia. Julia was accustomed to being sacrificed for others' benefit with no concern for her own happiness. In the Bardings' welcoming embrace, she might be manipulated into agreeing to marry Peter.

Miles could not countenance his favorite brother

being condemned to a distasteful marriage when he himself would marry Julia happily. *What?* Where did that thought come from?

"I need to talk to you both," he said. "We can be private in that little chamber at the other end of the gallery." Charfield Hall having been built in many stages, sometimes without much forethought, the rambling structure was a warren of rooms. He and the Stretton boys had spent hours attempting to find a priest's hole or hidden room filled with treasure. Being deep as well as long, the house possessed several small, enclosed courtyards to provide light and air to interior rooms without windows in the outer walls. The one he was thinking of was pleasant and overlooked one of the little courts.

"We can speak freely here." He could not recall the room ever being used during the years he had lived at Charfield, and the furniture gave no clue, consisting of a settle, several armchairs, and a side table holding a branch of candles.

When they were seated, he began, "I believe we all know that Georgie may not live. If Popejoy does not have another son, Peter will be the family's last hope. He is willing to marry to do his duty to the family. The dowager countess came up with a scheme that you should marry, and that if you had married secretly before Jeremy's birth, Jeremy would be legitimate." Julia's raised eyebrows indicated she was unaware of Lavinia's plan. Her raised chin showed what she thought of it.

"I have the greatest respect and affection, too, for Lavinia, Lady Barding, but…"

"That was my reaction as well, Mistress Perry. I

pointed out the several problems: the likely unwillingness of one or the other of you, the need for a certificate of marriage and entries in the parish register. They would have to be forged, and even that would not help if there were no way Peter could have been in the country at the relevant period."

"Unfortunately, I could in theory have returned for a short time."

Miles smiled wryly at Peter's glum tone. He was probably wishing he'd lied about where he had been and who had known of it. "It has been pointed out to me that, with a wedding under the Rules of the Fleet Prison, we would need only a certificate. Peter is amenable to an arranged marriage, and you, Mistress Perry, have no maternal connection or interest in Jeremy."

She started to speak.

"It's not a criticism, ma'am. It works to our advantage. Given those two factors, if I can find a young woman whose whereabouts is unknown during the months Peter might have been in England, she could be Jeremy's mother."

"Assuming she were willing to take part in such a deception, Mr. Halliwell."

"And assuming she was acceptable both to me and to my mother and grandmother."

"Also assuming I can find a forger. I have been given the name of a man who may be able to help. I think we have to try, although I do not like the idea of committing multiple crimes and misdemeanors. Peter, would you care to wager that you would not give in to Lavinia and your mother's desire you should marry Julia if no other option presents itself?"

"Uh, no."

"Mistress Julia?"

She bit her lip. "The Bardings have been so good to me…"

"They have said they will try to find a suitable girl, but one in their level of society would not make it possible to allege a secret marriage and pregnancy. Legitimating Jeremy is important to Caroline, Lady Barding, but though she says she will give the notion up if she must, I believe Lavinia will make a push to accommodate her."

"Meaning they might press me to marry Mistress Perry."

"What makes you think I would be willing to marry you, Mr. Stretton?"

"Would you refuse?" Peter asked.

Julia began, "I…" Her voice trailed away.

Miles understood: her choices were so few that she might agree to marry Peter.

"Would you refuse?" Miles repeated the question.

She sucked her lower lip, a sight almost too much for Halliwell's composure. "Perhaps not, Mr. Halliwell. They've all been kinder than I could have expected. It might be my only chance to marry."

"Still, that's no reason to feel you must oblige them. I have no doubt that you will attract a man of good birth with the family's help. It will be better to find Peter some other bride.

"Peter, would you be willing to agree to my finding a bride for you in order that Jeremy could be made to seem legitimate? Mistress Perry, would you object to another woman claiming Jeremy?"

She replied first. "As you have mentioned, sir, I

have no attachment to the boy—to Jeremy. I would gladly have surrendered him to a foster family. Janet Campbell is devoted to him, and I believe she will not give a straw whose child he is said to be, though she would not want to be parted from him. I will sound her out, however."

Peter waved a languid hand. "I don't mind an arranged marriage if the lady is acceptable to, er, all concerned."

He really should bring up one last point. "Mistress Julia, their ladyships and I discussed whether your family would oppose any pretense that Jeremy is not related to them. It was my opinion they would not want to risk revealing one of their daughters had borne an illegitimate child. No matter which young lady was the mother, the scandal would affect all of them. The truth would undoubtedly come out, as the Bardings would not tolerate their interference."

Miles Halliwell did not say he feared the St. Johns would attempt blackmail, she noted. He really was decent, in spite of the impassive face he showed the world. She smiled in acknowledgment of his courtesy. "An attempt at blackmail, you mean? You need not mince your words."

"That was my meaning. I am sorry to ask, but do you think it possible?"

"I hardly think so, Mr. Halliwell. Your reasoning was sound. 'Tis not as if they have any personal interest in Jeremy. Their stake in him begins and ends with providing a connection to the Bardings. If they can claim acquaintance with the earl and his family, they will not care. I wish I could say otherwise, but I won't gloss over the facts."

"It might be awkward if they knew we were passing the boy off as Peter's and some other lady's."

"I doubt my father and stepmother will care or even hear of it. I believe nothing more is required than the earl and his countess inviting my family to an entertainment or two in London."

Peter Stretton was frowning, sunk in thought. Julia wondered if he had even heard them.

"Peter, do you have any objection to what I have proposed?" Halliwell inquired.

He looked up. "No. I owe my parents and Grandmama something for having deserted them for so long. For their misapprehensions about me, too, which must have been a source of discomfort. And I have already agreed to an arranged marriage. I would want to meet and approve my prospective bride before you raised any expectations, however."

"Of course."

"Then I think you should set the project in motion rather than waiting for Grandmama and my mother to begin bringing young ladies home as if they were stray kittens. I fear all of them would be young and silly."

"Peter, you are not in your dotage."

"No, but my nature is serious, and in my experience, young girls tend to be shallow. Nor do I think Mistress Perry and I want to be subjected to my mother and grandmother's hopeful glances, as we will be, if my mother has set her heart on legitimating Jeremy."

"I agree," Julia said. " 'Tis uncomfortable to see Lady Barding and the dowager Lady Barding watching us and finding excuses to throw us together."

"Hear, hear!" Peter Stretton agreed.

"Then I will leave for London tomorrow and find out if it's practicable."

"I'll come with you, Miles."

"You only just arrived at Charfield."

"If this plan of yours and our grandmother's is possible, you'd be sending for me to meet my prospective bride, wouldn't you? You wouldn't bring her here."

"That's true."

"I'll be ready to leave in the morning."

Miles sighed inwardly. He met Julia's eyes and murmured apologetically, "I fear I will not be able to ride with you tomorrow, Mistress Perry."

"Of course you must set the plan in action as soon as may be. I shall look forward to our ride at your next visit, as I have been invited to remain with the earl's family and intend to do so."

The promise her smile implied made his heart give a thump. He ignored a certain mocking twinkle in Peter's eyes.

Chapter 20

The last cheerful dinner at Charfield had been before Miles and Peter departed for town. The family's pleasure at the youngest Stretton son's return from Italy, their desire to catch up on the missed years, and his fund of amusing stories about his travels and the people he had met had made for lively conversation and even gaiety. Miles Halliwell's presence was welcome, too. His manner was grave, but his presence was somehow reassuring; one felt nothing could go very wrong when he was there to deal with it. Today talk languished.

Julia, seated between Verity and Eustacia, had an opportunity to reflect and no need to exert herself to find a topic to introduce. Verity was engaged in a discussion of the Poor Laws with the curate, as animated as Julia had ever seen her. Eustacia picked at her food and seemed unable to rouse herself to speak to anyone.

Timothy Sykes did his best to introduce a cheerful tone. He really was a nice young man. While on walks in the garden, Julia had seen how popular he was with Eustacia's daughters when they and their governess were taking the air and had observed the tutor's way with little Georgie. Soon after her arrival, she had watched Sykes coaxing Georgie to study a butterfly perched on a flower in the garden, explaining to him how the insect begins as a caterpillar. The child had stared at the pretty creature with dull eyes, visibly finding it less interesting than Julia did. Someday Sykes might be Jeremy Perry's tutor as well as Georgie's. She thought he would not hold the boy's illegitimacy against him.

The tutor's easy manners were as likely to appeal to an adult as to a child. He was able to converse with the taciturn Hilda Ernst and the shy Verity, both of whom posed some challenges for everyone else. Even he was finding it hard work to promote discourse at the table today.

In a momentary silence at the end as they nibbled fruit, sweetmeats, and cakes, Lavinia asked, "Did you find what you were looking for in Banbury, Eustacia?"

Eustacia's over-emphatic "No!" made Julia flinch, and startled the others as well. "I shall have to write to Halliwell to obtain it in London. 'Tis most vexing. I will need a groom to carry my letter in the morning."

"Oh, excellent," Caroline said. "I need one or two things which I would have requested you get at the haberdasher's, had I known I needed more silk thread before you set out. If I send a sample with the groom, the haberdasher can match the colors."

"The groom will be going to London, Mama-in-law."

"Is it so urgent? I thought you would have him take the letter to the Banbury receiving office. You would have an answer within a week, I suppose."

"I must have it sooner. He can wait while Halliwell obtains the things I need, and then bring them directly back. I do not care to trust them to a country carrier."

"With one of the grooms abed with a broken ankle

and one sent to the Cumberland property—"

Eustacia's shrill voice cut off the earl's reply. "When Halliwell is here, he is assigned a groom to carry his letters back and forth, and he is only a bastard and hardly better than a servant."

This outburst dropped into their midst like a cannonball, leaving behind a moment's shock.

"Then of course you must have a groom take it," Lavinia replied.

"If it is so important, I will have Davis wait on you in the morning to receive your letter and instructions," Barding said.

"Eustacia, dear, we know how you are suffering under the strain of little George's illness. Let me escort you up to your chamber. I believe we have some oil of mandrakes which will help you sleep." Caroline might have been speaking to a fretful child.

"I will go up, but I have syrup of purslane, which will serve to make me drowsy." Eustacia rose abruptly. "Excuse me, please."

What an interesting and unusual family. One might have expected tension between the dowager countess and Caroline, Lady Barding, but instead they were like mother and daughter. Or perhaps like fond sisters or aunt and niece? And how kind they were to Eustacia, who could be prickly. Now, with her son ailing, she must be frantic, poor woman.

If her own family had been like the Bardings, what would they have done? Somehow they would have dealt with Cecilia's mistake in some other way. Julia would never have met the earl's family or Miles Halliwell. She might have married Theo Manning whom she had known for years from parties and assemblies in their circle. She no longer regretted Theo's loss. He had been pleasant, but she knew nothing of his character. She knew Miles far better after little more than a month.

****

Julia rode with Verity almost every day. She wished Caroline's companion were willing to ride farther and at more than a trot, and that she possessed a livelier mind. She had ridden once with Miles Halliwell. They had even galloped without his displaying concern as to whether she was an accomplished horsewoman. Knowing Miles, he had probably questioned the head groom. He showed her more of the estate than she had previously seen.

When she saw a boy carrying an armload of sticks and small branches as they rode through one of the wooded areas, her eyes slid toward Miles uneasily. He grinned at her. "No need to worry for the child. The earl has not and swears he will not seek an Enclosure Act here or at his other estates. Neither will Lord Popejoy. The tenants and laborers still have their traditional rights, and I hope always will."

What a difference from other landowners, including her father, who had enclosed the open fields held in common and taken away traditional rights to graze animals on the common land and gather or cut firewood.

She also assisted Marcia Brant with the little girls' French lessons and occasionally with lessons in botany. Marcia had grown up in town with no garden whereas Julia had lived in the country and enjoyed gardens, if not gardening. While Eustacia had promised her daughters lessons in herbal preparations when they

221

were older and would have been the natural choice to teach them about plants, she claimed she was too busy at the moment. Helping the governess with the twins was diverting, as the girls were well-behaved but not lacking in liveliness.

Caroline and Lavinia Barding were preoccupied; they and the men were frequently in conference together, presumably to discuss estate business or investments. Perhaps financial matters were only a pretext: George and Eustacia's little boy was still ailing. It was impossible to assume it was only a trifling childhood illness when the doctor came every two or three days and had left word that he was to be sent for day or night in the event of any sudden change. It was unnecessary for him to add "for the worse."

Julia sometimes met the viscountess when she walked in the gardens or saw her at her work table in the stillroom. She commented to Verity on Eustacia's devotion to her pastime during one of their rides.

"Her remedies must be in demand among the tenants, to judge from the hours she spends in the stillroom."

"Oh, she does not make only the common remedies. She makes conserves and preserves of herbs with healing or strengthening powers, and candies herbs and flowers as well. She is spending more of her day working there recently." After a moment she continued, "It may be it occupies her mind while she is worried about dear little Georgie." There was nothing to say in response. The child's illness cast gloom over everyone at the manor. Even his sisters had grown subdued.

In spite of Lavinia and Caroline's acceptance, being an outsider in the midst of a family afflicted by illness was uncomfortable. She tried to be of assistance to both Ladies Barding, which eased her embarrassment at her presence somewhat and to Lady Popejoy also. In theory, there should have been nothing for her to do, as Lavinia had Hilda Ernst as a companion, and companions, as everyone knew, were meant to take on all the little tasks a lady found tiresome. However, Hilda had grown nearly to womanhood in Hanover and had been accustomed to think her family of considerable importance before their move to England. But as Hanover had been nothing but a principality before George Louis of Hanover was made king of Great Britain, few English people shared her belief. Hilda thought herself more a guest than a companion.

Verity, Caroline's niece, fulfilled the function of a companion in theory. In fact, Julia soon concluded that the paid post was only the countess's excuse for taking in a niece left destitute when her father died in debt. Verity happily performed any domestic task given her, but she was so timid she shrank from delivering baskets of food and other comforts to the estate's laborers and tenants who were ill, elderly, or had recently given birth. Caroline ordinarily enjoyed this duty, but at times her other responsibilities made it impossible. In other families, the heir's wife might have delegated for the countess, but Eustacia's anxiety over her son and her uncertain temper made her a poor choice. Julia was pressed into service as Caroline's surrogate, having often taken her stepmother's place in dealing with the St. John Underhill tenants. She also transmitted Caroline's instructions to the cook, who terrified Verity.

The girl might have been of some use in the

nursery as she claimed to be fond of children, but she was so affected by the mere thought of Georgie's illness that she could not bear to visit even his sisters. Verity never mentioned Jeremy, but Julia could hardly fault her for ignoring him, as she herself visited him only once a day, briefly, to see if Janet Campbell needed anything. She suspected Verity's avoidance stemmed from disapproval of bastardy.

The child should not be blamed for his parents' immorality. Julia pitied the boy but could not feel warmly toward the son of the man who had debauched Cecilia. His existence had stolen her own future. No, to be fair, her own family had done that. Though really, what difference had it made? She had already been unlikely ever to marry unless she had accepted Manning, as she might have done out of desperation, if he had ever got around to asking her. She might still be living in her father's house. On the other hand, because of Jeremy, she was at Charfield Hall and had begun to hope for a better future, impossible as it seemed.

She felt a little guilty for her improved circumstances when the family's conspiracy to pretend nothing was really wrong with Georgie was failing day by day. Dark smudges under Eustacia's eyes testified to her wakefulness at night, and she ate little at dinner and supper. She had lost flesh even in the time Julia had been at Charfield, and yet she was increasingly active, sometimes actually agitated.

The viscount watched her with worried eyes and encouraged her to rest and eat more. Her favorite dishes appeared at meals with great frequency, only to be picked at or ignored. Julia, often in Caroline's or Lavinia's presence, thus heard the latter question

Eustacia's maid.

"She takes no more than a cup of chocolate in the morning, my lady. I always bring her a roll as well, but she mostly only takes a bite or two. Her stomach bothers her, but she's taking a tonic for it," Alice said.

After she had been sent away, Lavinia admitted, "I cannot like questioning another lady's servant, but I am becoming concerned about Eustacia. She is distraught over her son, naturally enough, but it is affecting her own health as well."

Chapter 21

Job's Coffee House was smaller than some, humbler than many, and plainly furnished. But the servers were neat and quick, and the woman behind the counter was busily occupied with brewing more coffee, while a boy shook a pan of coffee beans on the hearth. The aroma filled the air, mingling with pipe smoke and the scent of pomade and sweat. The men at the tables were a mixed lot: laborers, tradesmen, prosperous merchants, a gentleman or two.

Peter gawked like a foreigner visiting England for the first time. He noticed Miles's amusement. "I don't think I was ever in a coffee house before I left on my tour." They paused inside the door. The man Hayes had described proved easy to find.

A fellow in a grass-green coat and blue waistcoat patterned with red sat by himself at a table in the left rear corner. No wonder Simon Hayes had mentioned his dress.

John Barlicorn saw them coming halfway across the room and watched as they threaded their way between the tables and the small groups of men who had stopped to address a chance-met acquaintance or were glancing around to find one or to choose a table.

"John Barlicorn?"

"Ay." The coat was old but well cared for; his shirt cuffs lacked ruffles but were clean, as was his neckcloth. The fine lace on it showed signs of wear and imperfect repairs. It might be in its fourth or fifth use. Lace was expensive and seldom discarded. Like brandy, it was often smuggled. He waved a hand to invite Miles and Peter to be seated. He made another, slighter, gesture to summon a waiter.

Neither he nor Miles spoke. While Halliwell was wondering if he should simply launch into his question or whether he should wait for the other to ask his business, a boy of twelve or fourteen bustled over with a tray containing pots of chocolate, tea, and coffee and coffee bowls. Miles requested coffee. Peter asked for tea. His right hand twitched as if yearning for a paper and chalk or pencil to record Barlicorn's face. The rogue gave him a hard look that prompted Peter to flatten his hand on the table and hold it still. Barlicorn's flashy, vulgar clothing was deceptive, obviously no more than a disguise to make him recognizable while distracting attention from his face.

When the lad had served them and whisked away to refill other customers' cups, Barlicorn spoke. "Who sent you, and why've you come to me?"

"Simon Hayes recommended you as someone who might be able to advise me. He says you may be able to, er…" *Supply what I need? Procure a female willing to marry to oblige my client and incidentally commit a misdemeanor?* No way of phrasing it could make it sound reasonable.

"What d'ye need?"

"The matter is extremely confidential."

"This table is well away from the others, and there's naught to bring a server 'less I summon one. Keep your voice low and no one'll hear."

"I need a young female, hmmmm, between twenty and thirty years of age, though an upper age of five-and-twenty would be best, who is genteel and has no close family or friends." He cleared his throat. "She must be honest, discreet, and not stupid."

"Kind, too," Peter added. Miles scowled at him.

"You want a rum mort who'll be mum and who's willing to undertake some job for you. I'll need more than that before I decide if I'll oblige you." Under the coarse speech, the ghost of good diction lingered.

"It's complicated. Is what I'm asking even possible?"

"Probably." After an uncomfortably long pause while Barlicorn studied them, he asked, "Is she in danger of injury or degradation?" There it was: some education under the sloppy, canting speech.

"No, none. She will have a position in society and live very comfortably."

"When you say 'a position,' do you mean she will be a mistress?"

"No. Her place will be permanent and secure."

"How?"

"She will be the wife of a gentleman."

"Me." Peter again. Miles had warned him not to speak unless spoken to. It was Miles's business to handle negotiations for the family. *Though not exactly like this.*

"Can you not find your own wife? A gentry-cove who can offer a woman marriage and a comfortable life seldom has difficulty finding a bride."

"I have not been in society here. And, er…"

"The situation is unusual," Miles allowed.

"Men come to me to arrange a mort o' different

things. What they want and why they want it is always plain. Without I understand why you need a woman to marry, I won't help you."

Halliwell was considering what he could safely divulge and how to explain it when Peter spoke again.

"My brother died leaving a bastard. My mother would like the child to be legitimate and part of our family, rather than growing up feeling unloved and unworthy."

Peter's words hit him like a punch in the gut. Those terms exactly described how he had felt as a child. *Only as a child?* Something changed in Barlicorn's face.

"In order to accomplish it, I must appear to have married the child's mother before his birth and the bride must be willing to support the lie."

Barlicorn sipped his coffee, which must by now have been cold. "What of the squeaker's true mother?"

"She will surrender the child. I can't marry her."

Peter was making a far better job of it than Miles could have done, and in fewer words.

"You're willing to do it? Accept another man's brat and wed some woman who's willing to agree?"

Peter made one of those subtly foreign gestures. 'Twas definitely past time he was home in England. "I have been a disappointment to my parents for many years. I would be glad to fulfill my mother's wish. I don't mind an arranged marriage, which are common enough in any case." He smiled ruefully. "I would rather not expose myself to a hunting pack of mamas and their daughters."

"Ha!" The rogue's short laugh was echoed by Peter's. "Life's easier in my part o' town, sirs." He turned his eyes to Halliwell. "What's your part in this?"

"I represent the family's interests. Though I see I might as well have left it to…er, Mr. Smith."

He had amused the rogue. Barlicorn said, "No need for names. If I want to find out who you are, I can, and no need for you to worry: I keep my clients' secrets. Have you taken thought as to the legalities? Do you mean to do no more than to claim you married while abroad? Easy enough to lose the proof of it and hard to get confirmation of it from foreign parts."

No wonder Simon Hayes had sent him to John Barlicorn. The man had deduced Peter had been on the Continent from that one unwary motion. Halliwell said, "We'll need proof. I understand the difficulty involved. In addition to a certificate, there's the problem of a parish register. Someone suggested that a Fleet marriage would be the simplest to, er…"

"Forge. Ay." His eyes focused on the wall behind Miles, who imagined gears turning in his brain.

"You want a bride who's intelligent, not one to blab, kind, and honest, but not so honest she won't agree to your plan. Younger than you," Barlicorn added for Peter's benefit.

"I don't think I care if she is a year or two older, if it comes to that."

"Do you insist on a virgin? Or a beauty?"

"We'll take what we can get if she's suitable otherwise, as long as she's not poxed," Peter replied.

Miles said, "She must be presentable in appearance and able to pass as well bred. We appreciate that all those qualifications alone will be difficult to fulfill."

"How comfortably will she live?"

Peter turned to Halliwell, brows raised. When he had been sent off on his tour, the earl had arranged an allowance appropriate to support a boy of eighteen on his travels. Peter might suppose he would be living on the same amount here at home.

"She will not have her own carriage, but she will live in a well-to-do gentleman's house, dress like a gentlewoman, have a maid, servants, and adequate pin money. I can attest that Mr. Smith is not violent and not given to drinking or gambling to excess."

"Not too hard to find you possible matches, then."

"Except for one additional detail." Which was the one thing that might make it impossible to achieve. "She would have to be in some out-of-the-way place, where no one could swear to her circumstances and the absence of a pregnancy and a child."

"The dates?"

Peter answered. "The five or six months prior to mid-October 1738 would do."

"But—"

"I've thought about it, Miles. The marriage has to have taken place by October 1738 when Jeremy was born, meaning he would have been conceived in December 1737 or within the month following. However, the pregnancy would not show until about April 1738, judging from what I know of how ladies' figures change when they are enceinte. Soon after the birth, his mother would naturally have turned the baby over to a wet nurse for fostering and resumed her ordinary life. That reduces the period she would have had to be in hiding to April to about November, 1738. If that makes it simpler?"

John Barlicorn sat contemplating his steepled fingers for several minutes. Miles did not interrupt. He had never cherished much hope the man would be able to find a suitable candidate. Yet Peter would be reluctant to give up if there was any chance at all. He wanted badly to fulfill his mother's wish.

At length, Barlicorn raised his eyes. "I'd have said you wanted the moon tied up with a pretty bow. But mayhap there's a chance. Can I trust your offer is in good faith and that you can guarantee your promises?"

"Simon Hayes will speak for my integrity, I believe."

"Oh, he has. He let me know he'd referred you. I know he's honest, and he'll tell you I am. Or rather, that I keep my promises." He grinned, revealing white, slightly crooked teeth. "It may be worth the risk to the lady. You'll both come in a carriage with the curtains drawn and a blindfold over your eyes. You won't remove it until I return you to your lodgings. If you accept those conditions, I'll make arrangements. Whether your proposal is accepted or not, I'll charge you a guinea and see you safe home. If you reach agreement, I'll charge you for my work. Getting the proofs and whatever else has to be done. Twenty-five pounds should pay for all. And that's only because I will employ the most trustworthy men and women."

"The secrecy seems unusual for what is essentially an employment interview, Mr. Barlicorn."

"Just 'Barlicorn' will do. If your requirements were not so mysterious and fantastickal, mine would be simpler. You know my name, and you know I can be found here on Tuesdays and Thursdays. However, it is best for certain others to remain anonymous. Hence my precautions."

"Very well. Tonight?"

"No. Where do you lodge?"

"The Red Lyon Inn, Holborn."

"A good location for our purpose. Be there and prepared to go out any of the next seven evenings. You'll get no message afore time, so be ready. Won't be later than half after nine. There's folk as rise early."

"The sooner, the better, Barlicorn."

"If the lady agrees to your proposal, I can arrange proof of the marriage. That's where the greatest expense will come. I'll get documents for the marriage settlement, too, to protect the lady's interests." The rogue smiled satirically. "What, did you think there would be no need for a settlement merely because she will have no dowry? Too many women trust their future to men who are foolish or thriftless and leave them in poverty."

They did not speak of the meeting as they walked back to the inn. Miles turned the matter over in his mind while Peter studied the beating heart of London. Leadenhall Street to Cornhill to Poultry to Cheapside, then to Newgate Street, Snowhill, and finally Holborn, everything fascinated him.

"You really didn't spend much time here before you departed for Italy, I gather."

"No. I was more interested in landscapes and classical architecture, fool that I was. In the Low Countries and Italy, I discovered a kind of art we seldom see in England. Street scenes, peasant festivals, people working at their trades. Far more interesting than depictions of mythical themes, battles, and landscapes. I wonder how I can draw all this"—he made a sweeping gesture that missed striking a well-endowed market woman's bosom by inches—"without making a spectacle of myself. Or becoming prey for a pickpocket."

"Rent the use of an upstairs window for a few hours or a day. Someone will oblige you for a few pence or a shilling."

In their parlor at the inn, Peter took out his sketch book and crayon before saying, "I thought the Italians produced colorful rogues. I perceive London has at least one. What do you think of him?"

Miles took his time answering. That question had occupied his mind during their walk. "Simon Hayes, a reputable man of business, vouched for him. The fellow's not a common criminal. Someone important in that class."

"Originally gentry, is my guess." Peter's drawing took on life with a few swift strokes: Barlicorn's roguish grin, shabby but clean second-hand clothing. "Why do you think he did not appoint a set day for meeting with the woman?"

"He probably doesn't want to be followed to wherever we're going."

"You aren't concerned?"

"He wouldn't make much money by robbing us. Besides, apart from Hayes's recommendation, my instinct tells me Barlicorn is honorable. In his way," he qualified.

Chapter 22

Eustacia had been nervous and irritable all day. Now she stood up abruptly and looked around, face blank. Her mouth opened and closed, and a ribbon of spittle drooled from the corner of her lips. Then she fell to the floor, limbs jerking rhythmically. Julia sat frozen, as Verity, who was seated nearest Eustacia, gave a little cry and threw herself to her knees beside her, tugging the viscountess's petticoat down over her ankles. Julia sprang to her feet and stood, hesitating.

Lavinia said, "Julia, please tell the footman to summon Dr. Broxon as quickly as may be, then request the viscount and the earl attend us."

By the time Julia returned, with the men close behind her, Caroline was kneeling by her daughter-in-law's side. Eustacia's eyes were open and blinking.

"N-nothing wrong with me. Just, just giddy." But she was plainly disoriented.

The dowager countess said, "I think you should rest, Eustacia. Perhaps if she can be carried up to her bed?" The question was directed at Popejoy.

When Popejoy and Barding assisted her to stand, Eustacia herself admitted she felt weak and unwell. She refused to be carried but permitted them to lend their arms. Caroline followed.

Julia, left with Verity and Lavinia, did not feel she could say anything. Had a connection of hers suffered such an attack, she would not be fobbed off with a claim it was no more than a swoon. Verity sat folding and re-folding her handkerchief, a nervous habit Julia had seen before.

Lavinia sipped from her bowl of tea and set it down. "We will wait upon the doctor's opinion."

Before we panic, she means. Julia could not quite imagine Lavinia and Caroline actually panicking, but Eustacia's collapse was worrisome.

"Verity, will you pour out the tea?"

The girl served them more tea and seemed steadied by the task.

Caroline returned and said, "I have instructed her maid to stay with her tonight. Barding and Popejoy are awaiting Dr. Broxon in the library."

The air was thick with uncertainty. Finally, Caroline voiced a suggestion that Verity might wish to go to bed. Her niece took it in the spirit it was intended—as an order—and made her good nights. From the alacrity with which she went, Julia suspected she found it a relief.

"Perhaps I should also withdraw, my ladies."

Lavinia and Caroline traded glances. "We will not keep you if you wish to retire." Lavinia put a slight accent on the "wish." "However, we count you as one of the family and a sensible woman. My daughter-in-law and I mean to put our heads together, and three heads are better than two." Her smile was no more than a quirk of the lips. "Any insight or observations you have may be useful."

The footman whose station was the bedroom wing burst into the room, white-faced, and blurted, "Lady Popejoy's in a fit, and her maid's all to pieces."

"Inform their lordships. We will go up and see what's to be done." Lavinia rose and, as the footman bolted out in the direction of the library, remarked, "He's one of the newer servants. He has not yet had time to perfect the bland, unruffled manner. Come."

The convulsions had stopped by the time they reached Eustacia's chamber, but the maid was weeping hysterically. Caroline took her down to the housekeeper to be soothed or bullied into rationality.

"Julia, would you fetch clean sheets from the linen closet? I would rather not involve more servants than necessary. We must help Eustacia out of bed while we change her night-rail and the bed linen."

The task was accomplished, and Eustacia settled in bed again, still dazed. Caroline returned to report the maid was not yet calm enough to be questioned. Julia was dispatched to let the men know Eustacia's second attack had passed off. She found Popejoy loitering in the passage, hesitating to go into his wife's bedchamber but reluctant to leave. Julia suggested he enter; there was nothing now to cause a man to seek refuge in brandy and male company. The earl had retreated to his study.

The doctor came at last and was taken up to examine Eustacia. Caroline remained with the doctor and Eustacia; Julia and Lavinia went downstairs.

When the physician came down, he was escorted to the drawing room by Caroline and Popejoy, and the earl followed close on their heels, summoned by a footman.

"Dr. Broxon has some questions, Mother."

The doctor made a rather informal bow and, at Lavinia's invitation, sat down. He wasted no breath on greetings or inanities. "My ladies, I understand Lord

Barding and Lord Popejoy were not present at either of the occurrences. Lady Popejoy's maid was of little assistance. Would you describe what you observed?"

The earl poured him a glass of Madeira, which he accepted absentmindedly.

Lavinia spoke crisply. "Eustacia stood suddenly and fell to the floor. Her limbs moved in a repetitive manner. She was unconscious, but before we could try sal volatile, her eyes opened and she was aware of her surroundings."

"Do you all agree?"

Caroline nodded. Julia said hesitantly, "It seemed to me that her arms at least began to tremble before she collapsed. Before she rose, she set down her teacup abruptly. See, a little splashed into the saucer." In the confusion, her tea bowl and saucer had not been cleared away.

"Thank you, Mistress Perry. That observation may be of assistance. Did her body arch during the fit?"

It had not, they all agreed.

"Has she suffered a head injury in the last few months? Or anything resembling an apoplexy?"

Head shaking all around. "If she had, we would have called you in, Doctor," Barding stated.

The physician frowned and said, "I will be frank: diagnosis where no obvious physical injury exists can be difficult. The falling sickness begins in childhood, as a rule, though in one case I heard of it beginning in an elderly person who had survived an apoplexy, and in another, after a head injury. Though in the latter case, I believe he eventually ceased having the attacks. Lady Popejoy is sleeping now, and I do not apprehend any new occurrence tonight. In the morning I will have the apothecary send a bottle of Syrup of Stoechas, which is supposed to be helpful for all sorts of palsies, tremblings, convulsions, and the falling sickness. According to Culpeper's *Physical Directory*, it works upon all infirmities of the brain arising from the cold, wet, or melancholy humors." He paused. "I am not convinced of all we are told by the ancients. I hold astrology in abhorrence and doubt many of the claims about the four humors. However, there must be some particle of truth to them. 'Tis certainly true that the patient's habits of mind affect the outcome of his illness, and equally true that Lady Popejoy has cause for melancholy over her son's ailment. She should be coaxed to take a more cheerful view of Master George's condition, if possible."

"Under the circumstances," Popejoy began, and stopped.

"Just so. Well, there's naught more to be done tonight. I'll return in the morning to see how she fares. She was not able to answer my questions tonight." With a nod and another brief bow to the company, Dr. Broxon took up his medical case and strode out.

"Something of an eccentric, but a very good doctor," Lavinia remarked.

Julia, suppressing a yawn, was glad to go up to her chamber.

Chapter 23

The days felt like the Roman church's purgatory. On the third evening after they finished supper, Halliwell gave up trying to write notes on a client problem he and Bryden had discussed earlier in the day. Thank God, there was only the one matter that was out of the ordinary, and his assistant could deal with it once Halliwell had given his instructions. Tonight, he could not concentrate; he would write them out in the morning and have them delivered. Peter was reading back issues of *The Gentleman's Magazine*, the inn possessing several years' worth. He had spoken only once in the last two hours, to say, "I missed these when I was in Italy."

Miles stared at the opposite wall. At intervals he rose and twitched the curtain aside to watch for a hackney coach. If he could not find a suitable female to marry Peter, poor Julia might be coaxed to sacrifice herself again. He would advise her against it. Somehow he had to make things right for her, and Peter, and the Bardings.

He jumped like a startled cat when an inn servant tapped at the door.

"There's a footman asking for you, sir. Says your coach is waiting."

Peter tossed Miles his tricorne and snatched up his own. "We'll go down."

Outside stood a well-kept carriage, the horses sleek and the coachman and footman in respectable livery.

When the footman opened the door and set down the step, Peter fairly vaulted in, followed more sedately by Halliwell. The windows were curtained, but by his voice, Miles knew the man sitting with his back to the horses was Barlicorn.

"Please put these bags over your heads, gentlemen. They're less likely to slip than a blindfold. No need for you to know where we go."

They complied, bound for an unknown destination in company with a man who had at least one foot in the criminal world, if not both. Still, Hayes knew and vouched for him. The coach jerked into motion, headed west. A few minutes later, they turned, this time to the south. After the fifth or sixth turn, Miles lost his bearings.

When the team pulled up and the door opened, his nose told him they were not in a good section of town. In warm weather, all parts of London smelled to some degree, if only of coal smoke and horse droppings. Several more layers of olfactory offense were evident here, including infrequently dredged bog-houses and a pungent reek from some workshop.

He felt his way through the door and down to the ground. Barlicorn took his elbow. "Three steps forward. Now there's a step up." He knocked, and Halliwell heard the door open, releasing an odor of fried onions, small beer, and mutton. Behind him, the footman was guiding Peter. Once inside, the door closed—a stout one by the sound—and a bar dropped into place to secure it. Judging by faint stirrings and two voices speaking quietly at a distance, people were present in the room. From the smells and the warmth, it was a kitchen.

Another door opened. "Come." They were led through it, into a room that felt smaller and smelled of cured meat and cheese and herbs.

"The young lady will enter, and we will be private. It's the pantry, and the walls are thick. The one window is closed and shuttered. There's a chair behind each of you. Sit, and I'll bring her in."

They heard the same soft voices, nearer this time, then a rustling of clothing and a light footstep, and someone brushed past. From the sounds, that someone sat in another chair. A man followed. They heard the door close.

"May we remove the bags?" Peter inquired.

"Do both of you swear as gentlemen you'll put them on at the end of your appointment here?"

"Ay," Halliwell said. Peter's agreement came a second later.

"Remove them."

Halliwell pulled off the pillow cover swathing his head and found the pantry illuminated by a pair of candlesticks. Barlicorn lounged against the pantry shelves, arms crossed on his chest.

Peter gazed at the young woman sitting opposite them. Turning his own attention to her, Miles saw a female a few years too old to be called a girl, her features regular, her hair the color of barley-sugar candy, midway between yellow and brown. She was dressed neatly in the sort of dark gown a maid might wear.

"I am told you may have respectable work for me." Her voice gave the first clue that her origins might qualify her for their purpose.

"It is not work in the ordinary sense. I don't know how much Barlicorn told you about it." Miles had warned Peter to let him question the woman.

"He said a gentleman was in need of a wife, but that you would explain in detail if I suited your requirements."

"Good. Then before I tell you what it is, will you tell me something about yourself and your reasons for being willing to consider such an unusual offer? It may be that something you tell me would disqualify you as my client's needs are very specific."

"Very well. My name is Rachel; my father is a squire of good reputation in our county. By your leave I will not give my surname or my family's home unless it proves necessary."

"That's adequate for now." Halliwell did not need to know it. Not yet.

She had been walking back from the village one afternoon when she met a young gentleman riding. He dismounted, claiming he needed directions, and accosted her. She fought him off and ran home weeping, her bodice torn. Her father had bellowed and visited the nearest manor, where a number of profligate young men were known to be staying in the absence of their host's parents. They swore they had spent the day together. None of them matched her description.

Her father assured her he believed her and thought the boys, most of them still at university, were lying. He meant to report it to a neighboring magistrate. Rachel's mother forbade it. The manor belonged to a viscount, and they must not incense him. The incident was all Rachel's own fault, Mama claimed, for dressing like some yeoman's daughter and for going to the village without an escort. Though, a chaperon had never been thought necessary before.

Once word got around, she would be ruined and the younger children would be harmed by the scandal. "I must do what I can to save you," Mama had said, and her father reluctantly yielded to her reasoning.

"My mother's great-aunt, Lady Helen, needed a companion. She was old and said to be wandering a little in her wits."

As it happened, Lady Helen was pleasant, not in the least confused, and happy to have Rachel with her. She expressed her opinion of Rachel's mother in terms direct from the free-spoken court of Charles II. They did not go about in society; Lady Helen walked with a cane and no longer enjoyed going out, except occasionally to the homes of elderly friends. Their amusements were limited to cards, gossip, tea or wine, and sometimes music if someone played the harpsichord.

"I was not unhappy. I did not see much of London because there was none to escort me, and Lady Helen considered it unsafe for me to go out without a gentleman as well as a maid. From what I did see of the town, she may have been correct. Her library was well stocked, and I had time to read, which Mama had not liked me to do. Lady Helen's friends were often very amusing, even if they were elderly, and she took an interest in two or three charitable activities. Though not," the girl said, "of the knitting-stockings-for-the-poor variety. She gave money to a little free school which taught poor boys to read and cipher."

Then Lady Helen died of lung fever following a

bout of influenza. Her great-nephew was her heir. "I will call him Roland Smith," Rachel said, amusement in her voice, "because it is not his name."

"A mortal lot o' Smiths about," Barlicorn muttered sardonically.

Smith's only visit to the house, the day after Lady Helen's death, convinced Rachel she could not stay. Before she had his measure, she asked Smith to advance coach fare, to be repaid by her father. She could not return home permanently, but her father would surely let her stay long enough to make other arrangements.

"Not likely. You'd not have been sent to nursemaid the old cat if they wanted you. I mean to lease out this barn, but I'll want a housekeeper in my rooms."

His expression reminded her of the libertine who had tried to force her. "I don't doubt he would have done so then, except that there were still servants in the house."

Smith dismissed most of them that same day. Rachel feared to remain longer. She could write her father once she had found lodgings. She possessed almost a pound from her last quarter's wages. But what she had would not support her until she heard from her father or could find another position of some sort. Lady Helen had been ill since a few days before the new quarter day, and so had been unable to pay Rachel.

"I knew where Lady Helen kept her money, as she sometimes sent me out to buy embroidery silks or some other trifle."

She stole five pounds. Having been Lady Helen's companion for near two years, Rachel knew where her benefactor's pin money from her quarterly income was kept. Rachel herself had sometimes tucked it away for the old lady. In spite of the small purchases, occasional gifts to servants and charities, Lady Helen never spent it all. The sum now amounted to almost fifteen pounds. At every quarter day, adding the current payment to the bandbox in which she kept the letters from her late husband, Lady Helen would say, "I really should donate some of these riches. But then, if Becky gives notice and marries her journeyman carpenter, I shall give her five pounds for a wedding gift. Well, we will let it go another quarter." Lady Helen would not have begrudged Rachel the means to escape her great-nephew.

"I had written Papa and Mama the day Lady Helen died, then wrote again the following day, to let them know I had found a room in a decent house some distance away, and my reason for doing so. I commenced to search for employment." A month passed with no reply, which worried her somewhat, but in spite of the claims of the General Post Office, mail to and from the country could be slow, and sometimes post boys were robbed. She wrote a third and then a fourth time. When another month went by, with neither answer from the squire nor offers of work, Rachel realized she must do something before her little store of money was gone. Her father might not have received her letters or he might have cast her off completely at her mother's insistence.

She paused in her story to collect herself. There were worse things than growing up a by-blow in a kind if not affectionate family, Miles considered.

"I am sorry to say it, but Mama and I never got on well. I don't know why."

Before he could speak, Peter took advantage of the silence following this statement. "Mistress Rachel, may I ask when you left Lady Helen's home?"

"Near the end of December, almost two and a half years ago. I lived in lodgings for a little over two months. I found employment here before Lady Day in March 1738."

A spark of hope ignited in Miles's chest. He glanced at Peter, who was staring intently at Rachel. His right hand lay on his thigh, making slight, abortive movements. Miles knew the signs: Peter wished to hold a pencil or crayon and draw.

"I could not get a position as either a companion or housekeeper because I had no reference from a previous employer." She could have asked the Reverend Mr. Roke of St. Anne's for a letter testifying to her good character and her post as Lady Helen's companion. She discarded the idea, fearing she might be found by Smith. Cautioning Mr. Roke against revealing her direction to him would not guarantee he would keep silent. The parson would never have divulged her address to some scurvy-looking fellow, but he would suppose Lady Helen's connection to be a gentleman and obligated to assist Rachel. He believed that families should care for their own and would ignore her fears about Smith, assuming her to have misinterpreted his words. He would almost certainly inform Smith if the question ever arose.

She admitted her fear was founded in part by her guilt over having appropriated that five pounds. "Which was foolish of me," she said with a twisted smile. "Smith can't have known about Lady Helen's little horde of coin. None of the servants did, since her maid died. She never bothered to hire another, as I could do whatever she needed."

The landlady of the lodging house came upon her weeping after a cit's wife refused her work as an attendant for the woman's aged mother. She had not hesitated to call Rachel a pert hussy who would plunder her charge's belongings for anything she could sell. The landlady, a placid and kindly widow, extracted the whole tale from Rachel, who held back nothing but the theft.

"There's few men as has power over a woman that won't take advantage," she said flatly. She'd seen it too often, though she'd never let either of her husbands get the upper hand. She agreed that without a reference, finding work would be all but impossible.

Frowning into her tea bowl as they sat at the kitchen table, Mistress Lefever said, "I knew a similar case. She went to live with her married sister when her mother died. Her brother-in-law was not a good man, and my friend decided the girl should go into service." The woman snorted. "Try finding a place without no character! Well, you know how it is. Then one day she came to me to say her little sister had got a position in a decent household, all thanks to a reference written for her by a man who makes a little business of it. It cost a couple of shillings and was well worth the money, she said."

"When I asked her if it was truly a decent household and not something worse, she patted my hand and said, 'I know what you mean to say, Rachel. No, I visited it myself and spoke with the cook. It's the home of a City man, and my friend's girl is still there. She works in the kitchen and has no complaint. Before you ask, I know how to contact the man who writes characters.' "

Rachel had had to meet the man herself, for he preferred to know for whom he was working. The thought of meeting a criminal terrified her, but Mistress Lefever accompanied her to a shabby church in a dismal street, where a curate smiled at them and pointed out a man in a pew near the front. Her landlady sat in the last row, far enough not to hear their conversation and the curate retired to the vestry.

"I spilled out the entire story, including the theft. It was a relief to tell it; this must be why confession is said to be good for the soul. I was afraid Smith would find me if I took work as a companion in London. What else could I be, after all? I had no experience to qualify me even to be a scullery maid. I needed a place where I would be out of sight of anyone from my earlier life."

Barlicorn was willing to provide a reference but suggested a place where she might apply. The curate was one of its trustees, as was a man of business whose direction he would supply. It need not be a permanent position, but if she stayed for a time, she would have two references, and would be able to move on to some better neighborhood. She had now been employed here for over two years.

"So I am not unfamiliar with peculiar opportunities, sir." Her smile was tinged with sadness.

"Do you like children?"

"I do. My employment brings me much into contact with them."

Halliwell did not miss the warmth in her voice, which boded well for what they would ask of her, if Peter agreed. Given her circumstances, her theft of the money suggested common sense and a willingness to lie if necessary. As it would be! He glanced at Peter, raising his eyebrows interrogatively.

"May I ask you a few more questions?" Peter asked.

"Certainly."

His half brother's probing brought out things Halliwell would never have thought of, and did it without seeming rude or prying, even without questions sometimes. She enjoyed country life. She had never gone into society beyond that found near her family's home, meaning people she had known since her childhood, except for the old lady's limited circle of friends. She did not think she would be shy among strangers, as she had not felt ill at ease either on moving to Lady Helen's home or when she was hired for her current post. She spoke French and could sing but did not play an instrument. One of Peter's stories, casually introduced, made her laugh with real enjoyment.

"I wish I might hear more of your foreign travels, for I envy you the sights you have seen." She sighed.

"Would you object to accepting a child as your own? Posing as the child's mother, I mean?"

"I hope I would treat a stepchild as if I had given birth to him."

"This would entail claiming the child was actually your own," Halliwell interposed, in case she had not understood.

She gave a wry little chuckle. "I could be hanged for stealing those five pounds. The penalty for perjury cannot be greater."

Peter said, "I think I would like to talk longer with Mistress Rachel, Barlicorn."

The archrogue frowned. "Not unchaperoned."

"No," Halliwell agreed. "Perhaps they might walk somewhere with the chaperon at a little distance?" The question would be, where? They should avoid places where they might meet someone who would recognize Peter.

"I will want my own people present."

So Peter and he could not steal Rachel away for their own nefarious purposes, without paying Barlicorn? Or out of an abundance of concern for Rachel's safety?

"The lady will be perfectly safe with me."

Miles had never heard his youngest half brother speak in such a hard voice; he had taken offense.

"A reasonable precaution," Miles said. "I will be present as well."

The watch had called "Twelve o' the night, and a fine, clear one," before the coach pulled up before the inn and Barlicorn bade them goodnight. They went upstairs in silence. As they shed their hats and coats, Halliwell said, "I thought we agreed you would leave the talking to me."

"We did. I suppose I grew used to acting on my own in the last seven years. I apologize."

"No need. I forgot you'd grown up. 'Twas a good thing you joined in with your questions. She spoke with you more easily than with me."

"Miles, I told Grandmother I would seek the family's agreement to my choice of bride. How am I to do that? I scarcely think we can take Rachel home to be approved, and the idea of bringing any of them here to meet her…"

Picturing either of the Barding ladies in the pantry

with Rachel, Barlicorn, Peter, and himself, Halliwell barked a laugh. "Preserve us! Though I think Lavinia and John Barlicorn would get along. Very practical people, both of them. When we decided to attempt this solution, Lavinia at least foresaw the problem. She told me they will accept my judgment as to your bride's suitability."

Chapter 24

The following morning, Eustacia suffered another convulsion. Dr. Broxon was sent for; fortunately, he was at home and already preparing to set out. Julia was with Caroline when he entered the hall. Caroline said, "The convulsion has ended but   "

They all heard a maid cry out, "Her ladyship's fitting again." The doctor took the stairs two at a time, calling to the footman to bring up his medical case.

The day's activities were suspended while the family waited on word of the viscountess's condition. Dinner went largely uneaten. The dining room had long been cleared and the housekeeper had timidly inquired of the countess what she wished them to do about supper, when the doctor entered the drawing room and stopped a pace inside the door. On his earlier visits, Julia had liked his pleasant manner. In her experience, physicians were often rather pompous and stood firmly upon their dignity. No one demanded to know how Eustacia fared; the doctor's gray, strained face was answer enough.

"I'm sorry."

The viscount made a sound in his throat and looked down, blinking.

Barding went to the console table and poured two glasses of brandy. He passed one to the doctor and the other to Popejoy.

"I'm no medico, as they say in Italy, but I prescribe a restorative. Sit down, Broxon."

"Was it the falling sickness?"

Dr. Broxon swallowed and then breathed out gustily. He met Lavinia's eyes. "My lady, I cannot say. I have observed cases of epilepsy. The falling sickness, as 'tis commonly called. We have little understanding of its cause, though Hippocrates believed it was a disorder of the brain. Some think it contagious, but while it may occur in family members, I have not known it to spread to servants or unrelated persons, even if they live together.

"Lady Popejoy exhibited various symptoms I have not seen or heard of before. While she was still conscious, she complained of muscle cramps. She vomited several times, and her heart rate was tumultuous. She became agitated and belligerent, making it difficult to examine her. I gave her a dose of laudanum to calm her. I resorted to bleeding, a procedure I seldom use, but it seemed called for, if indeed it is a brain ailment, as apoplexy is. She suffered more convulsions and became lethargic. I did everything I could think of. Nothing was of any assistance. She did not regain consciousness before the end came. I have never seen anything like it, and hope I never see it again." He drank off the remaining brandy.

"Is her maid with her yet? We should prepare the body."

"The maid is indeed there. But if you would delay for a few minutes, Lady Barding? Both Lady Bardings and my lords? I would like to ask a few questions about Lady Popejoy's health and behavior. There may be some indication as to what caused her death. Until the last time you called me in, I do not think I had seen her as a patient above four times. My impression was that she was strong and vigorous. What signs have you seen that her health was in decline?"

"Certainly she used to be in good health," Caroline said slowly. "But it seems to me that began to change some time ago. I am sorry to say, I cannot recall when. It was not a sudden alteration."

Lavinia's gaze turned inward. "Her appetite declined, but she had already mentioned some minor complaints. I encouraged her to eat more, but she told me her stomach was uneasy. I had hoped…but we decided it was no more than worry over Georgie's health."

Popejoy emerged from his private reflections. "We have all been concerned, but she was distracted with fear for him. Understandably so. She did not sleep well and was troubled by nightmares recently." He turned red, realizing he had revealed he had been in his wife's bed and observed the nightmares.

Men could be utterly ridiculous, Julia reflected. Now, if they had not been man and wife, his presence in her bed would be something to blush for.

"Did she describe them to you, sir? Sometimes one's worries are expressed in one's dreams, and they may shed some light on one's health as well."

"No. She did not speak of them."

"Ah, well. Which brings me to another question, Lord Popejoy. Your wife's maid mentioned she was taking a tonic of some sort. I would like to know what it was, and for what purpose she was taking it. The maid showed me the cabinet in which it is kept, but 'tis locked, and she does not know where the key is. Do you have it? Or a spare key?"

Popejoy's puzzled expression left no doubt he knew nothing of it. "Cabinet?"

"A Chinese cabinet with painted scenes upon it."

"Oh, that. I assumed she kept fripperies in it. Is it important?"

"It may be, as I cannot account for Lady Popejoy's death. Some of her symptoms are suggestive, but I should like to be able to correct any misapprehensions that might arise."

No one else understood this statement either, Julia saw.

"I think you must speak plainly," Barding said. "What misapprehensions?"

The physician frowned. "Believe me, my lord, I would not raise this issue if it could be avoided. However, in the event a magistrate should inquire about your daughter-in-law's cause of death, I would like to be able to testify I have reason to believe it natural."

Lavinia was the first to speak. "You mean someone might claim it was not a natural death?"

"Magistrate?" Popejoy stared at him with the same stunned expression Julia had once seen when her half brother regained consciousness after falling down several steps.

"People will talk when there is a sudden, unexpected death. As Lady Popejoy did not consult me about any ailment which might have caused death or indeed, about any symptom or illness, I can't in good conscience say I can account for it." He studied their appalled faces for a moment. "Her maid told me Lady Popejoy made the tonic she took for her stomach. Was she in the habit of gathering wild herbs?"

As most of the group shrugged or shook their heads mutely, Verity spoke. "She did occasionally, though not often. The physic garden is supplied with almost everything one could require, if it grows in England. The last time I can call to mind that she went out to harvest a wild plant was in the fall, when we rode out together to pick juniper berries. She told me they are good for a number of things, including coughs and looseness, which is very common." She blushed.

"It is, indeed. Did she or anyone else gather greens or vegetables outside the garden? Or purchase any, perhaps?"

Lavinia answered for all. "I am sure they did not. Our kitchen garden supplies our needs. Why?"

"It occurred to me that several of the signs I observed were what one would expect in hemlock poisoning. It is easy to mistake for parsley. Some wild plants are held to have greater medicinal powers than the commonly grown sort. I suppose she might have believed the same true of parsley and mistaken one for the other."

"She was very knowledgeable about herbs," Lavinia said. "However, I am not familiar with the appearance of hemlock. Is it very similar to parsley?"

"It would be very easily mistaken for parsley if one did not know the appearance of hemlock. I would like to know what tonic she was taking, to see if it contained parsley or any other simple which has an evil impostor."

"Then we had best open the cabinet, even if we must force the lock." The earl's voice was grim. Popejoy nodded.

The dowager countess added, "It should be in the

presence of all of us as witnesses."

Neither Julia nor Verity had meant to join the group, but Lavinia and the doctor insisted on their attendance as potentially less biased witnesses.

They contemplated the sheet-covered form on the bed. After her first glance, Julia turned her attention to the chamber. It was much as she would have expected: over-elaborate furnishings and too many knick-knacks.

The earl's gaze moved to the corner, where the maid stood sniffling into a sodden handkerchief. "Alice, we would like some food. Cheese, bread and butter, cold meat, biscuits, whatever the kitchen maid can manage easily. Bring it to, ah…"

"The ladies' parlor," Lavinia said. "A very good idea, Barding. We will all be better able to think and do whatever must be done after we have something to eat. We will want tea also."

"A good idea, indeed, my lord," the doctor said after the maid was gone. Did he mean sending the servant away and thus eliminating a witness who might gossip? What did he expect to find in the cabinet?

Popejoy made a quick search of places the maid thought her mistress might have hidden the key, without success: her little writing desk, her sewing box and jewelry case and the like. Finally, the lacquered double doors were pried open. Lined up two deep were bottles, each with a carefully written label.

The doctor picked up the first on the left, and read aloud, " 'Strengthens the womb and does all the good a woman can desire.' Hmmm." He pulled out the stopper and sniffed, then passed the bottle to the viscount, who was standing at his shoulder.

"Faugh. Disgusting."

They went through, bottle by bottle.

"Mother-wort. 'Makes women joyful mothers of children and settles the womb.' Some of these bottles contain remedies for bad digestion or sleeplessness, but most have to do with conception. Did any of you know she was dosing herself with so many things? If she was? Or mayhap she tried one, did not find it efficacious and stopped taking it before trying another?"

Caroline said, "I knew she was taking something for her stomach. It seemed not to do much good. When she needed something to help her sleep, I believe she took syrup of purslane."

He stood frowning and chewing his lip. "The labels are not an apothecary's."

"No, they're in Eustacia's hand," Popejoy agreed.

"Where did she get all these medicines?"

Popejoy shrugged.

"Why, she made them."

From the faces around her, Verity's words were a surprise to everyone but Julia.

"I know she makes, made, delightful lotions for the face and hands and scented soaps. I taught her what I know, and she surpassed me in those things," Lavinia murmured. "Of course, she also made the common remedies for coughs, aches, and chills, as any good housewife would do."

"She spends—has been spending—part of the day in the stillroom," Caroline's niece added timidly. She did not like being the focus of all eyes.

"How could we not be aware of this? I don't doubt you, Verity, but…" But Caroline's doubt was plain in her voice.

Julia's hesitant "Ummm" fell into the silence. "Since my arrival, I have often walked in the gardens behind the house. They're not as elegant as the formal garden, but I find them more interesting for the variety of colors and scents. It's more convenient to visit them by way of the door from the kitchen passage."

"The stillroom is located in that hall." Lavinia interpolated for the benefit of the doctor.

"I often saw Lady Popejoy working there."

"It was her especial interest," Verity said. "Though she only began devoting so much time to it quite recently. Within the last few months, I think. Since we have been in mourning, certainly."

Popejoy asked, "How could we not be aware of it?"

Disconcerted for once, Lavinia answered, "Between us, Caroline and I supervise the upper servants and household, review the housekeeper's and butler's accounts for this house and those of the other properties, and see to the welfare of the tenants and laborers. They were not things Eustacia enjoyed." She sounded almost defensive. She did not speak of her study of investment documents, but Julia had seen her reading them. Perhaps even Lavinia hesitated to speak of her financial dealings.

"Eustacia had no turn for adding and subtracting. She did not know the servants and the tenants as well as Lavinia and I do, and she was…" Caroline paused to consider. "…awkward with them."

Apologetically, from the viscount: "She had no experience with tenants or a large household until we married."

Julia's earlier feeling that Eustacia did not fit into

the family was confirmed. She herself had seen how the viscountess raised the servants' hackles.

"Then I must ask to examine the stillroom. I cannot tell from her labels what most of these bottles contain. If one did include wild parsley, there is at least the possibility she picked hemlock by mistake."

Did anyone else think the doctor's "at least" signified some anxiety about the cause of death? Perhaps, as no one asked if it could wait until morning. They all sensed the urgency in the doctor's words.

They brought two candle stands with them, Dr. Broxon having said he would need a good light. However, they found the work table provided with a pair of handsome bronze oil lamps.

"Even better," he said. "A good, strong light. Very sensible."

Verity, who had gone to instruct the maid to bring the tea and food to the stillroom, returned in time to hear the doctor's comment. "She only used them on overcast days, or I suppose in the winter if she was working here in the late afternoon." Lamps were a luxury, with whale oil so expensive. Still, if one needed a bright light, there was nothing better except daylight. No doubt the estate could bear the cost.

The shelves held an array of apothecaries' jars, the names of the contents in blue, surrounded by ornate borders in blue and gold. Plain crocks, tightly lidded, bore labels pasted on. Large bottles held medicinal cordials and oils. The doctor smelled each one. He frowned at one labeled "Oil of Wormwood." Another, "Compound water of wormwood, the greater," was nearly empty. A shelf of smaller bottles and jars held the sort of remedies any prudent lady might keep to hand for ordinary ailments and injuries.

"Lady Popejoy had a very extensive pharmaceutical collection." He turned his attention to a bookshelf.

Lavinia came forward to stand beside him and reached out to touch the worn spine of a small leather-bound volume. "This contains treatments and remedies written down by Barding's great-grandmother who had copied many of them from her mother. Barding's grandmother added to them. His mother died too young to contribute much to the collection. I wrote some notes and suggestions in it, too, before I gave the physic garden and stillroom into Eustacia's charge. The garden had come to be too much for me, and she took pleasure in it." She opened the book and leafed through it. "She has added some of her own observations and receipts, but my eyes are not good enough to read them. That was one of the reasons I gave up making the household's medicines."

"Culpeper's herbal. Culpeper's *English Physician*. Culpeper's *Physical Directory*." Many slips of paper and a folded sheet stuck out of the latter. Dr. Broxon removed the *Directory* and opened it on the work table. Unfolded, the paper listed remedies with notes by each. The doctor set it aside and opened the book to the first place marker, then to the second. "May I borrow this?" he asked. "I would like to see what pages Lady Popejoy consulted, and it would be easier when my own eyes are rested."

Pressed by the earl and Lavinia, after they had taken their hasty, informal meal (during which Dr. Broxon examined the stillroom's tools and utensils while eating), the doctor was invited to sleep in a guest room for what remained of the night. No one rose before midmorning, and even then, Julia doubted anyone had rested easily. The breakfast table was silent, and the doctor was abstracted and drank several cups of coffee without saying a word. At length Barding asked if he had come to any conclusion about Eustacia's death. His reply was that he had still to review her notes and compare them to the pages she had marked. After he took his leave of them, a meaningful look passed around the table and Barding, Popejoy, and the Barding ladies retired to the library as if with one mind.

When they emerged, a groom was dispatched to London with a letter.

Chapter 25

The visit to Chelsea in Barlicorn's coach went well. Two men dressed as footmen attended them, one on the box with the driver, the other standing on the perch at the back. Rachel was accompanied by a maid with a scarred face. Conversation inside was limited to the weather and the sights along the way. Once they reached their destination, however, Peter and Rachel walked together among the chestnut and lime trees in the grounds of the Chelsea College. The footmen lounged at a distance, while Halliwell and the maid followed out of earshot. The couple's conversation appeared to be lively. Once the breeze carried a peal of laughter to Halliwell's ears.

When they turned back, Peter said, "Rachel and I are agreed we will suit." The words were formal; his grin at the lady was not.

"We will." She smiled back at him.

"Have you explained the, er, situation in more detail, Peter?"

"Rachel knows I need a wife because of the succession."

"You did mention at our first meeting I would have to claim a child as my own."

"Ay. You would be claiming the—the love child of one of Peter's brothers who is now dead. Our intention is to make it appear you and Peter were secretly married before the birth so the child would be legitimate. Can you accept such a pretense?"

"Peter has told me his mother is exceedingly unhappy his brother had no legitimate son. I should be shocked at the idea of passing off a bastard as legitimate, but is it really worse than the noble families in which the wife's child from an adulterous affair inherits a name and title to which he has no real right? Under the circumstances, I am willing to lend myself to your plan." She added, "It's not much worse than lying about the little boy being my own. As we seem to be in agreement, we can meet Barlicorn at once. If that suits you, sirs?"

Barlicorn had done better than Miles expected. This young woman would do very well indeed.

They found Barlicorn at Simon Hayes's office, where a clerk showed them to a room set aside for meetings with clients. Hayes himself was out. Further explanations proved to be necessary. Both Rachel and Barlicorn had questions about how the marriage could have taken place. The archrogue suggested Rachel had fled Lady Helen's house straight to the arms of her suitor. The timing worked for the child's conception as well as for Peter's theoretical presence in England.

They moved on to arrangements. They would need settlement documents drawn up to assure Rachel would receive an income if Peter died. Halliwell would draw them up.

"What of the certificate and entries in a parish register?" That appeared to be the remaining problem.

"I know the very parson to have conducted a Fleet ceremony." Barlicorn's speech had altered out of recognition in the well-furnished meeting room. He was also dressed in good but plain clothing.

"How much of a bribe will he require, Barlicorn?"

"It won't be a bribe; he's old and forgetful and no longer performs weddings. His sister needs money to support him and won't know or care why I'm providing it. He won't have to do anything. I can get hold of his register long enough to add the entry. The forger will sign the parson's name on the certificate and date it. The bride and groom will fill in their names. The reverend has long suffered from arthritis, so a number of his later certificates and register entries are in others' hands except for his signature. The forger is trustworthy, but there's no need for him to know who the certificate is for. Do I need to provide witnesses?"

"I'll sign." One more crime added to the rest could hardly count, Miles reflected. If only George, Viscount Popejoy, could have another son. Better yet, several, so there would be no danger of Jeremy ending as the heir. That was the thing that most offended him about the whole irregular proceeding.

"William can be the second witness. My brother," Peter explained. "He's dead, but I'm sure we have a sample of his signature."

"I do," Halliwell agreed.

Rachel bit her lip. "It will not be a valid marriage. If it were called into question and disproved, I suspect the settlement would be overturned, too. What would become of me then?"

Rachel had foreseen the problem neither he nor Peter had thought of. Ay, she would fit into the Stretton family like a key into a lock.

Apparently Barlicorn had. "There will be a true marriage to protect Rachel's interests."

"I'll tell you how to apply for a special license, Peter. You and Rachel will marry before we return to the manor. Rachel is correct that she must be protected before she leaves her current position." His caution in not naming Charfield was wasted. He recalled Barlicorn saying he could discover Peter's name if he wished to know it. He would need to know it in any case to make the entry in the register. "A Fleet marriage might suffice for two young lovers, but now that they are older and wiser, they will naturally wish to make their union regular. Your mother will have to be content with a quiet celebration in honor of your bride, given the circumstances." That would wrap things up neatly.

Peter said, "Need our marriage be so hole-and-corner? Would a few guests not make it more like a real wedding?"

"It will be a real wedding," Halliwell and Barlicorn replied almost in one voice.

Barlicorn grinned before continuing, "A young lady does like her wedding to be solemnized with some ceremony. Having guests of the right sort would make it more believable."

"We could not invite anyone who knows the family," Halliwell objected.

"I wasn't thinking of them," Peter interpolated.

"By the 'right sort,' I meant respectable people who would not disbelieve you had married secretly several years ago." That was Barlicorn.

"Can you supply some, Barlicorn?" Miles asked without enthusiasm.

"As it happens, I can," Peter replied. "Friends from artistic circles who are not sticklers for social customs and have never met any of my family. If they do in the future, all they will be able to say is that Rachel and I wanted to renew our vows more formally as our original hasty marriage was celebrated under the Rules of the Fleet." He added, "Because Rachel had to flee the old lady's heir and I was to return to Italy almost immediately, we had no time for a more traditional wedding."

"That and the artistic disregard for propriety would explain it," Halliwell agreed.

"Artistic be d—hanged," Peter retorted. "Under the circumstances it was, that is, would have been, the most sensible way of preserving my beloved's reputation."

Peter had entered into the spirit of the thing wholeheartedly. Rachel had, also, judging from her approving gaze.

"She will need appropriate clothing. Not new, and not too rich. I will see to its purchase." To Rachel, Barlicorn said, "Easier to keep it quiet if I manage it— at your expense, of course, gentlemen. We won't send you to your husband's family looking like a serving maid in her Sunday best."

"A maid, too," Peter said. "I'm sure my mother would expect her to arrive with a maid. Or I suppose one could be hired once we're home."

Ordinarily Miles would agree that a maid should be hired from among Charfield's tenants or relatives of the Barding servants. "A local girl might gossip if Mistress Rachel makes some trifling mistake in her presence."

"Susan, who accompanied me today, is trustworthy. She has been working with the orphans but was accustomed to serving ladies before she was scarred in a fire. She cannot get a post as a maid now for that reason. If you've no objection, Peter?"

"None." Peter kissed her hand, which made her peep up at him from under her eyelashes.

"When will all be ready?"

Barlicorn thought. "Two days for Rachel's wardrobe, to allow for alterations, mayhap three to arrange for the documents. Four days in all, most likely."

"Getting the license should be possible within two days, and the inn can supply a wedding breakfast for your guests, Peter, as soon as you know how many. Swear them to secrecy, however."

"I'll tell them I don't want it getting back to the family before the deed is done. Parental disapproval, you know."

****

The several days before the wedding required more effort than expected: arranging for a parson and for the wedding breakfast, reserving a room for Rachel and her maid to share the night before the wedding, ordering a coach to take them to Charfield. He also dispatched a groom from the Barding town house to reserve rooms and a private parlor at a good posting inn where they could break their journey. There were the settlement documents to execute, and Peter had to make a will.

The day before the ceremony, Peter discovered he had not thought of getting a wedding ring, and that he must get money from his bank for it and for the journey. And a gift for his bride apart from the ring; what would she like? A necklace, yes, but not a necklace such as you would see at any gathering of beau monde ladies. The earldom had a fine collection of those, some of which she would be able to borrow. It must be different. Miles went to buy his own wedding gift for the couple, while Peter, unexpectedly flustered for a man of calm temperament, went to the bank and a jeweler one of his friends had mentioned, who might have something of interest.

Halliwell doubted he had spent fifteen minutes choosing decanters and tumblers for George and William. For Peter and Rachel, he wanted a more personal gift. After considerable thought, he purchased a handsome mahogany tea caddy with silver mountings and three kinds of tea to fill the caddy's compartments. The couple would need a tea caddy no matter where they lived.

Halliwell consulted his pocket watch. It was now too late to visit his office if he were to be at the inn before the bride arrived. He had tried to see Bryden every day but had now missed two days. No matter. If anything urgent had come in, Bryden would have sent it to him by their messenger. Tomorrow, after the wedding, would be soon enough.

He found Peter already drinking tea in their private parlor at the inn. He greeted Miles with a cheerful nod, saying, "I had forgotten how much I enjoy tea. Italian wines are all very well, but there's nothing like tea for comfort." He displayed the necklace he had chosen: a choker of silver stars set with crystals, supporting pendants of opaline glass depicting the phases of the moon. "Its artistic merit is greater than its intrinsic value, but it seemed appropriate. I've commissioned matching earrings. The jeweler didn't expect ever to sell the necklace. He made it as a display piece."

"No other lady will have one like it, and no one who sees it will forget it," Miles agreed. The ring, a simple ruby, was appropriately understated.

Rachel and her maid arrived at the inn in time for supper, with two trunks and a bandbox containing Rachel's wardrobe and a valise for the maid. Mistress Rachel soon joined the men in the private parlor.

"Barlicorn did better than I could have done. I don't know how he knew what clothing would be suitable for a gentlewoman without much money. None of it is new, except one night-rail." She turned rose pink. "He even included a few pieces of jewelry, just a cameo and a pretty enameled bracelet, and a kerchief pin. And Susan has three neat, plain gowns and several aprons and caps."

Miles hoped the trinkets had been purchased rather than stolen. Presumably the rogue would at least have taken care they could not be identified by a previous owner.

He had also provided a folded, slightly crumpled certificate of marriage. It had already been signed by Rachel, with forged signatures for the parson and William Stretton as witness. Miles and Peter signed at the inn. Once the ink was dry, Rachel refolded it and tucked it into her sewing box.

****

Lord Popejoy had drunk himself into oblivion the night following the inquest and was now suffering cruelly from a throbbing head and a very uneasy stomach. His valet was plying him with restoratives and responded blandly when questioned, that "Lord Popejoy, having been up very late, means to keep to his chamber until the day is more advanced." His true condition had been described to Julia by the maid who had gone in to lay the fire and found him "groaning and still as a corpse, he was."

271

It took no great perception to understand why, given the exceptional gloom at Charfield. The cause of Eustacia's death being uncertain, an inquest had been held. Dr. Broxon testified he was still trying to determine the cause of Lady Popejoy's death. The coroner, a paunchy, red-faced attorney, demanded to know how the good doctor thought he would be able to learn anything more than he had discovered from first treating the decedent, then examining the corpse.

The doctor explained that Lady Popejoy had apparently been in the habit of dosing herself with various medicines and tonics which she made from instructions in an apothecary's manual. "Having found upwards of a dozen preparations in a cabinet in her bedchamber, I am still studying the manual and her notes to see what they contained, for what conditions she was taking them, and how regularly she took them."

"Don't her maid know? Or someone in the family?"

"No, sir. Before the last few months, she had been very healthy and proud of it. More recently she admitted to indigestion, for which the maid was aware she took some remedy. Sometimes men, and women too, are reluctant to speak of their pains or indispositions lest it make them seem weak. I have never known a patient to employ so many medicines, and all without acquiring them from an apothecary who would be able to tell us what each was intended for."

Here the coroner showed some interest. "Is each not intended to treat only one thing?"

Julia heard Lavinia give a soft cluck at such ignorance and sensed, rather than heard, Dr. Broxon sigh. Both Ladies Barding, as well as Julia and Verity, had been summoned to give testimony regarding Eustacia's expertise and work in the stillroom, her lack of appetite, and her initial fit.

"No, sir. Many, perhaps most simples, the herbs of which medicines are made, are used to treat a variety of ills. The same is true of medicines. The same remedy may be held to strengthen heart, stomach, liver, and bowels, help colic and bloody flux, stop the nose from bleeding, and disperse fretting, choleric humors."

"Does a single medicine work for so many diverse illnesses, doctor?"

"I am inclined to think not, sir." After a pregnant pause, he added, "I wonder if Lady Popejoy, failing to get relief from one remedy, took a second and a third and so on, and the combination of many substances eventually ended in a fatal shock to her organs."

"An interesting suggestion, but I require something more substantial before asking these jurymen to reach a decision. I hereby adjourn this coroner's court until Dr. Broxon has completed his review of the decedent's medications. You will advise me when you are done, doctor, which I trust will be within a fortnight."

"I will, sir."

That night Lord Popejoy chose brandy as his remedy of choice.

Neither Lavinia, Lady Barding, nor Caroline, Lady Barding, was surprised, both agreeing that men would do it sometimes and it was best left to their male attendants to minister to them. Caroline kept thinking of things that must be done immediately, such as the ordering of mourning rings for those who attended the funeral—whenever it might be held—or else wondering if some task had been done. She would start for the kitchen to speak with Cook about reducing the number of dishes to be served at dinner for the next few days because none of them had any appetite and be found later inventorying the supply of black-edged paper and black sealing wax and wafers. She also wandered up to the nursery several times a day.

It was considered by all a mercy that Eustacia's death, having followed William's by less than three months, would not much prolong full mourning. Verity, unrelated to the Bardings except through Caroline, was wearing half mourning, and Julia had been considered exempt from any form of mourning, though she had chosen to return to her sad-colored gowns for the present. This had provoked a slight smile from Lavinia and a quip that the dull blues, grays, lavender, and browns were mourning enough for anyone.

Chapter 26

Peter and Rachel were married in the presence of Miles and two of Peter's friends and their wives. They were of good family, if not members of the beau monde, and like Peter they were interested in the arts. One was a sculptor, the other a painter, and their wives were practical, cheerful, and untroubled by the whims of the artistic class. The guests were given to understand that the couple's earlier marriage had been rushed for practical reasons, and the current reaffirmation of their vows was being kept secret because the family was in mourning and would not have approved of the Fleet marriage. Afterward, they sat down to a substantial and elegant wedding breakfast before the couple set out for Charfield.

Miles saw them off and made his own way on foot to his office, congratulating himself on how well it had gone. The stroll was soothing after the worries of the last several weeks. He was in complete agreement with Barlicorn's remark when Halliwell paid him for his services. "Didn't expect it to be as easy as it was. Piece o' luck all around, I'd say. Though 'tis helpful to deal with intelligent men—and women."

The pleasant conviction that all was now well lasted only until he reached his office. When he entered, Bryden shot up from his chair.

"Mr. Halliwell! There's been an urgent letter for

you from Charfield." Vertical lines showed between Bryden's brows, and his lips had tightened with concern.

This seemed an extreme reaction. Adam Bryden was ordinarily as cool as he was himself. "What's wrong?"

"I don't know. I didn't open it because it was marked 'confidential.' It came two days ago by one of the earl's grooms. I sent our boy to deliver it to you on his way home. I fear"—he pulled a long chain holding several keys out of a waistcoat pocket and unlocked one of his desk drawers—"I trusted too much in young Graham having his mind on his work so late in the day." He held out the letter.

Halliwell took it but did not break the seal at once. "What went wrong?"

"I told him you were at the Red Lyon in Holborn, which is almost on his way home, but he delivered it to your lodgings, which are farther out of his way. I think he did as horses do when you customarily ride them on a certain route: he was accustomed to taking messages to your rooms and delivered this without thinking. 'Tis only this afternoon the fellow who keeps the place sent it back by his servant who had taken the letter from Graham. As soon as I learned of it, I sent Graham to find you, but I did not entrust the letter to him again. I am very sorry for it, sir. I should have questioned Graham more carefully the next morning. Instead I only asked if he had delivered it, and he said he had, though you were out."

"Very likely there's no harm done. We often hear from the earl or dowager countess about one thing or another. What seems desperate to them very seldom is."

Except for Jeremy and the succession, of course, both of which actually were of critical importance. He opened the sheet. Georgie's death, if that were the subject, could hardly be considered an emergency. They all expected it, probably even Eustacia, though she behaved as if her son would recover if cosseted enough.

"My God. Lady Popejoy is dead."

"What a terrible thing, and she not even thirty?"

"Several years less. The earl wishes me to return to Charfield at once. Is there anything you cannot deal with here?"

"No, sir. It's been quiet, as most have gone to their estates."

"Then I will travel post as soon as I can pack and pay my shot at the inn."

"Is there to be an inquest? I hope the family is not much inconvenienced."

"There's no mention of it. Still, the doctor is not sure of the cause, which must be of concern to all." He did not mention the real reason the earl had written: *As George will marry again within the year, there is no need for Peter to sacrifice himself to marry immediately. My lady has agreed to give up her hope of seeing Jeremy legitimated, so we can look about us for a truly suitable young lady for Peter.*

Barding had added, *It would be best if the question of Eustacia's death were laid to rest, if I may phrase it thus, before George begins to look for a wife. It might otherwise have an odd appearance.*

"I should think it would be," Bryden commented. "Is there anything I can—wait a bit. I suppose it has nothing to do with the matter, but Lady Popejoy did write to request that we send her something from an apothecary. She could not get it in Banbury."

"What was it? I don't recall we've done the like for her before."

"Let me bring the file." He went to the cabinet where the boxes holding correspondence with the Bardings and Strettons was kept. "Here it is. One pint, oil of wormwood." He opened another box and withdrew several sheets of paper. "Here are the bills. I had to go to three different apothecaries to get the full amount. I packed it all very carefully, hmmm, three weeks ago yesterday, and the groom who brought the message took it the next morning."

"I'll mention it to the doctor, although I don't suppose it's important." He might be able to catch up with Peter and Rachel to warn them of Eustacia's death and suggest they stay over a day at the inn to give him a chance to arrive before them to break the news that the marriage was already accomplished.

****

His life had turned into farce. By the time he had packed and Bryden secured him a post-chaise, he was several hours behind the happy couple, which should have brought him to the Laughing Cat Inn while they were yet at supper. Instead, on inquiring for the Strettons, he was informed primly that they had already eaten and retired. The innkeeper evidently knew they were on their bridal journey and had no intention of disturbing them. He did admit they'd left instructions for their coach to be ready at nine in the morning. He appeared to think such early rising was odd, even suspicious, for a new-married couple. Halliwell said affably, "By leaving early, they can reach their

278

destination tomorrow." Better the man not think he was in pursuit of an eloping couple.

Miles requested that Mr. Stretton be informed of his presence at the first opportunity in the morning. If it was too late to stop the consummation of the marriage, why bother them? As he thought about it over his own supper, he concluded that the marriage was more desirable than not. Rachel Ambleton had impressed him and, more to the point, impressed Peter. Lavinia would certainly approve of her. There might be an equally suitable young lady in the pool of eligible girls Lavinia and Caroline knew, but Miles doubted it.

"Miles?" Peter found him in the inn's public room the next morning because there had, alas, been no available private parlor. He was drinking bad coffee and wondering how he could ever marry. A baron's daughter could not marry a bastard. He could not marry the sort of woman for whom Halliwell would be a good prospect. Unless he could find a genteel girl who was herself an unacknowledged by-blow?

"Miles, why are you here?"

Before Halliwell had finished explaining, Peter was laughing.

Utterly unseemly to laugh at a death but easy to understand. The intervention of God or Fate in their plans, not Eustacia's demise, gave rise to Peter's amusement.

"Man proposes, God disposes." By then, the waiter had brought Peter's coffee. He sipped it and remarked, "I'm glad you didn't catch us up earlier. I would not have changed my mind, but Rachel's conscience might have troubled her. She might have insisted we not, er, make our marriage irrevocable until I'd spoken with the family. Nothing has changed. I needed to marry, and this way we can fulfill my mother's desire that Jeremy be legitimated in the eyes of the world."

"Still, you might have found a lady of the beau monde who was to your taste and came with a dowry."

"You can't help thinking that way, being a man of business. No, I couldn't have found a better bride than Rachel, because no young lady in our family's circle would have been through the fire as Rachel has. She has a strength that awes me. I don't know how I would have survived, working as a servant with no hope of ever escaping drudgery. Besides, we think the same way about many things. In Italy, I grew accustomed to less formal ways than would suit more eligible girls. And despite her courage and fortitude, Rachel needs to be cherished." Another sip of the weak coffee. "If you had arrived earlier and persuaded us to have the marriage annulled, what would have become of her? She would have been willing to return to Barlicorn's orphan house, I'm sure, but I doubt Barlicorn would have been pleased with us."

"We would have settled her somehow. The Bardings take care of their dependents."

"A little annuity and a cottage somewhere? No. She would be utterly wasted. As Mistress Stretton, Rachel will be an asset to us. And I, mmm, can be comfortable with her."

His little brother had fallen in love despite his claim of having no romantickal notions. Almost at first sight, which Miles would have thought impossible.

"And where is Mistress Stretton this morning?"

"She'll be down soon. She wasn't quite ready when the maid brought our chocolate and informed me that you were here." He glanced over his shoulder. "There she is now."

They rose, and Miles bowed to his brother's bride. She was rosy and bright-eyed, and her jacket and petticoat became her well.

"My sweet, Miles brought me some news from the family."

In her wary "Oh?" Halliwell heard her fear that her good fortune would be snatched away. No, her happiness. He did not doubt that she had been happy. Before he could reassure her, Peter spoke.

"My sister-in-law has died suddenly. It does not change our plans. Does it, Miles?"

"You may wish to enjoy your honeymoon elsewhere. With the house sunk in mourning…"

"Should I not be there to lend my support?" Peter's lack of enthusiasm, and who could blame him, was unmistakable.

"If you are needed there, we must go." Rachel rested her hand on his arm.

"I don't think it necessary," Miles said. "Your marriage is a happy event and will please the family"—or so he hoped—"but you should have time to enjoy your new state before you go to a house disarrayed by the recent death. The estate in Cumberland would be a good choice, unless you prefer some other place. I've brought you additional funds. In a month or two, when things are more settled, your return will raise their spirits."

"The family did well enough without my presence when William died." Peter gave an Italianate shrug. "Would you like to visit Cumberland, Rachel? The roads are terrible, but we need not travel fast. The manor is comfortable, and the hills and lakes offer fine views."

Miles waved them on their way after a substantial breakfast and set out for Charfield. Peter was correct: it was as well his marriage to Rachel had been consummated. To try to annul it when they had created evidence proving an original wedding at the Fleet two years previously could only create problems. The questions raised by the attempt would be far worse than Peter marrying a girl from the gentry rather than a nobleman's daughter. Barding, or his mother, had not known how quickly the matter could be managed. Halliwell had been surprised, himself, and he'd been present at the negotiations.

All was well. Peter was happy with his bride, and Caroline would be delighted that Jeremy could be made to appear legitimate. Jouncing along the familiar road, he grinned to think that he was now glad to have accomplished the task he'd been set, when he originally deplored the idea. He was going home; if Charfield was not precisely a haven of peace and sanity at any time, it did hold most of the people he cared about.

****

Over the door, the hatchment which announced William Stretton's death had been repositioned to make room for Eustacia's. Miles knew how upside down the household was when the door was opened by a maidservant. She bobbed a curtsy and squeaked, "Their lordships is just back from riding over to Sir Randall's, sir. Their ladyships don't want to be disturbed. They was all fair put about at you not coming," she added gratuitously. "Mistress Perry's in the little parlor."

Wonderful. "I will see Mistress Perry before I

make myself tidy."

Caroline, Lady Barding, appeared at the other end of the long entrance hall as the maid took his hat and gloves. "Halliwell, we have urgent business to discuss. Shall we say the library in half an hour? I will let the dowager countess, Barding, and Popejoy know." The butler emerged from the back of the house almost at a trot, followed by a footman. "Adams, washing water for Mr. Halliwell."

He had lost his chance to see Julia alone. A footman brought hot water to his room within minutes; he must have taken the servants' stairs two at a time. Halliwell washed his hands and face, and the man ran a rag over his shoes and brushed his coat. Even so, he was in the library before the others. He rather wished he had gone by the little parlor on his way. The door opened and Lavinia marched in, followed by Caroline, the earl, and Popejoy.

As Miles murmured, "My ladies, my lords," and bowed, the earl's curt, "We'll dispense with the courtesies," warned him of the severity of the problem. "When is Peter coming home?"

Halliwell's satisfaction with the success of their plans vanished like dew on a sunny morning.

They took seats around one of the long tables which made the library such a convenient place to meet with the family. This was not quite as Miles had anticipated announcing the news. "Not for some time. He is on his way to Cumberland with his wife. Your letter reached me too late for the wedding to be stopped. Yet if I had received it in time, I think I would have ignored it."

They listened to his explanation of how easily

everything had fallen into place, the delay in receiving the letter, and how he decided the most recent bereavement made it preferable to send the couple north. When he asked if they had any questions about the bride, Lavinia answered.

"If you approved her and Peter likes her, I'm sure she is a good choice." She followed with a non sequitur meant as an apology: "Eustacia's death and the questions about it have thrown us into confusion."

And affliction. George, Lord Popejoy had said nothing after a nod and brief greeting to Miles. Of course, he had loved Eustacia in the beginning. He might have fallen out of love, but her death must have been a far greater shock than it would have been had it occurred in childbirth or from a known disease.

The earl said, "Letters came by messenger this morning. The coroner sends his apologies for the short notice and advises that the inquest will reconvene tomorrow afternoon."

"I wonder we have not heard from Dr. Broxon," Caroline remarked.

"When he was here two days ago to see Georgie, he told me he had been instructed not to speak of his conclusions to anyone until the inquest resumed. He was only to send word to the coroner he had completed his investigation. I'm sorry. I meant to mention it, but with one thing and another, it went right out of my mind." Lavinia made a wry face. "I must be getting old."

Chapter 27

There was no question about the family's attendance at the inquest. Julia sat beside Caroline to lend her support in place of Verity, who had been reared to believe it unsuitable for a lady to attend any occasion of notoriety like an inquest or trial unless she had to testify. She had been a witness the first time. She had not been summoned to testify today, therefore she would not attend. As well Peter had not married her: fond as Caroline might be of the girl, Verity would not be acceptable as a Stretton bride. One could imagine Lavinia or Caroline on the battlements of a medieval castle, commanding its defense in the absence of their lord, but not Verity.

Hilda Ernst and Julia would lend their support to the Barding ladies, not that they needed it. They sat together, backs straight, faces impassive. At the dowager countess's side, Hilda placidly knotted a fringe. Knotting was easy to transport and work anywhere as the thread, shuttle, and completed fringe fitted into a drawstring pouch. Julia, next to Caroline, tried to emulate her posture and dignity and conceal her curiosity. She wanted to hear what the doctor had concluded, but she was not truly apprehensive. Julia could not believe Lord Popejoy would poison his wife or anyone else. Still, any unexplained death left some cause for concern.

Miles Halliwell had contrived to sit on Julia's left side. His presence was oddly reassuring. He gave an impression of being solid, not so much in body as in character. Though his form did give an impression of strength. She studied his right hand as it rested on his thigh. Her only suitor, Theo Manning's, fingers had been rather stubby. She preferred Halliwell's long fingers. Preferred them for what? Logically considered, hands were just hands. Miles Halliwell's looked capable. He also smelled delightfully of faint, pleasant eau de cologne. The sooner the inquest began, the better, because her thoughts were straying wantonly. What a pity he seldom smiled.

She stole a quick glance at him. As if he had felt her gaze, he turned to her. His smile was only in his eyes: a serious demeanor befitted the occasion. She fanned her heated face. So many bodies packed into the inn's assembly room made it uncomfortably warm, though the day was not hot. The viscountess's unexplained death was the most exciting thing to happen in the area in a century. She preferred not to think about any other reason for her flushed face and body.

Then the coroner took his place, and the jury filed in to take their seats, ending the rustling and shuffling of feet, coughs, and whispers. The preliminaries accomplished, Dr. Broxon was called to testify. After summarizing his previous testimony briefly, in case any had forgotten it, he began to describe how he had reached some conclusions about the unfortunate death of Lady Popejoy.

"In more than thirty years as a physician, ten of them in London, I have never heard of a doctor or apothecary treating a patient with so many remedies. I have never had a patient who acted as his own apothecary, compounding medicines beyond the usual home doses women make for the colic, or coughing, or a fever." He paused. "Lady Popejoy owned several books adequate to train an apothecary. She made oils of herbs and flowers, as well as decoctions, syrups, and conserves of the same."

"Then she could not have made an error?" the coroner asked.

"In the general way, and in the preparation of any one compound, I would say no. However, we might liken her mistake to that of Icarus, who flew too near the sun."

The coroner was not amused. "I think you had better tell us what you mean by that, Doctor."

"Fortunately, the viscountess kept exact notes of every medicament she made, and Lord Barding and Lord Popejoy lent me her notes and books to try to determine the cause of her death. It has taken some time, given the number of remedies she was taking. She also left a list of simples she used, and for what purpose." He glanced apologetically toward the family. "Lady Popejoy was concerned about her difficulty in conceiving, and thus many of the medicines she took were to encourage conception. Others were for dyspepsia or nausea and for sleeplessness."

The jury and spectators waited. No one shifted in his seat or coughed. Did anyone even breathe?

"I considered the components of each and the quantity she took each day, and calculated the amount of the various ingredients she was ingesting. It was the most complex arithmetickal problem I have performed since I was in the schoolroom. I formed two hypotheses. The first was that some combination of substances was poisonous. The second was that the quantity of a single substance rendered it poisonous. May I pass to you the chart I drew up?"

The coroner accepted the sheet and frowned over it. "I am no expert in the apothecary's art, but if all the parts are wholesome, how can they have done harm, in combination or in quantity?"

"I cannot answer the first part of your question, unless the natures of different elements were so opposed as to war with each other. But as to quantity, a wholesome thing like strong drink may do ill, sir. A glass of brandy fortifies and raises the spirits, so to speak." There was a scattering of chuckles before Broxon continued. "Yet too much taken at one sitting may render one dead drunk. Or indeed, truly dead, as happens when someone drinks an excess of smuggled over-proof spirits undiluted. Will you take note of the entry for artemisia, also known as mugwort and wormwood?"

"Ay. Lady Popejoy appears to have taken a good deal of it, for several complaints."

"Not surprisingly, as it is valuable in the treatment of female disorders among other ills. In Culpeper's useful book, *A Physical Directory*, he says that one may take a drachm at a time. I would instruct a patient to take one drachm a day and believe most would do the same. Does anyone take into account all the tonics and remedies the patient is taking, some perhaps without the doctor's or apothecary's knowledge? I do not know.

"Much may depend also on whether one takes a spoonful of the powdered herb in wine or 'a quantity of the juice,' as Culpepper says, or a decoction of the herb in wine. Or as a syrup or conserve or in some other form. I found in Lady Popejoy's notes that she recently substituted oil of wormwood in some of her preparations. The oil would be much stronger than powdered wormwood or juice. It is impossible to be precise as there are three different kinds of this plant, and they vary in strength."

"She was certainly exceeding a drachm each day if your figures are correct and she was in fact taking all of these preparations."

"They may be low, for several plants are said to be good for the same purposes having to do with women's ailments, and Lady Popejoy was using all of them. I cannot help but wonder if their similar uses mean they are similar in composition, and all contain some element which taken in excess is harmful."

"Is a poison not fatal very quickly?"

"One like arsenic is. But it may be possible for the effects to come on over a longer period, if the dose is small. We do not yet know the answers to all questions of life and death. I can state that wormwood can cause death in rats. I paid a farthing for each well-grown rat the neighborhood boys could bring me. I gave some of them a tiny dose of the oil which seemed to have no effect. Others I administered a slightly greater quantity, and there was little effect. A bit more in the third group caused convulsions. Some of the fourth group died. All of the fifth expired."

"Could the decedent make the oil herself? Is that not a complicated procedure?"

"She could and did. She possessed the tools, the instructions, and from her notes it is clear she had prepared oil of wormwood." He frowned.

"Doctor?"

"But I cannot account for the quantity of oil of wormwood I found in the stillroom."

Beside her, Miles Halliwell tensed.

"Is it surprising, when she could make it herself and used it often?"

"I found a bottle with near a pint of it. 'Tis difficult to imagine how she could have made that quantity, for her still was a small one. The instructions in *A Physical Directory* call for a pound of dried wormwood and near two and one-half gallons of water. She could have reduced the quantities, but I would expect a pound of wormwood to yield no more than a few drachms of oil at most. Nor could her physic garden have supplied enough wormwood to make such an amount. I spoke with the apothecary in Banbury from whom she purchased medicines and some simples. He had sold her eight drachms—an ounce—within the past month, which was as much as he could spare, as his stock was low."

"You cannot account for the larger quantity?"

"I questioned the other apothecaries in town. Lady Popejoy had not purchased from them."

"That is very troubling. I had expected to conclude this matter today—"

Miles Halliwell rose. A frisson ran through Julia as the wide skirt of his coat brushed her arm.

"I beg your pardon, sir. I can explain where Lady Popejoy obtained such a quantity of the substance."

The audience stirred at this interruption. After Halliwell identified himself and his employment was confirmed by the earl, he was permitted to make his deposition and answer questions.

No, he had not been in London when his office received Lady Popejoy's instructions. As they had sometimes made purchases on behalf of the earl's family when they did not have a regular supplier of some item in Banbury, her ladyship's request was not considered odd. He did not have the letter or the bills of sale with him. They were in London, with the family's other correspondence. He had not realized they might be important.

Bills of sale? More than one? Yes, as his assistant had had to go to several apothecaries to obtain the amount ordered. Had none of them commented upon the amount? Adam Bryden had not mentioned any remark upon the subject. Had Mr. Halliwell not thought the order unusually large? He had not, knowing Lady Popejoy's interest in simples, decoctions, and remedies, and knowing nothing of what it might be used for.

"Doctor, given the amount of the wormwood oil left, can you say whether the amount might have been fatal?"

Broxon had been scribbling with a pencil on the back of some letter or bill. He scowled at it before saying, "There are a number of factors to be considered, and there are too many variables to state it as a certainty. Did she employ some of it in preparations she was not taking? Perhaps. The most I can say is, it is hard to account for the amount missing from that pint. Even before Mr. Halliwell's testimony, I was satisfied that the remedies which should have helped her were responsible for killing her. I suspected the wormwood in particular because of the number of formulations she took which contained it. Now that I hear of her purchase of a pint of it, it seems more likely yet that it was at fault. As I have told you, it killed rats. I do not know if rats and human beings react in the same way to oil of wormwood. However, if my estimates are accurate, Lady Popejoy may have been ingesting an amount of the oil equivalent to that which caused convulsions or death in the rats, proportional to their sizes. Er, if the jury understands my meaning?"

"If I understand you, 'tis like giving a child a smaller dose than an adult would take?"

"Yes, sir, precisely."

The jurors traded glances and nods. Dr. Broxon had treated many of the jury or their families and enjoyed an excellent reputation. Nor would anyone want to offend the Earl of Barding, whose family bought from local craftsmen or merchants when possible. When the coroner requested their verdict, it took no more than five minutes for the foreman to announce they found it to be an accidental death resulting from overuse of medicine. Perhaps the verdict was a foregone conclusion anyway. The decision was none the less welcome for that.

If Julia had not been so close to Halliwell, she would not have felt his almost imperceptible sigh. She need not see the countess or the rest of the family to know they were unlikely to show any emotion, no matter what they might be feeling. It must be a relief to Lord Popejoy, however, who had shown signs of distress at home.

Chapter 28

Relief did not lead to a celebratory mood at Charfield. No one wanted to discuss the testimony or any other topic.

He could have left for London the next day but for the earl's unexpected question when they sat over their port after supper. George had already excused himself. Sykes had gone, too. He seldom took more than half a glass, and not always that much.

"Where are Peter and his bride to live, after they return from Cumberland?"

"Ah…"

"You didn't think of it." Barding smiled faintly as if he had scored a point, poured himself another glass, and slid the bottle to Miles.

"Er, no, sir." He could not tell the earl that Peter would not be willing to live at Charfield as William had done.

"He and his bride will need a house. It is necessary to have my heir at the Hall to consult with him over decisions relating to the estates and our business interests. He has a right to be included." The earl stared at his wine and harrumphed. "I don't think living here benefited William or his marriage. We should have pushed him out of the nest."

Halliwell maintained a diplomatic silence.

"We have several properties which are not entailed.

There's that little farm we bought for the grazing. The house is plain but pleasant, and it's got a stable and barn, an orchard, plenty of room to grow vegetables and for gardens. It's not close enough to visit too frequently. They wouldn't be living in our pocket. There's the one in Lincolnshire if they'd rather be farther away. The house isn't as comfortable, but the tenancies bring in a fair amount. Or there's the London property we bought, hmmm, when Whitacker was still acting for us."

"The street near Bloomsbury Square."

"Ay. The owner was fairly done up, poor fellow, with all his debts. It seemed a terrible expense at the time, but Mother and Caroline both agreed with Whitacker it was an excellent investment. There's the house at the end of the row, the one we let for the parliamentary term. It's older, but it faces a more fashionable street."

"It's also larger and has a better garden. You'd be giving up the rent, but you'd also not be responsible for its upkeep. I don't know. You should ask Peter which property he would prefer, sir."

"I will. My lady and my mother both agree we should make them a gift of one or another, or of enough money to buy some other property. George was not available to talk about it. I don't know what ails him, now the inquest is completed."

Lord Barding did not assume it was grief. Neither did Miles. The consideration Popejoy had shown his wife did not prove he loved her, and she must at times have tried his patience. "May I inquire if you have asked the ladies their opinion?"

"They said he would get over it."

Either less perceptive of them than usual or they did not care to share their thoughts with the earl.

"I can only guess at Lord Popejoy's emotions, sir. I may be wrong."

"Get on with it, Halliwell. I do not know why my heir is suffering. I may not be clever about such things, but I don't think it's all grief."

"My lord, have you ever felt guilty for something when it was no fault of yours at all?"

Barding sat back in his chair, tapping one finger on the arm. "I suppose I have, on occasion." He smiled wryly. "A parson would probably say it's an inheritance from the guilt of Adam and Eve."

"No doubt. Lord Popejoy may be feeling that guilt, or at his relief Lady Popejoy's death was no one's fault—"

"Except her own."

"Ay. Or if he feels relief that she is dead. I don't think theirs was a happy marriage."

"It must sometimes have been devilish uncomfortable. Well! I think we must ask you to stay long enough to write out descriptions of the properties to send to Peter so he and his wife can consider which they would like. They could look at the Lincolnshire property and the London house on their way back from the Cumberland estate. There's no hurry about their return, after all."

He could have completed the project more efficiently by returning to London. But the earl preferred he remain until it was possible to discuss the choice of properties with Popejoy. Miles did not regret having to stay, though he did not examine his reasons.

The earl was finally able to talk with George on

Saturday afternoon. Caroline pointed out that it was too late to set out for London, and Lavinia added that Halliwell would not wish to travel on Sunday. He would have been willing to do so and suspected Lavinia had no qualms about traveling on a Sunday either, provided she was anxious to reach her destination. On the other hand, it meant he would be able to ride with Julia the next day.

****

Julia had accepted his invitation to ride after church. They were not even accompanied by a groom. Lavinia commented when he approached Julia that a groom would be unnecessary. "I have never known of a lady compromised while riding, and in any event, our Miles will not give offense, Julia."

She rode well despite having only recently resumed the pastime after two years without a horse. "Is there any particular direction you wish to explore?" he had asked when they set out.

"I have not yet been very far from the house and home farm so any direction will do if the ride is long. I would love a gallop, too."

Ah, because she had been riding with Verity, an unadventurous rider. "Then let us ride around the boundaries of the property. 'Tis not as large as some, but there is a variety of scenery. I know several places where we can give our horses a good run."

And they did. But mostly they rode side by side, talking, once they overcame the constraint caused by being alone together. He began by pointing out places the boys had played (or got into mischief), the derelict hut reputed to be haunted by the ghost of a former gamekeeper where they often hid and had meant to sleep one night, having sneaked out of Charfield Hall.

The owl's hooting did not worry them, nor the odd rustlings in the brush. 'Twas other strange noises that caused them to run for the house.

"What kind of noises?"

"A rapid panting was the worst, I think."

"And what was it, did they find out?"

"A ghost, no doubt." He kept his face serious.

Julia's eyes widened. "Really, Mr. Halliwell?"

"I suspect it was a hedgehog. It's this time of year they mate. No doubt if we were outside in the park at night and kept still, we would hear them."

She blushed delightfully, whether at the idea of mating or at being in the wood at night…with him, for instance. "Things can seem very different in the dark." A pause. "But what of your own boyhood adventures?"

"They were much the same. I also grew up in the country. You did, as well, I imagine." Most parents would leave their children in the country rather than take them to London.

"I did, but I never had adventures."

"Was it all nothing but learning your lessons, sewing samplers, and practicing to curtsy? Did you have no daydreams about whatever little girls wish for?"

"Well…yes."

"I'll tell you mine if you tell me yours."

She laughed ruefully. "Bear in mind I was very young and foolish."

"So was I, once."

"I used to pretend I was a princess or perhaps a duke's daughter who had been misplaced and any day my real family would discover me. Silly, I know."

That would have been after her mother's death, he supposed. "Not at all. I sometimes pretended I was the son of an earl."

They traded wry smiles and paused under the willows by the stream to let the horses drink.

"Now I understand that a princess probably leads a very restricted life and has to mate—um, marry—for reasons of state."

"As do noblemen's sons, I fear." He grinned at her. Clearly, mating was on her mind, as it was on his. "Now that Jeremy's future is assured, the Ladies Barding will see you established."

"They have said so. I cannot imagine how."

"Once you are again in society, you will meet suitable men and can take your pick."

"At my age?"

"Why not? You are pretty and possess character and intelligence. Any sensible man values those qualities…as I do. What would you look for in a man?"

She kept her eyes straight ahead, focusing between her horse's ears. "Kindness. Intelligence and character, a sense of humor."

"Not a title or wealth?"

"My family is not distinguished or well connected. I may have a dowry, but I don't know how much. Thus I must cut my coat according to my cloth, if I ever get any cloth." She did not look at him.

"You will, Mistress Julia."

She did not turn her head, but he sensed she was studying him out of the corners of her eyes.

To break the fraught silence and before he said anything to create awkwardness, he gestured with his crop. "Look, we are almost back to our starting place.

Shall we canter?"

The better he knew her, the more he wished he had something to offer Julia. He had seen her blossom from the sad woman in dreary gowns to a glowing, lively lady. Yet perhaps there was a chance for him.

They were drinking tea in the drawing room after dinner, the vicar recounting an amusing incident about his son's visit with a friend in Scotland and the language difficulties to be encountered even in the Lowlands.

"He had never seen the dish before so he asked what was in it, and the gaffer replied, 'There's the draughts and liver intil't, and onions and oatmeal intil't.' 'But what's intil't?' asks Harold, and the Scot returns, speaking very slow and rather loud, 'Haven't I just told ye, ye fule, there's draughts, liver, onions, and oatmeal intil't, boiled up intil a sheep's stomach.' "

A commotion in the passage cut through their laughter.

"Damme if I care a twitch of Old Nick's tail! I'll see him now, by Gad."

The door was thrust open, and a stranger strode in, a footman following in his wake, remonstrating, "Sir! Sir! You cannot—"

The newcomer halted in the middle of the room, booted feet apart, crop in hand, hat still on his head. He was dusty, a little less than average height, whipcord lean, and browned by outdoor life. Angry as a hornet, too.

Verity squeaked. The earl, viscount, and Halliwell rose while the vicar murmured that he and his mate must take their leave. They slipped out, keeping as much room as they could between themselves and the newcomer.

"I do not believe we are acquainted, sir." The earl's bland observation might have been uttered in a coffee house or assembly.

"I'm Ambleton."

The name conveyed nothing to Barding or Popejoy.

Miles said, "Mistress Rachel's father?"

"I am, damme, and where is she? By God, sir— begging your pardon, ladies—" He seemed to note the presence of females for the first time and whipped off his tricorne. He hesitated for a moment as if wondering what to do with it, before tucking it under the arm that held his crop.

Miles had not gone into detail about Rachel's background when he told the family about Peter's marriage. He had merely mentioned she came of the gentry and had found herself on her own after the death of the old lady.

"My lord, may I present Mr. Ambleton, Mistress Rachel Stretton's father?"

"You admit knowing of my girl, then."

The earl executed a slight bow. "Mr. Ambleton. I'm Barding. Please be seated. Will you have brandy? Tea?"

Ambleton let out a breath. "I could do with a drink of ale. I've had a long, thirsty ride. What I want most is to know—"

"My dear sir, please do sit down, and let us put off any serious talk until you have your ale." Lavinia patted the place beside her on the settee. An old lady's magic! What an asset she would be in Parliament. Ambleton settled onto it with a sigh.

The footman stood like a stock, all but wringing his hands.

Caroline said, "James, take Mr. Ambleton's hat, gloves, and crop."

He departed at Barding's curt, "Ale and, er, other refreshments for our guest, and see to his horse."

Halliwell completed the introductions, hoping neither the earl nor the viscount would try to explain anything. He trusted the countess and Lavinia not to speak unwarily.

At a glance from the dowager countess, Hilda and Verity excused themselves, but when Julia made to follow, Lavinia stopped her with a shake of her head. Julia resumed her seat.

Caroline inquired about the state of the roads. Although chafing at the delay, the commonest good manners forced Ambleton to reply, and to apologize for bursting in upon them, ending, "I trust you will pardon a father for his anxiety, my ladies."

The ale and a hastily assembled tray of cold chicken, cheese, pickles, and jam tarts arrived then, and Caroline directed the butler to have a room prepared for their guest.

"No need of that, my lady," he said, coming up for air. "I make no doubt there's an inn nearby."

"We cannot permit my son's papa-in-law to stay at an inn. We have much to discuss, and then it will be time for supper."

This completed Ambleton's conquest. Before he could speak, however, the earl said, "You were inquiring about your daughter, Rachel. We have not yet had the pleasure of meeting her. Halliwell, here, my man of business, has and I am sure can address any questions you have."

"Any questions? You may be sure I have a good many. My daughter has been lost to me this last two years and more, and now I have received a letter from someone styling himself Peter Stretton, son of the Earl of Barding, informing me he has married my daughter. Apparently that is true?—although I can scarce believe she lives, and this is not some imposture." He bit savagely into a leg of chicken.

Why the devil had Peter written? No, he could guess: Peter might have acquired a habit of informality in his travels, but he would think it necessary to apprise Rachel's family of her situation. Mayhap she had wanted to reassure her papa, too, even if he had ignored her when she had begged for his help. "Sir, may I inquire when you last heard from Mistress Rachel?"

"We, my wife and I, received a letter from her written the day my wife's great-aunt went to her reward. Rachel had been living with her as her companion. I wrote to tell her I would come to take her home and received no reply, but I thought nothing of that, as I would be there in less than a week, too soon to expect a letter in return."

"Did the recent letter not explain why Mistress Rachel left Lady Helen's house after her death?"

"No, by Gad, and I want to know. Stretton wrote naught but a curst statement he and Rachel had married not long after Lady Helen died. Where's she been all this time, that's what I want to know. My girl added two or three lines at the end, but nothing to the point. 'I am well and I hope you are all well' was the sum of it. But it was in her hand, which kept me from dismissing it as a cheat."

"Then I think I can explain. She did not receive your letter as she left the house almost at once to safeguard her virtue. Soon after the old lady's death, her heir came to inspect it and made an indecent proposal to your daughter. She did not have enough money for coach fare, as Lady Helen, being so ill, had not paid her at the quarter day. He claimed not to believe her without reviewing the accounts and refused to lend her the fare. The heir cannot have given you a true account."

"Stop my vitals, I'll take my horsewhip to him," Ambleton snarled before coming down to earth abruptly. "Suppose I'll have to buy one in London, as mine is at home. When I arrived, there were no more than two or three servants in the house, who claimed Rachel had gone, though they did not know where. They directed me to Lady Helen's relation. He said he had seen her only briefly and thought she had returned to us. I went to the nearest coaching inn with service to our part of the country. She would have known of it, as 'twas the one we arrived at, when I brought her to London. No one recalled her."

"Will you not take a cup of tea now you've quenched your thirst, Mr. Ambleton? Tea is so soothing."

He accepted a tea bowl absent-mindedly. "Thank you, Lady Barding. Where did she go?"

"She and Peter Stretton had become acquainted, and he was courting her." Halliwell hoped Rachel's fond papa would not ask how they had met. "Fearing Lady Helen's nephew would return…"

"Ay, ay, no need to draw me a picture."

"She fled, taking only what she could carry, and

303

went to Mr. Stretton."

"As any sensible young lady in such dire circumstances would do," Lavinia remarked.

"Are they truly married?"

Halliwell hem'd apologetically, hoping his powers of dissimulation were adequate. "This is the part which was not conducted quite as it should have been, sir. Mr. Stretton was anxious that they should be married at once instead of letting even one night intervene in which the lady must stay alone at an inn, which would not have been proper."

"Zounds! Indeed not! By license?"

If this worked, Rachel's father's support, as well as the Bardings', should carry the day. "He was not sure of how to get one, or whether it could be accomplished that same day. They wed under the rules of the Fleet Prison, without banns or license. Peter's brother William and I acted as witnesses."

"Hmmpf. Not what I would have chosen, but better than nothing. Why did she not write us?"

" 'Twas my understanding she did write." Miles paused. This was where they might founder if the letters Rachel had written from her lodgings were still in existence. Likely not. "Mistress Rachel, Mistress Stretton now, assumed you had cast her off when she received no response to her several letters to you."

"Letters? I never had any letter from her after the one informing us of Lady Helen's death."

"Ah, that would explain it," Miles said wisely.

"She wrote to us?"

"Yes."

Miles let Ambleton ponder this, until he said, "I cannot account for it. The mail is not always reliable, but all her letters lost? And why have I now received one to inform me of the marriage?"

Undoubtedly because it had been written by Peter. "Mr. Stretton had arranged to visit Italy for a prolonged stay before this difficult situation arose and was to depart almost at once. Naturally he took his bride with him. Now they have returned to England, they must have felt they should try once more. I was present when they reaffirmed their vows on their return. They felt they would be more comfortable after a traditional wedding, though there are thousands of Fleet marriages every year. They could do nothing while in Italy, of course, with no Protestant clergyman available."

"My poor, poor girl." Ambleton slumped. "Stretton's letter did not say where they were going. Can you tell me where I can find them? I assumed they would be here, if the story was not a gull."

"They meant to come here but received word of Lady Popejoy's unexpected death. It was decided they should instead visit friends for a time."

Ambleton muttered embarrassed condolences. "I do beg your pardon. I did take in the signs of mourning here, but in my worry for my daughter, I felt forced to ignore them. You must miss Mr. Stretton's support at such a sad time."

Lavinia, spoke up, for which Miles was profoundly grateful. He was having difficulty thinking of a convincing explanation.

"Believe me, we all encouraged him not to bring his bride to a household as distraught as ours. This was our second bereavement in three months, and we have been all topsy-turvy."

Seeing him unpersuaded, she went on, "But they

did send us their little boy with Mistress Julia, a friend of Rachel's."

Halliwell hoped Ambleton did not notice the moment of thunderstruck paralysis gripping the rest of them.

"The nursery is not much affected by our mourning, and young children do not enjoy long coach journeys. Jeremy is a particularly bad traveler. Would you care to see him?" Lavinia offered.

"Rachel has a child?"

If Ambleton were taken in, a whist player would say Lavinia had won the trick.

"Children do often result after a marriage," Caroline said kindly. "I'll take you up now, if you wish."

"You will want to review the settlements," Barding said. "We have a copy here somewhere, I think, Halliwell?"

The earl knew they did; Miles had brought it from town.

"I will find it while Mr. Ambleton meets Master Jeremy." It was a pity to let the man think the boy was his grandchild, but what else could they do? The deceit solved so many problems for the Stretton family.

Ambleton rose to follow Caroline. "As to settlements, my Rachel has a dowry. 'Tis not a fortune, but it should be a welcome addition to a second or third son."

No one said anything after the countess led Ambleton from the room until Julia, evidently feeling the silence had gone on too long, remarked brightly, "Well! Rachel will be pleased to know she was not abandoned by her family."

"Or at least, not by her father." Halliwell permitted his gaze to rest upon her, hoping she would read both sympathy and admiration in it. If he could not court her in earnest, he could at least show her how desirable she was.

"All very satisfactory," Lavinia said.

Chapter 29

Lavinia sat in her parlor, an unread book of sermons in her hand, lost in thought, a cooling dish of tea beside her. Verity remained nearby in case the dowager countess needed anything, as Hilda had gone into Banbury to visit a friend. Lavinia permitted Verity to take her usual companion's place, Julia suspected, because Verity did not chatter but merely sat sewing infants' and children's garments for needy families in the parish.

The earl and Popejoy were riding the estate with Ambleton and Miles. Caroline had given it as her opinion they would return only in time to tidy themselves for supper. Because the countess had been wandering the house in search of distraction, rather than remaining in Lavinia's or her own parlor at the back of the house, it was she who heard the coach wheels. She entered the room with less than her usual composure and actually broke in on an idle question of Julia's about the curate's clothing project.

"A coach has drawn up, and 'tis neither one of ours nor a hired carriage. I do not recognize the crest. And there is another behind it," she added.

Meaning, it was unlikely to be Peter. If Caroline did not know the heraldic device, the coach could not belong to a neighbor. Nor would anyone in the vicinity be unaware of Eustacia's death and that the family would not be receiving visitors.

"How very peculiar," Lavinia commented, roused from her brown study. "Do sit down, Caro. Adams will inform the caller of our mourning, as he has failed to notice the hatchments over the door, and he will be on his way."

But why two coaches?

"Could it be some distant relative?" Verity inquired timidly.

"I hardly think it. We wrote our friends and connections to inform them about William and then about Eustacia. I cannot think any of them would intrude at such a time."

With a shiver of dread, Julia wondered—

Ralph, the footman, appeared in the doorway and cleared his throat.

"My ladies…"

"What is it, Ralph?"

"Mr. Adams says Lord and Lady St. John and Miss Cecelia St. John have called. He wants to know, do your ladyships want to receive them?" The footman's hesitant voice made plain his opinion of those who ignored obvious indications of mourning. He had also referred to Cecilia as "miss," a term usually reserved for young girls. Julia took it as his judgment on her half sister's deportment.

Lavinia turned to her inquiringly.

"I had no idea." Julia would willingly have sunk into the earth. They must have received her letter. Why would they do this? The prospect of embarrassing her would not have stopped her father and stepmother, but she would not have expected them to flout the rules of common courtesy.

"Be easy, dear, it never occurred to me you knew of it. Shall I have Adams send them away?"

"Lavinia…" Caroline protested.

"You are correct, Caroline, I can scarcely deny them access to Julia. And Jeremy, of course," she added ironically.

Julia stood up, hoping she could persuade them to leave. Mayhap they had not observed the signs of mourning? No, they must have: if they had overlooked the hatchments, surely they had noticed the butler's and footman's black armbands.

"We will go down to greet them," Lavinia said.

This horrible situation had at least put a sparkle in the old lady's eyes. If it chanced to be slightly malicious, Julia could not blame her. It was better than her earlier absence of expression.

"They are in the reception room, my lady," meaning the little chamber off the front hall, where tradesmen and unwelcome visitors were penned unless someone deigned to see them. "Shall I show them to the drawing room?"

"By no means. Caroline? Julia? Verity, you need not come with us. Please tell Adams to inform Halliwell immediately upon his return." Lavinia swept out, her daughter-in-law and Julia following obediently.

Her papa was gazing out the window, hands clasped behind his back. Augusta rose with stateliness from an uncomfortable armchair. Cecilia was caught in the act of examining a Dresden china ornament and put it down guiltily and rather too hard on a side table.

Julia managed to make the introductions as if the St. Johns were merely acquaintances rather than her family. They could not mean to acknowledge her.

Her stepmother's and sister's curtsies were unexceptionable, her father's bow exactly right. To his credit, he appeared slightly uncomfortable. Maybe all would pass off without much difficulty.

"We were on our way to our estate and could not resist stopping to see Julia," Augusta burbled. Charfield was not precisely "on the way" to St. John Underhill. Julia did not know how many days' travel this deviation must add but suspected that they would either have to return to London to join a main road, or else continue north on some less frequented route.

"And little Jeremy, I assume?" Lavinia did not sit down.

"Yes, of course. We have been concerned for Julia's and Jeremy's welfare."

"In our house?" Lavinia's voice chilled. Julia could almost see frost forming.

"No, no, only because we have not visited our daughter for some time," her father hastened to explain. "And Cecilia has missed her sister."

Why were they acknowledging her? Papa's letter had made it clear they meant to cast her off to avoid any hint of scandal. Impossible to believe they cared about her. The relief she had felt since writing to him began to shred away. If he had not received her reply, she would have to face his wrath when she told him what she had decided. She could not think about it now. First she must get through the next few moments.

"Papa, I think you and Stepmama must be unaware that Lady Popejoy died recently. Coming so soon after Mr. William Stretton's death, the family has been plunged back into the depths of mourning."

"Gadzooks, I did not know there had been a second

death so recently." He did appear chagrined.

"Oh, dear, we had no idea." Augusta's gaze drifted to Cecilia.

"How could you? I cannot think the notice has yet appeared," Caroline responded.

Halliwell had suggested it not be published until after the inquest determined the cause of death and preferably after the beau monde had all retreated to the country. Perhaps not then, if the coroner's jury had brought in a verdict of homicide.

What was there about mention of a notice in the newssheets that rang a faint bell? Not William's obituary, something more recent. Cecilia was fidgeting. However had she kept quiet so long? She was due for some ill-considered utterance.

Lavinia said, "We cannot offer you much amusement, I fear."

"Oh, we were hoping only for a good visit with Julia," Augusta said.

This was a broad hint that Augusta hoped to be invited to stay for a day or two, or several. As it was midafternoon, the most threadbare good manners would require they be invited to stay to supper, and after that, it would be impossible to send them on their way tonight.

Caroline's eyes slid toward Lavinia. Julia knew the dowager countess well enough to see she was amused. The visitors would not recognize Lavinia's subtle signal, but the countess did.

"Then please do break your journey here," Caroline said. "The nearest inn is really not fit for gentlefolk."

"Thank you, Lady Barding. I do hope we can lift

some of your burden from you."

"I will just let the housekeeper know you will be staying," Caroline murmured and went out, rustling petticoat whispering offense.

"I know it is not usual after a death, but what are friends and connections for," Augusta inquired, "if not to offer their help and sympathy in times of trouble? A house in mourning is such a depressing thing. 'Whither thou goes, I will go,' you know. I've always thought Ruth must have been such a comfort to Naomi," she chirped.

" 'And where thou lodgest, I will lodge.' " Lavinia completed the quotation. The prospect seemed not to cheer her.

Julia hoped she was not grinding her teeth.

The housekeeper came to show them to their rooms, where they would wish to rest or visit with Julia until supper, at Lavinia's suggestion. Augusta and her father preferred to rest, wash, and change clothing.

"Do come to my chamber, Julia. It's been too long since I saw you." At Cecilia's urging, she could do nothing else.

Her sister kept up a stream of chatter about the entertainments she had attended in town as she washed her face and hands and her maid unpacked. As soon as she was done, Cecilia sent her away. The door was hardly closed behind her when she pulled Julia over to the window seat to sit side by side.

"You must wonder why we are here—"

"I did, rather, and I'm sure the Barding ladies do, too."

"Such news, Julia! I am to make the grandest marriage!" Her sister was bubbling with excitement.

"You will never guess to whom."

Julia ignored the invitation to speculate. "I'm sure I cannot."

"To Peter Stretton, the third son of the earl! Or mayhap he's the second son, now, as Will is dead. Is it not wonderful?"

"Peter Stretton?"

"Yes! Mama is in high good humor." Cecilia preened while Julia stared at her. Her sister mistook her speechlessness for amazement.

After a moment, Julia regained her wits and inquired, "How did this surprising event come about?"

"Well, it hasn't really been agreed yet. There will be all the tedious talk about settlements first."

"Wherever did you meet him? He has only been back in this country a short time."

Cecilia fluttered back to reality with a bump. "I haven't actually met him. But Papa saw in the newssheet that he had returned from Italy and mentioned it to Mama. He will be ready to marry, she says, and if he meets me, how can he resist? Especially since you are now on terms with the family. Won't it be delightful?"

In other words, Cecilia had built herself a fine castle in Spain.

Just then, Augusta entered Cecilia's bedroom without knocking. "Talking secrets? I hope you are not rattling on, Cecilia."

Before her half sister could stammer out the truth, Julia replied, "Cecilia has been telling me how much she has enjoyed London."

"She has indeed been a success. My dear girl has been courted by any number of very eligible

314

gentlemen."

And yet had not received an offer?

"Now it is time you were changing for supper, as they keep country hours here. I can't imagine why you have not already done so. You will wish to look your best. I'll send your maid to you." Augusta cast a disparaging glance at Julia in her plain, blue-gray gown.

Julia escaped with a word or two and a restrained smile for her half sister.

****

They entered the house through the side door nearest the stables.

The earl said, "There is plenty of time before we must change for supper. We'll go directly to the library if you do not object, Ambleton. Miles, will you fetch the descriptions of the properties we think might do as a wedding gift for Peter and Rachel? As soon as they have chosen one, we'll set the transfer in motion."

When Ambleton had studied the list of properties and all his questions had been answered, Rachel's papa declared the proposed gift was more than generous.

"I only wish I could give Rachel a dowry of more than two thousand pounds. Good enough for a country gentleman, but a paltry sum for the son of an earl."

Popejoy said, "Some considerations in choosing a wife are more important than the dowry."

Such as the ability to give Jeremy the Stretton name.

"A bond of affection, sense, a good temperament," the earl went on. "To marry only for financial gain or family connections can be a cold bargain."

"It can, indeed." They moved on to purely social matters, and Miles excused himself.

His satisfaction at the accord between the family and Ambleton lasted until he came downstairs, washed and clad in a suit Bryden had sent by the groom when Miles discovered his stay was to be prolonged. It was one of his better ones; apparently his assistant considered it more appropriate for a visit to an earl's estate than his ordinary wear. The footman on duty in the front passage was suspiciously blank-faced, the first sign of something amiss.

His stately "Good afternoon, sir," was uttered in his usual firm voice. "Beware the chit" was delivered quickly, sotto voce. His meaning became plain when a yellow-haired charmer emerged from the drawing room more hurriedly than elegance required.

"Oh, Mr. Stretton, I have been so eager to meet you." She came forward, extending her hands.

"I beg your pardon, ma'am?"

He did not take her hands as she seemed to expect, and his chilly tone caused her to check.

"Pray forgive me, sir. I am Cecilia St. John, and since your papa has taken my dear sister into your home, I count you as quite one of our family." She dipped a pretty curtsy before adding, "Mama often chides me for being impetuous, but I cannot help following the promptings of my heart."

"Your mother is quite correct. I am the Bardings' man of business, Miles Halliwell." He made a slight, stiff bow.

"Oh!"

What she might have said on recovering from her surprise he was never to learn, as Caroline swept into the passage from the direction of the dining room.

"There you are, Cecilia. In case you have not been

introduced, may I present Miles Halliwell, our man of business? Halliwell, this is Mistress Cecilia St. John. The St. Johns arrived this afternoon."

He bowed again. How the devil had Cecilia St. John and her family come to be at Charfield?

"Let us await the others in the drawing room, Cecilia. No doubt you will join us shortly, Halliwell?"

"Ay, my lady, as soon as I see to one last bit of business with Lord Barding."

She gave him an approving nod, linked arms with Cecilia and bore her off. When they were out of earshot, Miles muttered, "What the devil—?"

Ralph said, "The young lady and her parents came to visit Mistress Perry, they say." He gave the last phrase a fine, ironical turn.

"Good God. I'll make sure the earl and Lord Popejoy know."

Chapter 30

It cost Julia no struggle with her conscience to seek out Lavinia. She found the dowager countess in her bedchamber where she was making her own preparations before supper. Her laconic, gray-haired maid would have sent her away but for a word from Lavinia.

"Leave us, Jenner. I need only put on my mantua, and there is plenty of time for that."

The woman curtsied and retreated to Lavinia's dressing room.

"Sit, Julia. You are standing there like a maid waiting to be scolded."

"My lady." Julia sank onto the chair nearest the dressing table. Lavinia was scrutinizing her face in her hand mirror. She had clearly decided to armor herself against meeting with the St. Johns at supper, as an elaborate mourning gown lay across the bed. Since Eustacia's death, the Barding ladies had not bothered with a formal toilette except for Sunday dinner.

"It's about your people, I suppose?" Lavinia set down the mirror with a little sigh.

"I do not like exposing my family to censure, Lady Barding, but under the circumstances, I have no choice. My half sister sometimes speaks indiscreetly."

Lavinia dabbed on a little scent, a light floral evocative of a summer garden. She did not care for musky perfumes. "Did she confide the reason they have imposed themselves upon us?"

There was no use in trying to put a better face on it. "I learned from her that my father heard of Mr. Peter Stretton's return from Italy. He and my stepmother think Cecilia has a chance to enthrall him."

Lavinia, Lady Barding, laughed. "Her luck is out, then."

Julia sat with clenched hands, knowing the danger was not past. Lavinia arched her eyebrows interrogatively.

"He is safe from Cecilia, but I wonder if my stepmother will aspire to see my sister married to Lord Popejoy instead, now she has heard of Lady Popejoy's death."

The dowager countess tilted her head, studying her image in the mirror hanging on the wall over the dressing table. "Nothing is more likely. Your stepmother and papa will not wish to waste their trip, when there's the chance of securing Barding's heir for their little romp. I apologize for referring to Mistress Cecilia by such a term, as you may be fond of her."

"No need, ma'am. I know she is still somewhat childish." Cecilia was as beautiful and sweet as an angel even as a child. She was never too plump or spotty, and her nose never ran. Julia was fond of her in spite of her occasional lack of consideration for others. "She is a little spoiled. I do not know how any parent could resist indulging her. It's for me to beg your pardon for my family." Refusing Cecilia anything was like denying a treat to a toddler. Certainly Julia had wanted to escape the reproaches of her father and stepmother and out of concern for her half brother. But

Cecilia's pleading had weighed heavily. As had her own guilt at failing to foresee the necessity for chaperoning Cecilia at all times, even when she seemed to be involved in a lively game of Pope Joan with half a dozen other girls and boys her age.

"You bear no responsibility for their conduct." Lavinia paused in the act of putting on a black pearl earring. "The chit is very pretty and misses loveliness only by the lack of character and—pray forgive me— intelligence in her face. We can do without beauty but not without those traits. You may be at ease; there is no chance we would agree to Popejoy marrying your sister. Unless you think your family or mayhap only your sister might try to force the matter?"

Julia wished she could deny it. " 'Tis not out of question, I fear."

"Thank you for warning me. I will advise Barding and Popejoy, and the others, too, to be alert to such schemes." She was talking more to herself than to Julia. "Now, we must hit upon a way of keeping George out of her company, as he is the only prey left with Peter on his way to Cumberland. Do they know Peter is married?"

"Not from me. Nor did I mention he was not here, as my stepmother interrupted us and I could not let her know Cecilia had divulged the reason for their visit."

"Has it occurred to you there is a more immediate problem, Julia? Our other guest—"

She had forgotten Ambleton. "Oh, no." With Rachel's father believing Jeremy her child and the St. Johns knowing he was not, opportunities for disaster were breeding like rabbits. "What can we do?"

Lavinia's face showed no sign of discomposure.

"My dear, I have not the vestige of an idea. My reliance is on Miles. Yours should be, as well."

"Mr. Halliwell is devoted to your family's interests, my lady, but even for him, this may be an impossible challenge."

"We shall see. Supper should be amusing." She eyed Julia critically. "I wish you will put on a prettier gown. You need not wear mourning, after all. Hilda and Verity do not. The meal will be far less depressing with some spots of color among the crows."

While Julia would prefer to remain inconspicuous in her stepmother's presence, she had nothing to fear from her or from her father now that she intended to remain at Charfield. Too, the idea of her own family seeing her dressed becomingly was appealing. And Miles had not seen her newest gown yet.

For some reason it took longer to dress than usual, even with a maid's help. Was her hair perfectly neat? Was she revealing too much bosom? Julia was the last to enter the drawing room. With luck, she could slip unnoticed into a small, friendly group, perhaps one that included Miles Halliwell. She wanted to see his expression when he first beheld her. She stopped just inside the door. To her dismay, the usual clusters had joined into one circle. Miles and Lord Popejoy were near the door but so, alas, were Augusta and Cecilia.

Miles chose to join the group early rather than wait almost until it was time to enter the dining room. Apart from the risk of Lavinia's displeasure, he felt a certain morbid curiosity to see how the meeting of the St. John family with Ambleton played out. He reached the drawing room as Lavinia was presenting Julia's family to the earl and viscount. Then she introduced Ambleton to the St. Johns. To his regret, Julia was not yet present.

Caroline brought to mind a cat listening for mice. The ladies would anticipate fireworks at the meeting. After he had discharged his task in the library, it had been too late to speak with either lady or with Julia. He doubted Barding and Popejoy had managed to do so, either.

Barding acknowledged Miles with a nod. "You have not met Mistress Perry's family, I think? St. John, Lady St. John, Mistress Cecilia St. John, may I present Miles Halliwell, our man of business."

Their responses were as he could have predicted: a dismissive "Halliwell," from St. John, a slight inclination of Lady St. John's head, a shallow curtsy and "We have met" from Cecilia. Hard to guess whether their coolness had its origin in his being in Barding's employ or because they had somehow heard he was Barding's bastard.

St. John and Ambleton remained at the earl's side. Lavinia gathered Lady St. John and Cecilia to her and inquired about the state of the roads they had encountered, while Caroline spoke quietly with Verity and Hilda. Miles suspected she had been warning them against discussing Peter or Julia or Jeremy or Ambleton's visit. The countess turned to Halliwell and Popejoy and gave them a tight smile. "I trust all is well?"

"I believe the situation is in hand," Miles said with more confidence than he felt. Where was Julia? He did not feel he could ask.

"I hope so," the viscount muttered.

Verity moved to join Lavinia and her captive St. John ladies, and asked Cecilia some question. Perhaps about her pretty flowered gown, to judge by the girl's gesture at the petticoat of her robe à la française.

St. John was haranguing the earl about the state of the government and the scaff and raff getting above themselves and the reluctance of juries to hang felons. The earl dealt with his diatribe about what Parliament should do to suppress unrest by murmuring, "Do you think so?" and "That certainly bears thinking on," at intervals. Ambleton gave no clue as to his thoughts on the matter.

Lady St. John made some remark to Lavinia, curtsied, gave Cecilia a minatory glance, and crossed the room toward Caroline, Popejoy, and Miles in a spuriously casual manner. If Augusta St. John's unspoken message to her daughter was to join her, it failed. Cecilia grew nervous, but evidently she did not know how to detach herself from Lavinia and Verity.

"Popejoy, let me offer my condolences upon your recent bereavement. My heart goes out to your family, suffering two losses in so short a time, as I told Lady Barding earlier."

"Thank you, Lady St. John. It has been a difficult spring and summer."

"And your son is ailing, too, I believe?"

Popejoy's face froze. "He is being treated for green-sickness."

Miles saw Ambleton's eyes shift and followed their gaze. Julia was standing alone by the door, seeming even prettier and younger than he recalled.

The first words Julia heard on entering were Augusta St. John's as she cooed to Lord Popejoy, " 'Tis sad to think of your son unwell and without a mother to comfort him."

What he might have said in reply was lost at Augusta's abrupt demand. "Where had you that robe volante, Julia? I do not recognize it." She peered at the moss-green gown with its embroidered stomacher.

Before she had to stammer out some explanation, Lavinia spoke. "I really could not bear the sight of Julia in the gowns which were all she brought with her. In the interests of my digestion, I arranged for more pleasing garments. I cannot think how she came to choose such unflattering tints, as her taste otherwise is excellent."

The criticism chafed Augusta, who replied through compressed lips. "For an old...maid...to be getting herself up as though she were still a girl would be unseemly."

Julia's pleasure in her new clothing was burned away by shame. The moment was endless.

The earl commented jocularly, "If all old maids were as pretty as Mistress Julia, they would be in short supply."

Augusta turned an unbecoming shade of pink which did not flatter her hair. Stepmama was furious. Surely she would not disgrace herself with an outburst here.

Halliwell detached himself to go to Julia and made a leg, saying, "That green becomes you very well." He was pleased to see her expression brighten at the compliment.

St. John's voice, overloud, carried. "As a magistrate, Ambleton, you must agree that leniency breeds crime."

"What a pity we cannot give a dinner to make you known to our neighbors," Caroline interjected to give the conversation a different direction. "We are still all unsettled because of my daughter-in-law's death. Apart from being in mourning, the inquest only recently concluded."

Her words penetrated even St. John's absorption in his subject. "What? Inquest?"

Conversation was silenced in the wake of the countess's artless remark. Had Miles not been so appalled, he would have been forced to simulate a fit of coughing to conceal his amusement.

"An inquest was necessary, given the uncertainty surrounding Lady Popejoy's death," Barding said repressively.

"It was not a natural death?" Baron St. John realized too late this seemed to imply the wrong thing. "I mean, from an obvious cause?"

"No. No one had any idea she was ill. If she was," Lavinia added as an afterthought. Her eyes were bright with mischief. "Our doctor investigated the matter. Happily, it is all resolved now, and all's well that ends well." Delicate-minded or courteous guests would have found some reason to cut short their stay at a house where a suspicious death had recently occurred. Halliwell thought the older Lady Barding was overestimating their good breeding.

Augusta's self-satisfaction did not fall away, though it was diminished. "If the viscountess wasn't ill, what killed her?"

"My wife's death was tragic and unnecessary, the result of dosing herself unwisely for several complaints." No one could have mistaken the ice in Popejoy's voice.

"That was the finding of the coroner's jury,"

Lavinia agreed. Her comment seemed less reassuring than it should have. Was she hoping the St. Johns would suspect poison and leave post-haste? The remark was ill-advised in front of strangers, particularly in the presence of a magistrate. Then Halliwell saw the twinkle in Ambleton's eyes. One of the guests at least understood.

The awkward pause caused several to shift back into discreet gatherings. Verity rejoined Hilda, who had seated herself and taken out her knotting. Whatever did she do with it? She must have yards of the stuff.

Caroline took the space by George's side Halliwell had vacated. Miles had no doubt Lavinia and Caroline would succeed in herding the guests into the places they wished and hoped he could sit beside Julia.

Augusta St. John recovered her poise enough to fish for information. "You are also visiting here, Ambleton?"

"Yes. Lord Barding and I had a matter of business to discuss." He smiled blandly.

St. John's heavy brows rose. "You have commercial interests?"

"We all have financial interests of one sort or another, my lord."

"Do you live nearby?"

"My home is a few miles northwest of Worcester, outside the village of Sermon End."

"Is it a long sermon, Ambleton?" St. John guffawed.

They must have been hoping Ambleton was not staying in the house, fearing another guest would complicate their scheme. Unless they were considering Ambleton as a potential husband for Julia? They might feel they no longer needed her as a connection to Barding. Miles wanted to growl, then remembered Ambleton's wife disqualified him as a suitor and found himself beaming at Julia. He was trying to think how he could explain why he was grinning at her when Lavinia caught his eye and beckoned Miles to her side. Perforce, he must obey. "I'll be back," he whispered to Julia, who blushed and smiled. That boded well.

Lavinia Barding was some distance from any of Julia's relatives but kept her voice low. "Did your meeting go satisfactorily?"

Of course she was anxious to know as there had been no opportunity to inform her. But it was too complicated to explain here. "He will assess the situation and decide what to do. We—that is, your family, my lady—should say nothing about Peter or Rachel or Julia's circumstances."

"I see." Perhaps she did, as Ambleton had evaded answering why he was at Charfield. The dowager countess would need no more explanation for the present.

Adams announced supper, to Halliwell's relief. The food would be a distraction from awkward topics.

"As we are ill-supplied with gentlemen today, we will not stand on ceremony. Barding, if you will give Lady St. John your arm?" Caroline turned to Lord St. John. "Sir, if you will lead Lavinia, Lady Barding, in? Ambleton, will you escort Julia? Popejoy, Cecilia. Halliwell, you may give me your arm. Hilda and Verity, you must go in together."

Dinner was not as much of an ordeal as Miles had anticipated; the manners drilled into all of them as children held at the table. Miles had secured a place next to Julia, which in his opinion greatly improved the gathering. Her stepmother would not notice or care, as he was not an eligible suitor for Cecilia. Julia had Ambleton on her other side. For all his seeming like a simple country gentleman, he was well-informed on a number of topics.

Lady St. John sat beside Barding, and St. John was honored with the place to Caroline's right. Ambleton was seated between Caroline and Julia. Cecilia, between Lavinia and Popejoy, was devoting her kittenish charm to Popejoy and ignoring Lavinia entirely, probably a tolerable state of affairs from the dowager countess's point of view. Hilda was seated to the left of Miles. With Lady St. John on her right, the chances were Lavinia's companion would converse with him or not at all. Hilda did not approve of him.

Julia's face glowed with enjoyment. Whether she had feared the disclosures Ambleton might make or suffered humiliation for her family's graceless behavior or both, the worry had begun to drain away when Ambleton escorted her into the dining room and he himself managed to nab the chair on her other side. He wished he might have reassured her beforehand, but surreptitious glances at her set him at ease. She and Ambleton were discussing the relative merits of dogs and cats in a household. Her lively sense of humor was a surprise.

With Ambleton and Julia engrossed in their debate and Hilda occupied with her food, Miles was able to follow other conversations. Caroline was interrogating St. John at length which must be a relief to Verity, as the baron's remarks tended to be equal parts ponderous and patronizing. At the other end, Lady St. John had been describing St. John Underhill to the earl, who listened affably and did not respond with details about his own property. This may have led the baroness to suppose she had impressed him. Although Barding controlled his expression admirably, Miles thought he had formed a fair opinion of the members of the St. John family.

Chapter 31

Julia was weary to her very soul when Lord and Lady St. John rose after drinking a cup of tea in the drawing room after supper. Augusta had dark circles under her eyes, hardly surprising after their day's travel. She bore away Cecilia, still bright-eyed, and St. John bade the company good night, saying he would see his lady and daughter upstairs. Hilda and Verity followed a few minutes later.

Julia made no move to follow. The earl, Popejoy, and the Barding ladies would want to meet to discuss her family's arrival. Miles would undoubtedly be present. Her own presence might not be required, but she would attend if they permitted. If they did not want her, Lavinia or Caroline would suggest she must be tired, too, and should seek her bed.

Ambleton gazed around the room and stood up. "Time I was retiring," he said. "Lord Barding, Lord Popejoy, I hope we may be able to continue our discussion tomorrow. Servant, ladies, sirs." He bowed to the room in general and strode out.

No one spoke. After an interval sufficient for Ambleton to reach the guest wing, Lavinia said, "Shall we adjourn to the library?" Her glance at Julia included her in the question.

As they filed in, the earl spoke to the footman he had instructed to light more candles. "Aaron, you will wait outside and not leave for any reason. If some young lady should faint in the passage, or the house catch fire, you may tap on the door and inform us. This should not take long."

The release of tension on being private was palpable: the relaxation of postures, a sigh of relief, and a suppressed whistle from Popejoy.

"My heart was in my mouth," the countess said. "If Lavinia had not given me a sign that it was under control, I think I must have swooned away from pure terror. And Julia, too, seemed unconcerned."

"I was worried at first, my lady, but then I saw how calm Mr. Halliwell was." She stole a look at him.

His face was grave, but his eyes glinted as he responded. "I beg your pardon, my ladies. Once I had spoken with Lord Barding, Lord Popejoy, and Ambleton, there was no time to let you know what was decided. Her ladyship has said her heart was in her mouth, which exactly describes my feelings when I met with their lordships and Ambleton after learning of the St. Johns' arrival."

"Go on, Miles. Do not keep us in suspense." Lavinia, seated beside him at the long table, tapped his wrist sharply with her fan.

"I walked in on them with only the length of the passage between the hall and the library door to decide what to say. I could only think of one possibility."

"Miles." Caroline was too far away to admonish him with her own fan.

"Halliwell is too controlled to relieve his feelings by swearing." Popejoy grinned for the first time since Miles's return. "Pray let him amuse himself a little, Mama."

"You are being pompous and long-winded, Miles. Out with it," the dowager countess admonished, halfway between laughter and annoyance.

"I told him the truth."

"All of it?" Julia was startled into speaking when as an outsider she should have kept silent. She shrank into herself in embarrassment.

Caroline laughed. "Exactly my question."

"Not quite. Ambleton is a magistrate, after all. I admit it was a risk. However, from talking to him and even more, listening to him, I judged him a practical man. He is also exceeding happy to have his daughter restored and married into a noble family. While he never said as much, she seems to have been his favorite."

"I confess, you gave me some uncomfortable moments," the earl admitted. Popejoy nodded.

"I told him where Rachel had really been living after leaving Lady Helen's house. I explained whose son Jeremy actually was." He nodded apologetically at Julia. "He was hot as fire about that."

"Oh, dear. Perhaps you should not..." Her heart thudded.

"I had to tell him. While Lord and Lady St. John are unlikely to say anything about Jeremy, would you care to wager Mistress Cecilia will not let it slip? I have it on her own authority she cannot help following the promptings of her heart."

Male chuckles; the Barding ladies' lips twitched. Julia closed her eyes briefly in embarrassment for her sister. However had Cecilia happened to confide such a mawkish sentiment to Miles? Really, she deserved to have her ears boxed.

"He was not angry about our initial lie to him, Mistress Julia. He harrumphed about it, but what raised his ire was your family using you to save your sister's reputation. I did not go into detail about how Peter and Rachel met. The rest was easy: they liked each other very well, Peter's family had been encouraging him to marry, and it was to Rachel's benefit to marry a man able to support her in better circumstances than those in which she had been living. Ambleton could not have hoped to find a husband of better family for her, and the settlements we'd made were generous."

Popejoy had served the ladies glasses of sherry and poured out brandy for the men.

Miles paused to drink. "He did not reject outright my proposal to pass off Jeremy as Rachel's and Peter's, though he gave his opinion that it was 'Damned irregular,' which is true enough."

The earl smirked.

"I told him we made up the story about the Fleet marriage to reassure him about the way Rachel survived the last two years. His chief concern was the legalities, if Peter adopted Jeremy. Needless to say, I did not mention we meant to make the boy legitimate. He was concerned that Peter would be giving Jeremy precedence over any children of his own and Rachel's."

Barding said, "We had already dealt with the inheritance issue, of course. As Peter's estate includes neither entailed property nor title, Jeremy will not receive more than the hypothetical other children. We have the resources to establish as many children as the couple may have, and we can draw up documents tomorrow to guarantee the same. And no, my dear, we did not mention your argument that being William's son, Jeremy would take precedence over Peter's first son."

"I suppose it would not have impressed a magistrate." Caroline clucked her tongue irritably. "The law is sometimes perfectly unreasonable."

Miles said, "His concern that the truth would out was not as easily addressed. But the only people who know Jeremy's real parents are those of us at this table, the St. Johns, Peter, Rachel, and Ambleton. It is unlikely ever to come out unless one of that limited group speaks of it. Mistress Julia's people have shown no interest in the boy except as an excuse to scrape acquaintance with the Bardings. They would not want it known that either of their daughters had had an illegitimate child. It would make it difficult to fulfill their social ambitions. I imagine if they eventually learned Peter and Rachel had adopted him, they would hardly give it a second thought. Do you agree, J— Mistress Julia?"

"I do, sir. In fact, I cannot imagine they will ever hear about it, as being able to claim acquaintance with the Earl of Barding does not mean they will be moving in the same circles." She eyed her hosts and hostesses shyly.

"Indeed not," Lavinia responded with a little laugh. "Then Ambleton accepts what we have done, Miles?"

"He has not yet given us his final decision, though he did say he would not cast doubt on our story until he made up his mind. The whole account gave him a great deal to think about and too little time to consider the matter before supper. I think between relief his daughter is alive, safe, and creditably married, and disapproval of the St. Johns, he may agree to ignore the deception. He seemed mighty taken with Julia at supper, so it may also weigh with him that letting it seem Jeremy was Rachel's would help Julia."

Several nods and a grunt of approval from the earl. The dowager countess said, "Very good, Miles. You never fail us."

He inclined his head, acknowledging the compliment. "I should add that Ambleton called us the most arrant bunch of rogues he had ever met outside a courtroom. He swore if any of us ever came before him in his official capacity, he would not hesitate to find us guilty. I think he was joking."

The ripple of laughter in the dim room was comforting.

"There is just one more thing." Caroline's soft statement sounded apologetic. "How are we to protect Popejoy from the girl? I do not think one of us or a servant can be with him every hour of the day. I trust you will lock your door at night, George, and have your valet sleep in your dressing room, too."

After a long pause, Miles said, "It pains me to admit my brain is as empty as a pauper's pocket."

"Is there any sickness in the village or among the tenants?" Julia asked.

The earl nodded. "When I went to see about the hay barn leak, I heard the Ruckles at Long Barrow Farm had come down with a flux."

"Something they ate, I apprehend," was the dowager countess's tart observation.

"Really, Joan Ruckle's kitchen and habits don't bear thinking of." Caroline sniffed. "No one else is ill except for a head cold or two."

In the thoughtful silence that followed, Julia

murmured, "Lord Popejoy must suffer from some illness that confines him to his room, and a flux would ensure no one wants to visit him. Only his valet need know the truth."

Miles smiled at her, making her heart give a little skip.

"A very good notion, Julia," the dowager countess allowed. "And one reliable maid to empty the mythical slops. I know just the one. But it should be dysentery, not merely a passing flux from something he ate. George, you will not leave your chamber in the morning. Explain to your manservant, and I will send for Dr. Broxon. I am sure he will oblige us with the correct diagnosis."

"Yes, Mama. Er, if there is nothing else to discuss, I confess I look forward to my bed."

They all looked toward the end of the table where Lavinia and Miles sat. Seen together, Lavinia Barding and Miles Halliwell were oddly alike with their strong features and hooded eyes. Julia wondered what color Lavinia's hair had been before it turned to silver-white. If she sought out her portrait in the Long Gallery, would she find it had been chestnut?

The old woman pondered and inquired, "Miles?"

"We should not let them know of Peter's marriage. If they still have hope of him, they may not push so hard to marry the girl to Popejoy. Let us say he has gone to Scotland to hunt stags with an old friend rather than going to Cumberland for his honeymoon."

"He wouldn't, Halliwell. We could never induce him to hunt with us."

"The St. Johns don't know that, Lord Barding. Hunting is a good reason to go to North Britain, and it's too far for them to follow or for him to be back soon. They'll have to give up and leave."

More nods around the table.

"Then perhaps we can bring this to an end, Barding. As an old lady, I protest I need my sleep." Lavinia yawned discreetly behind her fan.

"After today, I think we all do," the earl replied. "Good night to you all. Popejoy, I will walk you to your chamber."

"And come in to search it, too, I hope, sir."

Barding laughed. "Indeed. I really cannot have my heir compromised."

Leaving Aaron to snuff the candles, they went their separate ways, most to the stair leading to the family wing, Julia and Miles to the guest wing stair.

"Is it always like this?" she asked when there was no danger of being overheard.

"No, thank God. Not this bad, anyway. While the earldom's affairs are extensive and complicated, as a family, they are not troublesome."

As they reached the staircase, he rested his hand on the back of her waist. The touch caught her breath in her throat. Even through her gown, corset, and smock, his touch felt intimate. The gesture was only to steady her: climbing stairs was difficult when a lady must use both hands to hold up her petticoat. The light was dim, too, with the candles in most wall sconces extinguished for the night. Despite knowing he meant it only for her protection, the light touch made her want to wriggle like a lapdog begging for attention. She could sympathize with the little canine. How unseemly. The memory of their ride did nothing to subdue the feeling.

When they emerged on the first floor, he dropped

his hand and offered his arm instead. She accepted it. Walking with Theo Manning had never made her heart beat faster. Certainly Theo had never aroused such sensations of, of…well, of something. Best not to think of what they meant.

At her door, she paused. "Good night, Mr. Halliwell. Thank you."

He stood frowning down at her. "Mistress Julia, I would like very much to kiss you."

She almost did not hear, he spoke so softly. Her family and Mr. Ambleton had rooms on this passage.

"I am not a loose woman, sir, no matter how it may have appeared to some." Though she now had a greater understanding of how some ladies fell into—call it, bad behavior.

"I have not thought you were since shortly after we met. I should tell you I am the earl's by-blow, however."

And therefore below her? How did one weigh a nobleman's illegitimate son against a spinster at her last prayers? How much would Miles weigh— If she colored up, the fact should not be apparent in the dim light from the nearest sconce. She swallowed and managed to say, "You are not to blame for his actions."

"Yet in general bastardy is considered to taint the character."

"Your character appears to me to be first-rate, as my half brother would say. It's an expression of approval relating somehow to naval ships."

"I have heard the term. Thank you for your good opinion, ma'am. It applies equally to you."

"I wish you would, sir."

"Hmm?" He continued to gaze at her intently but

made no move to oblige; had he not understood?

"Kiss me. I mean, I wish you would." Wasn't that where this conversation had begun?

It started as a gentle pressing of the lips. Then his arms were around her, and it felt so good to be held that her arms twined around his neck without her bidding. Sensations overwhelmed her: warmth, his beard stubble, a scent of something herbal, the firmness of his body. Many of the men her family knew in London were fleshy and big-bellied from too little exercise and too much food. Clearly Miles Halliwell's was not a sedentary occupation.

She wished it would never end. Ridiculous, of course. They could not stand here wrapped in each other's arms forever.

He must have realized it at the same moment and broke the kiss. But in spite of their lips parting, they remained embracing for a few moments longer.

"I beg your pardon, Mistress Julia. I hope I did not give offense by taking greater liberties than you expected."

"No."

"No?"

"I'm not offended. I wanted you to kiss me, and I enjoyed it."

"So did I."

"But I'm not unchaste, and I think I must retire now."

"I was not attempting to seduce you. We should talk in the morning."

She smiled a little uncertainly and whispered, "Good night, Mr. Halliwell," before slipping through the door.

****

The softness of her lips, the way she felt when he held her, stayed with him as he trudged the length of the passage to his own bed. He had not meant to enfold her in his arms, but upon their lips meeting, he had lost his wits. Not entirely: if he had, he would have picked her up and carried her into her chamber, confirming the world's worst opinion about bastards. Her bosom had been heaving as if she had been running. She had claimed not to be offended.

This was different from the kisses he had casually bestowed on females in the past. They had been no more than pleasant diversions which sometimes led to informal connections. What if Ambleton had happened to open his door? Or one of the St. Johns? Discovering Julia in his arms would have given Julia's parents endless opportunities to castigate her. What would the earl think if he had come upon them? Barding's disapproval would have reduced Miles to ashes. The countesses…

The countesses would think they were courting. Good God, was that what he was doing? He must be. The thought was at once appealing and alarming.

He had given up all thought of having his own family years ago, after his loss of Letitia Bellingham in his callow youth. If he could not have her, what was the point? Looking back, he wondered why he had been captivated and concluded that youth accounted for it.

When he had called on her the day after the assembly, it was her father who received him, not in the drawing room but in his study. He was not unkind. "Best to begin as we must go on," Attorney Bellingham told him as he showed him out. As a junior clerk with no expectations, Halliwell would not be permitted to pursue an acquaintance with Letitia. Mr. Bellingham did not speak of Halliwell's base birth, but it was implicit in Miles's lack of family connections.

Now Letitia seemed pallid and insubstantial by comparison with Julia St. John. He stopped inside his door trying to herd his thoughts into order and trying not to think about carrying Julia into her bedchamber. Even with his brain half scrambled, he would never have imposed on a lady, any female at all, under the earl's roof. Most especially not Julia.

He and Julia really must talk after he had time to think.

Chapter 32

"Fiddlestick," Caroline muttered at breakfast, folding the sheet and slipping it into her pocket. "Here's two lines from Peter to let us know he's gone to stay with his school friend, Cunningham, in Scotland. For the hunting, you know." She spread marmalade on the bit of toast remaining on her plate.

"I am sorry we will not be able to meet him." Lady St. John's sharp glance at Cecilia was not lost on Julia. Her half sister had been warned not to burst out with any spontaneous remark.

"Where are the gentlemen this morning?" Augusta inquired as if she had just noticed that apart from herself and Cecilia, only the two countesses and Julia were at the table. The absence of Hilda Ernst and Verity Winston did not interest her.

"Barding is visiting tenants. Halliwell and Ambleton have ridden to Banbury." Lavinia sipped her gunpowder tea. "Popejoy is keeping to his chamber today with some indisposition."

So there would be no discussion with Miles about what had happened last night, or whatever it was he had thought they should talk about. The morning no longer held any promise.

"I hope Lord Popejoy is not ill," her stepmother said.

"The doctor says 'tis dysentery. It will pass"—Julia

concealed a choke of laughter under a cough—"in a week or in a month or six weeks, no matter how we dose him, Dr. Broxon says."

Caroline sighed. "It is terrible to hear the way my son groans."

Cecilia ventured, "I heard him as I came downstairs. I wish I could do something to relieve his suffering."

Cecilia had no business in the family's wing. Evidently she realized this observation left her open to censure, for she rattled on, "This is such a large house, I mistook my way this morning trying to find the stair."

Which she would have passed on her way to the other wing.

Augusta tittered. "My little Cecilia has no sense of direction, I fear."

"In a house this size, that could be a grave affliction," Caroline replied. Lavinia merely sipped her tea.

The viscount had proved to be an accomplished actor. A footman admitted to the conspiracy was stationed outside his door and tapped a signal when he heard anyone approach. Popejoy would then moan very movingly, as Caroline had confided that morning when they were alone before Augusta and Cecilia appeared.

"Alas, I fear nothing but time and the gentle remedies our doctor prescribes will cure him. He is trying syrup of quinces, brandy, and beef broth."

"What a pity, when the day is so fine." Cecilia's mouth drooped.

"Perhaps you and your daughter would like to visit the nursery, Lady St. John?" Julia heard the acid in Lavinia's smiling offer, if her stepmother did not.

Cecilia fidgeted. Her mother asked, "Might we stop there as part of a tour of this fascinating house?"

As if Cecilia were affianced to some member of the Barding family. Augusta had always wielded her superior lineage to get what she wanted. Her manner alone sufficed with those of lesser birth, but to try to impose on a countess was a flagrant offense against good manners.

Caroline responded smoothly, "Why, certainly, if you can do without my mama-in-law or me as your guide. My niece Verity knows the house well and would enjoy showing you its best features." From her silky voice, no one would guess Caroline's thoughts.

"Alack, Caroline and I are engaged in planning to furbish up some of the chambers and the work must be completed before we leave for London in the autumn," Lavinia said.

Please, Cecilia, do not ask if you may assist, as if you have a right to an opinion. The thought flickered in her half sister's eyes and was extinguished by another glance from Lady St. John, who could recognize encroaching ways unless they were her own.

"I'll send for Verity so you can begin after you finish your breakfast, if that will be convenient."

Augusta St. John thanked her graciously. Lavinia rose and wished the unwanted guests a pleasant morning. She paused at the door and addressed Julia.

"If you would join me in my parlor when you are done here, I need your help with a little task."

"Of course, my lady." *Had she somehow learned of that passionate embrace last night?*

"Julia, do not keep Lady Barding waiting. You have surely eaten enough, particularly as you appear to

344

have put on a great deal of weight since last we saw you." Augusta's pointed order would have compelled Julia to excuse herself if she were still hungry. As she had finished all but a fragment of the bun Lavinia called a London wig, she was happy to leave Augusta and Cecilia to Caroline.

Once they were private, the dowager countess said, "We will wait for Caroline. I must say, I cannot like your stepmother."

Julia could not say she did not like her either, but any response was unnecessary, as Lavinia had not finished.

"To speak to you as if you had grown fat, when you were almost bones when you arrived!"

Caroline arrived then, saying as she seated herself and arranged her petticoats, "On the theory that Verity might have difficulty controlling two ladies, I instructed Adams to send Hilda along."

"A good thought. Cecilia will not be able to escape her."

"Even my stepmother would not have Cecilia force her way into the chamber of a man suffering from dysentery," Julia protested. "I think."

"In any case, Popejoy's privacy will be guarded by his valet and a footman. We need not protect him long, I hope," Lavinia said. "Now, to the reason I asked for your presence. When Barding instructed Halliwell to go to Banbury this morning, Miles had a word with him about another matter. My son requested that I convey Halliwell's apology that he could not meet with you this morning but means to do so this afternoon or evening."

"Oh." Julia swallowed.

"Barding feels, and Caroline and I agree, that we must stand *in loco parentis* to you."

"In *loco*—?"

"In place of your parents, as a lawyer would say. You are under our roof, and if I may speak freely, my dear—"

"As if anyone could stop you." Caroline laughed.

"—your own father and stepmama are perhaps not as much assistance to you as they might be."

It was true, but it ill became a daughter to agree. "I'm sure they mean well."

Two pairs of eyes skewered her. Caroline gave a ladylike snort. "Actions say more than intentions."

"In any case, Miles wants to court you. Before you say anything, know that we are all pleased with the idea and would be glad to welcome you as a relation. We regard Miles as part of our family."

Before she could stammer out a response, if she could think of one, Caroline added, "Which is not to say we are pressing you to marry him, if you should not care to. We think well of him, and I believe he would be a good husband, but it's a very personal decision. I know there is some prejudice against natural children."

"Miles was brought up here with George, William, and Peter. We can all testify to his steadiness and good character. He is also able to support a family." Lavinia patted Julia's hand.

He was reared at Charfield? No wonder he seemed to be at home.

She went on, "He was not quite sure how you felt about it. That was the impression I received from Barding's account of their conversation. I cannot be sure whether Miles was actually stammering, which

346

does not seem like him, or whether it is only that the message was filtered through another man. They are seldom good at talking about feelings. I suppose it seems unmanly to speak of their affections. Have I embarrassed you? Were you not aware of Halliwell's interest?"

"Not really? That is, I wasn't sure?" He had seemed to enjoy kissing her, but men kissed girls all the time without meaning anything by it. So she understood, though she had gone largely unkissed, herself. Theo Manning's one kiss had not given her any great interest in the pastime.

"You may wish to think about it today." Caroline's eyes sparkled.

"We will support your decision, whatever it may be."

"Thank you, my lady. My ladies. I do like Mr. Halliwell very much, but…"

"But?" The dowager countess repeated the word.

"I'm not sure I have a dowry." She should have one, unless it had been added to Cecilia's, on the theory that an old maid did not need a portion. She wished the thought had never crossed her mind, as it would never have done if she had not had reason to distrust her father. Augusta would think increasing her dowry would improve Cecilia's chances.

"My dear Julia, it will make no difference to my grandson. He is in a good way of business, and I am sure has no thought at all of marrying for a dowry."

"There, now," Caroline said briskly. "Don't you feel better?"

Julia gave a slightly shaky laugh. She did, indeed. The knowledge Miles Halliwell meant to court her with the approval of the Bardings was as comforting as a warm mantle and a hot drink on a chill day.

Would her own family object? To them, Halliwell was no more than a professional man at best, and a cit at worst. If they knew he was the earl's illegitimate son, which would influence them, his bastardy or his connection to the earl? She could readily imagine Augusta's pursed lips. If they disliked the connection, she hoped it would not lead to recrimination and raised voices. But why should they object, when she had been gone from the St. John home for two years? Then she thought, *I was scarcely part of the family then. I am of age, and the Bardings approve of the connection. What does it matter if Papa and Augusta rail against it?*

****

"I told Lord Barding I have a few questions for you before I make my final decision, Halliwell," Ambleton said.

"I'll answer them if I can, sir."

Ambleton sat his raw-boned gelding as if they were one. He did not glance at Miles, riding beside him. "Didn't care to ask these questions in company. You met her once, I think you said."

"Several times, in fact. I was present at their initial meeting, again during a coach ride to and from Chelsea where she and Peter strolled in order to have some time to get to know each other, at their wedding, and then the following day."

"Tell me about her. How she looked, how she sounded, what you thought of her."

Halliwell produced as detailed a word picture as he could, ending "She impressed me as well-suited to be the wife of an earl's son."

"The place she was working, what was it like?"

This was a more difficult question. Best not to mention all he had seen of it was the pantry. "We met her after the day's work was done. The orphan house appeared to be well-run and carefully managed. A well-regarded man of business is one of the board of directors." He dredged up a memory of something Rachel had told them. "Most of the children your daughter taught their reading and numbers were between five years and ten or eleven."

"Ay, she'd be good at that. Needle-witted and always wanting to know more. Could think rings around her brother for all he went to the old vicar for tutoring and she only had a governess. Her little sister was prettier, but Lord! Not an idea in her head except what the ladies were wearing and her own next gown. What I want to know is, how did she get such a post, with no reference or experience?"

Miles replied easily, "The landlady at the house where she lodged after fleeing Lady Helen's house happened to know one of the governors. She went with Mistress Rachel to the interview. The curate who volunteers at the home was also present." Substantially true; the curate was in the church at the time, and John Barlicorn played some major role in the management of the place.

"This last…I have to ask. Is the boy Jeremy hers in fact? Did Peter Stretton seduce Rachel?"

"No, he did not. He's an honorable gentleman and would not ruin any female."

"Gentlemen have been known to do things when cup-shot they would not when sober. The child does resemble Popejoy and Barding."

"The truth is as I told you: William Stretton got Jeremy on Cecilia St. John. William was dissolute, and the St. Johns are ambitious to worm their way into the earl's circle. They decided to sacrifice Julia St. John to save Cecilia's reputation."

Ambleton nodded, deep in thought. "Thank you. I had to know, because whatever my girl's life has been since she vanished, part of it is my fault. When I found her gone from Lady Helen's, I remained in town for near two weeks, trying to find her. I questioned the servants and the nephew, went to the parson at the church they attended, asked at the coaching inn. If I'd gone to the magistrate instead, he might have been more successful."

"Sir, she was afraid Lady Helen's heir would pursue her. She found respectable lodgings at some distance for that reason. She did not go to the parson as she did not trust him to believe her and not to tell that blackguard where she had gone. When you did not respond to her letters, she gave up and sought work before her little store of money ran out. She was safe enough among the orphans. I hope I have addressed all your concerns?"

"I do have one last question." Ambleton turned his head to look at Miles. "With Rachel hidden away in the orphan house and Mr. Stretton newly arrived from the Continent, how did they meet?"

He had dreaded that subject, but now it was raised, the answer came easily, thanks to something Peter had mentioned.

"Mr. Stretton was deeply impressed by the foundling home in Florence. He visited the children's home where Mistress Rachel was employed to see how our orphan houses compare with it."

Rachel's father accepted this explanation with a nod and a "Thank you." After a time, he said, "I'm glad to know the truth. It's weighed on me. I'd like to write to her to beg her pardon before I see her."

"Lord Barding will send it on."

"I'm not settled in mind about those letters. One might be lost, but several?"

Miles maintained a diplomatic silence.

"Rachel was always an honest girl. Too honest, sometimes. My wife despaired of her because she would not pretend to hang upon the baronet's son's every word. I couldn't blame her: he was a bottle-head. Still is. My wife wanted Rachel married. She believes 'tis important for the older girl to marry before the younger. She claimed Rachel wouldn't make a push to attract a husband and that our younger girl would be snapped up in a month. 'Tis only since coming here I've thought about it. There's no need to pay attention to women's talk about beaus and marriage, 'cept to make sure the suitor's the right sort. After Rachel disappeared, m'wife asked if Rachel's dowry shouldn't be added to her sister's. Told her I wasn't giving up on Rachel yet awhile, that no one's declared dead until they've been gone seven years, 'less there's a body." He frowned at the horizon. "The post is delivered in the morning, usually when I'm out before breakfast. I'll be speaking to my household."

"I do not envy you."

"I'm a magistrate, Halliwell. When I listen to testimony, I look for lies and evasion, and I find 'em, by God. Still, you expect to be able to trust your family."

They reached Banbury without another word spoken.

Chapter 33

Ambleton would have a look around the town. He had only come to question Miles in privacy, the reason Halliwell had been dispatched to Banbury with him. Now Miles would do a few errands, most of them trivial. The longest and most important was the choice of a small gift for Julia. He would not be able to give her anything very personal until they married, assuming she accepted his suit. Flowers, a book, or a fan were all acceptable, but the garden at Charfield Hall was now a riot of blooms, none of the books available in Banbury were likely to appeal to Julia, and the fans were either humdrum or suitable only for a village assembly. In London he could find a better one: chicken skin, perhaps, with ivory sticks. In a shop selling small wares and haberdashery, he found several pin-pillows made by the owner's daughter. They were of wool, rather than silk, but one was heart-shaped, embroidered with ivy and pansies. It reminded him of Julia. He bought it and a paper of pins, always a welcome gift to a lady. The plump, cheerful woman at the counter smiled at him in a knowing way as she accepted his money. To be expected, he supposed. How many men bought ladies' sewing tools, after all?

They did not return to Charfield until shortly before supper owing to Ambleton's desire to see the nearby manor, which was one of those Peter and Rachel might choose. This made it impossible to speak privately with Julia or give her the token of his esteem, as he entered the drawing room with only minutes to spare. Ambleton, less concerned about his appearance, was there first.

The two St. John ladies were discussing the tour of the house. He could not think of Julia being a St. John: she was too different from her half sister and stepmother. Well, she would soon have a new surname, he hoped.

Lady St. John was full of praise for the size and elegance of the rooms. The so-called queen's bedchamber met with Cecilia's approval, though the bed hangings and curtains would be prettier if they were a lighter color and silk rather than wool. "I suppose in Queen Elizabeth's time everything was old-fashioned," she remarked.

"I am sure that is true. But our Queen's Chamber was furnished for the anticipated stay of Queen Henrietta Maria in 1627. Charles I's queen, you know." At Lavinia's dry tone, Miles and Julia's eyes met and quickly parted lest one of them laugh, as Cecilia looked blank.

"She never actually came here, however, as it was decided to change her route," Verity explained.

Caroline inquired, "Did you visit the nursery? I made some changes to it when I was expecting Popejoy, as it was rather gloomy. After William's birth, I ordered substantial alterations to make it more convenient for the nurse and nursery maids. Part of it has been refurbished more recently, as well."

Augusta St. John uttered the tinkling little laugh that Miles loathed. "We thought it best not to intrude, as

I vow I was ready to drop with fatigue, and young girls are bored by domestic matters. When Cecilia marries, she will naturally take an interest in the management of her nursery."

Ambleton's face would have been a study had anyone but Miles observed it. After a moment during which Miles expected him either to growl or bark a sardonic laugh, Ambleton observed, "As a fond father, though only of three children who are now grown, I enjoy nurseries. I visited it t'other day and met a fine little fellow called Jeremy, though I'm sorry to say I did not see the other lad, who was napping. We rolled a ball back and forth. He would be a credit to any parent."

None of the St. Johns had anything to reply to this, and talk turned to Ambleton's visit to Banbury.

"I knew of Banbury cakes and Banbury cheese but did not know the town had a thriving industry." Ambleton had been impressed by the horse blanket manufactory's employment of several dozen workmen.

This topic occupied the men until supper. Halliwell noticed Julia took little part in the women's talk of the society to be found in the neighborhood and of London events. Unsurprising, given that Lady St. John's brisk interrogation of Lavinia and Caroline interspersed by Cecilia's naïve comments left no opportunity for Julia, Verity, or Hilda to add a remark. The Barding ladies could have ended the spate with a word or two, and he did not think they were merely exercising good manners. They were giving Augusta and Cecilia St. John enough rope to hang themselves, if indeed they needed more. Ambleton might have made up his mind when Augusta and Cecilia St. John convicted themselves of not caring a groat about Jeremy. Now they had a foothold in the Bardings' circle, Cecilia's son had ceased to exist for them. That, with the practical considerations, might tip the balance.

The men had scarce begun to drink their first glass of port when Dr. Broxon was announced.

"Halliwell, take the doctor up to Viscount Popejoy, please," Barding said.

Miles was glad to escape, since speaking with Julia would not be possible until the men joined the ladies in the parlor. Even then, it might require some clever strategy to lure her away.

"Any change in the viscount's condition?" Broxon asked.

"None," Miles replied. It was the truth; Popejoy was bored, catching up on his reading, and playing piquet with his manservant. By now, he should have finished the supper Cook sent up ostensibly for his servant but ample enough for two.

"I want to look in on Georgie first. Then I'll see Viscount Popejoy."

"I'll tell him you're coming."

The doctor grinned. "I'm sure he would appreciate a visit from you. When I came to see him before, he complained bitterly about being confined to his chamber."

Popejoy's first words when he saw Miles were, "I hope Grandmama and my mother have a plan to rid the house of Julia's people. I've been reduced to writing letters I've put off for weeks."

"They seldom fail in their objectives. I'll play a hand with you if you like while you wait for Broxon to finish with Georgie."

"I'd rather we talked. I may never play piquet

again. If we had been playing for money, my sharper of a valet would have won enough from me to set himself up for the rest of his life. Tell me what you did today."

Miles was saying, "I think Ambleton is won over to our side," when a tap on the door announced the doctor's arrival.

"How is he?"

"I will leave you," Halliwell said.

"No, stay, Miles. Please."

"If you wish."

"Doctor? How is my boy?"

"I am truly sorry, my lord. Barring a miracle, it is only a matter of time, and as a physician I have found miracles in short supply. I cannot encourage you to hope for his recovery."

"It is only what I expected."

A grave nod from the doctor. "I'll be on my way, then, after assuring your family you are no better."

"Doctor, one moment, please. Something has troubled me since the inquest concluded. I need to know…"

"Whatever it is, I will try to answer."

"Is it possible some tonic my lady gave Georgie…?

"Has caused his debility?" The doctor shook his head. "No. I went through her notes and the books she used page by page. That is why my review took so long. Lady Popejoy was extremely precise and thorough. If she made up an ointment for a servant's strained muscle, she wrote it down, with the ingredients and directions for use. In the last year, she listed a syrup for Georgie's cough last winter and dosed him for colic. She asked my recommendation for the syrup when I was here to see him, and the colic remedy was one she had used before. Neither contained anything harmful. She was exceeding careful with him. While I cannot assign a name to your son's ailment, it or something similar occurs occasionally in children and in adults. The colleagues I wrote knew no better than I what to do. I think Lady Popejoy resorted to too many remedies because she was overly concerned about her ability to conceive again."

"She wanted to give me an heir. Another potential heir, as young George was sickly. She need not have worried. If I had known how she felt, I could have reassured her. I knew Peter would do his duty to the family."

"Her anxiety may not have been only for the succession. I apprehend some women feel they have failed as wives and females if they cannot conceive."

On that thought, Dr. Broxon took his leave. Miles remained with the viscount for some time, hoping to cheer him. He recounted some amusing incidents from London's business world and finally they laughed about some of their childhood adventures.

Now he was free to address Julia, if only he could find a way of getting her alone. But she had retired with a headache as he discovered when he reached the drawing room. In courtesy, he could not leave at once and had to sit for half an hour making labored conversation with Verity and Hilda.

Chapter 34

Yesterday she had thought Miles wished to speak with her. After that embrace, she had expected or at least hoped his request meant…well, meant something more than talk. The Barding ladies said he wanted to court her. She had waited all day alternately anxious and hopeful, and he never sought her out. Granted, he had had to go to Banbury and had not come back until supper. Then he had disappeared. Dr. Broxon had come to see Georgie and the viscount, but Miles would have had nothing to do with that. He must have changed his mind. After only one cup of tea, plagued by a headache and unable to bear Cecilia's prattle any longer, she excused herself and went to bed.

She rose late, having been unable to fall asleep because of the early hour and memories of every encounter with Miles, wondering how she had come to suppose he cared for her. Why had he spoken to the earl about her if he were unsure about his feelings? Or had Lord Barding misunderstood? Miles Halliwell must have reconsidered his intentions, if he had had any.

She had thought Cecilia was building a castle in Spain on her hope of marrying Peter. Or mayhap Popejoy, once she knew he was a widower. Now she had made the same mistake herself on the foundation of a few words and that kiss. The castle had crumbled, but still, she had much to be thankful for: the earl's family were kind and had invited her to stay before Miles had spoken of courting her.

To her relief, her own family had not been as much of a trial as she had expected, apart from their unannounced, unwanted arrival. They were an embarrassment, but Julia no longer felt responsible for their behavior. They also ignored her, for the most part: they had come to thrust themselves into a nobleman's family rather than to waste time with her.

Their inattention was welcome. Her father had mostly ignored her all her life, and apart from a critical comment or two, Augusta had left her alone. The worst she had had to endure was Cecilia's unguarded remarks (when Stepmama was absent) about the grand marriage she expected to make.

The maid brought her chocolate and asked if she would like to breakfast in her chamber, an offer she accepted gratefully. Doing so would permit the servants to clear the dining room as everyone else had eaten, and also spare her the necessity of seeing anyone until she had composed herself.

"Their ladyships asked after you, ma'am, and said as they'd be in the ladies' parlor when you come down. Unless you was still unwell, and then I was to tell them so they could send for Doctor."

"It was only a headache. I will go down as soon as I dress." Which she could do unaided, if she put on jumps and a casaquin jacket. She liked the casaquin and matching petticoat Lavinia had ordered for her. They were simple, and the deep rose became her. She really did have much to be grateful for. Her life was better than it had been in Handley. The sun still shone, flowers still had perfume, and she had friends and things to do. This afternoon, she would assist Marcia Brant. They would make the French lesson enjoyable by inventing ridiculous dialogues. *Monsieur Lion, will you take a cup of tea? Mademoiselle Pony, you are fat. You do not require the seed cake.*

Buoyed up by the knowledge she was looking her best, she entered the pretty salon where the household's ladies gathered informally. It was smaller than the drawing room and more comfortable, with pale green walls and furniture of several different styles chosen for comfort. The upholstered pieces had been covered with the same dark green velvet in an attempt to unify the furnishings. The attempt failed as the many plump little cushions in various colors had been made by small girls still learning to embroider. Some of the watercolor pictures on the walls were beginners' efforts, too.

It was not to be expected that Augusta and Cecilia would be absent. But they would confine their attention to Lavinia and Caroline, leaving Julia to work on embroidering a pair of pockets. Her stepmother greeted her with a cool, "Julia," and her stepsister beckoned her to sit beside her on one of the settees.

Lavinia's "I hope you are quite recovered, Julia," and Caroline's "You are looking very pretty this morning" more than made up for Augusta's curtness. Julia sat beside Cecilia and took her embroidery from her work bag.

They had been discussing possible entertainment for the guests. Caroline said, "We do not feel we can attend the Banbury fair this year, but your family might. I expect Mr. Ambleton would go, and Miles Halliwell also."

"Oh, may we?" Cecilia exclaimed. "I do love a

361

fair."

Julia controlled her expression, a skill she had perfected as a child, at the memory of Cecilia's account of the Tottenham Court fair where she had met William Stretton.

"I feel we should not abandon you to your mournful reflections even for a day," Augusta protested.

"Please do not feel obligated to bear us company. You are not in mourning, after all, and I am sure your daughter would enjoy the jaunt."

Julia glanced at Lavinia's face and recognized a cynical glint in her eyes. Perhaps she was also thinking about the Tottenham Court fair.

"May we, Mama?"

"I'll speak to your father about it."

Verity entered precipitately and, without pausing to curtsy, broke into speech. "My ladies, Lord Barding sent word there's been an accident at the Andrews' barn. He's sent for the doctor, but Mistress Andrews is beside herself. There's a beam fallen, and they are still trying to lift it off the oldest boy's leg without anything more falling. "

"I'll go." Caroline stood up. "Her girls are too young to be any use. Is the boy the only one hurt?"

"Andrews was, too. They've half a dozen men there doing what they can."

"I would think the bailiff could handle a tenant problem," Augusta whispered, quietly enough that Julia trusted neither Caroline nor Lavinia heard it. "Now, Julia, I want to know how you dared write such a disobliging letter to your papa? You will return to Handley as soon as we can arrange it. You have imposed on the earl and his family long enough."

Lavinia stiffened; she had heard that remark, Augusta's voice having risen somewhat in her annoyance.

Caroline's stride on her way to the door checked briefly, then with a glance over her shoulder at Lavinia, she continued on her way, instructing Verity to have a box packed with a bottle of port and one of brandy and whatever buns, cake, or biscuits were available. "Have Adams send to the stables for a groom to hitch up the little cart and be ready to take me there. Tell Cook to prepare food and ale for dinner for the family and the workers. She will know what to do. I'll send the cart back for it." Verity pulled the door shut, failing to notice it did not catch and remained open a few inches. Julia rose, meaning to close it. Before she could move, Lavinia said, "We really cannot spare Julia. We consider her one of our family."

At these words, Julia stood still, hoping not to draw more of Augusta's wrath.

"It is gracious of you to say so, my lady, but it was only necessary that she deliver the child and remain long enough to see him settled. As that is accomplished"—and how did her stepmother know that, when she had not visited Jeremy in the nursery?— "she is needed at the Handley property. Even a small manor does not manage itself."

"High Farm consists of a cottage. There are no tenants and the sheep pasturage, though extensive, is leased to a man who oversees flocks for their owners. I cannot believe a four-bedroom farmhouse, with no one in residence save a servant or two, needs Julia."

Augusta St. John rallied quickly. "I meant to spare

my stepdaughter humiliation. She is our responsibility, and she must be an embarrassment to your family, as it will surely become known she is the mother of a bastard."

"We take care of our own, including by-blows and their mothers. In Julia's case, we choose to welcome her for her own sake. We all know who Jeremy's mother is." Lavinia turned a cold gaze on Cecilia, whose face first betrayed astonishment, as if she had forgotten Jeremy was hers, and then humiliation, as she voiced an almost inaudible "Oh!"

Thank goodness no one else was present! Cecilia's tacit admission left Augusta with no way to deny it. Augusta's affronted, "I suppose she has told you some ridiculous tale," came a few heartbeats too late to be convincing.

"Julia's reputation is unsullied and will remain that way. If any of our family should hear talk about her, we will put the record straight."

"I assure you, my lady—"

"When Barding received Lord St. John's letter, we naturally had your family thoroughly investigated. It was not difficult to discover the truth. We have invited Julia to remain with us. She is of age, and she may be too filial to tell you she prefers to live here. Besides, I have in mind an excellent marriage for her."

Julia stared mutely at the dowager countess. What could she mean? She had no hope of Miles now: it had been a day and a half since that whisper, "We should talk in the morning." He had changed his mind or not meant what she had thought. Peter was married, and who else could Lavinia be thinking of? Not Popejoy, certainly.

Augusta's mouth worked without any sound coming out, making her look rather like a fish. To be specific, the head and shoulders of a cod, a dish which had frequently appeared on the St. John table in London. The creature's expression had always made Julia nervous; now she knew why. Before her stepmother was able to speak, Cecilia sprang to her feet and shrilled, "Not Lord Popejoy! I am to be a viscountess and then a countess, not Julia!"

"And that lack of discretion, Lady St. John, is why no grandson of mine will ever under any circumstances marry your hoyden of a daughter. Not even if she managed to compromise him, which she will not." Lavinia Barding's iron voice left no doubt the discussion was finished.

Her breathtaking bluntness held even Augusta mute. Julia had once overheard an elderly lady say, "The freedom when one is an old woman is vastly amusing. An' you smile you may be as rude as you like. I vow one could almost commit murder, and the victim would be blamed."

A fit of hysterics by Cecilia would be welcome for once, freeing them from their paralysis. No doubt she would soon oblige as her bosom was heaving and her breathing was shallow and fast. If she were slapped now, she would dissolve in tears, but Augusta was still frozen, and if Julia applied the remedy, Augusta would upbraid her for cruelty to her sister. Lavinia, Lady Barding could do it without censure. That would be best.

Lavinia might have done so, if the door had not opened suddenly. Miles Halliwell stalked in. His face was thunderous, but he spoke lightly. "With all due apologies to Viscount Popejoy, I really could not permit him to marry the lady who is engaged to me."

She was as stunned by his words as by his sudden presence at her shoulder. He took her limp hand and gave it an encouraging squeeze. Did he mean it?

Cecilia squeaked, jarred out of her incipient outburst. "Julia!"

"Engaged?" Augusta uttered the word disbelievingly. "You did not inform me, Julia."

"Our betrothal is very recent, my lady," Miles replied.

Now Augusta's bosom was heaving, and her nostrils were dilated. "I must speak to St. John at once, if you will excuse me, Lady Barding. He will not be pleased that you have not sought his permission, Halliwell. Come, Cecilia."

Still goggling at Julia and Miles, her sister bobbed a curtsy to the dowager countess and flashed a half-apologetic smile at Julia before hurrying after her mother.

Lavinia's eyes snapped with amusement as she watched them go. Julia could not blame her. Her stepmother had deserved a sharp lesson for her scheming. She could only feel a certain amused exasperation with Cecilia, slightly leavened with sympathy. She did feel some compassion for her papa, foolish enough to be ensnared by Augusta. He should have wondered why a reasonably pretty young lady of excellent lineage was unmarried at four-and-twenty years. It could not all have been due to her almost red hair and long nose.

"Miles, there is a bottle of sherry and glasses in that chinoiserie cabinet. I need a restorative, and I expect you and Julia would be the better for one."

Miles surrendered her hand with a faint, rueful smile—had he really been clasping it this whole time?—and obeyed. Bereft of his reassuring presence, her eyes followed him until they met Lavinia's and encountered her tiny smile.

"I am very pleased for both of you, my dears. I thought you would make a match of it."

"But…" What could she say? She had hoped Miles meant to ask her to marry, but surely he had announced their engagement only to distract her stepmother and Cecilia.

Miles served Lady Barding first. When he pressed the glass into Julia's hand, he said, "I would have asked you, but this is the first chance I've had. Given what I heard when I approached a few minutes ago, it seemed best to presume upon your good nature. Will you consent to be my wife? If you do not care for the idea, you may disavow our 'betrothal.' But I hope you will not."

Julia swallowed the lump in her throat. When she was a girl, when she had still imagined being courted, she had never envisioned a proposal quite like this.

"Oh, don't blush, girl. Give him an answer, if you please. It's no use pretending you're indifferent to him: Caro and I have eyes in our heads. It may not be the moonshine and roses sort of offer, but I misdoubt Miles would do well at such a thing. He's no beau to be mouthing practiced flattery, but he's sound as a roast." She sipped sherry. "There's a deal to be said for a man who's responsible without being dull."

"Are you sure?" Julia stared into his eyes. They no longer made her think of dirty ice. They were more like durable, useful pewter. She read warmth and humor and something more.

"Absolutely, my doubting Thomasina. Will you marry me?"

"With the greatest pleasure."

Was he going to kiss her? Her glance slid to Lavinia. The same thought seemed to have occurred to Miles, who had turned his head toward the Barding matriarch.

"Ridiculous children," she observed. "Finish your sherry, and then you may stroll in the garden. I'm sure you can contrive to avoid the gardeners. Barding and St. John should discuss the settlements tonight, if Barding is not still taken up with the Andrews accident. Or in the morning; I expect your family will be anxious to leave, Julia. They won't wish to return for the wedding, will they?"

Julia found her voice. "I shouldn't think so." Her first, unmoored sensation had been replaced by a feeling of being caught in a great windstorm. "It would be a considerable journey for them."

"If all can be accomplished expeditiously, Barding can announce your betrothal at dinner tomorrow, but we will hold the formal celebration after your family have left. Popejoy will wish to be present, and he can scarcely recover from dysentery overnight. It would be lacking in tact. Don't stand there. Sit down and drink your sherry, both of you."

She found herself sitting beside Miles on the sofa facing Lavinia. He grinned at the dowager countess who smiled primly in return.

"Now, once Peter and Rachel decide which property they like, Miles, you and Julia can choose one of the others. St. John may already have used Julia's dowry for Cecilia's dowry or his own purposes, but no matter. Miles, after your mama died, Barding invested in the Funds for you the amount he had been paying her each quarter, until you came of age. It is a tidy sum by now. We thought it would be helpful when you married. Though I admit, there were times when I despaired of your ever forming a connection."

Julia heard Miles swallow as if he had something stuck in his throat. Lavinia Barding must often have that effect on those around her.

"Miles, I want you to know…" For once Lavinia, Lady Barding's voice sounded hesitant. "I have long known that of all my grandchildren, you are the most like me."

Neither said anything more for an uncomfortably long moment while Lavinia and Julia's betrothed studied each other.

The dowager countess spoke at last. "I hope you consider it a compliment!" She went on, "Now, when we go to London in the autumn, we will review suitable ladies for George to marry. You will investigate them, and he will be married by January, I trust. The sooner, the better, in fact, as he needs another heir in case…" The old lady's face clouded over. Then she added, "Besides, your conscience can rest easy once little Jeremy is farther down in the line of succession. Now run along and enjoy the sun and the roses."

Beside her, Miles seemed to give himself a little shake, gathering his wits as if they were as scattered as her own. "My lady, I sought you out originally to let you know Ambleton meant to go over to the Andrewses' farm to help. I should ride over to see if there is something I can do."

"Miles, we take advantage of you. Barding can do without your assistance this once. Shoo! Quick, before something else happens."

They took her at her word and fled.

A word about the author...

Kathleen Buckley has loved writing ever since she learned to read. After a career which included light bookkeeping, working as a paralegal, and a stint as a security officer (fascinating!), she began to write as a second career, rather than as a hobby. Her first historical romance was penned (well, wordprocessed) after re-reading Georgette Heyer's Georgian/Regency romances and realizing that Ms. Heyer would never be able to write another (having died some forty years earlier).

Warning: no bodices are ripped in her romances, which might be described as "powder & patch & peril" rather than Jane Austen drawing room. They contain no explicit sex, but do contain mild bad language, as the situations in which her characters find themselves sometimes call for an oath a little stronger than "Zounds!"

http://18thcenturyromance.wordpress.com

Thank you for purchasing
this publication of The Wild Rose Press, Inc.

For questions or more information
contact us at
info@thewildrosepress.com.

The Wild Rose Press, Inc.

www.ingramcontent.com/pod-product-compliance
Lightning Source LLC
Chambersburg PA
CBHW051127030726
47504CB00004B/741